CATACLYSM

THE LEGENDS OF THALARIA
BY LORE CASTA PENDRAGON

Chapter One

Cataclysm

Grand wizard Lore Casta Pendragon and his apprentice Aram Allheart stepped carefully through the snow to the summit of Mt. Muse, icy wind blew around them seemingly from all directions, an unnatural force directed by callous hands.

The mountain overlooked the land of Thalaria, many cities and villages could be seen from here including the tower of the magi, a tower built by the wizard's guild to train mages, it towered above the landscape, a testament to the power of the guild where Lore had trained in his younger years.

"Master Pendragon, we shouldn't be in this place!", Aram shouted above the roar of the wind, almost losing his footing on the ice.

Lore Casta Pendragon turned to him.
"We have to find him Aram, Guldamere didn't revive those mages and bring them up here for nothing, he's up to something sinister", Lore's voice cut through the wind, enhanced by powerful magic.

Lore stood strong, his long beard swayed in the wind, he had his feet planted as if magnetized by the stone, his apprentice Aram followed suit and found his balance with a reassuring sigh.

Continuing along a rocky slope they saw the fallen soldiers of the dark wizard Guldamere Godfear.

Lore looked them over then turned to Aram, "looks like they met some trouble here, we need to reach the summit swiftly".

As he turned back a dense black fog descended the mountain as if compelled by a will of its own, moving faster it swirled around the fallen men, turning shades of bright green as the men rose to their feet lifted by the black miasma, it penetrated into their bodies, their eyes turned black, their pupils green, they all turned to look in the direction of Lore and Aram.

"Necromancy?", Aram shouted, horrified, "how is he able to raise the dead from such a distance?".

The reincarnated soldiers drew their swords and with rasping growls, they advanced toward Lore and Aram.

Lore Placed his fists together with his knuckles interlocked, looking to Aram he said, "I'll need but a moment".
Aram nodded and drew a long ornate steel staff that was strapped on his back.

"Five on one, not great odds", Aram said.

Aram rushed forward hoping to catch one of the risen off guard, he raised his staff high above his head and jumped forward bringing the staff rocketing down at speed onto the crown of the first soldiers head, with a resounding crack the soldier hit the snow.

Aram wasted no time moving onto the second target, he slid down on one knee sliding across some ice-covered snow, he swept the legs from under it with a horizontal sweep of his staff.

The third wasn't far behind and struck forward with a broadsword toward Aram's face, Aram bought one end of his staff up to defend and as the two clashed the ring of steel sang out.

Aram turned his wrist and flicked the end of the staff down onto the soldiers wrists, another loud crack could be heard as the sword clanged along the ice, Aram followed up by stabbing his staff into the ground and stepping his foot around it, he coiled the staff around his hip and let the tension go, the staff shot around his hip into the side of the soldiers head like a tensioned spring taking the soldier clear off his feet, Aram spun on the ice with the momentum of the strike.

A fourth soldier ran forward with a short mace in hand as Aram withdrew the staff back through his hands, he launched forward using the superior range of the staff with a straight stab with the tip to the midsection, knocking his opponent backward.

He then raised the staff with his back hand to bring it around his head in an arcing motion and onto the top of the soldier's head, the soldier whiplashed forward then fell on his back.

A fifth soldier moved at Aram with dual broadswords, slashing from what seemed to be every direction in continuous slashing motions, Aram raised his back hand to his brow, his forward hand at the center of the staff in a defensive motion moving the staff side to side, he blocked each strike in quick succession.

The second soldier found his feet and was advancing to Aram's rear, Aram took a step back and as the soldier came close, he swung his staff around using his tenkan technique, a one-hundred-and-eighty-degree rotation on the back foot.

Aram's staff moved with the spinning motion, he collected the soldier in front across the jaw and took the legs out from the other soldier for the second time, with all five undead soldiers now floored he lowered his guard.
"Aram look out!", shouted Lore from a distance.

Aram turned to see all five soldiers rising again, black miasma pulling them to their feet.

by Lore Casta Pendragon

One of the soldiers had a broken arm and another had a crushed skull, yet somehow, they were still able to fight.

"This is no ordinary magic, something's off, it's much more potent than it should be", Aram said, fear creeping onto his face.

Lore Casta Pendragon raised one arm forward toward an ice sheet overhanging the cliff, grabbing his elbow with his other arm he grasped it hard, funneling his power into it. "Aram, get out of the way!", Lore shouted, Aram sprinted toward Lore and slid beneath his feet as Lore Casta Pendragon let fly a fireball the size of a cannonball into the side of the mountain, the ensuing explosion caused an avalanche, burying the five risen soldiers in ice and snow.

"Well done master Pendragon", Aram said panting knowing all too well that he did most of the work.

Lore grabbed Aram's hand and helped him to his feet.

"Those abominations can't be defeated like normal men, they don't bleed, there are few ways to defeat the risen, incapacitating them or making the bodies unusable is your best defense", he lectured, Aram just bowed taking in his master's wisdom.

"Thank you Master, we best be moving", they quickened pace and advanced up the mountain.

The dark wizard Guldamere observed Lore and Aram through the eyes of an undead Raven, His eyes whited over in a trance, he watched the battle as they drew closer to his location at the summit of Mount Muse.

Three statues of beautiful semi clad women stood nearby, they were immaculately carved as if these women had been turned into stone, not carved by it, all held their hands over a pool, from their hands flowed water of different colors, one was faintly white, one faintly green, and one faintly black, they swirled together into a whirlpool, seemingly holding a perfect balance one eliminating the other like a perfect trinity.

Guldamere blinked a few times regaining consciousness, his eyes returned to normal, he stood slightly stooped, a black full-length robe covered him, black hair fell to his shoulders and a pale looking face peered out from under it, ten black cloaked men stood in a circle around him, lit up by the glowing essence from the pool.

                    by Lore Casta Pendragon

Guldamere looked around at his followers and with a sneaky smirk said,
"he's almost here, our time is nigh, immortal life and power without limitation is at our
fingertips", he said in a breathy tone.

The cloaked men congratulated each other and showered each other with praise.
"together we will undo the seal, release the chaos within and the power will be ours to
control", Guldamere said.
One man chirped up among the ravel, "but all of our power combined together could only
scratch that statue, it would require at least a hundred more mages to accomplish the task of
actually destroying them".

Guldamere looked displeased at the naysayer, he looked over and pointed his direction, "that
scratch released enough chaos magic to allow me to raise our fallen dead from here!",
Guldamere spat at him.

"Imagine what we could do if we were to destroy all three", he said greedily, the men nodded
their approval but
the naysayer spoke up again.

"It took us all to the point of death trying to do just that, even if you could find a hundred
mages, they would probably die trying, no-one can wield that much power without sacrificing
their life force", he scowled.

Guldamere straightened up and walked toward the man, "you don't seem to realize how much
more powerful you are just from that small release of chaos magic", he smirked.

Guldamere held his hands out wide gesturing to the rest of his followers, "allow me to
demonstrate the power of chaos magic".

Guldamere placed his hands together as if in prayer, his followers did the same, black smoke-
like miasma reached up from each of them and flowed into Guldamere, he reached a hand
now blackened from the dark magic forward toward the naysayer, "wait!", "Please!", "Stop!",
He cried as his life energy was ripped from his body; he slowly became hollowed out, a husk
drained of any semblance of life.

Guldamere was engulfed in the black miasma, it moved with him like a shadow, dark claws of
smoke appeared around his hands, "those who don't believe in *my* divine power, will not be
privy to the spoils of *my* labor", Guldamere cackled.

The rest of the cloaked figures repeated their precept in a unison chorus, "immortality is the
gift of Guldamere", Guldamere smiled and whispered under his breath, "soon it will all be
mine".

Guldamere's followers backed into the shadows at the side of the cave leaving Guldamere alone in the glow of the muses smirking to himself.

Lore Casta Pendragon and Aram reached the mountain peak, at the very top was a small cave lined with healthy greenery in contrast to the ice and snow around them. Lore looked over at Aram, "be careful, our enemy is prepared, danger could be lurking around any corner", Aram nodded and grabbed the staff from his back.

Lore looked over the lands of Thalaria from the top of the mountain, lush greenery covered the land beyond the mountain.

"A good reminder of what we're fighting for", Lore said, then he noticed the tower of the magi, "one day I'll return to the tower and put right the wrongs I committed there", he thought to himself.

The cave was surprisingly warm compared to the harsh icy wind outside, the air was warm and humid inside. Lore and Aram look to each other perplexed then moved further into the cave.

Lore took the lead, lighting the way with a small fire in the palm of his hand, they descended down naturally formed stone stairs, they could hear the sound of scuttling from small exoskeleton covered creatures on the walls, descending further the darkness seems to get denser as if squeezing the light.

It began to move strangely, like it was retreating from the light instead of being illuminated by it.

Aram saw a shadow moving on the wall like a clawed hand, but it faded from view in the light before he got a good glimpse of it. "Master Pendragon?", Aram whispered, "I know, we are being watched", Lore whispered back, "there is foul magic being used here, but it has an obvious weakness".

As they descended further the clawed hands multiplied at the edges of the shadows, clawing on the ground but being driven back by the light, suddenly and without warning a black claw with talons six inches long on each finger shot out of the darkness toward Lore, he raised his fiery palm and blasted it away with a gout of flame.

Lore dropped to one knee and Aram grabbed him, "are you okay master?", Aram inquired.

Lore looked up as the darkness enveloped them, "took me by surprise is all", he said, "I put a little too much into the fire", "I'll be alright, I just need to rest a while", a shrill scratchy high-pitched voice came from the darkness around them, "we have been waiting", it said, startled by

the silence broken, Aram tore his sleeve and wrapped it around his staff then began channeling into it, Lore smiled, "you've been reading my books again, haven't you?", Aram smiled back and shrugged, Lore addressed the voice calmly,
"who's there?", "who were you waiting for?".

"We were waiting at the edge of reality, in the dreams of the living, trapped beyond the border, unable to pass, the deal has been made, the abyss is open, the boundary between our world and yours has arrived, the age of darkness will soon begin".

Aram summoned a small fire in his palm to light his staff and the light pressed out against the dark only to be repelled again like being squeezed into a smaller space, the only luminescence was the staff on Lore and Aram's faces, the voice seemed entertained as it giggled around them annoyingly, "we are so close, so very close", the creature giggled.

A clawed black hand reached around Aram's face, his eyes drew wide and before they could react it pulled him into the darkness, Lore Casta Pendragon slammed his fists together, life energy surged through his body, he extended one arm straight up grabbing it at the elbow with his other hand, his fist clenched and began to glow with a bright white light, it grew stronger and it pushed back against the encroaching darkness which forced itself against the light, the light grew until it enveloped the entire cavern, with one last push of effort, it exploded out from Lore's fist in a blinding flare of luminescence.

There was a shriek in the dark and the shadow claws were driven back by the light, Aram was sitting against one wall his staff now illuminating the room naturally.
"What was that thing?", Aram asked, "I don't know, but I think Guldamere may have already done something irredeemable", Lore slumped to the floor drained.

Aram looked at him concerned, "you didn't overdo it, did you?".

Lore looked at him confused, "no I'm fine, I've never felt chaos magic move so quickly or abundantly before, whatever Guldamere is up to, its effecting the flow of power, it also seems to be releasing creatures from the abyss, we have to hurry".

Lore tried to stand but was too weakened by his last spell, "go on ahead Aram, I'll be right behind you, I just need to catch my breath, I'll be right behind you, scout ahead a short way and tell me what you find", Lore asked panting.

Aram nodded, he moved down the corridor, the sound of scuttling creatures was no longer audible, only the dripping of water from stalagmites and the footsteps of Aram's boots.

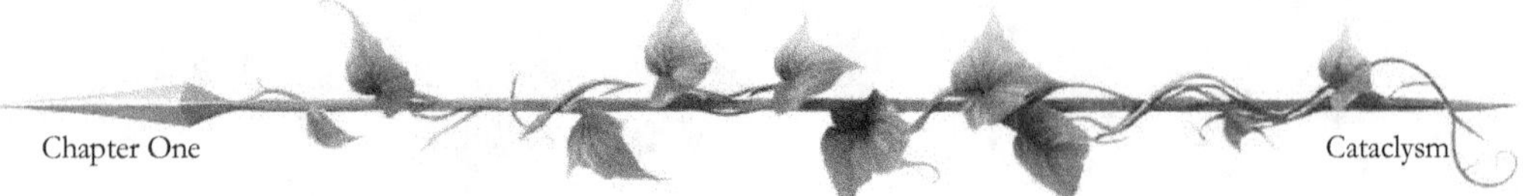

Aram found himself entering a large open cavern, three statues of semi-clad women were in the middle surrounding a luminescent whirlpool, at the other end was an opening overlooking an outside cliff face, one of the statues was slightly damaged and leaking out a smokey white miasma.

Out of the shadows stepped a young priestess.

"Hello squire, what brings you here?", she asked in a pitchy voice, Aram looked over to her suspiciously, "we were following a dark wizard, he raised prominent dead mages from across the land and brought them here with promises of immortality".

The priestess smiled at him, "well it's a good thing he's gone then", the girl said, Aram looked perplexed and asked, "where did he go?", "well in there I guess", she pointed to the whirlpool, Aram walked over to the pool and peered in, the priestess walked over to him, her voice changed into that of Guldamere as he said, "here take a closer look!".

Guldamere shoved Aram into the whirlpool, he put his hands together in prayer and a black miasma raised from the black cloaked figures as they stepped into the light, the black miasma flowed from them into Guldamere, Aram tried to escape but was fighting the current of the whirlpool.

"You're not Pendragon, but you'll have to do", Guldamere's voice echoed off the chamber walls, "you'll be the catalyst I use to enhance my power", Guldamere said raising one hand to the already damaged statue, then the other toward Aram.

The black cloaked figures started to chant as they channeled power to Guldamere, the black miasma reached toward Aram, dark shadow hands reached out from it, it held him firmly.

Life energy started to drain from Aram's body as the statue began to shake and turn to dust, the more it fell apart the stronger the mages seem to become as the room started to shake, sparks started appearing in the air like reality itself was becoming unstable.

Aram choked from the life being drained from his body, he looked to the entryway, standing there was Lore Casta Pendragon, fists clenched together he extended an arm towards Guldamere, grabbing his elbow firmly with his other hand, he launched a fireball at the dark wizard, sending him flying into the back of the cavern.

Lore shouted to Aram, "extend your staff!", Aram was weakened and struggling to stay afloat, but managed to take his staff from his back and extended it toward Lore, Lore grabbed the staff and pulled Aram from the water.

"Thank you master", Aram said looking drained, Lore looked over at Guldamere's chard corpse, the black miasma surrounding him swirled and picked him up from the ground, two of the black cloaked mages fell, drained of all of their life energy, Lore looked on horrified.

                                      by Lore Casta Pendragon

"Aram, the ones in black cloaks are amplifying his powers, we need to take them out first", Lore exclaimed.

Aram took his staff in hand, "time for some payback", he said rushing forward, he stabbed the point of the staff into the ground and somersaulted over it, launching himself into the air.

He lifted the staff over his head with him, as he fell, he brought it down with full force, the sound of crushing bone echoed throughout the cave as a black cloaked mage's head was caved in, the mage slumped to the ground in a heap the black miasma link between him and Guldamere wisping away.

Guldamere moved toward Aram but caught his own reflection in a shallow pool.

Skin was burned from his lower jaw, he growled with anger.

Summoning his power he moved with incredible speed and strength at Aram who brought up his staff for protection, a black miasma surrounded Guldamere's hand and made a sharp claw slashing at Aram, Aram managed to block the blow with his staff, but the force of the blow had him sliding backward toward Lore.

Lore slammed his fists together and pulled on his life energy to infuse it with chaos magic, the air began to move around Lore rapidly as Guldamere rushed forward to attack again, Lore moved his arms around using the lotus technique, full arcing circles around his body, as if collecting the air around him, he brought his feet a full one hundred eighty degrees and threw the air toward Guldamere.

Lore unleashed a torrent so devastating it threw Guldamere and his black cloaked acolytes backward against the far wall. Aram smiled at Lore astonished, "when were you going to teach me that one?", Aram said sarcastically, Lore smiled back, "maybe you haven't been reading my books enough", Lore chuckled.

Guldamere rose once again, his robes now in tatters, he growled with rage, the black miasma ripped the life from his remaining acolytes and they all fell to the floor, the smokey miasma coated Guldamere in a black and green hue.

It pulled him up, levitating him above the floor, making a shadow resembling a black hooded grim reaper with large taloned claws which grew to the size of wine barrels.

Guldamere flew toward the two men, lifting the black claws in an upward strike, he landed both hits on Aram and Lore, Aram blocked with his staff and Lore summoned a magic ward, a type of solid magic wall to protect himself, it shattered like glass on contact and they flew back and landed hard bouncing against the stone floor.

Guldamere flew forward and picked up Aram, he began to crush him in one claw, Aram screamed out in pain as the claw ripped into his flesh, he dropped his staff to the floor.

 by Lore Casta Pendragon

Lore rushed in fists together, then extending both hands out in front, he grunted with the effort as he sent multiple fireballs at Guldamere.

Guldamere saw him coming and dropped Aram, knocking the fireballs away with the shadow claws, as Lore came closer Guldamere tried to grab him in his clutches but Lore unleashed a fireball at point blank range, blowing even more of Guldamere's now decrepit face away.

Guldamere growled, "Fool!", and smacked Lore into the wall, Lore slumped to the ground.

Guldamere moved toward the damaged statue, he grabbed it in his blackened claw and he squeezed with all his strength, it began to shatter as light spewed forth from the cracks, chaos magic began to pour into Guldamere as the statue crumbled in his hands, astonished at the sheer power it yielded to him, he cackled, "with this power I will be nigh unstoppable!".

Aram stumbled to his feet blood dripping from his wounds, he walked toward Lore.

"Master, get up, we can't let Guldamere do this, get on your feet!", Aram shouted as he helped Lore up, blood dripped from Lore's mouth and he wiped it away with his hand.

Aram nodded to Lore as he picked up his staff and held it out in front of him, he channeled his life force into the weapon, then charged at Guldamere and threw the staff like a javelin at a rocketing speed.

A golden aura trailed behind it as it penetrating into Guldamere's body, the necromancer cried out in pain and Aram hit the floor from exhaustion.

Statue still in claw, Guldamere squeezed it with all his might, the cracks grew larger.

Lore could feel an influx of chaos magic pouring from the statue, "if Guldamere can use it to strengthen himself then so can I", Lore said, he slammed his fists together, electrical energy started crackling around him, he extended one arm and grabbed his elbow with his other hand, he pointed his index finger forward and aimed at Guldamere, "I can't allow this to continue", Lore yelled.

Electrical energy powered up around Lore, it crackled around him burning his robe and striking scorch marks across the floor.

Guldamere's eyes went wide, seeing the danger he was in, his black miasma claw extended from him, it picked up Aram and moved him into the path between Lore and Guldamere just as Lore was about to unleash his attack, "Aram, I can't hold it, you have to move!", Lore shouted, but Aram wasn't responding, his body was lifeless in Guldamere's clawed hand.

Lore's vision blurred from over extending himself, at the last minute he fired to the right to avoid hitting Aram.

                    by Lore Casta Pendragon

A lightning strike with all the force the master wizard could muster exploded forth launching Lore backward with such force that he was thrown into the wall behind him, the lightning strike slammed into another muse statue and it shattered into pieces releasing a torrent of chaos magic as Guldamere shattered the other in his claw, the power in the chamber began to build immensely.

Lore slammed his fists together, crosses his arms in a cross pattern in front of him and summoned a powerful magic ward around him with the last of his life force.

The room was overcome with bright golden light as chaos magic penetrated into Lore and Guldamere from the statues, the magical energy exploded outward, Guldamere was caught in the explosion, the flesh was blown from his body as it engulfed him and Aram.

The peak of Mount Muse exploded into a giant golden energy ball, Guldamere and Lore were thrown out from the mountain peak like missiles in opposite directions, the remaining statue shattered into five shards and were thrown in all directions, the giant ball of gold chaos magic grew massive in size and rose up above the peak of the mountain shooting giant golden beams of power over the land.

It melted through the stone, digging huge gorges into the earth as it released its power, cities and towns that were visible from the mountaintop were vaporized as people screamed out at the sight of the immense power burning everything in its wake.

A massive earthquake ravaged the land, mountaintops erupted into rivers of magma.

Bodies of water evaporated as everything was consumed by the blast, the energy ball got smaller as it released power, until, in one final coup de grace, it exploded into a dark shockwave that shattered the mountain beneath, leaving a crater where Mt. Muse once stood.

The shattered pieces of the final statue landed at five points around the land, magic wards shielded those area from the devastation, what was left was a desolate smoldering wasteland with five patches of land left unspoiled, the rest was completely ravaged.

Hours later Guldamere awoke, he rose to his knees in the remnants of a destroyed church in what was once the capital city of Thalaria.

Smoldering fires raged about him, the dark smoke around him was thick and dusty, he might have coughed if he had a throat left to do so, most of his flesh had been blasted from his bones, he looked down at his skeletal hand which he was still quite able to move.

"Interesting", Guldamere said perplexed as he turned his hand back and forth in front of his face, the black smokey miasma clung to him like his own flesh used to do, he caught his reflection in a broken mirror seeing his face mostly gone, his eyes now just smokey black miasma with gold pupils, his tattered robe still draped about him, the world was dark, the sky

      by Lore Casta Pendragon

full of dark clouds, he cackled manically in a raspy voice, "I did it, I'm immortal!", Guldamere shouted victoriously.

He stood and extended his hand out to test his newfound power, the people that weren't completely obliterated in the cataclysm around him began to rise from the rubble, the first few rose to see that he was reviving the fallen and they begged for him to rescue their loved ones.

Guldamere wrapped the hood of his cloak around his wounded face and held his head high, "I only revive those who worship me for I am Guldamere and even the gods fear my power", Guldamere proclaimed, the people began to kneel before him in reverence as he began to revive the fallen.

Days later Lore Casta Pendragon found himself awakened by a bucket of water to the face, his arms were held with thick magically reinforced chains that glowed with a golden light, he blinked blurry eyes as two people came into view.

Before him stood Aram, behind him Guldamere in his lich form, he seemed to be in some kind of cave with shimmering black walls and a large stone door, Lore spoke in a weak and defeated voice.

"Aram are you alright?", but Aram did not respond, his head down, the lich spoke.

"Now that the world knows who caused this cataclysm, I no longer have use for this wretch", Guldamere said waving a skeletal hand, Lore watched as Aram's risen body turn to dust and bone and fell to the floor.

Lore looked at Guldamere with fury in his eyes, "what have you done!", He growled, the lich cackled and replied, "Aram told everyone, well everyone who I revived, that it was you who caused the disaster and since he was your apprentice and with your less than reputable past, everyone believed him", the lich cackled at his own brilliance.

Lore fought against his chains attempting to break free, "you fowl worm, when I get out of here, you'll pay for this", Lore said, the lich smirked at him, "oh?", Guldamere laughed teasingly, "you're never leaving this place Pendragon", he spat at him, "you're going to be here until I find out how to extract the power within you, then I'll discard you like your little pet there", he pointed a skeletal finger to the pile of ash and bone that used to be Aram, Lore slumped down hanging from his chains.

"Fact is, this might just be the safest place for you, since I raised a lot of the peons from the dead, I am now somewhat revered as their savior, little do they know that I'll be harvesting

by Lore Casta Pendragon

their young to feed my own being", he cackled, "I am Immortal as long as I have them to give me more life".

Lore raised his head, a golden light shined in his eyes, he summoned the power within him and planted his feet firmly on the ground circulating his power as he did with his hands, then launched a kick forward knocking Guldamere out of the room with a powerful gust of wind, two circular steps of his feet and the wind slammed the stone doors shut one after the other in the lich's face.

Guldamere started feeling frantically around the door for a way to open it as golden runes appeared running down crack of the door, it burned Guldamere's skeletal fingertips to ash, the lich scampered back looking at his damaged hand.

He was locked out of his own prison, "fine Pendragon, you can't hide away in there forever and when you emerge, I will be waiting for you and I will take the power from you!", Guldamere shouted.

The lich extended a skeletal hand, black miasma swirled over it and coalesced into a raven, the raven perched itself above the doorway, the bird opened its wings wide and black miasma fell from them over the door sealing it from the outside, Guldamere then walked away, leaving pendragon imprisoned within.

                                        by Lore Casta Pendragon

Thalaria
Road
River
Iron halls
Ravenhill
The Living forest
Riverside
Paladins reach
Dawnshire
Dragons well
Gutfish lake
Necropyre
Torins well
The pit
Mt. Muse crater
The elven forest
Ruined tower of maal
Eastern desert
Bamboo forest
Oasis
The ronin city

Chapter Two

All heart

Ailyn Allheart was catching fish in the river near his home, he had short blond hair and wore rags and fishing pants, he waded in the water up to his hips standing as still as he could, he wiggled one finger in the water patiently waiting for a fish to swim by.

"You might actually catch one this time", taunted his older brother Aidem from the riverbank, "shh", his father Aethor whispered next to him, a fish approached, Ailyn stood still and eager, wiggling his finger in the water, the fish grew closer until finally it lunged, Ailyn curled his finger into the fish's mouth and pulled it from the water.

The fish thrashed about wildly as Ailyn bear hugged it, it was half the size of the boy of fifteen years, he struggled to keep hold of it as he stumbled on the smooth river stones and running water at his feet, he almost lost it as the slippery fish flicked out of his grasp, he caught it upside down, hugging it tightly, the fish slapped him in the face with a powerful wet tail and Ailyn fell into the water losing the fish.

Ailyn could hear bellows of hearty laughter from the shore from under the water and his face went red, he didn't want to resurface, "maybe I can just die in the river", he thought to himself embarrassed, he didn't resurface until he started to lose his breath.

Ailyn surfaced and stumbled to the river bank, his father Aethor helped him out of the water, "that was a big one for a first timer, Aidem's first one was no bigger than a carrot", Aethor said, Aidem grunted "least I didn't lose mine", Aidem said.

"Boys", the soft voice of their mother Asta called from their house near the river, "dinner will be ready soon".

Aethor carried a stick with a dozen fish tied to it back to the house, he was a thin man with a defined muscular build, he had light brown hair and trained often, working through martial forms.

He had a tree near the house with poles sticking out of it that he used as a sparring partner, working through katas, he frequently did strength training, his family often watched with admiration and his boys Aidem and Ailyn sometimes joined him, Aidem more often than Ailyn as he was five years older and much more capable.

Ailyn spent more of his time with his mother, tending to household chores and helping in the garden, playing with the various strange creatures he found there, while Aidem hunted, fished and trained with his father.

                    by Lore Casta Pendragon

Their house was small and modest and was located at the edge of the water in a place called Riverside, just beyond was the living forest, a dense forest created during the cataclysm full of fast-growing vegetation said to be cursed with dark magic.

Further downstream was the city of Dawnshire, a city controlled by the church of the god feared, a religious sect who worshipped Guldamere the god feared, the all-powerful ruler of Thalaria.

Aethor stored the fish in a barrel of salt outside the house, ready for transport to Dawnshire the next day, while the boys went inside, Asta ruffled Ailyn's hair as he walked in the door and he smiled at her lovingly, she was a homely woman with blond hair and blue eyes, her most defining feature was her kind heart, always there with a welcoming hug and words of encouragement.

Their house was small, just one large room with some beds at one end, a cooking pot and a fireplace elevated at the other end, the roof was made of large leaves from the trees around the living forest, straw and timber, for the most part, it kept out the rain and blended in with the environment which kept them safe from the nightmare creatures that roamed the blasted lands beyond, the fireplace was made of river stones and clay, the floor was made of stone and timber.

Aethor had built the house here in Riverside to get away from Dawnshire and the Religious insurgents that lived there, Aethor hated the church of the god feared and often attended political meetings opposing them, he was chastised his whole life for being a descendant of Aram Allheart, who assisted Lore Casta Pendragon in instigating the calamity known only as the cataclysm and so, chose to live outside of the safety of the fortified cities, relying on his own strength.

They sat around the fireplace as the sun disappeared and as they ate a hearty meal of fish and vegetables Aethor told them stories of heroes of old, including that of Lore Casta Pendragon, Aram Allheart and of the Cataclysm.

Ailyn was seated in front of the fireplace, sleepily he asked Aethor, "how long ago was the cataclysm?", "It happened well before I was born", Aethor replied with look of contemplation on his face, "I think about five hundred years or so, the cataclysm refaced the land and much was lost", he sighed.

"You know they say that our ancestor Aram Allheart assisted Lore Casta Pendragon in causing the calamity, they say they messed with powers they couldn't comprehend, if you believe the words of the church of the god feared", Aethor grunted looking into the fire, Ailyn could see the resentment on his face.

"Father, can I come with you to Dawnshire tomorrow", said Ailyn, "absolutely not", Aethor replied quickly, "I wouldn't go there at all if I didn't need to sell our produce and buy supplies", Ailyn looked disappointed then replied, "but Aidem always gets to go with you", he whined.

Aethor gave him a disapproving look and smiled at Asta, "I need someone with a strong back to help me move the wares into Wynn's shop and I need you to stay here and protect your mother while I'm gone", Asta smiled back at him.

"I'll be fine Aethor, it'll do him good to see the city and see how things work around here", she said, Aethor sighed deeply, "fine you can come", Ailyn's smile grew wide with excitement, Aethor looked him in the eye sternly and said, "we are protected for the most part here at the edge of the living forest, but beyond the lands are full of horrors, the blasted lands between here and Dawnshire are dangerous, so stay in the boat until we get to the city", "s-sure thing dad", Ailyn said grinning, "we leave at first light", Aethor stood, "come Aidem, we need to light the torches for the night", he said as Aidem stood to join him outside, Asta tucked Ailyn into bed, Ailyn looked to his mother, "mum why do we keep the torches lit at night?", she walked to the window to watch them.

"Because outside of the safe havens of the forest there are creatures that prey in the dark, I am thankful they are rarely seen here so close to the forest, but just in case, we light the torches, even the light retreats in fear of them, so we can tell if they are nearby", she explained.

Ailyn shivered at the thought of something so evil, "try not to dwell on it little one, you have a big day tomorrow, get some rest", Ailyn closed his eyes, "love you mother", he said as he fell asleep.

That night Aethor woke, Asta was asleep next to him in his bed, he brushed the hair from her face and smiled, he got out of bed and slipped on his boots, he felt something squishy splat between his toes, "ahhh", he groaned, "blasted shoe slugs", he muttered sleepily.

The shoe slugs liked to eat the dirt and dead skin from your clothes in the early mornings, while they typically retreated before the sun got too warm, sometimes they'll still be in there in the early hours, friendly and even cute creatures, they were often used to clean clothing, but not when you accidently tread on them.

Aethor walked outside and shook the slug juice from between his toes, scooping it out of his boot, his hand covered in slimy green goo, he washed his boot and foot with a nearby hand cranked water pump, then placed his boot on his foot and grabbed the torch on the sconce near him.

He turned to use the outhouse in the vegetable garden, the night was quiet and dark, he placed the torch on the wall sconce next to him then let out a sigh as he relieved himself.

 by Lore Casta Pendragon

When he was done, the light in the outhouse dimmed, Aethor looked at it alarmed and he grabbed the torch, slowly opening the door, he peered through the crack out into the garden then crouched down and moved low through the foliage.

Hidden by tall plants, he made his way back to the house which was now much darker than before, he placed his torch back on the wall sconce and left his boots outside, then slowly closed the door, placing a beam in front of it to secure it shut.

He made himself ready, moments passed in utter silence, until he heard trotting and panting running down the road close to the house, he looked outside through a window, several large doglike creatures with large sharp teeth and protruding jaws sprinted by quickly as if running down their prey.

Aethor ducked against the wall as they passed until the sound of running paws stopped, the light slowly returned to normal as the creatures faded off into the distance, Aethor gave a sigh of relief and kept watch for several more minutes before returning to his bed.

Hours later Ailyn and Aidem were woken by Aethor, "wake up sleepy heads it's time to pack the boat". Ailyn sat up groggily and rubbed his eyes while Aidem pulled the blanket over his head, Asta started preparing food for the boys to take with them, Aethor saw Aidem not rising so he went outside until he found a bunch of tickle worms clustered together in a nearby tree.

He covered his hand with a cloth then grabbed a few making his way back into the house, Asta noticed what he was doing and struggled to hold back a cheeky grin as Aethor lifted the bottom of Aidem's blanket and threw the worms under.

Aidem began writhing and thrashing with laughter under the blanket as the worms wriggled all over him, tickling him mercilessly, they all burst into laughter as Aidem's blanket was kicked off and he stumbled around trying to throw the worms off of him.

Aidem rushed outside removing his shirt, then dunked a bucket of water over his head to wash them all off, his hair now stuck down against his face, the rest of the family still roaring with laughter joined him outside, he moved the hair showing his father a very unamused pout of disdain, Ailyn, Aethor and Asta laughed even harder as Aidem grumbled sleepily.

They went down to the river to a small row boat with cart wheels strapped to the sides, the row boat could be converted into a cart for transporting goods by inserting the oars into the bottom like an axle, an invention of Aethor's.

They walked along a short wharf, throwing bags of vegetables folded into large tree bark and tied with string and two small barrels of salted fish with straps on them like a backpack into the boat.

        by Lore Casta Pendragon

"Farewell Asta we'll be back in a day or so", said Aethor, "yeah sure, tell Wynn I said hi, oh and try not to drink too much", Asta said waving them off.

"It takes only a few hours downstream by boat and its safer, but takes almost a full day to ride back by the road, we'll hire a Carribook to help us get home once we're in Dawnshire", Aethor said grabbing a long oar, Aidem grabbed one too and Ailyn sat in the middle.

They made their way downstream, the waters were calm, clear and level at first, but soon gained pace as they headed downhill.

"Keep her straight Aidem", Aethor said as the boat started rotating too much to the right, they stuck the large oars into the water, moving expertly down the rapids pushing the oars against the rocks to avoid any collisions.

A few hours later the river calmed and became darker as it widened into a large lake, "Dawnshire is on the far west side", Aethor said, "we are far from the protection of the living forest now, always be on your guard, even during the daytime".

An ashy dark fog permeated the lands outside of the five habitable regions of Thalaria, often referred to as the blasted lands.

Ailyn looked out at the water, a large serpentine finned tail moved through the water behind them, "dad", Ailyn said, "dad, there is something behind us", Aethor raised his oar and as the creature moved in closer, he splashed the water with it and it swum away quickly.

"Gullfish are skittish alone, but frenzy in groups, they are horrifying to look at, like an eel with a human skull", he said, Ailyn turned to look forward as the large gate and walls of Dawnshire's port came into view.

Standing ten men tall and made of stone, the walls surrounding Dawnshire were covered in sconces, "watch your words carefully in Dawnshire boys, these people are quite protective of Lord Guldamere and don't ever mention the cataclysm here, best not to stir up the church folk", Aethor said.

The voice of a guard called from atop the water gate, "what business do you have in Dawnshire?", the guard called down, Aethor called back, "we have wares, fish and produce for Wynn's shop".

A few moments past then the gates began to open up and they waded the boat inside the port, it was small and circular, five wooden wharfs with stairs leading up the stone walls, most the shops were made of wood and stone, wooden signs hung out in front of them indicating what was for sale inside, immediately in front of them was Wynns shop, on the other side of the street was a tavern called the slippery squid.

                    by Lore Casta Pendragon

Aethor, Ailyn and Aidem pulled the small boat onto a boat ramp at one side of the wharf, taking the cart wheels off the sides and sliding them into position on the bottom of the boat with the oars acting as axle points.

The boat now resembled a cart, they wheel it around to Wynn's shop, Aethor and Aidem strapped the barrels to their backs and Ailyn grabbed the bundles of tied vegetables.

As they pushed the ornate wooden door to enter the shop the bell on the door jingled, Aethor placed the barrels on the floor, "Aethor!", yelled a large burly man in an apron behind the counter as he slammed down a cleaver into a fish and moved to greet them.

He picked Aethor up and bear hugged him against his large belly and fishy apron.

"You look as good as you smell Wynn", Aethor struggled to say against the force of the man's hug, he placed Aethor down, "it is good to see you Aethor and you've gotten so big Aidem", Wynn said as he patted Aidem's hair with fishy hands, Aidem sneered and was very unimpressed with this as he picked fish guts from his hair.

On one wall of the shop was a taxidermized gullfish, it had a large human like head, protruding jaw and rows of large razor like teeth with the body of an eel, under it was an assorted display of prepared seafoods, on the other wall were displays of fresh fruits, vegetables and barrels of spices.

"What have you brought me today, Aethor", bellowed Wynn, "vegetables and salted fish", Ailyn interrupted, Wynn leaned over to get a better look at Ailyn, "you must be Ailyn, nice to finally meet you", Wynn said, his voice booming without effort.

His head was twice the size of Ailyn's and Ailyn shied back afraid of having fish guts smeared in his hair, "y-yes sir", Ailyn said nervously, Wynn straightened up and turned to Aethor, "he looks so much like Asta, how is the woman?", Wynn asked.

"As vibrant as the day I met her", Aethor responded, "she's made you soft Aethor", Wynn chuckled, "when I'm done with the shop, we should catch up at the tavern over yonder", Wynn offered, "I bet I can still drink you under the table", Wynn said with a wry smile, "you're on Wynn", Aethor said taking up the challenge with a wide grin, "boys take the cart round back off the street, I'm going to help Wynn with the goods", Aethor offered.

Aidem and Ailyn went outside and began to move the cart to the back of the shop, behind the shop was a small stable full of straw, inside it was a large two-legged winged creature with long feathers and a long neck.

by Lore Casta Pendragon

"Bacaw!", It squawked as the two boys passed it and put the cart down to rest, strolling past the back alley they overheard the voices of some figures dressed in the religious robes of the church of the god feared, one man was shockingly huge and towered over the other.

"Aethor Allheart has been seen entering the city", said one voice.
Aidem and Ailyn crouch behind a barrel to listen closer.

"truly", said the large man, "so, the trouble-maker has returned", "it's an insult that an Allheart still exists in this age", "well then, we'll set up a little welcoming party for our guest then, shall we?", The two men laughed as they walked out toward the street.

"What do they want with our dad", Ailyn said, "I don't know, we best be getting back", Aidem replied.

Wynn and Aethor walked out of the shop, "we'll stay in the inn tonight then head off in the morning", said Aethor.

"Nonsense Aethor, you can stay with me at the shop tonight and I'll lend you my Carribook Dimitri for the trip home", said Wynn, "he's fast and can make his way back to me on his own", "thanks Wynn, I owe you one" said Aethor.

Ailyn and Aidem ran up to their father, "dad, dad, we heard two men talking in the back alley", said Aidem, "they were talking about you", said Ailyn, "always the popular one aren't you Aethor", Wynn bellowed sarcastically, "I'm sure it's nothing boys, we won't be staying long, we'll rest up here tonight and head off first thing in the morning", Aethor reassured them, "come along now", he said looking around as they crossed the street and entered the slippery squid tavern.

They found a table and ordered food and ale.

Later that evening Aethor put his face down on the table with a thud, Wynn laughed heartedly into his cups, "you're still a lightweight Allheart", he bellowed, Ailyn and Aidem had already gone to bed above Wynn's shop.

A drunk at a nearby table turned to face them briefly, sneered then left his coin on the table as he got up to leave in a hurry, Aethor grunted and conceded defeat.

Wynn bellowed a victorious cry followed up by a massive throaty burp, "I win again, lets order you some water, can't have you driving the cart back drunk, can we?", Wynn said patting Aethor on the back.

A while later Aethor raised his head, "time to call it a night old friend", he said groggily, but as they stood up to leave, the patron that hurried out earlier barged in with a dozen other men in

by Lore Casta Pendragon

the robes of the god feared, one huge muscular man in a black leather vest with legs the size of tree trunks ducked through the doorway, he could barely fit through and stood towering above them, some patrons got up and left in a hurry, others stayed to watch the show.

"That's him there, the big one called him Allheart", said the drunk patron as the huge man put some coins in his palm, he then scampered out of the tavern away into the night.

"Allheart ay", he called to Aethor, "no doubt a treacherous dog just like that Aram and the rest of his ilk", the large man taunted.

Aethor sighed, placed some coin on the table and got up to leave, but as he tried to walk by, the big man placed a large hand on his chest, "why don't you stay a while, you still look thirsty", he said with a devilish grin, Aethor looked up at him angrily as Wynn walked toward them, he squared up to the man, looking up at him, Wynn was a big man, but this man was gigantic.

"Well, well, it seems the shop keep wants to pick a fight with the town guard, you sure you want to do that Wynndell?", Wynn stared at him, "leave him alone Harram Halfborn", Wynn warned.

One of the other men in robes grabbed a drink on a table nearby and threw it at Aethor, he moved his head one inch and it missed.

It showered another table of four patrons in ale, angrily they got up wiping the ale from their faces as the men moved into the room around Wynn and Aethor, a mug came flying into the face of the drink thrower from the angry patron nearby, shattering and knocking him out cold as all hell broke loose.

Aethor took a step back and used his side kick technique stepping his back foot behind his front foot then launching a powerful kick at one of the robed men, it hit him square in the middle, knocking him off his feet, the man folded and hit the floor unconscious.

The four men from the table rushed four of the robed men, throwing punches left and right, Harram Halfborn threw two punches into Wynn's bloated stomach then a heavy uppercut to his jaw, Wynn stumbled back and a robed man screamed as Wynn fell on top of him smashing through a table, squashing the man underneath him, the man groaned but didn't move.

Two robed men either side of Aethor came forward, one man swung a chair at him and Aethor threw a straight punch through the chair shattering it and knocking the man out cold, the second man tried to punch Aethor but he easily avoided him once then a second time, moving his head inches in either direction, as the third punch closed in Aethor intercepted it with a backfist under the arm and into the man's face, with a crack his opponent hit the floor.

Wynn got up as Harram grabbed a patron assaulting one of his men and raised him above his head, the patron screamed at being lifted ten feet in the air as Harram threw the man into Wynn and they both fell back through the bar counter, glass and liquor smashing everywhere.

     by Lore Casta Pendragon

Wynn got up with two large bottles of hard liquor in either hand as Harram came for him, he smashed them together from either direction at Harram's head but Harram had his guard up, the bottles smashed into his arms, glass and liquor smashed all over him, some of the liquor got into his eyes, it burned and he grunted, squinting and trying to see Wynn, Wynn raised a big hairy fist and landed a mighty punch to Harram's face sending him backward.

The remaining three robed men approached Aethor, one of them pulled a knife from his robe, Aethor saw the danger and turned to run, he sprinted up the stairs and they follow him in pursuit, he ducked into a room which joined directly with the room next to it and ran straight out the second door, two men followed him into the room and one stayed outside, a working girl screamed as Aethor dashed through the room and out the door, the door opened and he rushed at the robed man in his path delivering a jumping side kick sending him backflipping over the rail, he fell into a carriage wheel chandelier.

The rope snapped and the chandelier almost squashed Harram as it fell, Harram saw it coming and moved out of the way, Wynn took advantage of the distraction and tried to tackle Harram around the waist, but to his surprise Harram didn't move, Wynn was a big guy, but Harram was a monster.

Harram put his hands together and hammered down on Wynn's back, Wynn groaned out in pain but held on until another two strikes made him fall down to a knee, still holding on, Harram hit him again and again and eventually Wynn lost his drink, barfing over the floor, falling unconscious.

The two robed men pursuing Aethor come out of the room, then pointed toward him, Aethor took his stance and they were taken aback by his readiness to receive them.

As the first one came forward Aethor did a one eighty degree turn onto his knee, his other foot spinning in a powerful sweep taking his opponents legs out from under him, he turned with the momentum, crossing one hand over his body to his opposing foot and flipped upside down, his back foot went straight up in the air with one hand planted on the ground, his used the momentum to bring his foot plummeting down into his prone opponent to finish him off, then frog leaped himself to his feet.

His last opponent holding the knife slashed at him, Aethor blocked the blade with his outer arm to stop it hitting any vital parts, grunting as the knife cut his flesh.

He leaped backward, grabbing at the wound on his arms he glared at the man, anger is his eyes, the blood dripped down his arm to his hand and he brought his hand to his mouth and licked the blood.

His eyes changed to red as his opponent slashed at his throat, he backflipped and kicked his opponents knife hand up with one foot and connected with his jaw with his other foot, sending him in the air, the man landed on his back, the knife clanged to the floor.

           by Lore Casta Pendragon

Aethor ripped off his shirt and made a makeshift tunica, tying it around his wounded arm, his eyes returned to their normal brown, blood dripped to the floor from the wound.

No sooner did he finish this, Harram Halfborn came crashing through the door behind him knocking him through the rail and through a table one floor below, an oil lamp crashed to the floor setting the tavern on fire, Aethor got to his feet dazed and confused as Harram jumped down from the second-floor balcony.

Harram linked his fingers together over his head and charged forward with an overhead hammer fist attack, Aethor moved out to the side and attempted his spinning sweep to Harram's leg, which connected but failed to move the man's giant leg, which made him smile menacingly at Aethor's weakness.

Realizing his mistake Aethor did a backward handspring avoiding Harram's meaty fist, immediately following it up with his dragon kick, it hit Harram directly in his midsection knocking the wind out of him, but Harram grabbed his foot and pulling him forward violently grabbing him by the throat and lifting him up.

Aethor struggled choking as the tavern burned around them, Harram grunted and headbutted Aethor leaving a bloody gash on his head, the blood ran down his face and Aethor licked at it, he smiled as he looked into Harram's eyes his eyes going red.

Harram looked at him confused as Aethor placed his fingers at Harram's chest, Harram looked down as Aethor used his short-ranged punch technique slamming Harram's heart, his chest indented with the force of the blow and Harram stumbled back, dropping Aethor and holding his chest.

Harram dropped to one knee gasping for air as Aethor grabbed his neck from the pain, they looked at each other nodding and laughed with respect at each other's strength.

Ailyn woke to the commotion next door and ran to the window above Wynn's shop to see the fire burning in the slippery squid, "wake up Aidem", he shouted shaking his brother, they rushed down stairs and out of the shop to the tavern to see their father and Harram, the patrons desperately trying to put out the fire and wake the unconscious people.

Ailyn and Aidem rushed over to Wynn and helped him to his feet, "we have to get these people out of here", Wynn said obviously pained and struggling to move, Wynn ignored his pain and picked up a patron in each arm, he carried them outside and moved back in for more.

Ailyn and Aidem looked on as Harram charged at Aethor, Aethor used his weight and momentum against him by throwing himself forward and ducking into a ball at Harram's feet, he tripped on Aethor and crashed through the wall, falling from a ledge on the other side.

"ALLHEART!", He shouted as he crashed through a wooden wharf below, it splintered as he disappeared into the water beneath.

by Lore Casta Pendragon

Ailyn and Aidem moved to their father's aid, but he raised a hand to stop them, fire burned around him, he stood slowly fists clenched and shirtless, defined muscles glistened with sweat, looking like they were carved of stone, red eyes from his blood rage technique burned like the fire around him, the image was burned into Ailyn's mind, this was his father, Aethor Allheart, the warrior.

As they turn to leave Ailyn spotted a single raven, black smoke trailing its movements as it perched on the roof of Wynn's shop watching them.

They returned to Wynn's shop and dressed their wounds, "the church of the god feared", Wynn scoffed, "what a joke, nothing more than common street thugs", Aidem said with disdain as he helped to sew the cut on Aethor's arm.

"What did they want with you father", Ailyn said as he dabbed the wound on Aethor's head with a damp rag to clean it, "it was Aram's fault, my whole life I've been persecuted because Aram was named a heretic to the church of the god feared, having the name Allheart painted a target on my back, that's why I had to become strong, so I could fight to protect myself and the ones I love, one day, mark my words, I'll have my revenge against the church of the god feared", Aethor got up.

"Wynn, we have to be going, no doubt this will cause more problems for you if we stay, will you be alright?", Aethor asked, Wynn was laying down on his stomach shirtless with a bucket in one hand unable to move, large bruises covered him from where Harram had struck him.

"I'll be fine Aethor, just hand me a drink from behind the counter, I'll just stay drunk until I wake tomorrow, that should dull the pain", he tried to bellow out a laugh only to stop and wince in pain, he coughed a few times then waved goodbye.

"Take the Carribook, get out of here, but be careful on the road, there are much worse things creeping around in the darkness beyond these walls at night, just release Dimitri when you're done with him, he'll sprint right back to me".

Aethor thanked Wynn for everything and they move out of the shop, they strapped Dimitri the Carribook to their boat-cart and climb in, they started to trot down the road, the tavern fire was just quenched by the local patrons.

A carriage of city guardsmen in the robes of the church of the god feared came past them as they made their way along the city street, Ailyn looked in the window and saw a man with a black wide brimmed hat and scars all over his face looking back at him, he stuck his head out of the window of the carriage lifted his hat so he can see better and gave the three a good once over as he passed by, he grinned wide and then sat back into his seat.

They made their way to the north road gate, a guardsman atop the parapet called down, "it's

late, nightmare creatures lurk in the dark beyond the wall, head back", Aethor whistled to get his attention then flicked him a gold coin, the gates opened to let them out and closed behind them.

They lit some torches and continued up the north road which paralleled the river they came down on.

Some ways up they met a crossroads, a sign pointed left and right, on the left the sign said, beware! The Living Forest lies ahead, on the right it said, Riverside, pointing directly at a stone bridge crossing the river away from the forest.

They took the right to cross the bridge but about midway over they heard howls coming from the other side, "barghasts!", Aethor shouted.

"I saw them running past our house the other night, it seems they've caught our scent, YAH!", he yelled as he whipped the reins, Dimitri let out a squark and started to run at speed over the bridge, they turned down the road and a few minutes later their torches dimmed, Aidem spotted a barghast running to their right, Ailyn spotted another to their left, they converged behind them, catching up with them, "YAH!", Aethor yelled, pushing Dimitri to run faster.

The barghast's started to gain on them as they began to move downhill between a rocky gorge, large dead vines crisscrossed overhead, the barghast's jumped from one to another, quickly advancing overhead, as they started to make their way back uphill, they lost speed and a barghast pounced at them.

Aethor stood up and with a straight kick, knocked the beast away, it whimpered, rolled, roared then got back up and continued chasing them, the other barghast moved in front of them, Aidem ripped off a thick branch from a passing dead tree and as the barghast tried to take a bite out of Dimitri he threw the branch into its gnashing teeth, Dimitri fluttered into wings, jumped and kicked the beast into the ground as the cart rolled over it.

The sound of cracking bones crunched under the cartwheel sending the cart bouncing upwards, Ailyn fell over the side, Aidem grabbed his hand and helped to pull him up as the remaining barghast ran up and snapped at Ailyn's feet.

Ailyn grabbed onto the side of the cart, but couldn't lift himself up, "Ailyn!", Aidem shouted as the barghast came in for more, he leaped from the cart onto the barghast's back, it thrashed to shake him off but he held onto it, then kicked off the barghast launching himself forward and the barghast to the right, it crashed into a fence and rolled down a hill, leaving deep claw marks as it fell.

Aidem rolled to a stop dust kicking up around him, Aethor pulled the cart to a stop, the barghast got up and ran back the other way to devour the easier meal left behind in the chase, Ailyn and Aethor pulled Aidem back into the cart, "are you alright Aidem?", Aethor asked,

Aidem just nodded and sat down in the cart, with a flick of the reins they sped down off the road.

Many hours later they arrived at first light back at Riverside, Asta heard the carriage approaching and jumped out of bed, she covered her mouth in shock as she saw them.

"What happened to you?", she said, Aethor jumped down from the cart and embraced her, "we were attacked by soldiers in Dawnshire, then chased half way home by nightmare creatures, I don't think we'll be returning to Dawnshire again anytime soon", Aethor explained.

Asta helped the boys down from the carriage, she hugged them tightly then led them inside for much needed rest.

Aethor gave Dimitri and big juicy carrot from the garden and removed the ropes tying him to the cart, Dimitri gave a happy squawk and sprinted off much faster than he was able to while dragging a cart and three men disappearing quickly down the road.
"Be safe my friend and thank you", Aethor called to him as Dimitri the Carribook rounded the bend.

Chapter Three

Silent Silus

Salin Silus stood lined up at the end of his pallet bed at the end of the room, his sheets folded, his nightwear packed away neatly in a lockbox at the base of his pallet, he wore leather fingerless gloves, rags and a flat tweed cap, looking the very image of a street rat.

Next to him was Cinder Crowler, a pretty young girl wearing the same outfit with the addition of a dirty red scarf hiding half her face and short dark hair.

The workhouse man strolled into the room, a dozen beds with children lined up military style in front of him, he assessed each one as he walked past, making sure that not a single thing was out of place.

As he approached the center of the room, he noticed one child had kicked his nightwear under his pallet instead of folding it, he bent down till he was eye to eye with the boy.

"Ya think I wouldn't notice boy", he said in a voice that clearly dictated his intelligence, the boy started to sob as the Workhouse man grabbed a big thick leather blackjack from his back pocket, "hold out ya hands boy", the boy shook and sobbed as he lifted his hands up in front of him, with a clack the workhouse man slapped the blackjack down on the boys hands, he squealed in pain, sobbing loudly as he pissed his pants, "are you kidding me", the workhouse man said angrily as he slapped him again even harder.

He grabbed the boy by the scruff and threw him toward the door, "go wash up and when ya done you can scrub me floors ya just soiled", as the boy turned to leave the workhouse man addressed the rest of the children in the room making sure the boy heard him well, "I know one boy who won't be eaten tonight", he said looking back at him, utterly defeated the boy left the room tears streaming down his face.

The room was deadly silent, the rest of the children tensed as the workhouse man walked past, he stopped to inspect a child's bedding when Silus noticed a food wrapper tucked under Cinder's Pallet.

Silus took two rocks out of his pocket and threw them at the door at the other end of the room just behind the head of the workhouse man, they hit the door one after the other, making an audible knock, knock, as they hit.

"Huh", the workhouse man said, "who is it?", "I'm busy", no answer came and he walked briskly to the door and opened it looking bewildered, but he saw no one and grunted as he slammed it shut, Silus used the distraction to quickly move over to Cinder's bed pallet and shoved the wrapper in his pocket.

by Lore Casta Pendragon

He moved back into position just as the workhouse man turned around to continued his inspection, he noticed two stones on the ground and picked them up, he looked around the room slowly, then thought to himself, "surely not, I doubt they're smart enough for that, or would even dare", he dropped the rocks near the door as the boy from earlier came back with a bucket of water and a rag, "clean those up to piss pants", the workhouse man said to him.

Cinder Smiled at Silus and mouthed a silent, "thank you", Silus slightly bowed his head and smiled back.

The workhouse man turned to leave and as he walked out, he said, "work starts in an hour, ya working the market this morning, remember if you're caught, you ain't from here, I don't need to tell ya what happens if ya cause trouble".

The children of the workhouse did all sorts of work for the workhouse man and in return they got a roof over their heads and one meal at night usually consisting of an assortment of what they stole that day, things like fruit and bread were usually an easy steal, things like meat were more difficult as the children didn't have anywhere to cook so they'd have to steal it prepared, if you managed that, you were considered a hero in the workhouse.

The children who were caught were severely beaten by the town guardsmen, some lost their hands and were no longer welcomed back to the workhouse, those that ratted out the workhouse man were usually never seen again, usually killed, sold as slaves or imprisoned and sent to mine the pit.

Silus walked over to the door and picked up the rocks he threw earlier, he put them back into his pocket.

"You're mad", said Cinder shaking her head, Silus just smiled at her and walked out the door.

They convened in the marketplace a little while later, the workhouse man sat at a stall at one end, selling various wares that were probably stolen, once a week at dawn, the city of Ravenhill had a street market, vendors would use the stalls the city provided to hock their wares.

Silus was always excited to see what new things were for sale and the smell of food permeated the air, market day was always the best day of the week as it was the day the children of the workhouse had ample food to eat.

"Ok kids, time to go play", the Workhouse man said and a dozen children scattered in every direction, Cinder and Silus started walking down the main street checking out the stalls for any sort of blind spots, Cinder saw a fruit vendor talking to a customer and laughing, she used the distraction to pull a fishing line with a fish hook and sinker on one end from her pocket, the other end looped around her middle finger.

by Lore Casta Pendragon

She deftly flicked it out and hooked an apple in a basket on the ground out of sight of the vendor, she pulled it back and caught it, quickly pocketing it in a deep coat pocket.

"Nice one", Silus quietly muttered, "easy pickings", she said with a shrug of her shoulders.

As they walked down the street she took a bite out of the apple, Silus bumped into a man and spun around, pocketing a bag of coins, the man look back at him and shouted, "watch your step rat!", As he walked off, Silus lowered his hat and didn't turn back to him as he didn't want the man to see his face and kept walking, Cinder skipped ahead excited, "that was amazing, that will keep the gargoyle happy for the rest of the day", she said, she sometimes called the workhouse man a gargoyle due to his unpleasant angry demeanor and horrendous looks.

They spent the next few hours snatching food, jewelry and coin and delivering it to the workhouse man's stall where he threw it in compartmented barrels behind the stall with false tops, one part lifted a lid on top the other part lifted the whole false top revealing the goods at the bottom in case the city guard came snooping around.

Silus noticed a stall of meat skewers that smelled particularly good, so he approached it.

"I'd like twenty please", he addressed the vendor who looked at him with an eyebrow raised, "I can pay", Silus said as he laid some of the coin he had stolen earlier on the counter, the man's expression changed to a happy one, "right away little sir", he said with a wry smile and wrapped them up in a paper bundle.

As they walked away Cinder was nervous, "if the workhouse man catches you using his coin, you'll be done for", she said, but Silus didn't care, he knew that he would be a hero to the rest of the children in the workhouse, so he thought of an elaborate ruse he'd tell the workhouse man of how he acquired the food.

At the end of the day, they reconvened at the workhouse man's stall and help him roll the barrels back to the workhouse, they unloaded their haul and the workhouse man took the coin and jewels and the lion's share of the good food, returning to his quarters at the start of the hall.

The children were left with a banquet of food stolen from the marketplace, fresh fruits, vegetables and even a cooked meat skewer for each child, they feasted well and told each other the story of how they 'acquired', each the goods.

Silus told his lie about how he acquired the meat skewers and the children cheered aloud, patting him on the back, Cinder just looked at him arms folded, smiling and whispered, "you're so full of shit Silus", he smiled at her warmly.

The next morning the workhouse man did his usual inspection, the children lined up, beds made, clothes neatly folded, he stopped in front of Silus and bent down to look him in the eye, "I had a good yarn to me mate at the market, he said a boy of your description bought some of his wares yesterday".

     by Lore Casta Pendragon

Silus showed no expression, but inside he was furious at the betrayal, "I'll show you what happens when you waste me coin boy", he pulled out the leather blackjack, Silus showed no expression of fear, he didn't even blink.

"It was me", Cinder said, Silus's eyes grew wide with fear as the workhouse man turned to her, anger on his face.

He swung across with the blackjack to strike her face but Silus was fast, he leaped and grabbed his arm, swinging with the blow, slowing it down significantly, Cinder ducked and it missed, the workhouse man grabbed Silus in both arms and slammed him into the wall.

Cinder took her fish hook out of her pocket and began spinning it, "yer don boy, I give ya everything and ya betray me for this girl, you'll be working the pit till ya drop", the gargoyle said, Cinder flicked her fish hook onto his far shoulder and pulled it making the gargoyle cry out in pain, he dropped Silus to the floor and turned.

He grabbed the line and pulled Cinder in, slapping her face so hard she hit the floor in a daze, he pulled the hook from his shoulder, "to hell with both of ye", he grabbed them both by the back of the shirt and hauled them off to another room, he threw them inside and locked the door, then returned to his daily inspections.

The rest of the children had their heads down burning with anger, Silan Silus was a hero to them and a source of hope in an otherwise dark and abject existence.

"I had it under control", Silus said to Cinder, "I'm sorry, I couldn't let you take the fall after what you risked for us, for me", after a while she said, "what's going to happen to us now?", "Like he said, probably the pits for hard labor until I die, for you, probably a slave to some old perv", Silus replied, Cinder cringed and slumped against the wall.

A few hours later the workhouse man returned with a tall and lanky old man dressed in a black suit with the emblem of the church of the god feared on it and a wide brimmed black hat, Silus and Cinder stood to face them.

"Interesting specimens, are they any good", the lanky man said in what could only be described as a devious but well-spoken manner, "they've both got me some coin, more so the boy, but the girl has some interesting skills", the gargoyle said.

He looked them both up and down, "I'll take them", said the tall man handing over a bag of coins, "you'll be coming to live with me now, my name is Malacore, there's a carriage waiting outside, come along", he said turning to leave.

Silus and Cinder looked at each other confused, then headed after him down the hall, "what does a rich looking man like him want with us?", Cinder whispered, "he's probably going to have his way with us then kill us", Silus replied.

They stepped outside and waiting for them was a horse drawn carriage, Malacore offered them a hand up to get in then shut the door and turned to speak with the Workhouse man, "maybe

                                                                by Lore Casta Pendragon

this won't be so bad?", Cinder said, Silus looked out the window, "they always treat the animal well before they slaughter them".

Malacore finished his conversation and hopped into the carriage, "well, what are your names?", Malacore asked, Cinder responded in a friendly manner, "Cinder, Cinder Crowler", she offered a hand. Malacore kissed the back of her hand, which made Silus sneer, "and you", he addressed Silus, "Salin Silus", he said shortly.

Malacore sat back in his seat and signaled the driver, they began to move away from the workhouse, Silus stared out the window for most of the trip while Cinder made small talk with Malacore.

They pulled up at a large house at the other end of Ravenhill, Malacore helped Cinder down from the carriage while Silus leaped down behind her, the house was beautiful, it was like nothing they ever had the privilege to see before, they moved down a long path and through a meticulously groomed garden and inside the house.

"Line up", Malacore ordered and they did as he asked just as they did for the workhouse man every morning, hands by their side and still.

"The discipline is there, at least the idiot taught you to respect orders", Malacore looked them over, "let's play a little game, I will ask you a question or give you a task, if you get it right, you will be rewarded handsomely, if you get it wrong however".

He quickly revealed a knife and threw it in between the eyes of a taxidermized elk head on the wall, both Silus and Cinder's eyes widened and they shifted nervously.

"Let's begin", Malacore said as another knife seemingly just appeared in his hand, "who do you serve?", Cinder and Silus looked at each other, Silus replied first, "y-you sir", he stammered, Malacore slashed Silus across the face, Silus cried out in pain and dropped to a knee holding his face, Cinder reached into her pocket only to realize she no longer had her hook, Malacore held the knife out to her throat and she stopped still.

"Get up Mr. Silus, the correct answer was Lord Guldamere or the church of the god feared, I only gave you a shallow cut for being half wrong, try not to make such mistakes again", Malacore said glaring at them.

Silus stood up and Malacore gave him a handkerchief to hold against his bleeding face, "don't make a mess of my floor Mr. Silus and don't be too hasty, we wouldn't want you to bleed out on your first day here", Malacore said, Silus and Cinder stared at him horrified of what would happen next.

Malacore paced in front of them waving the knife around, he dropped another knife from his suit sleeve into his free hand and it seemed like it just appeared out of nowhere.

"You'll live quite comfortably here, provided you do as I instruct, I do NOT tolerate failure, you will be here in training until I deem you are ready, or until you die, in return you will

 by Lore Casta Pendragon

pledge your allegiance to me and the church of the god feared", Malacore explained and with a flash the knives disappeared from his hands.

"Again", he shouted, "who do you serve?", Both Silus and Cinder replied quickly in unison, "Lord Guldamere", they said, Malacore smiled, "well done, your reward is upstairs", he signaled for a servant in black robes, "escort them to their rooms, your clothes are laid out on the bed, dinner will be in an hour", he pointed to one of the robed waiting staff, "oh and tend to Mr. Silus's wound won't you", he ordered.

Malacore left the room and the two were escorted to beautiful rooms with four post beds and clean sheets, on the bed Silus found a suit, a black outfit and a black coat with a dozen knife holsters.

Cinder found the same and also a beautiful evening dress, a female servant helped stitch the wound on Silus's cheek, he fidgeted the whole time and the servant became frustrated with him.

"So, what does Malacore do to afford a place like this anyway?", He tried to ask the servant, but she just smiled, collected her things and left the room without saying anything.

Later that night they sat down at a long table with shiny silver wear, food laid out in front of them and servants standing by, ready to serve.

Malacore walked in briskly to join them and stood at the end of the table, he placed his hands together in prayer and urged them to do the same.

"We praise all mighty Guldamere, he who raised us from the dead after the calamity, he alone who gives us life and provides for us, who protects us all, Amen", Malacore took his seat which was much more ornate than their own and began eating his meal.

Silus and Cinder sat quietly waiting, "eat", Malacore said looking at them curiously, "you'll find it quite adequate", he took a mouthful of food, and groaned with pleasure at the taste of it.

They began eating and were very impressed with the food, they looked at each other eyes wide and happily began scoffing the food down, Malacore asked them of their days in the workhouse and what the workhouse man had them doing and stories of their best work, they were having a wonderful time talking and laughing.

Silus suddenly vomited up his food in a puddle of black mush, looking shocked Cinder tried to ask him what was wrong but then did the same, they both looked at Malacore, "you poisoned us!", Cinder shouted.

Malacore smiled wickedly, "well I'm feeling fine", he shrugged as he continued to eat unphased, Silus and Cinder fell to the floor in pain as Malacore finished his meal, "oh, it's only a little poisoned, don't be such babies", he said as he wiped his mouth and got up.

                                    by Lore Casta Pendragon

"Help our guests to their rooms and have them bathed", he said as he left them on the floor, the servants picked Silus and Cinder up and drag them out of the room.

The next day after a horrid night of endless stomach cramps, a servant came to greet them and get them ready for the day only to find Silus and Cinder already awake standing at attention at their doors, he then returned to Malacore.

"Well, where are they?", he said to the servant, "your protégé are waiting for you to inspect them", he said in a posh impressed voice.

Malacore spat out some of his breakfast into a napkin and got up quickly rushing upstairs, he saw the pair standing there and laughed, "while I do appreciate your discipline, it is not necessary here, come downstairs", he said amused.

They followed him downstairs and onto an outside balcony with a small round table, there was tea and an assortment of breakfast foods ready for them, Malacore sat and began drinking his tea and they sat nervously without touching the food.

After a while Malacore put down his tea and explained, "look, last night was an error on my part, I didn't account for the fragile nature of children and put too much poison in the food, it won't happen again".

"Too much poison!", Cinder exclaimed, "any poison is too much poison", Silus said angrily, Malacore looking very unimpressed glared at them, they moved nervously awaiting punishment, but he calmed down.

"I'm dosing you with small amounts of different poisons in order for you to build up tolerance to them, can't have my artists in training dying from something as pathetic as poison now can I", Malacore explained, Cinder and Silus looked at each other horrified and nervously picked at the food in front of them.

A few moments later a servant came by and whispered something into Malacore's ear, he then excused himself and left the two alone.

"He's trying to kill us", Cinder whispered, "we'll leave tonight", Silus replied, "while everyone is asleep", Cinder nodded her approval.

They explored the grounds around the house that day, accompanied by a servant, there were many training grounds surrounding the property such as an archery range and a fighting pit with an accompaniment of many different types of weapons, they both kept an eye out for places to hide and escape routes for later on.

Later that night Cinder sat in her room, feeling queasy from dinner, she heard two knocks on

                                  by Lore Casta Pendragon

the wall then slowly opened her door, Silus did the same, they snuck out quietly and closed the doors behind them.

They creeped down the stairs and toward the front door, they opened it and moved to leave, but as Cinder took her first step down the stairs a rope came down from a balcony above her, it twisted around her neck and lifted her up into the air choking her.

Silus moved to grab her but a knife flew down and speared him through his shoe pinning him to the ground beneath, Silus cried out in pain as he looked up to see Malacore hanging upside down on the railing above them, rope in hand, he let go of the railing and Cinder was pulled upward toward the balcony, Malacore landed smoothly in front of Silus and with a flash, his knife was in hand at Silus's cheek.

"Romantic midnight rendezvous?", he asked, "or were you trying to betray me?", Silus sputtered but couldn't make his words out through the pain in his foot.

"I'd think again if you thought you could escape the master assassin of the thieves guild", he slashed Silus's face with his knife giving him yet another wound, Silus stood there shaking too afraid to move as blood ran down his face.

Malacore handed him a handkerchief to stop the blood, "don't let me catch you two fooling around again, or you'll have more than just a few cuts on your face", he warned dropping the rope, Cinder came down as Malacore pulled the knife from Silus's foot and pushed him forward, she fell on top of him and they both hit the ground Cinder choking and gasping from the rope now loose at her neck, servants came out to clean up the mess and dress their wounds, helping them into the house.

Later that night Cinder approached the wall between their rooms, "Silus", she said softly behind tears, "yeah", he replied, "I think for now it's best we do as he wants, until we're strong enough to fight back", she said, a moment passed then Silus replied, "okay", they went to bed sore and sorry, not knowing what tomorrow might bring.

A few years later…

Salin Silus and Cinder Crowler stared at each other at either end of the fighting pit, Silus's face now covered in scars while Cinder had none.

Malacore and a few servants watched from the parapet, Cinder dropped a heavy blade tied to a rope to the ground, one end wrapped around her left hand the other to the rope tied to the blade.

      by Lore Casta Pendragon

She lifted it and began spinning it around, Silus flicked his wrists and two knives appeared in hand out of the sleeves of his coat.

Cinder turned with the weight of the blade and wrapped it around her elbow, she straightened her arm and the blade shot out toward Silus, he dodged left, slapping the flying blade away with his knife then threw his other knife toward Cinder as he dashed to close the distance.

Cinder did a pirouette out of the way, the knife shooting past and slamming into the wooden wall behind her, she pulled on the rope and the blade came rebounding back to her, Silus narrowly avoided being hit in the back of the head by throwing himself to the ground, another pirouette and she used the momentum of the blade to bring it around for a vertical strike.

Silus rolled to the side avoiding it, he threw his other knife at Cinder and with yet another pirouette she dodged, the knife stuck into the wooden wall behind her again.

Cinder pulled the rope and swung the blade above her head, Silus rushed to close the distance and with a flash two more knives were in hand, Cinder then threw the blade in a wide arcing low swing, Silus smiled as he thought the blade went wide but she pulled the rope through her hand and it sped up, coming in short and wrapping around his ankles.

The heavy blade entangled itself slamming into Silus's leg giving him a small gash at his ankle, Cinder pulled the rope, pulling Silus off his feet, she ran at the wall and kicked off, leaping over a support beam above them.

She sprinted toward Silus and the speed of her movement dragged Silus passed her then lifted him upside down hanging by the rope, she quickly wrapped the rope around a weapon rack fixed to the wall, then dusted her hands off smiling at Silus who was looking quite pathetic hanging upside down.

Silus sighed then grabbed his legs and pulled himself up enough to grab the top of the rope, he cut it then dropped to his feet, Cinder made a mental note to use an iron chain next time as Silus threw a knife at her, she turned her body narrowly avoiding the blade as it stuck into the wall near her face.

Silus moved in to attack and Cinder grabbed a spear from the weapon rack, she stabbed at him but Silus turned around the spear tip flicked his knife upside down, turning his hips back to her he cut the head off the spear.

Cinder jumped backward as Silus approached, he slashed to her face and she blocked it with the end of the spear that was now just a staff, she stabbed at his face but he turned again in the opposite direction and cut off even more of the staff, she stabbed again and even more staff was shortened until she only held a small piece of wood.

Silus smirked at her amused and she smiled throwing it at him, with a flash two knives appeared in her hands, they came together slashes seemingly coming from every direction, sparks flying as the daggers collided, they come to a stop with Cinder's knife at Silus's throat.

                                    by Lore Casta Pendragon

"Enough!", Malacore called from the parapet, they stood side by side and bowed to the master assassin.

"That will do for today, I have a few tasks I need you to complete", the two trainee assassins met Malacore on the parapet and he handed them both an envelope.

"Assassination missions, your targets are inside, be sure you are not seen", they nodded and moved to their rooms to prepare.

Cinder spoke up, "you're still letting me win, aren't you?", "Barely", Silus replied, "you don't want to end up with a face like mine do you", he smirked at her scars covering his face.

"He wouldn't dare scratch this face, it's too important to his missions", she said begrudgingly, "is he still making you seduce your targets?", Silus said sadly, Cinder sighed looking disgusted.

"I think it's time we put an end to this farce, let's do it tonight after the missions", "do it?", Silus replied with a cheeky grin, "you know what I mean Silus", Cinder drew her thumb across her throat, Silus's face became sullen, "do you think we can?", "He's always been two steps ahead of us", Silus said.

"We're stronger now, we can beat him, together", Cinder said as she looked at him with hope in her eyes, they stopped outside their rooms and she kissed him passionately.

"I'll see you tonight, don't die on me", Cinder said as she entered her room.

Later that evening as Silus got ready for his mission Malacore knocked on the door, "Mr. Silus, I have a request for tonight's mission, I'd like you to wear this costume, it's a mask and tabi clothes from the thieves guild, if you're seen, people will think you were one of them and not one of us", he said.

"Sure", Silus replied, "you read the dossier on the target?", Asked Malacore, Silus nodded, "this will be no ordinary target, you'll be fighting a professional, so don't hold back, report to me once the deed is done", Silus bowed and headed off to the location noted in the dossier.

Moving down back alleys always sticking to the shadows, he arrived at the location, a steel mill used for fabrication work, he moved inside through a sliding door, it was dark inside and as he entered a thin steel chain came down from a walkway above and wrapped around his neck, the unknown assailant jumped down and Silus was lifted up choking from the chain, he swung himself back and forth as he struggled then kicked off the door flipping himself upside down, he grabbed the chain and planted his feet on the bottom of the walkway, then pulled hard.

His assailant was pulled over the railing, they both landed on the ground hard, Silus removed the chain from his neck and with a flash his knives were in hand, he moved to attack, his assailant was wearing a mask similar to his own, but his assailant walked backward into the shadows and disappeared from sight, Silus stopped and listened carefully but could hear only silence.

by Lore Casta Pendragon

A sickle on a chain flew out at him arcing low from the right, he jumped to avoid it as it wrapped around a pillar on the other side of the room, Silus threw a knife in the direction of the attack, but hit nothing hearing the clang of the knife bouncing on the floor, again the room was silent.

From the other side another chained sickle arced out around his mid-section, Silus bent backward to the floor narrowly avoiding it as it wrapped around another pillar, he flipped onto his feet.

Silus realizing he walked directly into a trap looked around scanning the darkness, he was illuminated by moonlight through glass windows at the top of the warehouse but the walls of the room were shadowed.

He heard running steps and he launched a volley of throwing knifes into the darkness around the room, another chained sickle arced out low from behind, Silus jumped it as it wrapped around another pillar, chains now crisscrossing around the room.

He heard a lever crank at the far end of the room and a large steel mechanical pulley began to spin, all three chains pulled tight and the sickles tore free of the pillars, all three blades arced around Silus, he couldn't avoid them all so he jumped high, the lowest chain missed, but he was caught around the arms and ankles by the other two, the sickles wrapped around him and dug into his flesh, he hit the ground hard and was dragged toward the pulley wheel.

As he drew close to the pulley, he flicked a knife into the gears and it slammed to a hold, his assailant walked out of the shadows with a knife in hand to finish him off, Silus turned so his back was facing his assailant, he managed to wriggle an arm free loosening the chains, he pulled out a knife and rolled quickly toward his target.

Using his free arm he launched the knife at blistering speed into his assailant's chest, his opponent let out a breathy scream and fell back against a nearby pillar then slid to the ground.

Silus took out the sickles with pained grunts and freed himself from the chains, he limped over to his assailant and removed the mask, Cinder looked at him, blood trailing from her mouth, Silus's eyes grew wide with fear as he shouted, "Cinder?", "No!".

He took off his mask and frantically thought of a way to help her, "Silan", she whispered, "as usual he was one step ahead of us", she reached into a pocket and pulled out her dossier handing it to Silus, she coughed up more blood and Silus held her in his arms, tears forming in his eyes as she took her last breath, Silus screamed in grief and anger, "I'll kill him, I'll kill him if it's the last thing I do, damn you Malacore!".

Silus laid Cinder gently on the floor, and ran back to the house, when he arrived Malacore was waiting for him wearing his assassins black coat and his wide brimmed hat with his knives in hand, "you dirty rotten bastard, you'll pay for what you've done!", Silus screamed at him.

     by Lore Casta Pendragon

"Mr. Silus, you're the one who killed Cinder, not me, this is your punishment for plotting to kill me, surely you didn't think your actions would not have dire consequences", Malacore replied in a calm yet sinister voice.

Silus screamed out in anger and charged at Malacore slashing at him, Malacore returned each slash with one of his own, daggers sparked as they collided, each fighters' blades ripping holes into each other's bodies, blood spirting over the walls from every wound inflicted.

They started to slow as the pain and bleeding compounded, Malacore laughed as he shoved a knife into Silus's side, Silus's fury gave him strength and he returned the favor shoving his knife into Malacore's chest.

"It seems you are finally prepared to serve", Malacore said as he fell toward Silus.

Malacore took off his hat and put it onto Silus's head, "for four centuries I've done his bidding, now that I've found a suitable replacement, he will finally let me die", Malacore said as he collapsed to the ground.

Silus looked down at him, "see you in hell Malacore", he said dropping to his knees, blood gushing from wounds all over his body, his vision blurred as the light in the room shrunk as if being squeezed by the dark.

A dark figure in tattered black robes walked into the room and held out a skeletal hand, the world turned black and Silus fell into a dark river flowing rapidly, flowing fast, he moved with the current, not made of water, but of a ghostly representation of water, he could see at the end was a waterfall and beneath an abyss of darkness, Malacore smiled at him and drifted silently off the edge, smiling the entire way.

A large black clawed hand reached in and grabbed Silus out of the torrent pulling him from the brink of death, moments later Silus opened his eyes, his bleeding had stopped but his wounds were still fresh, he groaned in pain as he was addressed by the figure in black.

"I won't let you just die", A raspy voice spoke to him, he blinked blurry eyes a few times and regained his vision, A half rotted skeleton covered with a smokey black miasma and golden pupils stood before him.

He knew who this man was, though he had never met him before, "I will offer you a deal in return for your service", Guldamere said, "who are you?", Silus asked weakly, "I am your savior, I can bring her back to you", Silus's eyes opened wide, "anything, anything you want, just bring her back", "good", the lich cackled and pulled Silus to his feet using a black miasma claw.

"Firstly, you must find for me, a source of power, once lost long ago, only then will I have the power to raise the long dead from the abyss, only then will your beloved Cinder be by your side", Guldamere offered a hand and Silus took it, "I will, thank you Lord Guldamere".

 by Lore Casta Pendragon

Many years later…

"Master Silus, there has been a disturbance at the tavern, your skills are required", a raven made of black miasma spoke to Silus and he stood up from his writing table slowly putting on a black wide brimmed hat.

Walking outside he climbed into a carriage with a groan, old wounds still punished him from his fight with Cinder and Malacore all those years ago.

He wrapped Cinder's red scarf around him and tucked it into his coat as they headed downtown, Silus saw a strange looking cart pulled by a Carribook, half cart and half boat, he stuck his head out the window and lifted up his hat as a heavily wounded man with two children rode within it, he locked eyes with the younger child and smirked, taking note of them as he past.

Arriving at the scene, he saw Harram Halfblood climbing up from the wharf, covered in wounds and sopping wet, he laughed heartedly at Harram.

"Piss off Silus", Harram sputtered still covered in seaweeds, Silus chuckled, "want to tell me who's responsible for this?", Harram shook himself off like a dog, "one by the name of Allheart and that Wynn guy, the one who owns that shop over there", Harram grunted.

"Thanks, Harram, I'll pay Wynn a visit", Harram chuckled approvingly as he walked into the burned tavern from the hole, he made earlier to get a drink.

A bell rang and Wynn looked over from the table he was still laying on, "we're closed", he bellowed as Silus walked in, he attempted to get up but no sooner did he move a knife sunk into his hand, Wynn cried out in pain, over the road at the tavern Harram sat at what was left of the bar and heard Wynn's cry, he shuddered and took a swig of a drink from a broken bottle, "glad I'm not you friend", he said.

"We're going to get to know each other a little better, you're going to tell me who your friend is, the Allheart, or I'm going to start removing some of these fingernails", Silus said with a smile.

by Lore Casta Pendragon

Chapter Four

A kind heart

Kimba Kindheart stared contemplatively out the window of her father's two-story townhouse on a hill in the city of Necropyre, the capital city of the land of Thalaria, she was short and thin, had brunette hair, light brown eyes and small delicate features.

She huffed in boredom as she looked out upon the town seeing the denizens walking about, it was getting late, acolytes of the church of the god feared were lighting the street lamps using magic, Kimba often watched them with interest wondering how they did it.

Her father Kamdar worked in the reliquary of the god feared, A type of library where they kept magic tomes in the god feared cathedral which stood overlooking the city, only those deemed worthy by Guldamere the god feared and his acolytes were allowed to read them, it was outlawed for anyone outside the church to practice magic.

"Kimba", called Kamdar as he entered her room, "dinner is ready", he said, "I could eat", she replied as she turned to him from the window, he was a thin man with a soft and gentle nature, often with his head in a book, a trait that Kimba shared.

Before they could sit down, there was a frantic knock on the door, "let me in, let me in", cried Felix Flight, Kamdar opened the door and Felix came stumbling inside, "what's wrong this time Felix, did your shadow chase you?", Kamdar jested, "hilarious Mr. Kindheart", Felix huffed.

Felix was an oddity, he had a protruding jaw and large triangular ears on top of his head, he looked like a house cat, his people, the Felinine were mostly wiped out in the cataclysm, Felix's parents were murdered by bigots when he was young, but he found a home with a kind hearted engineer in Necropyre who kept him around to keep the rats at bay, but grew fond of Felix and made him his apprentice.

"I was making my way back from the workshop when I saw a pup get trampled by a carriage, I went over to help, but the acolytes raised the damn thing and it started chasing me down the street", Felix whined, "are you alright, did it bite you?", Kimba asked him concerned, "I'm fine Kimba", he smiled back at her straightening up and dusting himself off.

"The acolytes from the cathedral thought it was a sight to behold, I think one of them fell in the dirt from laughter", Felix explained.

Kamdar grinned wide and put a hand on his shoulder, "that's because you run and scream like a girl", he teased, "well I'm sorry, but the risen just give me the creeps, especially the ones that walk around when they should have been buried a long time ago", Felix said.

                                      by Lore Casta Pendragon

"Have you seen the old man who lives in the outpost outside of town, the other day he was at the tavern where I was playing my lute and his whole arm came off, just fell on the floor in front of everyone, then he didn't like my song so he threw it at me!".

"Well, you probably deserved it, I've heard you play", Kamdar laughed, Felix huffed as Kimba spoke up, "don't worry Felix I love your songs, what are you working on at the warehouse lately?", Kimba said scratching behind his ears to comfort him, Felix purred softly.

"Oh something amazing, I can't give out details just yet, but it's something that will put the Flight name in the history books", Felix said, "you didn't even take a break all day did you?", Kima asked, "why don't you join us for dinner Felix?", Kimba offered, "that sounds amazing thank you Kimba", Felix replied, leaving Kamdar to grunt and frown, "is that ok father?", Kimba said looking up to her father with puppy dog eyes, "don't look at me like that, your mother used to do that to me and I could never say no, you remind me of her more every day", "see I told you it works every time", Felix whispered to Kimba and she smiled back at him playfully.

The three of them sat down and talked about Felix's work and japed at his terrible music until the conversation turned, "so what do they have you doing at the Cathedral these day Kamdar", Felix asked, "lately we've acquired manuscripts from the late Lore Casta Pendragon", Kamdar said.

"The breaker of the world?", Felix replied stunned, "the very same, I'd love to read them, but they are keeping them lock away, the church are very protective of the use of magic", Kamdar said, "surely you must have peaked at a few tomes", Felix asked, there was a short silence, then Kamdar replied, "none, if the soldiers see me reading the tomes, they would incinerate me on the spot, the study of magic is reserved only for the acolytes of the church", Kamdar explained.

"I would love to see the library father, will you take me with you one day?", Kimba asked, "tomorrow should be fine, but most of it is just manuals, novels, histories, we collect what wasn't destroyed in the cataclysm, but nothing overtly interesting, it's all strictly monitored and anything that goes outside of church doctrine is usually burned", Kamdar said.

"Can I come with you?", Felix interrupted, "I need to look for a solution to an engineering issue I'm having, maybe those old books could shed some light", Felix asked, Kamdar grunted again, "ok, but if you get scared and scream like a girl, I'll stuff your gullet with scrolls and use you as a receptacle", Kamdar warned.

Kimba showed Felix to the door as her father cleaned up the table, she looked mischievously at Felix, "I know that look, what are you planning?", Felix asked raising an eyebrow, "I'm going to sneak a peek at those tomes", Kimba said with a smile, Felix tilted his head to the side, "are you insane, do you to want to be a pile of soot?", Felix warned, "and you're going to help me", she said, "of course I am", Felix rolls his eyes, "this isn't a good idea, but I can never

          by Lore Casta Pendragon

change your mind when you look at me like that", Felix said with a sigh, "see you tomorrow Felix", Kimba said as she shut the door.

Kimba sat back at her window and watched as an acolyte lit another lamp with nothing more than his empty hand, Kimba smiled, "tomorrow I'll find out how they do it".

The next morning Felix met them at the front door and they headed for the Cathedral, the streets of Necropyre were full of people, most healthy but there were some who looked so old, that they must have been well over a century in age, the city streets were narrow and full of two-story town houses, with cobblestone roads.

An acolyte of Guldamere stood guard at the entrance and checked Kimba and Felix as they entered, he laughed when he saw Felix, "if it isn't the screamer from yesterday, I just about pissed myself laughing as you ran down the street with that pup on your heels", he said with a devilish grin, Felix gave a sarcastic laugh toward the acolyte and an unimpressed grin.

"Good morning, Kamdar, Lord Guldamere has requested you find maps of the area surrounding Dawnshire and the living forest, be sure you hand them to me by days end", a soldier said to Kamdar as they entered the Cathedral reliquary, to their left was a large two-story room lined with books and scrolls, a large staircase was either side leading up to a second floor with more books.

At the back was a heavy locked door guarded by two soldiers in armor, a smokey raven sat perched on the railing above, looking down at them, Kimba looked at it, then look to Kamdar, "he's always watching Kimba, make sure you stay out of trouble", Kamdar warned.

Kimba sat with Felix at a table piled with various books on mechanics and engineering, "I have work to do, so I'll check back with you two later, if you're after anything in particular let me know and I'll find it for you", Kamdar offered but Kimba just gave her father a hug and slipped her hand unnoticed into his pocket, "thanks daddy", she said innocently, Kamdar raised an eyebrow at her and grunted as he walked off.

Kimba gave Felix a mischievous smile, "so the room at the back must be where they keep the magic tomes, we need to get into that room unnoticed", Kimba said, "and how are you going to get in that room with those two guards standing there", Felix asked her, "with these", Kimba lifted a finger and a chain of keys dangled from it, Felix swatted her hand down, "are you insane?", he whispered, "you're going to get us all killed", Felix said nervously, "that's where you come in, I need you to make a distraction", Kimba pointed to the front door.

The acolyte at the door was talking to a couple of soldiers wearing armor, Kimba snuck off and made her way behind a bookshelf, "I'm counting on you", she whispered to Felix as he scratched at his head with his foot.

by Lore Casta Pendragon

A few moments later a big dead rat hit him in the face thrown from the door, he caught it in his hand confused as the acolyte raised his hands in prayer and began whispering something, the rat woke from its extended rest and bit Felix on the hand, he yowled and swatted the rat off the table, the acolyte and his soldier friends started laughing as the rat chased after Felix who was now screaming like a girl and running away frantically.

The guards at the tome room door rushed to see what the commotion was, only to see Felix trip on a pile of books and fall down, the rat assailed him again and he yowled louder, the raven on the railing had its eyes fixed on Felix as Kimba moved on the door, she found the right key on the second try and made her way inside, closing the door behind her.

Inside she found books assorted by color, to one side are books made of a kind of fleshy black leather, some were blue hardcover books with latches on them, she unlatched one of the blue books and opened it, white trails of chaos magic flew out from the pages as she turned them, the title was.

'Discerning the nature of the occult, volume one, by Lore Casta Pendragon', "found you", she whispered as she tucked the book under her dress and moved to the exit, as she approached the door she saw the raven flying back her way through the bars in the door, so she ducked behind it, she thought she was caught but scampered behind a bookshelf as the raven perched itself between the bars of the door, slowly looking over the room from one side to the other.

The raven then flew across and perched itself on a table in clear sight of the door which was the only way out, "well I messed up, now how am I going to get out of here", she thought as she picked up a black fleshy book, she unlatched it, the title read, 'Guldamere's Necronomicon volume 1', the ravens eyes were immediately drawn to her location as a black miasma poured out from the book, she immediately shut it and left it sitting open on the floor next to the bookshelf.

Kimba scampered around another bookshelf staying out of sight of the raven which flew itself over to a table looking down the aisle she was just in, "If that bird spots me I'm done for", Kimba thought opening Pendragons book, she began to read, on the page were diagrams and lexicons explaining how chaos magic is all around them and when infused with life energy it was given a life of its own and made real.

Kimba continued reading and followed the instructions, she placed her fists together, knuckles almost interlocked and focused on the space between, she felt her own life force flowing from one fist to the other and back again until she saw thin white lines of chaos magic flowing between them, she then used her life force to pull on the chaos magic, the effort immediately left her exhausted, "too much, a little less this time", Kimba thought as she tried again and to her surprise she could see more of the chaos magic, she pushing her fists together interlocking them then followed the directions of a spell in the tome, her hands became less visible as if disappearing under cloudy water.

                    by Lore Casta Pendragon

She increased the amount of life force used and her body was covered in a foggy veil barely visible to the eye, the raven moved back to the door and scanned the room, it found nothing and exited back through the bars, with a sigh of relief Kimba opened the door and moved out, she made it past a yowling idiot now being accosted by Kamdar for being too loud and stupid.

Slipping the keys back into Kamdar's pocket she moved past the acolyte and guards at the front door, she ducked down a side alley out the front of the cathedral and released the spell, the world went black as she collapsed to the ground.

Felix woke her sometime after and helped her to her feet, "I hope you got what you were looking for miss Kindheart because you certainly owe me for that, I've never been so humiliated and your father is furious", Felix said, "I got it", she whispered groggily as she showed him the book, a huge smile of satisfaction on her face.

They walked back to Kimba's townhouse and Felix excused himself, "I think I need to take a bath", Felix said with a shudder still thinking about the dead rat crawling over him, "thank you Felix", Kimba said as she gave Felix a kiss on the cheek, Felix's mouth and eyes went wide open as Kimba shut the door giggling at him.

Later that night after dinner, she waited for Kamdar to go to sleep then she lit a candle and continued to read Pendragon's tome, after a few hours study, the light of the candle flame grew brighter as the words on the page began to rearrange themselves before her eyes, they began to form into a sentence.

"Pendragon lives", Kimba said the words aloud then said them again "Pendragon lives?", Her eyes widen as the words rearranged again and formed a new sentence, "locked away", she said and again they rearranged, "Mount Muse", the words returned to normal and Kimba grabbed her coat, she hurried downstairs and out the door, on the roof of her house sat a smokey raven with golden eyes, it pursued her unnoticed into the black of the night.

Kimba arrived at Felix's house and knocked on the door, the raven perched on a rooftop close by as he answered wearily, wearing a pointed pajama hat over one long ear and holding a candle, his eyes barely open, he perked up when he realized it was Kimba at the door.

"Pendragon is alive!", She said as she pushed her way past, "what?", Felix said sleepily, "come in, why don't you", Felix said as he fixed to get them both some tea, Kimba recounted what happened with the tome in her room.

"Pendragon died five hundred years ago after messing with powers he couldn't control and took most of the world with him, he was a power-hungry dark wizard", Felix stated.

"That's what the church of the god feared tells us, but what if he never died, what if Pendragon was sealed away?".

by Lore Casta Pendragon

"What about all the stories of Pendragon before the cataclysm, he was thought of as a hero of the people, A warrior against the powers of chaos, that's why the church has been collecting and destroying histories before the cataclysm", Kimba retorted, "even if the book tells the truth and Pendragon is alive, Mount Muse was destroyed during the cataclysm, it's nothing more than a crater now, so he can't be located there and besides why would you want to find a man who destroyed the world?", Felix asked.

Kimba looked at him sadly, "because the church of the god feared took my mother, they said she had chaos sickness, so father took her to the cathedral to see Guldamere, she never came home, I think something happened to her, but I was very young, I also think it's why my father chose to work for them, he's still trying to find out the truth of what happened, I think Pendragon can help me find the truth and the first place to look will be the crater where Mount Muse used to stand", Kimba said.

"You've lost your marbles, there are nightmare creatures out there, you'll be dead before you even get close", Felix stammered, "there are less monsters out during the day, so that's when we'll go", Kimba said, "we?", Felix said in a high-pitched whiny tone, "of course, you wouldn't make a hapless young woman do this alone would you?", Kimba looked at him with big doe eyes and Felix stood there unimpressed, "how dare you use my own tricks against me, but of course, I will help you", he said in as manly a tone as he could muster.

Kimba smiled at him, "besides I've got this", she held up Pendragons tome.

The raven outside Felix's house exploded into black smoke and the Lich Guldamere stood from his thrown in the cathedral of the god feared, he floated down the stairs and walked down a corridor running his smokey skeletal hand over each door as he passed, seven acolytes acknowledge his presence and begin to follow him downstairs without a word spoken, they convened at the main doors and Guldamere addressed them in a wicked raspy voice.

"The Kindheart girl has stolen something valuable from us, bring her to me alive", raising a hand, black smoke gathered around it forming into a raven, it flew ahead of the Acolytes as they bowed and left lined up in two rows of marching formation, they made their way down the street following the ravens lead, the lights dimmed as they passed, people stumbled and ran from their presence as they headed downtown to Felix's residence.

Kamdar saw the lights dimming from his bed as they passed, he looked out the window to see the acolytes marching downtown, he took three candles and put them together to make a larger flame to compensate for the dimming light, he then walked down the hall to check on Kimba.

He knocked on the door and waited, there was no answer, he cracked the door to peek inside only to find her bed empty, "Oh no, no, no, no", Kamdar said as he ran down the hall, his mind raced to all the possibilities which panicked him further.

Kamdar already lost his wife, he couldn't lose his only daughter, not to them, not again.

He changed into his robe and grabbed a notebook from under the floorboards in his room then rushed out the door in the direction of the acolytes.

The acolytes arrived in front of Felix's house and placed their hands together as if in prayer, black miasma poured from them as they extended a hand toward the house, flames appeared in their palms, they came together in a semi-circle and extend the fires in their hands towards the center, it conjoined into a fireball the size of a cannon ball.

Felix set Kimba up on a pallet bed on the floor, "see you in the morning miss Kindheart", he said tenderly, she blew him a kiss and he smiles, "goodnight, Felix", Kimba said looking at him lovingly, but as Felix turned to leave, he went to blow out a candle near the door, as he brought his lips to it, it grew very dim, as if the darkness was pushing in around it, "that's odd", Felix said looking puzzled.

Kimba looked up at the light and her eyes grew wide with fear, the front door of the house exploded into pieces of flying wood and fire, Felix was blown into the room, then jumped on top of Kimba to shield her from any falling debris with his body.

As the dust settled the acolytes stepped through the door, Felix helped Kimba to her feet and they both ran for the back door, as they moved Felix opened a cupboard and pulled on a rope, "I hope this still works", he said as a trap door opened in the front room of the house and hundreds of little furry worms fell out from the ceiling covering two acolytes as they began to laugh hysterically, overwhelmed by the tickling creatures they hit the floor giggling, another Acolyte raised a hand and purged the room with fire, burning his colleagues, the worms and the house as Kimba and Felix rushed outside into a narrow alley.

Felix opened a small shed and pulled out a small bag and a bicycle with a strange contraption attached to it he got on and helped Kimba onto his lap, three acolytes appeared in the alley as Felix pulled out a flint from his pack.

He struck it and a wick began to spark as the acolytes each raised a hand, fire sparked to life in their palms, the wick burned into the contraption and it exploded into life, sparks flew everywhere as a piston attached to the rear wheel spun wildly, they speed off down the alleyway toward the acolytes as the acolytes blasted small fireballs towards them, one connected with the front wheel and it bent the wheel frame as the bicycle rammed into them at tremendous speed knocking them flat,

Felix maneuvered the bicycle as they skidded around the corner onto the street, two acolytes saw them as they sped off down the street, the bicycle wobbled uncontrollably on the broken wheel as they made pace, Felix couldn't control the damaged bike and they crashed into a wall sending them hurtling over it rolling onto the pavement, bruised and grazed.

by Lore Casta Pendragon

"What the hell, FELIX!", Kimba yelled at him, "I'm sorry miss Kindheart, it still needs some work", Felix said sheepishly, they heard the footsteps of the acolytes running down the street after them and got to their feet.

The acolytes started firing fireballs from the wall and they ducked into an alleyway between two shops, they rushed down the alley only to find it ended abruptly, they turned to leave but two acolytes stood to block the exit.

"Miss Kindheart, Mr. Flight, you're coming with us, Lord Guldamere wishes an audience with you", one of them said with a tone of authority.

Felix pulled a small metal cylinder out from his pack with two buttons on each side, he squeezed them and the cylinder sprung out into a staff, the acolytes placed their hands together and black miasma extended upward from them it joined together then hit the ground in front of them, it formed an inky dark hole devoid of light, a long limbed lanky humanoid creature with hollow black holes for eyes clambered out of it.

"It's a Fake", Kimba whispered horrified backing away, the acolytes backed away from it and out of the alleyway, the creature screamed a horrifying cry and advanced on them on all fours, long front arms like an extra-long pair of legs.

Felix growled, hair standing on end, 'I have to protect her', he thought then moved to intercept it, "be careful Felix!", Kimba shouted, icy fear gripped them both as the creature came close, its foul breath stank of death.

Felix stabbed at it with his staff but it grabbed it with an effortless reflex and pulled it out of his grasp, it threw the staff to the ground in one quick movement and continued to advance on Felix.

Felix began to whimper as he stepped backward not able to match the nightmare creature's strength, the creature grabbed him lifting him eight feet up against the wall with one lanky arm, its mouth opened wide revealing a dark void within as it began to suck the very life force from Felix's body.

Felix's face became gaunt as his life was being stripped away, Kimba grabbed Pendragons tome and started flicking through pages frantically trying to find a spell she could use to stop the creature.

Just then a sudden burst of wind blew through the alley and they heard two loud cries of pain as both of the acolytes hit the wall of the alleyway, there stood Kamdar notebook in hand, dust kicking up around him, Kimba's mouth opened agape, she couldn't believe what she saw, "father?", she asked confused, never in her wildest dreams would she thought her timid father could be a wizard.

Kamdar slammed his fists together then extended both arms toward the nightmare creature, light began to glow on his palms and started to engulf the entire alleyway in a blinding array of

light, the creature let out a screech, dropping Felix to the ground, then climbed the wall of the building to escape over the roof.

"Are you alright Felix?", Kamdar asked helping him to his feet, "I'm, I'm fine sir, thank you, you saved my life", Felix said, "no, thank you Felix, you saved my daughter", Kamdar said, he regarded Felix with a newfound respect as he pats the dust from his tailcoat, then he regarded Kimba.

"I'll be taking that", Kamdar said as he snatched the tome from Kimba, "do you know what you've done, I told you he sees everything and you completely ignored me", Kamdar scolded, "I'm sorry father, why didn't you tell me you knew magic?", Kimba said unable to look him in the eye head down.

"I've been keeping notes from Pendragon's tomes for years, every time I've had a chance, but Guldamere and his, minions, keep such a close eye on me, I've hardly had time, I still don't know what happened to your mother, but I'm convinced Guldamere was responsible", Kamdar explained.

"Pendragon is alive father", Kimba said as she looked up at him, "that's impossible Kimba, it's been five hundred years since Pendragon broke the world, he's long gone, stop this charade, we are going to the church to give this back and beg for forgiveness", Kamdar said grabbing Kimba's hand and turned to leave.

"It was in his book, it told me, he's imprisoned at Mount Muse and besides, Guldamere and his ilk have been around since the cataclysm, so why not pendragon also?", Kimba pleaded to him pulling back.

Kamdar stopped in his tracks, "if anyone would know what happened to my mother, it would be a man like Pendragon", she started to sob.

Felix saw she was upset and perked up, "well, it's not like we have much of a choice now anyway, the church won't let us go now that they know about us borrowing their precious book", he pointed to the end of the alleyway, the acolytes were gone, across the street a raven was perched above the alleyway, watching intently.

Felix fetched them some hooded coats to hide their faces as they made their way to the city gate, crouching behind a peddler's cart, the guard at the gate was talking to a merchant, "no one is permitted to enter or leave at this time", the guard said.

"How are we going to get out?", Felix asked, "we can use the tome", Kimba said, Kamdar took out the tome reading from one of the passages on the manipulation of light and water molecules, they placed their fists together and a cloud of blurry water made them almost completely invisible, like looking into a dirty water trough.

"Well, that's all good for you, but what about me", Felix asked, "stay in the city, lay low for a while and we'll be back in a day or two", Kimba said stroking Felix's furry face.

"Okay, take my pack miss Kindheart, there are some supplies in there for the road", Felix responded with a sigh as the two headed to a guard door next to the main gate.

As a guard unlocked it and walked out, they slipped in behind before it closed then headed out into the blasted lands beyond the city, it was dusty and devoid of life, ruins from an age before the cataclysm dotted the landscape and the howls, growl and maniacal laughter of nightmare creatures echoed out over it.

Not long after they left the gate Kimba dropped to a knee exhausted from holding up the veil of the cloaking spell, Kamdar released it as well, panting from the effort as they faded back into view.

"We'll head east, toward the crater of Mount Muse, we'll look around for any traces of Lore Casta Pendragon there", Kimba said, they headed off as day broke over the horizon, a raven following not far behind.

They travelled sticking to the light for the day before coming to the crater it was deep and shrouded in a dense black fog, in the middle they could faintly make out a waterfall from a rocky ledge, they headed down the chasm and into the fog, the rocky ledge was narrow and treacherous.

As Kimba stepped it crumbled away, it was hard to see and the sound of howls and scurrying creatures could be heard nearby, Kimba shuddered, this was no place for living things.

"It's no wonder no one ever comes here, it's a home for nightmare creatures", Kamdar said regretting his decision.

"Father, we should remain unseen", Kimba said nervously grabbing Kamdar by the hand, the two placed their fists together and faded from sight, they made their way to the bottom of the cliff face, then started toward the center of the crater, they walked along a path with footsteps in the muddy ground that looked like it had been regularly used.

They came to a rocky spire that leaned over a pool with an impossible waterfall flowing over it, the water seemed to originate from the rocky spire itself, the path took them behind the waterfall and into a cave behind, it was warm inside almost inviting, with green vines growing just outside.

Inside they found a large black obsidian stone door, it had golden runes down the center and was covered in a thick black miasma, looking up they saw a raven perched above, draping black miasma over the door.

"This has to be the place", Kimba said, "Guldamere wouldn't be keeping watch here for nothing", Kamdar replied, he sat on a stone in front of the door, pulling out some food and a

　　　　　　by Lore Casta Pendragon

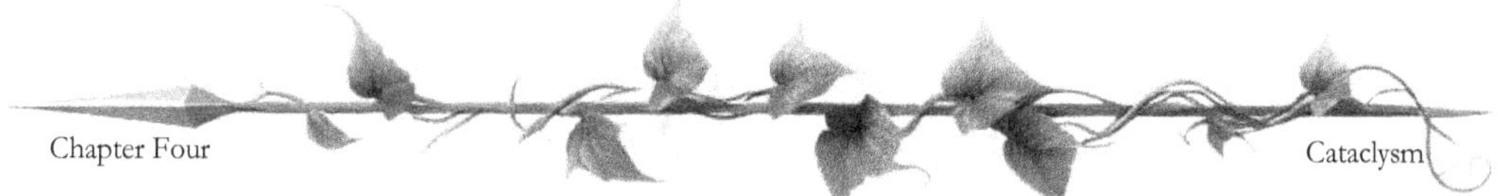

flint and steel to start a fire and cook their meal, Kimba walked back out to fetch some of the deadwood from outside for kindling.

She bent down to pick up a rotten log when she thought she heard a wailing sound from out in the dark fog and looked up, she looked around but couldn't see anything, she headed back in quickly and helped her father get a campfire started.

"So how do you think we get inside", Kimba asked Kamdar, "it looks to be sealed magically, my guess is we have to use magic to open it", Kamdar said, "it's no wonder Guldamere didn't want people knowing how to cast magic, he didn't want people like us being able to open this door", Kamdar said.

Kimba opened the tome and flicked through the pages, the words began to change, "Father come look!", Kimba shouted, Kamdar rushed over and looked at it astonished as the words formed into a sentence; it said, 'Kill the bird'.

Kamdar slammed his fists together, he pulled on his life force as he extended his arms out toward the bird, the wind picked up around him and a powerful gust of wind blasted out toward the raven, it fluttered its wings and blew the torrent back toward them knocking them down next to the sparking fire, the wind picked up embers and blew them around the cave and back toward the bird, it squawked wildly as an ember singed at its wing.

"Flick through that book and see if you can find any information on fire", Kamdar asked Kimba, she turned through the pages until she found a page containing information on how to manipulate combustible gases in the air and condense heat.

Slamming her fists together she pulled upon her life force and extended a hand toward the camp fire, up jumped a bit of fire resting in her palm, it burned through her life force pool quickly like paper to a flame, she realized the amount of raw power and how exhausting it would be to create a fireball the size of the one that blew up Felix's front door.

"I'll help", Kamdar said, they both interlocked their knuckles and pooled their life force together, they reached a palm outstretched toward the fire, the flames jumped up into their palms and they both increased their output, Kamdar grunted from the effort and Kimba panted wildly.

They pushed their palms next to each other and the fire exploded from a small flame into a ball of fire, "now Kimba, we can take it down", Kamdar shouted as they aimed up at the bird and let it the fireball go, it shot out like a cannonball and hit the bird directly, it exploded into black smoke with an echoing squawk, disintegrating into feathers which then smoked away into nothingness.

The cave began to rumble and shake as the black miasma which fell over the door began to dissipate, they heard a wailing from outside the cave as ghostly robed creatures flew in carrying long scythes.

by Lore Casta Pendragon

They flew toward Kimba and Kamdar, the golden runes on the obsidian door glowed brightly then shattered like glass and a line of golden light appeared at the join of the door, "Kimba, those nightmare creatures are wraiths, they're harvesters of souls", Kamdar shouted as the door began to open, a bright light shot out from within lighting the cave, the creatures were eviscerated by the light as Kimba and Kamdar were engulfed by it, the light shot out of the cave in a beam of iridescent brilliance, destroying a small army of nightmare creatures waiting outside.

Kimba shielded her eyes with her hand and dared not to look beyond it lest she go blind, the light faded and her vision cleared, standing there in the doorway was Lore Casta Pendragon looking old, grey, agitated and disheveled, "Is that you Guldamere?", "Did you enjoy my welcoming gift you coward!", Lore said in an old timey voice, Kimba looked at Kamdar, then back to Pendragon, "I'm Kimba Kindheart, and this is my father Kamdar, we found your tome".

Pendragon raised a bushy grey eyebrow and looked them over, "hmm, it seems like some of my magic still exists in this world, would you mind helping an old man out of these chains?".

                    by Lore Casta Pendragon

Chapter Five

All Hearts Break

Ailyn Allheart was exploring through the living forest close to his home at Riverside, foraging for the sweet fruits that sometimes grew there, he climbed up a large tree wrapped in vines, below him he could see his father Aethor and his brother Aidem training in a circular area cleared of vegetation and lined with rope made of vines.

Aethor was instructing Aidem in his form of martial combat, it consisted of powerful full body kicks and intercepting your opponent's attack while avoiding at the same time and on top of that Aethor had a powerful technique that was passed down through the Allheart bloodline called blood frenzy, consuming his own blood and infusing it with his life energy enhanced his physical abilities for a short time, like adding pure oxygen to a flame.

Ailyn admired his fathers' ability and sometimes trained with him, but his childish nature often got the better of him and he would become distracted, today, he just felt like something sweet to eat, he licked his lips thinking about the sweet fruit as he peered through the forest looking for the plant which harbored his prize.

His mother Asta was hanging clothes nearby to dry, she said she would join him earlier that day to look for fruits, she had a tricky way of getting Ailyn to do his training that made it fun for him.

Ailyn spotted a bush on the forest floor that looked like it had some berries on it, Ailyn smiled and swung down from a branch onto a large vine below, he slid down it in a show of youthful acrobatics and dexterity.

He often played at the edge of the forest, but dared never to enter too far, the living forest was an unforgiving place, the forest grew rapidly and often people found themselves trapped in walls of vegetation if they stayed in the one place too long, it was best to keep moving, it was an omnivores paradise and provided an endless supply of food to the animals and people living nearby.

Ailyn made his way to the forest floor quickly, his small size allowing him easy access around the tight spaces between trees and vines, he saw the bush he was after nestled between two large trees, he licked his lips as he moved toward the bush.

Reaching up to grab one of the berries the sun shone down from the canopy into his eyes and he squinted to see in the darkness behind the bush he thought he saw a large figure silhouetted there, he pulled his hand back and tried to focus his eyes, no sooner had his eyes adjusted a large hard grabbed his whole head in one gorilla like palm lifting him.

by Lore Casta Pendragon

Asta heard Ailyn's scream and dropped the basket of clothes she was holding, she rushed into the forest as fast as she could, "Ailyn?", Asta called out, she vaulted over and ducked under vines and foliage as she ran as fast as she could toward Ailyn's screams, she arrived at the location of the noise when she saw a very large man holding Ailyn by the head out toward another man in a wide brimmed hat with scars over his face, "Silus, this is one of the Allheart brats, I saw him at the tavern in Dawnshire", Harram Halfborn said to Silan Silus.

"Where is Aethor Allheart?", "If you tell us we promise not to hurt you", Silus said.

Ailyn struggled against Harram's iron like grip, kicking his legs and punching at his arm, trying desperately to escape, "that's fine, if he doesn't want to tell me we'll just have to start making things a little less comfortable for him", Silus said pointing to a vine bush covered in sharp thorns.

Harram smirked as he tossed Ailyn toward it, Ailyn cried out as he was thrown.

Asta came flying across at speed and caught Ailyn mid-air in her arms, without losing a step she continued running the direction she was moving, jumping from root to root and ducking vines.

"Shit!", Harram cursed and the two men started after her, Silus flipped over roots and swung from branches in a show of acrobatic mastery while Harram stormed through swinging his large arms, breaking branches and crushing the smaller vegetation under his bulk.

Asta noticed Silus gaining on her and she changed direction behind a tree and out of sight, Silus moved at pace past them, Asta noticed him out of the corner of her eye then leaped upwards from branch to branch with Ailyn cowering in her arms, "mother I'm scared", Ailyn said, "don't worry my little one, I won't let them hurt you", she said throwing him over her shoulder.

Silus realized they were no longer in front of him and turned back spotting them in the tree moving higher.

Asta moved to a higher branch and made a run for it, Silus grunted looking down at his bad leg then made after them leaping up the tree and running up the trunk, he made it half the distance to them before backflipping from the tree onto a nearby branch, then sprinted up the branch looking to cut them off.

Asta scrambled up a branch growing over the river upstream from their house, Ailyn still on her shoulder, Silus was closing the distance fast behind her, with a flash Silus had his knives in hand and as Asta reached the end of the branch, she turned, Silus was right there, a grin showing from beneath his wide brimmed hat, he ran forward and slashed at her, Asta had no choice, she threw herself back over the edge falling from the tree.

Ailyn fell from her shoulder and she screamed, "Aethor!".

by Lore Casta Pendragon

Aethor and Aidem looked up to see Asta and Ailyn falling from a very high tree above the river not far from them, a strange man in a wide brimmed hat was standing at the end of the branch.

Silus grabbed a vine and dived, pushing off from the branch, he planned to capture Asta mid-air.

Aethor grabbed a training staff and hurled it with all his considerable strength to intercept him, Silus saw it coming and twisted the vine he was holding like a cat tail in the air twisting his body to avoid it.

Asta and Ailyn hit the water hard, Asta came up first and looked around for Ailyn, then dived down, he was dazed from the landing, she grabbed him and pulled him to the surface as the water carried them downstream back toward the house.

Silus swung from the vine and flipped himself onto a lower branch of the tree landing gracefully, "that man is dangerous", Silus thought to himself.

Aethor and Aidem met them at the river bed and helped them out of the river, "what happened?", "Is Ailyn Alright?", "Who is that man?", Aethor asked Asta.

"I'm fine dad, thanks to mum", Ailyn said smiling at her, Asta smiled back with a worried and relieved expression, "I don't know, I've never seen him before", Asta replied, "I have", Ailyn said, "where?", Aethor responded.

"In Dawnshire as we were leaving, he was in a carriage with the emblem of the church of the god feared on it", Ailyn explained, "an assassin working for the church?", Asta questioned, "how did they find us?", Aidem questioned, the four looked to each other and all came to the same conclusion at once, "Wynn", they all said at the same time.

"They must have tortured him, Wynn wouldn't rat us out", Aethor said," well they've found us now, but I'm not going to let them attack my family and get away with it", Aethor said turning to face the forest.

"I can help father", Aidem stood by his side, "I can fight too", Asta said.

"Asta, I'd prefer if you found a place to hide with Ailyn, he's too young to fight, I'll come find you once this is over", Aethor said, Asta nodded knowing too well that if she fought then Ailyn would try to protect her and would be in danger, her first priority was Ailyn's safety.

Asta and Ailyn moved back to the house as they heard the sound of breaking and snapping branches coming from the forest nearby, into the clearing stepped a very agitated Harram covered in twigs and leaves and a large blood sucking leech, he ripped the thing from his arm then shook off the leaves off like a dog.

As he walked toward Aethor and Aidem, Silus swung down from a vine and landed gracefully near him retracting his knives in the blink of an eye.

by Lore Casta Pendragon

"ALLHEART!", Harram called, "I've come for a little payback for the trouble you caused in Dawnshire", Harram swung a large arm in circles rubbing his shoulder to emphasize his point.

"Also, my colleague here would like a word with you", Harram said smugly extending a hand toward Silus.

As they approached, Aethor and Aidem walked to meet them and took up their fighting stances as they drew close, Silus stopped and bowed deeply, "I am Silan Silus, officer of his royal highness lord Guldamere", Silus straightened up as Aethor replied, "we have nothing to say to you or your kind, leave here now", Aethor warned.

"I thought you'd say so, but my little friends here have other plans", Silus flicked his arms out to the sides and two knives appeared in hand, Harram let out a battle cry, then charged toward Aethor.

Asta and Ailyn looked on from the window of the house, "will father be alright?", Ailyn asked, "I don't know Ailyn, but I won't let anything happen to any of you", she replied.

Aethor tried to avoid Harram's tackle, but the man's reach was too wide and he caught him, tackling him into the ground, Aethor grabbed a hand full of dirt and threw it into Harram's eyes causing him to let go of his waist to try to free the debris from his vision.

Aethor kicked off Harram's face and rolled backward, pushing up with his hands and straight up onto his feet, a knife smashed into Aethor's shoulder as soon as he rose sinking hilt deep.

Aethor cried out in pain as Silus walked forward with another knife in hand, "oh that looks like it hurt Allheart", he smirked.

Aidem rushed forward with a flying kick but Silus effortlessly moved aside, Aidem followed up with a flurry of speedy kicks, Silus moved left and right, ducking and weaving.

Aidem attacked furiously but hit nothing but air, Silus seemingly toyed with the boy's lack of experience, a big smile plastered on his face, like he was enjoying himself.

Silus slashed Aidem across the chest and the boy stumbled back in pain, blood dripped from the shallow wound, "Aidem!", Aethor yelled as he pulled the knife from his shoulder, he moved to help his eldest son, but Harram punched Aethor to the ground with a meaty fist, "your fight is with me Allheart", Harram said mockingly.

Aethor frog leaped to his feet and bicycle kicked Harram right under the chin, the big man's head whiplashed upward as Aethor followed it up with a spinning jump kick, hitting Harram across the jaw, Harram reeled from the force of the impact placing one hand on the ground to stabilize himself as he stumbled to regain his footing, Aethor danced around the big man staying light on his feet.

Harram swung his large muscular arms in large arcing hooks, Aethor dodged each one and landed a few straight punches to Harram's face and ribs.

Becoming increasingly frustrated Harram charged at Aethor once again, Aethor saw what was coming and tried to leap away but Harram caught him by the arm and swung Aethor back into him wrapping his arms around him, arms like tree branches bear hugged him against his large muscular chest.

Aethor raised a knee to Harram's chest in order to counter the attack but Harram's strength was overbearing, making Aethor's him cry out in pain, Harram heard a Aethor's back crack then smiled smugly and swung Aethor by one arm like a ragdoll and launched him through a nearby wooden fence.

Aidem licked the blood from his wound and looked at Silus, a flicker of red passed over Aidem's eyes for a few seconds and he moved at incredible speed using the dragon side kick his father taught him.

He speared Silus in the guts, Silus's eyes grew wide as he was completely taken by surprise by young Aidem's increased speed and flew backward, sliding across the dirt.

Harram strutted over and picked Aethor up by the back of the neck and rammed him against a nearby tree, Aethor growled with anger as he tried it again but lifted both legs and kicked off the tree, he flipped backward out of Harram's grip landing behind him, he kicked at the back of Harram's knee dropping him to a kneeling position.

He put a choke-hold on Harram, only to find the big man's neck was too muscular to get his arms around properly, Harram laughed and grabbed Aethor's arm, he swung him over his shoulder and into the ground, Aethor landed on his back knocking the wind from him, he squirmed on the ground clutching at his back in tremendous pain.

Silus slowly got up holding his mid-section, "not bad young one, you've earned my respect, now I'm going to take you seriously", Silus said putting his knives away in an instant and darted forward.

He threw a faint with one hand and Aidem moved to intercept it but Silus changed directions and ducked down slamming a fist into Aidem guts, Aidem let out a breathy pained cry as he curled over from the blow and hit the dirt in a ball.

"Aidem, get up!", Asta whimpered watching from the house, Aethor saw Harram approaching as he came to finish the job, he used his tatsumaki sweep, spinning his legs around like a top and raising himself from the ground.

He collected Harram on the side of the knee and made him stumble sideways, but as he found his feet, a knife plunged into Aethor's back and he dropped to his knees screaming in pain, Harram slammed him in the face with punch, knocking Aethor down again.

"No!", Aidem gasped from the ground trying to find his feet, Aethor struggled to stand, shaking with the effort, the pain in his back was overwhelming, Silus smirked then shook his

by Lore Casta Pendragon

head, then threw another knife, it slammed into Aethor's back and Aethor hit the dirt face down.

"Leave them alone!", Asta shouted as she rushed across with a staff in her hand, she struck at Silus, he dodged and with a flash more knives were in his hands, he slashed at Asta and she raised the staff blocking him at the wrist with the bottom half of the staff, Asta flicked the staff forward and with a loud crack she hit Silus's face making him drop a knife.

Asta raised the staff for an overhead strike but Harram grabbed the staff from behind her and snapped the staff in half with one hand, "nice toy you got there", Harram said teasingly, "I'll be happy to play with a pretty girl like you", Asta spat at him in disgust.

Harram snarled at her, he grabbed her violently, when she resisted, he slapped her face viciously.

Asta went limp in his arms, "that's more like it", he chuckled then tucked her under his arm, "take care of them, I got plans for this one", Harram said chuckling to himself as he started walking toward the house.

Silus looked at him in disgust but didn't stop him, he raised a hand and made a signal, a raven that was perched close by flew off down the path, Asta started to sob, "no, please don't do this", she pleaded.

Aethor opened his eyes, they flashed red, he raised his shaking fingers to his mouth and licked his blood which had now begun to pool around him, Aethor's eyes began to burn a vibrant red.

Aethor felt his life force start to burn like paper to flame, he pushed off the ground and landed on his feet, he shot off with an explosion of movement, "what?", Silus said.

In seconds Aethor was right behind Harram, Harram turned his head to noticed him but too late, Aethor delivered a powerful close ranged punch to Harram's spine grabbing Asta and sending Harram flying though the stone wall of the house.

Another knife flew toward Aethor's back, but he turned and caught it between two fingers, putting Asta down gently, he regarded Silus, "is that all you can do, throw knives into people backs, you coward!", Aethor said.

Harram groaned from inside the house, clearly in pain holding his back, Ailyn tried to hide himself behind the kitchen table as Harram got up and turned to face Aethor teeth clenched with anger.

Aidem got to his feet and limped over to join his Asta's side, "are you alright Aidem?", Aethor asked, "I'm fine, you're in worse shape than me, that Silus is a tough one", Aidem warned.

                    by Lore Casta Pendragon

"Harram is hurt, help your mother, I'll take care of Silus", Aethor said as he sprinted at Silus launching at him with a flying kick, Silus narrowly dodged to the side he eyes wide as Aethor's foot missed his face by an inch, "If that hit's me I'm done for", Silus thought to himself.

As Aethor landed Silus threw another dagger at his back, Aethor dodged it then did a backward handspring away as Silus threw a volley of daggers one after another, Aethor sprinted off to the left outpacing the daggers, he closed the distance at alarming speed and slamming a fist into Silus's face sending him flying off his feet, Silus hit the ground and bounced.

Harram stepped out of the rubble of the stone wall, "no more playing around Silus, we need to finish the job or there'll be hell to pay", he said in a low menacing tone.

Silus leaped to his feet gritting his teeth with anger, blood trickled from his mouth, he reached in and pulled out a tooth, grunting as he threw it away.

Silus opened his hands and extended them in front of him like he was using a marionette puppet, he began circulating his life energy and a black miasma started leaking from his fingers like small tendrils, Aethor stood ready, fists clenched, muscular frame and red eyes burning wildly.

Silus moved his fingers and swung his hands left then right, all the knives Silus threw previously suddenly came to life surrounded by a black miasma, they flew toward Aethor.

That was his plan all along, to get Aethor at the center of the trap, Aethor couldn't dodge them and he raised his arms to protect his face as a dozen knives sunk into his flesh from all directions.

Aethor cried out a mighty roar of pain as he sunk to his knees, "I can't lose, I can't let them hurt my family, I can't", he thought to himself as he pulled a knife from his chest and licked it.

The knives ejected from him in all directions, blood splattered around him making a blood-stained circle, his pupils glowed red as Aethor pushed the last of his life force into the blood rage technique.

He charged at Silus like a human missile, spear tackling him at tremendous speed, Silus cried out in pain as they crash through a cobblestone fence and into the river beyond.

"Aethor!", Asta cried, Ailyn watched from the safety of the house, horrified by what was happening to his family, Harram took advantage of the distraction and grabbed Asta and Aidem by the hair, "poor Allheart, he won't survive those wounds you know, it's time I was done with the two of you", Harram said.

Asta and Aidem struggled against Harram's grip but the man was just too strong, he walked them down to the river bank.

by Lore Casta Pendragon

"Run Ailyn!", Asta cried out as Harram plunged them into the water holding them under, Ailyn watched terrified from a crack in the door not knowing what to do as Asta and Aidem struggled.

Asta reached over and grabbed Aidem by the hand, Aidem looked at her with horror and grief in his eyes, she smiled at him and mouthed, "it's ok", then their eyes closed and they went limp.

Harram let them go, and he watched as Ailyn's mother and brother floated lifelessly downstream, Ailyn began to sob uncontrollably as Harram slowly walked out of the river and started heading back toward the house.

Ailyn's fear of his inevitable demise at the hands of Harram Halfborn gripped him and he ran out the door toward the living forest, Harram saw him and started running after him but his back injury twinged from his fight with Aethor earlier and he stopped unable to keep up.

Ailyn made his way to the forest and expertly traversed the trees and vines, Harram got up and fumbled after him, crashing through the vegetation.

"You think you can escape us boy, we will find you and when we do, you'll join the rest of the Allheart's in the Abyss!", Harram called out after him.

After searching for a while, Harram realized he wouldn't find the boy and turned back, after about an hour of running through thick vegetation, Ailyn slumped down in a nook of a tree and let out a terrible mournful cry, he was all alone, he'd never train with his father or feel the loving embrace of his mother's hugs or play in the river with his brother again, his loved ones were gone forever.

Ailyn laid there in the nook of the tree, he just wanted the forest to take him to, long hours past and the forest was mostly silent but for the rustling of trees, Ailyn closed his tearful eyes and went to sleep, hoping to wake from this terrible nightmare.

Ailyn's stomach began to hurt from hunger, he opened his eyes, to his surprise there were some fruits and nuts laid out in front of him, he greedily ate them up and got up to look around to see who put them there but there was nobody around.

He made his way downhill till he found a fresh stream of water and took a drink, above him he heard the rustling of a tree, he looked up and the sun bloomed through the tree, a silhouetted figure moved out of sight as his eyes adjusted to the light.

"Who's there?", Ailyn called, but there was no response, Ailyn waited but heard nothing, he was alone again, tears welled up in his eyes and he wiped them away with his sleeve.

"I'm safe here in the forest, I doubt the god feared church will try to find me here, but if I'm going to survive, I'd better make a shelter", Ailyn said.

He had helped Aethor and Asta fix the house many times over the years, so he had a basic knowledge of how to make a good shelter but the forest grew fast, so whatever he made would have to be made high above the ground.

He climbed up a tree as high as it would go and picked a decent spot between several branches, he used vines to pull logs up from the ground and place them together to make a floor, then tied vines around them, "It's not home but it'll do for now", Ailyn said to himself.

"I'd better work on catching some dinner and making a fire", Ailyn said as he made his way down to the river and waded into the shallow water, there he waited still as a stone, wiggling one finger just under the water's surface just as Aethor and Aidem had shown him.

A fish swam up and tried to latch onto his finger, he hooked it into the fish's mouth and pulled it from the water, it began to struggle but Ailyn grabbed it by the tail and slapped it against a nearby stone, the fish went limp and lifeless, Ailyn smiled briefly as this was his first successful attempt at catching fish by hand.

He looked up for approval from his brother and father but realized they were no longer with him and his smile faded, tears dropped down his face and dripped into the water, he slowly made his way to the shore and tied the fish to his pants with a small vine.

He noticed a gathering of some thick grass piled on the ground nearby which looked to be semi weaved into a basket "there must be some people living around here", Ailyn thought to himself, he finished the weave and used some vines to strap it to his back like a backpack, he found a collection of rocks and clay and kindling at the base of the tree as well.

Ailyn looked puzzled, someone was helping him, but they hadn't let him see them, he made his way up to his treehouse, piled the rocks up enough to make a small fireplace using rocks and clay and cooked the fish, "blah", Ailyn said as he picked at the fish, he hadn't gutted it and it tasted horrible, "tomorrow, I'll make some tools", he thought to himself as he curled up on the floor, the night was cold, but Ailyn was too exhausted to care.

The next day Ailyn awoke to find the vines had already begun to overtake the treehouse; one side of the treehouse had vines, weaved and knotted to grow upwards, Ailyn was alarmed that someone had been here while he was asleep but saw what they were trying to do and caught on, he began to weave the vines so they'd grow into the shape of a house.

Over the next month, Ailyn survived by living with the ebb and flow of the living forest, he grew stronger and the trauma of his families passing haunted him less with each day, though the memory remained raw to him.

One evening while he laid on his bed made of reeds, he heard a strange sound like laughter, he looked out the window of the tree house to find strange looking small green humanoid creatures with long pointy ears holding spears, climbing up his tree.

by Lore Casta Pendragon

"Be careful, boiled human is a delicacy to goblin-folk", Ailyn looked up startled by the silence suddenly broken, on a branch nearby casually sat an old man in tan clothing with long platted brown-grey hair.

"Who are you?", Ailyn asked, "there will be time for introductions after we deal with them", the stranger pointed at the goblins climbing up the tree, Ailyn nodded and asked, "what do I do?", "We let them go, they're much weaker than we are", the stranger said, Ailyn gave him a puzzled look, "It doesn't really seem like we're in the position to do that", he said confused.

The stranger smiled and stood up, putting his hands in his pockets, he dropped down off the branch landing directly on top of one the goblins, the thing squealed as he kicked it.

It fell from the tree then he landed on top of another one, each goblin dropping to the ground far below as he stepped from one to another.

Taking his hands out of his pockets he grabbed a vine and swung around the tree kicking goblins as he swung, he stopped suddenly as one goblin stabbed at him with a spear, the stranger moved ever so slightly backwards with a look of supreme confidence on his face and the goblin over extended trying to get at him with the spear, the stranger pulled on the spear gently and the goblin looked at him and whimpered as he tilted forward and lost his footing, falling to the ground.

The stranger pulled on another vine and a branch broke free from above, the vine he held pulled him upward to the treehouse as the branch plummeted down and collected two more goblins on their way up.

Ailyn looked at him mouth wide and in awe, he had never seen anything like it, the man didn't even use any effort at all and they were all clutching their wounds at the bottom of the tree, "how did you do that?", Ailyn said, "I didn't do much of anything, I just let them go", he gave a small chuckle as the goblins got up and ran away.

"They are actually very skittish creatures, mostly afraid of their own shadow, nothing like nightmare creatures", the stranger said, they both watched as the goblins faded into the distance, "you're the one who was helping me aren't you?", Ailyn questioned the stranger, "I just gave you a push in the right direction, you did the rest", he smiled.

"You're a weird guy", Ailyn said directly and they both chuckled, "so who are you anyway, do you live here?", "Are there any others", Ailyn asked, "my name is Den, there used to be a few of us but now I live alone in the temple nearby, I've been keeping watch on you since you got here, you're lucky to be alive, it's dangerous out here, where are your parents?", Den asked.

Ailyn looked down sadly, "they were killed, by men from the church, I came here to hide so they wouldn't kill me too", he said, "I'm sorry to hear that", Den said, Ailyn wiped the tears welling up in his eyes and after a while replied ,"It's ok, there's nothing that can change that now", Den smiled at Ailyn, "that's very grown up of you, you have wisdom for one so young", Den said.

"So why do you live here in the forest?", Ailyn asked him, "I've lived here my whole life training at the temple of the Aikitai, I took over from my late master many years ago, back then the temple used to be a place of pilgrimage, but the church banned travelers from entering the living forest, so these days I mainly just tend to the temple and train alone", Den explained.

"Train, like martial arts?", Ailyn asked, "sort of", Den said, "Aikitai is more of a way of life then a martial arts style", Den explained, "how so?", Ailyn said.

"The whole world in is harmony with its surroundings, as water flows it moves with the path of least resistance, so does the wind, so do the animals and the insects, when things interrupt the flow, they invite conflict and chaos, interrupting the flow of the nature order, if one moves with the flow, one can make it through life much easier, that's what we call Aikitai", Den said.

Ailyn begun to understand a little and said, "it's taking the path of least resistance", "exactly", Den winked at him, Ailyn pondered what old den said and asked, "could you show me how it works?", Den smiled at him gratefully, "I'd be happy to, but it's not easy, there's a lot more to it than just a philosophy, come to the temple, we have rooms there, they are a bit more welcoming then your tree house", he said, Ailyn nodded and he followed Den toward the temple of Aikitai.

On the way Den explained to Ailyn how living in harmony with the living forest is great training in the art of Aikitai, as it constantly invites new challenges and new understandings.

As they arrived at the temple there was a bridge over a river, it was fashioned by vines wrapped around themselves grown into shape, just as Ailyn was doing with his treehouse, there was a waterfall running over the temple itself, it looked like it was made of limestone carved from the redirected water flowing over it, stairs where fashioned the same way as the bridge, made from the natural growth of the forest.

"So, this is what he meant by living with the flow of the living forest", Ailyn thought to himself, there was a large greenhouse made of vines containing all sorts of fruits and vegetables, the temple was beautiful, it had an open courtyard, water running either side of it with pictographs etched into the limestone.

At the back were a series of caves carved into the mountainside which opened up into various rooms, Den showed Ailyn to a room which had a comfy looking bed, a wardrobe and a writing table with a lamp hung above it, it was small, but also warm and quiet.

"First things first, we'll have to get you out of those rags, I'll get to work on that", Den said to Ailyn, "if you're going to learn to practice Aikitai, you'll have to dress the part, we'll begin your training in the morning", Den turned to leave but Ailyn stopped him.

by Lore Casta Pendragon

"Thank you, Den, it's been a long time since anything nice has happened to me", Den turned to him, "that's master Den and you're welcome, get some sleep Ailyn, believe me when I say you're going to need it".

Ailyn woke to the faint sound of rushing water outside the temple, his whole body felt relaxed, like the very air itself was purifying him, he even managed to put aside his grief for a moment and smiled.

Den had laid out his new uniform on the desk, strangely enough it fit him perfectly, he moved to the temple courtyard where Den was waiting for him.

"These clothes fit so well, how did you know my size?", Ailyn asked.

"The fibers I used are made from a particular vine here in the living forest, they're semi parasitic, it'll gain it's nutrients from your body, more-so your dead skin and sweat and repairs itself over time with a little help from you, as long as you keep training, it'll keep feeding on the water, salts and ammonia your body secretes and the bacteria in the fibers turns the ammonia into nitrates, it uses those as food and will also keep you clean, it's stretchy and durable and it's a great insulator, it'll live on your body and grow with you", Dan explained.

"That's amazing", Ailyn proclaimed, "one of the many benefits of living in unison with nature", Den said, "your first lesson is going to be how to present yourself when you're faced with conflict", Den squared up, his hands close to his face, his palms facing Ailyn, "I want you to attack me", Den said.

Ailyn squared up and took the stance his father showed him bouncing on his heels, Den just stood there, staring at him with the intent of a lion about to jump on its prey.

Ailyn saw no opening at all, no opportunity to strike, he knew that the moment he moved, Den would destroy him, "I, I can't", Ailyn said, "do you know why?", Den replied, "there's no opening", Ailyn responded, "wrong!", Den said, "I'm not moving, I'm an open target, what you feel is intent, this is my 'sema', my warrior spirit manifested, and the form is called sagaan".

"How's it work?", Ailyn asked, "by focusing and sharpening your mind to a single purpose, your intent manifests into a force of its own, and if you add a bit of life energy into the mix, it heightens the effect".

Den opened his hands curling his fingers back to look like animal claws, Ailyn felt a pressure on him like he never felt before, a primal fear that if he didn't get out of this man's way, he was going to die.

"You are truly terrifying Master", Ailyn said, Den dropped his guard and smiled, "good, you get the point", Den came to stand next to Ailyn and showed him how to stand in the sagaan form.

by Lore Casta Pendragon

"The first step to mastering Aikitai, is learning to move with nature", Den explained as he showed Ailyn a series of footwork for him to copy, Ailyn moved with him copying his every step and after several days of practice Den moved Ailyn over to one side of the temple where a small waterfall fell, he pulled on some vines close by and a series of bamboo tubes moved streams of falling water around.

Den stood under the water flumes, "I want you to pull on these vines, try to hit me with the falling water", Den asked, Ailyn walked over and Den took his position, Ailyn pulled on the vines and the tubes moved the water around, Den moved his feet using the footwork they had been practicing over the last few days, no matter how hard or fast Ailyn moved the tubes, Den moved around the flowing water in a show of mastery that Ailyn would be hard pressed to follow.

Eventually Den stepped away, not a single drop of water had touched his clothing, "now it's your turn", Den extended a hand and Ailyn took his position, as Den moved the tubes Ailyn managed to dodge the first of the falling water using the footwork he was shown, but his movements were jerky, not fluent like master Den, he got soaked by the second tube.

Pushing his hair out of his face, now sopping wet, Ailyn looked at Den with a look of hopelessness, "again", Den commanded and Ailyn nodded with a sigh, he tried again realizing just how difficult the task was.

Ailyn did a little better this time but used the wrong movement and got doused in water, "you made it look so easy", Ailyn said, "It's easy for chaos to destroy balance, one wrong move could mean the difference between life and death", he said, Ailyn looked at him pondering such a profound statement, but realized the truth in his words, he gained a new understanding of the technique and he bowed to his master as they continued their training.

Silus opened a door and moved to join Harram in a small room in Ravenhill, in front of them a raven made form black miasma was perched, they knelt before it and the raven spoke in the raspy dead voice of the lich Guldamere.

"What information have the prisoners given you Silus", Silus bowed his head and responded, "they didn't know anything about the lost power, I used my most effective techniques, I'm certain they don't know of its location", Silus said.

"No matter, we have another more pressing issue to deal with, Lore Casta Pendragon has broken free, helped by the Kindheart's here in Necropyre", the raven said, "the clerk?", Harram questioned.

"The very same, it seems he was planning to betray us this whole time", the raven responded, "what should I do with the prisoners?", Silus asked, "send them to the pit, they can work till they die", the raven cackled.

by Lore Casta Pendragon

"Umm, you see, the thing is", Harram sputtered nervously, "what is it Halfborn", the raven spat, Harram responded timidly, "the youngest Allheart child got away, escaped into the living forest, I tried to pursue him, but the forest was too dense and I", Harram trailed off, "FOOL!" the raven spat at him, "I will not allow the progeny of Aram to continue living in MY land!".

"Order a battalion of soldiers and a few acolytes to go and kill the runt", Guldamere commanded.

"Silus, Pendragon has one of the third of the power, in order to get what you desire you'll need to use everything at your disposal to bring him to me, once I extract the power from within him, I'll be strong enough to return even your beloved Cinder to you", the raven said.

Silus looked up at it longingly, he served Guldamere for one reason and that reason was to see his Cinder returned to him, Silus nodded and left Harram and the raven in the room.

"That guy, he gives me the creeps, if you give the girl back to him, how do you know he'll stay loyal to us?", Harram questioned, "I've held his leash this long, I can string him along a bit longer, if it comes down to it, I can always just have you kill him and raise him as a thrall", the raven croaked quietly, "now go", the raven burst into black fog and Harram left the room with a smile on his face.

At the Cathedral in Necropyre a young boy was being escorted to the throne room of Guldamere's cathedral, "welcome young one, you must be excited to be joining the ranks of the church of the god feared at such a young age", the boy looked at Guldamere, who was veiled in his robe disguised in a more human looking visage, "yes your lordship, a, a great honor", the boy stuttered, "good, it is always a good idea for a young altar boy to differ to his betters", Guldamere smirked, flashing rotten teeth.

"Y-yes sire, I can read and I can work and I know most of the histories we're taught at school, I, wasn't the best student, but I promise, I won't let you down", the boy said taking a knee, Guldamere waved his hand standing from the throne, he walked slowly toward the boy, the room seemed to darken as he drew closer.

"Then let us begin the acceptance ritual", Guldamere said as he placed his hand on the boy's shoulders, the room went black and the boy started to scream as Guldamere ripped the very life from him, his face turned gaunt and hollow, then he fell to the floor, nothing left but an empty eyeless husk.

"That's a good boy", Guldamere said, "clear this one out and bring in the next, he ordered", two acolytes dragged the body into another room to the side of the chamber then threw him down a shoot, the body fell into a pile of rotten husks as another of the citizens of Necropyre was led into the throne room, each one drained as the last until Guldamere regained some semblance of his humanity.

   by Lore Casta Pendragon

"My lord should we get more offerings", a soldier asked, "no, I'm done", the lich sat on his throne, "now that Pendragon is finally free, I can claim the power I've sort for so long, no more will I have to resort to draining the living to sustain my eternal life", Guldamere said.

"You can also give to us what was promised", a female voice said from under a black robe as she walked over to offer a hand to Guldamere, "indeed, you will also have life eternal without the need for resurrection", Guldamere promised, his congregation in black robes clapped agreeingly, while Guldamere drummed his boney fingers on the arm of his throne.

The spark of life had long left him, every moment seemed drawn and tedious, every conversation had been spoken, every tidbit of knowledge researched, his long years searching and waiting had him exploring every city in Thalaria, speaking to every idiot with a theory about the origins of chaos magic, it was all just so, "typical", Guldamere said out loud, "typical sire?", A veiled man with a katana strapped to his waste replied, "nothing", Guldamere said, "I have a task that requires both of your attention".

                                             by Lore Casta Pendragon

Chapter Six

The missing pieces

Lore Casta Pendragon sat down and put his fists together under the sleeves of his long multicolored robe, the blown-out fire burst into a brilliant flame as he sat to warm himself.

He looked up from the fire toward Kimba and Kamdar, Kimba was startled by his steely gaze under those bushy grey eyebrows, "tell me girl, what has become of the world, it would seem, I've been gone a long time", Lore said to Kimba.

"I don't know much, I've not travelled far from home before now, but I've read quite a lot, what I do know is, not a lot survived the cataclysm five hundred years ago, all we know from the ruins of the old world is that most of it was destroyed, there are extremely large gorges separating the lands, in its center a crater of what was once Mount Muse", Kimba replied thoughtfully, "was the devastation truly so powerful?", "*that* was caused by the release of chaos magic?", Lore thought to himself out loud.

"The land is mostly baron and full of nightmare creatures, although there are fortified cities scattered about and people live in the green zones that are mostly unaffected by the blasted lands outside, nightmare creatures rarely travel there, they prefer to stick to the darker places", Kamdar added.

"I see", Lore got up and slammed his fists together, the air around Kimba and Kamdar became denser as if pressing in on them, they struggled to breathe, "what are you doing?", Kamdar gasped, "I can't move", Kimba said panicking.

"I doubt anyone could have survived a cataclysm of such immensity", Lore shouted, "you must be one of Guldamere's risen, come to claim my power", Lore said as he squeezed them tighter, Kimba and Kamdar fell to their knees gasping for air, "some, in, the, green, zones, survived, the, blasts", Kimba said breathily.

Lore released the spell and they fell to the floor panting, "we should never have come here", Kamdar said to Kimba, "he destroyed the world once and he'll probably do it again", Kamdar said staring daggers at Lore.

Lore sat back down with a concerned look on his face as they found their feet, "I'm sorry, but the fate of the world rests on my shoulders, I can't be caught or the world itself might end", Lore said putting his face in his hands.

"Despite what you may have been told that is not entirely true", Lore said, "I tried to stop him, we both did", Lore's face looked down sadly, "stop who", Kimba asked, "Guldamere", Lore said angrily, "it was he who broke the seal, there was a war eons past to hold back the dark and seal away the abyss and chaos magic itself, Guldamere wanted their power for himself and it

by Lore Casta Pendragon

wasn't the first of his atrocities, every power hungry lord in the land tried to break the seal and each time they tried a little more chaos leaked into the world, the more chaos, the more chaos magic", Lore explained.

"So, you took it for yourself instead", Kamdar spat at him, Lore raised a bushy eyebrow toward him, "no, let me explain", Lore said.

"I documented the use of chaos magic so it could be used to help the world, my words are written in that tome you hold", Kimba took out Lore's tome from her pack, "but there were others who used it as a weapon to dominate", Lore went on, "my apprentice Aram and I swore an oath we would stop them at any cost, by the time we found out about Guldamere's plan however, he had already amassed a small force of powerful risen necromancers and convinced them to help him.

We fought him, but we failed and in the ensuing battle the muses seal was broken, it released a tremendous amount of magic into the world, too much all at once, Guldamere gained one part of the muses power, I gained another and I suspect the other was likely claimed by someone else, Aram died in the cataclysm and if Guldamere had two thirds of the power he would have lifted the seal long ago to claim the part that I hold", Lore explained.

"So that's what really happened, the church has been lying to everyone for hundreds of years and covering up the truth", Kimba said astonished.

"Guldamere made himself out to be a godlike figure to the people of Thalaria, bringing back the dead, healing the sick, most people revere him", Kamdar said.

"He's holding them hostage more like it", Lore replied.

"Tell me, how did you end up in here?", "Why did it take so long for you to be free?", Kimba asked, "Guldamere brought me here, at the time he was still a mage of subpar talent, he planned to keep me prisoner until he learned to extract the power I held", Lore shifted uncomfortably.

"But I sealed the door from the inside and slowed the passage of time from within while the outside world continued forward, unfortunately Guldamere sealed it from the outside as well, a bit of an oversight on my part, I have no idea how long I was trapped inside, I just know it was a very long time, I hoped by now Guldamere would have perished, so I asked you to break the seal through my book, I honestly had no idea who would be waiting for me on the other side of that door, I'm sorry I attacked you but I have to be careful, I'm glad it was you two and not Guldamere waiting for me", Lore smiled at them.

"So how has Guldamere stayed alive for five hundred years?", Kamdar asked, "when Aram fought him, he drained the life force from him, he may have stayed alive using the power and extracting the life from the living, have people gone missing around him?", Lore questioned thoughtfully.

"So that's what must have happened to mum", Kimba replied sadly, Kamdar got up and slammed his fist into the cave wall, "damn that bastard!", "If it's the last thing I do I'll have revenge for what he did to her!", Lore got up from his seat, "then we have an accord, I'll help you dispose of Guldamere, although I don't know the extent to his power now, he's been free for five hundred years and his power would have only grown since then", Lore explained.

"So, the first thing we should do is locate the missing power before he does, I'll use it to defeat him once and for all", Lore said, "how do we do that?", Kimba asked.

"You mentioned green zones that were unaffected by the cataclysm, I believe they may be a good place to start, some sort of power must have protected them from the devastation, else they would have ended up blighted like everything else", Lore said.

"We should be going as soon as possible, no telling when more nightmare creatures may show up, with that raven gone Lord Guldamere will know something is up".

They made their way to the front of the cave and began the long hike out of the crater of Mount Muse.

"Many stories tell of your exploits with Master Aram", Kimba said to Lore, "Master Aram?", Lore chuckled heartily, "Aram was very talented, it's the reason I took him on as an apprentice, he wore the moniker of Allheart well, but I'd hardly call him a master, he was more like hired muscle", Lore started.

"In fact, his use of magic was very modicum", Lore added, "he was said to have been one of the greatest warriors who ever lived", Kimba said, "no doubt, he used his power mostly for combat enhancements, I could always rely on him in a pinch, he was a dear friend", Lore said looking down visibly upset.

"I failed him", Lore said, "I'm sure you did everything you could", Kimba said trying to comfort him, Lore rustled her hair with a smile.

"I need to take a break", Kamdar said urgently as he rushed off to find a place to relieve himself, "so you've been reading my book have you, how about you show me what you've learned", Lore asked, "oh I haven't been studying long, Guldamere and his acolytes kept the books under lock and key, I only just got my hands on this one before we got your message", Kimba explained bashfully, "nevertheless, you managed to kill the bird, so you must have a rudimentary knowledge of fire manipulation, try a fireball at that dead tree", Lore pointed over to a nearby deadwood at the edge of a ledge.

"I only just summoned a fireball for the first time back there in the cave, and I didn't summon the fire myself", she said trying to find an excuse not to embarrass herself, "I see", Lore raised a bushy brow. "Do as I do", Lore slammed his fists together and Kimba did the same, "your

                    by Lore Casta Pendragon

knuckles should be interlaced forming a tight seal, otherwise your life force wont flow directly", Lore tutored.

After fixing her posture and hand position he instructed, "pull on your energy and feel it circulating, build it like your pouring water from a bucket into a small cup, too much and you'll waste it, too little won't be enough", Lore said.

The air around Kimba grew colder with the increase of her power, "very good, now hold it, you should be able to feel the chaos magic around you, the wind, the earth, the sky and even the temperature fluctuations in the air", Lore said.

"I can feel it", Kimba replied surprised, "now keep circulating your life energy by quickly extending an arm like this and grabbing at the elbow like this", Lore extended one arm outward and grabbed his elbow to demonstrate, Kimba nodded and followed suit, "this way you can continue pouring in energy as you build the flame, pull all of the heat from the air and add your life energy to it, focus on the point just beyond your palm".

A fireball erupted from Lore's hand floating in the air just beyond his palm, he released the spell and it snuffed out with a wisp of smoke.

"Your turn", Lore said as he pointed to the deadwood, Kimba pulled on the heat around her and sparks flickered at her palm, then a small flicking fire, she laughed triumphantly.

"You've got the fire, now give it the fuel it needs to burn", Lore said and Kimba poured her life force into the flame, it burst into a small fireball the size of her palm.

"I did it!", she yelled, "don't put too much of yourself into it or you'll burn yourself out, only use half at most, now aim at the deadwood just between your two fingers and between your knuckles then give it a push", Lore instructed lift her arm up slightly.

Kimba lined up the tree, focused, aimed, then pushed, the fireball shot from her hand and the deadwood exploded into splinters, Kimba jumped up and down with excitement and Lore chuckled with her.

"WHAT THE HELL!", Kamdar shouted from behind a rock on the other side of the tree, desperately trying to pull up his pants, Lore and Kimba couldn't hold back their amusement and let out a hearty laugh.

"I'm sorry, I didn't know you were there", Kimba said after she regained her composure, "you could have killed me girl, you certainly made the process of evacuation my bowls much faster", Kamdar said struggling with his pants, which made Lore and Kimba laugh harder, they continued onward in good spirits.

Once they reach the top Lore launched a fireball and blew a large scorpion like creature into embers, other nightmare creatures around them retreated to escape a similar fate, Lore looked

by Lore Casta Pendragon

out at the land and the devastation around him and sunk to his knees, he grabbed the pointy hat from his head and grasped it at his heart, "it's all gone, all of it, there's nothing left of what was, just baron wastes and monsters", he said in despair.

"There are still cities and towns closer to the green zones, we'll head for Riverside village in the northwest, I heard there was a resistance gathering somewhere there", Kamdar said.

Kimba walked along then suddenly tripped a wire along the path, knives came flying at her from every direction, Lore slammed his fists together and stalagmites of earth pull up around them, the knives collided with it.

Lore slammed his foot down and the earth crumbled away, "well, well, aren't we perceptive", Silus said dropping down from a nearby tree, he dodged suddenly as a fireball ripped just past his face, he looked up to see Lore's palm still smoking. "Patience is a virtue you know, at least let me introduce myself", Silus said.

"I'm afraid you've already worn out your welcome", Lore said angrily as he fired another fireball at him, Silus did an aerial flip to the side and hid behind a boulder, "your very decisive, I can see why you gave my lord trouble, I'm Silan Silus, officer of Lord Guldamere, it's nice to finally meet you Lord Pendragon", Silus said readying a knife.

He heard no reply only silence, he peered out from behind the boulder to find nobody there, "oh, you sneaky scoundrel!", Silus shouted.

Lore, Kimba and Kamdar were veiled and running down the road, they reached a rocky overhang and stopped to rest, dropping the veil, panting Kimba fell against the rock wall, "quick thinking young one, we'll make an apprentice of you yet", Lore said to Kimba.

"Silus, he's one of Guldamere's inner circle", Kamdar said, "I heard he's a master of tracking his enemies, and also Guldamere's chief interrogator", "that doesn't bode well for us", Lore replied.

Silus took out a small statue of a raven and threw it into the air, it burst into black miasma, the smoke swirled and coalesced into a raven, he then pulled out another statue of a humanoid werewolf.

The raven cawed as it flew past the three hiding beneath the rocky overhang, "he found us", Lore said, "how do you know?", Kimba asked, "those ravens with the smoke trailing them are Guldamere's eyes", Lore answered, "we can't hide from him with that bird following us, we'll have to face him", Lore said.

They hid alongside the road behind whatever covering they could find and waited, Kimba looked down the road from behind a rock, as she turned back a knife pressed against her throat and her eyes went wide, it lifted her to her feet as she tried not to get cut by the blade.

Kimba got up slowly and turned to see Silus behind her, "where are your friends' girl?", Silus said impatiently, she turned to face him and the knife in his hand got red hot.

                                                      by Lore Casta Pendragon

"Shit!", Silus cried as he dropped the knife, it turned to a puddle of molten steel on the ground and he backed up to avoid the sparks, Lore and Kamdar walked toward him, all three of them fists interlocked and ready for battle.

Silus continued backing up, "hold on a minute, I have something for you", Silus smirked, suddenly a massive powerful nightmare creature launched itself from the dust fog on their left, it grabbed Lore by the shoulder in its toothy maw and razor-sharp claws ran off with him into the decayed forest.

"Lore!", Kimba shouted, but the creature was too fast and it was gone before they could react, Silus smirked and raised a hand, several hidden soldiers in armor came forth and charge at them.

They were trapped and outnumbered, Kamdar summoned wind while Kimba summoned fire both complimenting the other causing a giant bout of forceful flame, three soldiers were caught alight and screamed a blood curdling cry as they burned, Silus threw a knife cutting Kimba's thigh and the flames ceased, she fell with a scream toward Kamdar, he grabbed her before she hit the ground and the soldiers rushed in surrounding them weapons inches from them.

Lore was being dragged from a bloody wound across the ground, he cried out in agony as the beast dragged him in its maw, the old man slammed his fists together and a dead tree uprooted and fell in front of them a branch clotheslined the werewolf across the neck, branches snapped as they broke through, the werewolf let out a whimper getting caught and let Lore go, he flew through the air, fist together he held his breath then pulled the air around him making it denser, he slowed his descent and landed on his feet with a gust of wind.

The beast got up and shook off the blow, Lore's blood dripped from its mouth, "I hope you liked that meal because it's the last one you're ever going to have!", He shouted, the beast accepted the challenge and charged at him on all fours, it was so fast.

Lore raised his hands to the sky, rock and broken branches rose up from the ground all around him, Lore threw his hands forward and the chatter shot out, piercing the beast's flesh from every angle, it let out a final death growl as it crashed into the ground and slid to Lore's feet.

Lore huffed and fell to his knees grabbing at his wounds, then with a grunt he closed his eyes and began circulating life energy at the wound, slowly the wound began to stitch together leaving a nasty scar from where the teeth and claws had sunk in.

Lore fought to get to his feet and kicked the werewolf in anger, "you hideous runt of a mother's cud", he shouted in anger as he stumbled back toward his companions.

Kimba and Kamdar had their hands tied, armed men pointing sharpened weapons at their faces, Silus searched over them and pulled out Pendragon's tome, Silus paced in front of them.

"According to our laws you are in possession of illegal magical contraband to which the punishment is", he turned to them, "death".

Two soldiers kicked the back of their legs and they fell to their knees, with a flash two knives appeared in Silus's hands as he stood in front of Kamdar and reached up high with his blade to deliver his judgement, thunder rumbled loudly from the sky above, Silus looked up confused as the clouds above turned a darker black.

Lore came walking into the clearing, hands raised to the sky, electrical energy crackled about him, lightning struck down around them, exploding at the ground where it landed kicking up soil and dust, Silus and the soldiers turned stiff like stones for a moment then all of them dropped simultaneously to the ground unconscious.

Lore used his magic to unravel their bindings, Kimba and Kamdar embraced each other tightly, "that was too close", Kimba said, "thank you Lore, we thought we were done for", Kamdar said, "I thought I was too", Lore responded showing them the holes in his robe letting them see his scars.

"How are you still alive?", Kimba asked, "I've faced much bigger foes in the past", Lore chuckled, "that was the biggest nightmare creature I've ever seen", Kamdar said, "you really are something else Lore", Kamdar said impressed.

Lore just smiled and Kimba grunted in pain, Lore hushed her moving her hand away, "shh, shh, shh, let me take a look", he said, Kimba pulled up her dress and showed the slice Silus's knife had left on her thigh, it was bleeding badly, "that one will leave a mark I'm afraid, but I can show you how to heal it", Lore said.

"You can't do it for her?", "Like you did for yourself?", Kamdar asked, "afraid not, the act of healing comes from within, if I were to fix it myself, nothing would be in the right place, the body is made of thousands of small cells, so many that I could never place them back together myself, but if we do it ourselves, our body naturally knows where things belong", Lore explained.

"Focus on the wound, feel the pain, your body is pointing you to the exact places that need to be mended, use your life force to help your body's natural healing process along and feed it chaos magic to amplify the effect", Lore said.

Kimba nodded, before Kimba's eyes, the wound began to stitch back together leaving a small scar.

"Thanks Lore, what should we do with them?", Kamdar asked, "I'll finish them off quickly, we can't afford to have them report back to Guldamere", Lore said, he begun to summon a fireball, it burst to life in his palm and he aimed it at Silus, but as he fired, the raven that was following them swooped down and landed on top of Silus, with a loud caw, black miasma fell over Silus enshrouding him, the fireball snuffed out as it collided.

      by Lore Casta Pendragon

"You're stronger than ever Pendragon", a dead raspy voice said from the raven's mouth, "Guldamere", Lore said, his bushy eyebrows fell to a frown.

"Now your back I'll be taking my power, see you again soon old friend", the black miasma thickened then faded away with the sound of Guldamere's dead cackle, Silus disappeared.

"We need to leave; his forces are everywhere, they won't be far behind us", Kamdar said, Lore and Kimba nodded and they moved off quickly down the trail.

A raven flew into the cathedral of the god feared at Necropyre, flying awkwardly and looking diminished.

It crashed into the floor at the steps of Guldamere's throne in a burst of black miasma, as the smoke cleared, Silus was laying on the floor, "get up fool", the lich commanded, a black miasma claw grabbed Silus by the back of the coat and lifted him to his feet, Silus was semi-conscious, struggling to stay upright.

"You failed me", the lich said, "My lord, Pendragon's magic is overwhelmingly strong", Silus said in a defeated tone, Guldamere dropped Silus who struggled to stay on his feet, the black miasma claw faded away in a wisp of smoke.

"My lord, my defeat was not entirely without merit", Silus explained weakly, the lich's expression changed to one of interest, Silus brushed himself off trying to regain some of his dignity, "based on their current direction they're heading will be one of four possible destinations, Dawnshire to the east, Riverside to the northeast, the living forest beyond that or Ravenhill in the north, I doubt they'll be coming here".

Guldamere pondered for a moment then responded, "for five hundred years I've sent my forces into the green zones in search of the missing power, the living forest is a hostile place, especially for those like us who are touched by the abyss, it rejects our kind outright, should Pendragon reach the living forest he might just find the missing power and bolster his already heightened magical ability, if that happens my reign may end at his hands", Silus looked at him with concern, "my lord, I've never heard you utter any doubt in that regard, this missing power, is it really that strong that it could rival you?", Guldamere tapped his boney fingers on the arm of his throne.

"If Pendragon were to obtain it before I do, his power would exceed my own, needless to say if that happens Cinder would remain bound in death forever, for I am the only one who can bring the fallen back to life", Guldamere said.

Silus's expression changed at the mention of Cinder, "how do we know the missing power is in the living forest and not one of the other green zones?", Silus asked.

"My only concern is recapturing Pendragon!", The lich spat at him, "summon my generals, gather all available forces, if I remove Pendragon from the equation then there won't be anything left to oppose me", Guldamere said standing and pointing toward the door.

Silus turned and hurriedly limped out, as the door closed, Guldamere slumped back upon his throne taking a glass crystal decanter from a table next to it, he let out a roar of anger while he threw it across the room shattering it into a thousand tiny pieces.

At the Aikitai temple, Den instructed Ailyn on combat techniques, Ailyn's hair had grown out longer and he wore it in a que just as Den did, "tell me what you remember of the forms so far", Den asked, Ailyn put a hand to his chin in thought, "Sagaan is the form of defense", Ailyn said, Den nodded.

"Ukemi is the art of avoiding damage", Den nodded again, "taisabaki is the art of moving", Den nodded a third time, "you're a fast learner, but let us see if you can put them into practice", Den said.

He threw a punch at Ailyn's mid-section, Ailyn turned using the tenkan technique Den had showed him moving his foot one hundred eighty degrees behind him, putting him at Dens side, the punch moved past without making contact.

Den backed away quickly then followed up with a kick, Ailyn slid backward out of the way, Den launched another attack to Ailyn's face, Ailyn used Kaiten, doing a slight slide forward turning one hundred eighty degrees with his hips, the punch narrowly missed him.

Den unleashed a volley of attacks and Ailyn slid back, holding Sagaan posture, he effortlessly pushed each attack to the side with his palms, each one missing him by an inch.

Den grabbed Ailyn and attempted to throw him to the ground, Ailyn moved with the force of the throw and redirected the power outwards instead of down pulling Den along with him, Ailyn rolled to the floor and Den came flying over the top with twice the force.

Den broke the contact, rolled into a ball then expanded his body, he sprang up and slid backwards, the centrifugal force completely dissipated.

Den smiled brushing the dirt from his clothing, then regarded Ailyn, "well done Ailyn, that's all for today", they bowed to each other and Den excused himself, "oh Ailyn before I forget, why don't you try the Ai se shin mediation", Den said as he left.

The Ai se shin mediation was a form of mediation done under the pressure of a waterfall, they didn't usually do that type of training that early in the day so Ailyn looked a bit confused, then Ailyn sniffed his armpit and realized that he needed to take a shower and chuckled as he headed to the falls on the eastern side of the temple.

Ailyn was deep into his meditation, his focus being challenged by the waters pressure, which seemed to grow heavier and colder over time, he delved deeper into his mind to escape the distraction, visions of his late family clouded his thoughts, their memory still weighed heavily on him.

 by Lore Casta Pendragon

Ailyn opened his eyes after a while and found he was short on breath, he decided to take a walk to ease his troubled mind.

Following a path down the cliffside, gigantic trees towered over making the area dark and shadowed beneath the temple, the sun shone briefly through the canopy of foliage, revealing the rock wall next to him.

The cliff face showed petroglyphs of men with their hands raised towards the temple, Ailyn moved some leafy vines and above the image was the visage of a beautiful woman with her hands extended to them, "a deity of some sort?", Ailyn pondered.

He wandered further down the path which ran behind the waterfall, pushing aside heavy vines he entered a large overhang, vines curtained the overhang, the ground was carpeted in a soft green moss and fireflies moved around within illuminating the space.

In the center was a calm pool occasionally being splashed with drops from the waterfall, Ailyn sat at the edge of the pool and looked in, it seemed so serene but the air grew colder, the light retreated and his reflection clouded over.

A vision of a silhouetted figure casting dark clouds swept through the forest, vegetation wilted and died as he passed, behind him walked thousands of people, behind them the people got more stooped and ever more they stumbled, shambling and crawling, eventually turning into shadow and the silhouettes of nightmare creatures, beyond that everything was engulfed by darkness.

Ailyn fell back away from the pool, horrified from the vision he saw within, the pool darkened, but after a few moments the light within the cave seemed to brighten again, a mote of white light slowly floated up from the water, it floated above it, hovering like a seed pod in the wind, then came to rest on the surface.

The mote dimmed showing a wisp, a creature of made of light and pure energy.

The pool brightened again and the wisp took off, hovering above it, "Ailyn", a voice said in an echoing tone, Ailyn was startled by the mention of his name, the voice who said it sounded familiar, he knew that voice, "mother?", Ailyn asked.

"No, I'm not your mother Ailyn, what you are hearing is a voice that is calming to your soul", the wisp replied, "who are you then?", Ailyn asked cautiously.

"I am a remnant of something long lost, you could say I am part of the forest itself", the wisp responded, "what I just saw in the pool just now, was that you?", Ailyn asked, "this pool has been magically purified, it can do many things, prophecy or fate, a reflection of one's soul, it can see the lands past and the lands beyond, there are few like it in this world", the wisp said dancing on the water's surface as it spoke to Ailyn.

"Can it show me my family?", Ailyn asked.

 by Lore Casta Pendragon

The wisp stopped and stayed silent but eventually responded, "that which crosses the abyss should never return from the lands beyond, for it brings with it fearful darkness".

The wisp grew brighter and dimmer as if agitated by the suggestion, "I'm sorry", Ailyn said, the wisp continued dancing on the surface of the pond, illuminating it with the touch of thin light filled tendrils, "do you like it here?", Ailyn asked, "I'm bound to this place, my power diminishes the further I roam from here", the wisp responded, "how did you know my name?", Ailyn asked, "I know of most the creatures who dwell within the forest and even some that dwell beyond it".

"There are strangers approaching the forest, I can't stay here much longer, but come back and speak to me again before you go", the wisp said and with a flash of light the wisp was gone and Ailyn was alone again in the overhang. Ailyn pondered over the words the wisp had spoken then began the climb back up the cliff face.

A few days later Kimba, Kamdar and Lore made their way into Riverside village, there were only a few houses that made up the village and most were spread far apart from one another along the river bank, towering beside it was the living forest made up of large trees wrapped with huge vines that constantly moved and grew, if you stopped and looked at it, you could see the forest moving like watching clouds moving slowly through the sky, "I can see why they call it the *living* forest", Lore admired, "there is definitely some magic at work here", he said admiring it.

They continue walking until they found the ruin of a house along the road, an etched sign on a stone wall read Allheart's.

Lore stopped in his tracks, "surely not", he thought to himself as he pushed a small wooden gate open and continued toward the house, "what's going on master Pendragon?", Kimba asked but Lore didn't respond, Kamdar and Kimba looked at each other, shrugged then walked in after him.

There was a giant hole in the wall, Lore looked over the property, he took note of the training equipment, the destruction and the things left behind, most of it had been stolen by neighbors and passersby, but the sentimental things remained, "whomever lived here must have fallen victim to bandits or nightmare creatures", Kamdar assumed.

"Not surprising when you live all the way out here without the protection of the city walls", Kimba responded, Lore grumbled then said, "there was a battle here", pointing at the ruined house, "how can you tell?", Kamdar asked.

"There were weapons left lying around everywhere outside, mostly knives and they stink of dark magic", Lore assessed, "it seems Aram had progeny who survived all these years just to be snuffed out by assassins", Lore slammed his fist into the stone wall in frustration.

  by Lore Casta Pendragon

"We can't shelter here, it's too exposed", Kamdar said as he picked up one of the knives and placed it in the back of his pants.

"Then onward into the forest", Lore said, "wait we're actually going in there", Kimba said nervously, "how else are we going to find the power", Lore said.

As they approach the forest they heard a cawing noise in the distance, Lore turned to look back down the road to see a black miasma raven circling the path above.

"Guldamere has caught up with us", Lore said, around the bend Ghouls came running down the road at speed shrieking as they saw the three of them, Lore slammed his fists together then extended an arm firing a fireball the size of a cannonball at the leading Ghoul, it exploded violently into viscera and shattered bone flew out in all directions, a femur bone stuck into a tree next to Lore's head and his eyes grew wide, "run", he said quietly at first, then he found his voice as the ghouls continued advancing and he shouted, "run!".

The three of them turned and ran into the forest, Kimba being the smallest of them had less trouble making her way through the thick vegetation, Kamdar and Lore followed behind.

The Ghouls snarled and gnashed and shambled their way behind them, one of them fell off a large tree root and skewered itself upon a broken tree stump, it explodes into viscera, bone shards shooting from the corpse, Lore slammed his fists together and made a magic ward behind them, the bone shards rebounded off it.

"Nasty, vile things, Guldamere's work", he said as he turned to continued running the Ghouls not far behind and in great numbers.

Kimba tripped on a vine and it constricted around her foot, she tried to free herself with her hands, but the vine started constricting tighter and winding its way up her leg, Kamdar took the knife from his belt and cut the vine freeing Kimba, Lore and Kamdar helped her up and they ran with the Ghouls right on their heels.

Lore noticed some loose earth on a ledge above and slammed his fist together, he threw out a hand and a boulder crashed down and smashed into a tree with another dead tree resting against it, with a loud crack it fell behind them, they took cover behind a cliff face as it landed on the Ghouls behind them. The tree exploded into blood, wood, viscera and bone shards, taking out more Ghouls behind them in a chain reaction of bloody mess, leaving the forest floor looking like a slaughter yard.

"I didn't think nightmare creatures could enter the green zones", Kamdar said, "these aren't nightmare creatures, these are the risen of Guldamere, that bought us some time but we have to keep moving", Lore said pushing them onward deeper into the forest, Ghouls still shrieking in pursuit.

                                        by Lore Casta Pendragon

a large black carriage with the symbol of the church of the god feared made its way into Riverside accompanied by five hooded figures in robes on horseback and six battalions of the churches armed forces.

As they marched their way to the forest edge the presession stopped, in the carriage Guldamere held a black flower, he whispered something to it and it oozed with black smoke as the carriage door swung open, black miasma poured out from the flower and the grass wilted away under it.

Guldamere bent down and planted the flower into the ground, dark roots began to grow from it killing all the other vegetation around him, the five hooded men on horseback lined up as the lich stepped forward with his hands clasped together in prayer, everyone of Guldamere's forces took a knee other than the five on horseback as Guldamere approached the forest, a raven sat on his shoulder.

As Guldamere walked into the forest as it died around him, turning into rot, cutting a path for his forces to follow.

by Lore Casta Pendragon

Chapter Seven

The Dying Forest

Ailyn walked through the forest, he practiced his Taisabaki footwork as he moved, ducking, spinning, dashing, avoiding vines and branches, moving around trees, it was like a dance.

He became entranced by the movements and closed his eyes, he felt the forest around him, he felt like flowing water, he felt his life energy circulating around his body.

Ailyn heard a branch crack above; he rolled out of its way then rose to his feet as it crashed down behind him.

Opening his eyes, he took a deep breath to center himself, there were sounds of shrieking in the distance, then an explosion, Ailyn was confused, it was not a sound he usually heard in the living forest.

He moved toward the sound as it grew louder, coming to the edge of a cliff face, he looks down below to see three small figures were running from a large group of shrieking creatures moving quickly below, to his left was a small gorge leading up the mountain which then curved to the right and connected to the pathway leading up the same direction.

A dozen creatures followed behind the three figures and dozens more veered right, the mountain on the right of the gorge continued upward in a clear path.

At Ailyn's vantage point he could see the creatures were about to cut them off in a pincer, they would be cut off.

"No, not that way", Ailyn tried to call out to them but he was too far to be heard, "so, there you are", Den said as he jumped down next to Ailyn, "what are these people up to, being this far into the forest?", Den wondered.

"They're in trouble, we should help them", Ailyn said, Den looked over the cliff, "they certainly have gotten themselves into a pickle", Den remarked then turned to face Ailyn, "well, what are you waiting for?", Den said, pointing downhill.

Kimba, Kamdar and Lore came to a cliff face, "this way", Lore shouted following alongside the cliff wall, "we'll find a way up here", Kamdar said as they moved upward through the rocky pass.

They slowed having to climb over large boulders and thick tree roots, the ghouls behind them gained ground shrieking and groaning, they crawled on all fours over the obstacles easily, digging their sharp gnarled fingers into the rubble.

"Against the wall", Lore said as he slammed his fists together, several large boulders came loose on the cliff face rolling downhill toward the ghouls, most of them moved out of the way,

but a couple weren't looking where they were going and got caught, exploding into a bloody mess, bone shards flew out in every direction collecting a few more ghouls in the process.

They made it to the right hand turn in the gorge, they could see the top of the hill not far ahead of them when a dozen ghouls crested the hill, they stopped in their tracks, a dozen more came up behind them.

"What do we do?", Kimba asked, "we've no choice now, we have to stand our ground", Lore said, they stood back to the wall and surrounded as the ghouls advanced closer.

"Any chance for more of that lightning", Kamdar suggested, "the sky is blocked by the canopy of trees and even so I can't cast it, when they're this close to us", Lore replied.

Kimba slammed her fists together and said, "follow my lead", she began to fade from sight like fading into murky water, Kamdar and Lore followed suit, the ghouls came closer.

They moved silently while the ghouls reached out with long gnarled hands, listening out for any sign of movement, they swiped at the air trying to find them.

Kamdar stepped back to narrowly avoid a boney rotted hand and stepped on a stick with a crack, the noise drew the attention of the ghouls and five of them leaped toward Kamdar's location, he dropped the veil and the wind picked up around him, he extends his arms out at the last minute and the ghouls were blasted away by a powerful gust of wind, they shrieked and now all the ghouls were focused on him.

"Don't worry about me, I'll be the bait, I'll take as many of them as I can, just make your way out of here", Kamdar said, Kimba opened her mouth to object but Lore extended a hand and muted her voice with magic, "No father, please", she mouthed muted as the ghouls moved on Kamdar.

He slammed his fists together and they glowed with a bright light, he put his hand to his elbow and funneled his life force into the light.

The gorge filled with blinding brightness, the ghouls shielded their eyes unable to look into the light, Lore turned and pulled Kimba away and up the gorge and as the light faded, Kamdar dropped to a knee having exhausted his life force, the ghouls all shrieked at him in unison and moved toward him, they approached him on all sides as he drew the knife from his belt.

An old man in tan clothes and long braided brown hair swung past on a vine kicking a ghoul as he passed, a younger man wearing the same outfit with long braided blonde hair did the same on the other side, the vines tangled together as they swung from opposite directions and pulled them around in a circle, they kicked at the ghouls as they swung around in tighter and tighter circles, kicking one after another as they swung around Kamdar.

They landed on either side of him, grabbing him under the arms while holding the twisted vines.

                                                   by Lore Casta Pendragon

They ran downhill baiting the ghouls to chase after them, they pulled on the twisted vines and they acted as a spring, swinging them back the other way.

They launched themselves over a large group of ghouls giving them an opening to start sprinting up the hill, Lore and Kimba drop their veils and move to intercept them.

They slammed their fists together and placed a hand on their elbows, they extended the hand closest to each other and stood back-to-back arms extended toward the ghouls.

Waves of heat started to coalesce into their palms and a giant fireball exploded to life in front of them and they aimed up at the edge of the gorge and let it go, the fireball exploded into the cliff face, sending rock down to bury the ghouls with falling stone and earth, the five of them fell to the ground covering their heads hoping not to be crushed, then all was silent.

As the dust settled, they slowly got up and observed the destruction, Den turned away in disgust, "this is what happens when you play with chaos magic", he said then walked up the path back toward the temple.

"Thank you", Kimba called after him, Den just waved a hand and kept walking, then she turned to Ailyn and hugged him tightly, "thank you, you saved my father", Kimba said, Ailyn patted her on the back, "erm, you're welcome", he said awkwardly.

"Thank you, stranger, I didn't think we'd see anybody this deep in the living forest, but I'm sure glad you were here", Kamdar shook Ailyn's hand, Lore stepped up to Ailyn with a bushy brow cocked and looked him in the eye, Ailyn took a step back nervously.

"It can't be, you look just like him", Lore said, "what's your name boy?", Lore questioned, "um it's Ailyn", Ailyn says confused, Lore bonked him on the head, "your full name!", Lore said impatiently.

Ailyn rubbed his head and responded, "Ailyn Allheart", he grumbled, Lore smiled, "I knew it, you're the spitting image of Aram", Ailyn looked surprised by the old man's words, "you know the stories of Aram and Lore Casta Pendragon?", Ailyn asked, "you could say that, I was the one who wrote most of them down", Lore said looking at him in hope that he'd catch on.

Ailyn looked over the old man, his colorful silk robe, pointed hat and long beard, "you look just like Lore Casta Pendragon from the stories", Ailyn said, "he is Lore Casta Pendragon", Kimba said putting a hand on Ailyn's shoulder, Ailyn eyes grew wide.

"What?", "How?", "You died five hundred years ago", Ailyn said confused, "not quite", Kamdar chuckled, "we found him in a sealed cave in the valley of Muse", Kimba explained, "does that mean Aram is alive too?", Ailyn asked, Lore looked to the ground.

"Aram didn't survive the cataclysm", Lore said, "oh", Ailyn said disheartened, "who's your grumpy old friend", Kamdar asked as Den crested the hill, "that's master Den, he's an Aikitai master from the temple, probably the last one living, the vines were his plan", Ailyn said.

by Lore Casta Pendragon

"I see", Lore mumbled, "I have some questions for master Den, may we join you?", Lore asked, but Ailyn was distracted looking at Kimba, he'd never seen a girl so beautiful or so close to his own age, she was talking to Kamdar and smiling, then noticed Ailyn staring and looked away.

"O-of course!", Ailyn said excitedly, "we've never had visitors, so it'll be nice to have people come by", Kamdar noticed Ailyn's lingering eyes and stepped between him and Kimba.

"I'm Kamdar Kindheart, this is my daughter Kimba, thank you again for helping us", he said, "if you follow me, I'll show you the path to the temple, it's best not to linger long in the living forest, else you'll end up trapped or buried or strangled or eaten, or poisoned or put in a pot and boiled by goblin", Ailyn paused, "it's a dangerous place, just, just try to stay close".

Kimba took that as an invitation and grabbed Ailyn by the arm as they made their way up the hill, Kamdar and Lore looked at each other and groaned.

A raven watched as they crested the hill from a high perch then puffed into a black smoke.

"I apologize for master Den, the precepts of Aikitai are very strict on the use of chaos magic, it goes against everything Aikitai stands for, we avoid chaos in order to live in harmony with the world", Ailyn explained while walking them down the trail.

"I can attest to the damage chaos magic can inflict upon the world, his views aren't without merit", Lore responded, "I imagine the one who destroyed the world would have firsthand knowledge of such things, I am interested to hear your story", Ailyn said.

Lore coughed and cleared his throat abjectly, Kimba interrupted him, "that's a common misconception, master Pendragon wasn't the one who broke the world, he was fighting against lord Guldamere, who was the one who destroyed the muse statues and released all that chaos magic into the world at once", she explained.

"Not entirely true", Lore interjected, "the fact is we both had a hand in destroying them, although it wasn't entirely my own fault that the second statue was destroyed, the third was shattered in the ensuing explosion of energy and its power has been lost ever since", Lore explained.

"That's the reason why we came to the forest, to look for it, I need to ask master Den if he has any idea where the missing power might be", Lore said, "and why are you looking for this missing power?", Ailyn asked, "Guldamere is searching for it, he already possesses one part of the power, if he gains more, he will become nigh unstoppable".

They came to a clearing with a large vine bridge over to the temple and began to cross, "this place is beautiful", Kimba exclaimed wide eyed, "the Aikitai have been tending to the temple for hundreds of years, it used to be a place of pilgrimage before the church banned travel here", Ailyn explained.

                                    by Lore Casta Pendragon

"You live here?", Kimba asked, "master Den brought me here a few years ago and started training me in the ways of the Aikitai, before that I was living in the living forest alone and was almost goblin food", Ailyn said.

"So why were you living here alone?", Kimba asked, "that's enough questions Kimba", Kamdar interrupted, Kimba had a kind heart as her namesake suggested, but she was a curious type and as such she lacked a certain social etiquette at times, Kamdar knew that all too well.

They neared the temple, Den stood arms folded at the end of the vine bridge, "those who practice chaos magic are not permitted on the temple grounds", he shouted back at them, "it is imperative that I speak with you master Den, the fate of all Thalarian's is at stake", Lore bowed with his response.

Den appreciated the etiquette and gave a slight bow in return, "nevertheless, you cannot enter, turn back", Den said.

"Let me handle this", Ailyn put a hand on Lore's back, "master, I know magic users invite chaos, but would it be enough to have them vow not to use chaos magic while they are here?", "You should listen to what they have to say", Ailyn pleaded, "the use of chaos magic is against the precepts of Aikitai, chaos invokes destruction and hardship", Den replied.

"I know, but they're pilgrims, didn't you say the temple used to have many of their kind?", Ailyn argued, Den thought about Ailyn's words, "alright Ailyn, but while they are here you will watch them closely, any use of chaos magic and they will be expelled from the temple grounds", Den agreed walking back to the temple.

Ailyn waved over his new friends, "the use of chaos magic is forbidden here, please refrain from using it while on temple grounds", he asked, as they crossed the vine bridge.

"Master Den, please meet Lore Casta Pendragon, and this is Kimba and Kamdar Kindheart", Ailyn introduced them, they all bowed as they passed Den, Ailyn showed them to the caves in the back of the temple to some spare rooms, they lowered their packs and got comfortable, it felt like forever since they actually had time to rest and recover.

Later on, Den was training Ailyn at the water flumes, Ailyn closed his eyes and his life energy flowed, he could feel the water as it fell around him almost in slow motion, Den moved the flumes around and Ailyn moved between the water spouts using the taisabaki footwork he had been practicing.

"Well done, Ailyn", Den said, Ailyn opened his eyes took a deep breath in and bowed, "it seems you've finally got the hang of taisabaki".

Ailyn noticed Kimba, Kamdar and Lore watching nearby and became nervous, Den saw his apprehension and put a hand on his shoulder whispering in his ear, "know your strength Ailyn,

let it be your foundation, fear plays on weakness, conquer your fear and you conquer your weakness", Den said.

Ailyn bowed as Den patted him on the shoulder.

"Impressive", Kimba said smiling as Ailyn approached, "I'm nothing compared to master Den, but I'm getting better", Ailyn responded, "I've been learning from master Pendragon, so I know what it's like to compare yourself to someone who's skills far outshine your own", Kimba said, "you both have big shoes to follow", Kamdar added.

Den walked up to Lore, "master Pendragon", Lore bowed his head slightly while lightning a long pipe, Den got a serious look on his face, "it can't be you, you died hundreds of years ago", Den said then assumed his fighting stance.

"Ailyn, he is risen!", Lore felt a sudden pressure from the man not felt moments earlier, like if he moved the wrong way, he would die.

Lore jumped back and slammed his fists together preparing himself, Kimba ran between them, "hold on, let us explain", she said facing Den, he lowered his stance and waited.

Kimba pulled out Lore's tome, "this book was originally written by Lore Casta Pendragon centuries ago, it still contained his magic, he used it to ask us to free him from his time prison at the valley of Muse, he's been stuck there since the cataclysm over five hundred years ago", Kimba explained.

Lore released his seal letting his hands drop, "it seems I have some explaining to do", Lore said.

The group sat on the stone ground of the temple listening to his story, "so you were trapped in there for five hundred years, but for you it wasn't that long?", Den asked, "indeed, the passage of time was far faster for me then it was for the outside world", Lore added, "it is truly amazing that you managed to stay sane trapped in an empty cave for that long", Den said, "when one has a magic to pass the time, one is rarely bored", Lore said smiling wryly.

"I have a theory", Lore perked up, "that these forests are able to grow due to a magic catalyst", "the forest is a force of nature", Den interjected, "I know it might seem so to you, but before the cataclysm, the land was covered in forests, none of which ever grew this tall or this fast, I believe the missing power may be the catalyst for its growth", Lore explained.

The sound of clanging armor emitted from the other side of the vine bridge, "shh, do you hear that?", Kamdar interrupted.

Den and Ailyn stood up, the noise got louder and the forest darker as the sound drew closer, black miasma started pouring over the cliff ledge on the other side of the vine bridge, vegetation began to rot and fall away, the vine bridge collapsed as Guldamere appeared out of the haze, behind him five hooded men in robes on horseback rode out of the smoke on black horses followed by lines of soldiers armored and ready for battle.

"Found you!", Guldamere said from the other side of the gorge, "I'll be taking my power now Pendragon!", Guldamere said clasping his hands together in prayer, the horses of the hooded riders turned to smoke and were consumed surrounding the riders in black miasma.

They shot off over the gorge at speed toward the temple then crashed on the other side into five plumes of black smoke, Kimba, Ailyn, Lore, Den and Kamdar all stood and faced them.

"Do not dare use chaos magic on these grounds", Den shouted, Guldamere cackled deeply as his troops brought him a seat to sit on to enjoy the show.

The first hooded figure in front of Kimba removed his hood revealing a scarred face and put on his wide brimmed hat, "I am Salin Silus, chief interrogator to my lord Guldamere", he said with a tip of his hat.

Ailyn looked at him, fear and anger welled up inside of him, "you killed my father you bastard!", Ailyn shouted, Ailyn was ready to charge at him then and there but Den held him back.

Silus smiled wickedly, "you remember me, but I don't remember you", Silus said.

An exceptionally large figure in front of Ailyn dropped his hooded cloak revealing a muscular chest in a leather vest and legs the size of tree trunks, "Harram Halfborn?", Ailyn said softly as the memory of his mother and brother being drowned struck fear into him, grief gripped his heart and all he could do was stare at the man in disbelief.

Den stepped in front of Ailyn, eyeing down the large man, "I've come to finish what I started, Allheart", Harram said.

The third hooded figure in front of Lore removed his hood revealing a man in a red velvet suit, "I am Stephan Stratomancer, master strategist to my lord Guldamere", he said taking a short bow, then pulled out an ominous looking box and placed it on the ground at his feet.

The fourth hooded figure in front of Den didn't remove his hood, instead he took out a jagged ceremonial dagger and revealed his bare arm, it was skinny and covered in scar tissue, with a throaty growl he said, "I am Charon, I am head acolyte of the church of the god feared, behold", Den looks at him warily, not sure what to make of him.

The hooded figure in front of Kamdar removed his hooded cloak revealing a creature who looked to be the result of several different people sewn together he had a spear and shield, "I am Petricus Postmortus, field commander to my lord Guldamere's vanguard forces, now that we have been formally introduced, the terms of engagement, you will lay down whatever arms you may be carrying and surrender yourselves to our lord", he commanded.

Lore slammed his fists together, "it doesn't seem like they're giving us much of a choice", Lore extended his arm and a fireball burst into life, he fired it straight ahead at Stratomancer and the

box in front of him jumped up to intercept it, it opened up and sucked in the fireball then sucked both Lore and Stratomancer into it.

"Lore!", Kimba yelled, Guldamere cackled in the distance, "too easy Pendragon", he called from across the gorge.

"Hold on we'll get you out of there", Kimba said, but as she tried to move to help, Silus threw a knife at her, she narrowly avoided it by stopping in her tracks, "you won't be escaping me this time, girl", Silus remarked.

"Ailyn, remember what your aikitai training has taught you", Den said, Ailyn nodded his head and they both took the aikitai fighting stance.

Harram chuckled as he swung a large arm holding his shoulder, "you know your brother looked at me the same way before I made him take a swim", Harram said, "just a shame I didn't get a taste of your mother before I held her under", Harram taunted, Ailyn's heart caught fire and his fear was replaced by fury.

Charon pointed at Den, Den squared up and faced him, then he sunk a ceremonial knife into his forearm and moaned a throaty cry as if he was enjoying it, he extended the arm out towards Den and twisted the knife, black miasma rose around Den and he grabbed his arm crying out in pain, "what in the abyssal hell is this?", Den said as Charon twisted the knife again, Den cried out dropping to his knees, "that knife, it has the power to make other feel his pain", Den said.

Ailyn couldn't hold back his rage any longer and charged at Harram, Harram threw a meaty left hook at him but Ailyn slid right under it taking Harram's dead side, Harram tried to turn to throw another strike, but Ailyn moved with him, perfectly mimicking his training with the water flumes, staying at his back.

Harram kicked behind him, but Ailyn moved, then lifted the leg onto his shoulder and ran with it over extending it, Harram groaned his legs split.

Ailyn jumped up and pulled Harram's shoulder back, the big man fell back and Ailyn moved out to the side as he fell to the ground.

Kamdar slammed his fists together extending one arm toward Petricus, fire flickered to life in his palm, "Yes!", Kamdar shouted as the fireball took shape for the first time, he launched it at Petricus, who raises his shield up to his head, the fireball slammed into the shield but was deflected over the top.

Petricus moved to one side and struck at Kamdar with his spear, Kamdar stumbled backward avoiding the first strike but fell, he clasped his wrist behind his back as Petricus followed up pointing the spear at Kamdar's throat, "weakling", Petricus said as he attempted to stick him.

Kamdar laid flat and brought his hand out from behind his back, another fireball ready to go, he let it go at point blank range, Petricus put his shield on the ground and tried to hide behind

by Lore Casta Pendragon

it, the flame exploded around him, then as soon as the flame subsided, he looked over the top of the shield to find Kamdar fading from sight, he tried to stab at him but hit nothing but air.

Lore found himself in a parlor, a chess board in front of him, Stratomancer on the other side of the board, all seemed perfectly normal, even peaceful, "what's going on here?", "Where am I?", Lore asked.

"Well hello master Pendragon, welcome to the tournament, the game is chess, the rules are simple, take your opponent's king to win the game, should you win, you will be able to leave, should you lose, you'll be stuck in this box forever, shall we begin?", Stratomancer said holding a hand out toward the board with a wry smile.

Lore slammed his fists together but nothing happened, "I'm afraid chaos magic doesn't really exist here, it's more of a realm of my own creation, you see rather than my cohorts outside I abhor violence, I prefer games of wit", Stratomancer explained.

Lore got up and tried to punch Stratomancer, but his arm turned into a floppy wet noodle and just slapped him slightly, "well that was mildly unpleasant", Stratomancer laughed "why did you slap me?", he said looking amused, "I like percussion", Lore grumbled sitting down on the chair in front of the board.

"The only way your leaving is if you beat me in a game, mind you, I've never lost, I'll even be so gracious as to give you the first move", Stratomancer smiled wickedly, Lore sat down with a grumpy expression and pondered his next move.

Kimba looked at Silus knowing that she was outmatched, "get him", she said to someone over to the left, Silus turned to look and Kimba ran, Silus sighed at falling for such on obvious dupe and chased after her, "why do they always run!", Silus said frustrated.

He threw two knives and they rebounded off the stone wall next to her as Kimba ducked into the caves at the back of the temple, he rushed in pursuit of her but slowed down as he got into the narrow corridor of the cave, "shit!", Silus shouted leaping back around the cave entrance as fire ripped past.

"Clever", he said.

Silus ducked back through the door, looking into rooms and down a hallway but couldn't see her, then he remembered her veil trick from the last time they met and he grabbed a lantern from the wall and threw it toward the entrance, it struck true, striking her shoulder, she screamed and fell to the floor dropping the veil.

by Lore Casta Pendragon

"Afraid that's not going to work this time", he said as he got close to her, Kimba slammed her fists together and extends an arm, Silus tried to advance on her but she fired a torrent of flames toward him and forced him back deeper into the caves.

Den got to his feet and ran at Charon, the hooded creature smiled devilishly as he twisted the knife in his arm, Den took the pain as he opened the wound further, as Den got close however Charon pulled the knife from his arm and sunk it into his own leg, Den fell down right near Charon in agony.

Charon removed the dagger and tried to finish Den with it, but Den caught Charon's arm at the elbow and put him into an armbar, Charon flicked the blade into his own wrist and Den flinched with the pain losing his grip.

Charon chuckled quietly blood running down his arms, Den felt exhaustion taking over as the blood drained from the both of them.

Charon extended his arm straight and sliced a big cut down his arm slowly, Den screamed in agony not knowing what to do, he thought about his Aikitai training, it never prepared him for an inescapable situation like this, if he couldn't hurt or detain his foe, then there was only one thing left he could do.

Den sprinted toward the skinny gaunt figure of Charon, Charon felt a pressure on him like he's in the path of a hurricane as Den ran in and picked him up onto his shoulder, Charon stabbed Den in the back again and again with the long ceremonial knife as Den stumbled to the edge of the gorge, with his last step he threw Charon off the edge.

Charon cackled and look Den in the eye as he fell, he smiled as he plunged the knife into his own heart, Den's eyes glazed over and his face slumped, "oh no", Den clutched at his chest then fell to his knees by the cliff face.

Harram got to his feet furious, he ran at Ailyn, Ailyn remembered his father's fight with Harram in the tavern and he curled himself into a ball, ducking down beneath Harram's feet, the big man tripped over Ailyn and fell forwards toward a water fall at the edge of the temple teetering on the edge.

Ailyn leaped to his feet and sprinted at Harram delivering a jumping side kick to his back, Harram growled as he fell form the ledge and splashed into the shallow water below landing on river stones with a loud crack.

Harram was hurt, he curled into a ball and coughed up blood grabbing at his side, Ailyn looked over to see Den throw Charon off the cliff face, wounds covered his back, he saw Den clutch at his chest then fall to the ground, "Den!", Ailyn shouted as he rushed to help him.

by Lore Casta Pendragon

Petricus had no idea where Kamdar went, he searched around stabbing at the air, "come fight me, coward!", Petricus screamed, suddenly out of nowhere a fireball struck him in the back, Petricus exploded into pieces and there stood Kamdar, palm smoking, "rot in hell corpse", Kamdar said turning from the smoldering pieces of Petricus.

Kamdar walked away unwary as a black goo formed out of the pieces that used to be Petricus and grab at one another slowly pulling themselves back together.

"How!", Stratomancer cried looking at the chess board, "how could I be defeated?", He whined.

"Well you challenged a five hundred year old wizard to a battle of wits", Lore taunted as he moved his final piece, "no!", Stratomancer cried as Lore got sucked back out of the box, he reappeared next to the box and looked down at it, "you were a worthy adversary, in all my years I've never seen someone use a strategy quite like that", he said to the box as he picked it up, he placed a hand on his elbow and summoned a gout of fire, the box caught and burned to ashes, "farewell Stratomancer", Lore said looking directly at Guldamere who sat on the other side of the gorge watching intently.

Silus was stuck in the caves, Kimba was guarding the entrance filling the corridor with fire whenever he showed his face, he made his way upwards and found a small room with a window, he kicked it out then dropped down to see Kimba hiding behind the wall occasionally looking in to make sure Silus remained inside.

Kimba knew she couldn't keep the fire up forever and was already feeling depleted, as she took another peek inside, but a knife appeared at her throat from behind, "get up slowly and put those nasty hands behind your back", Silus commanded.

Kimba did as he said, Silus tied her hands with a torniquet and told her to turn around, "pretty little thing you are, shame you wound up with this lot", Silus said, "I think you'll find you're the one on the wrong side", Kimba said looking over his shoulder, "fool me once, girl", Silus begun to say until he heard Kamdar approaching behind, no sooner had he heard, a massive gust of wind hit him from the side and sent him bouncing across the stone and rolling over a ledge.

Kamdar dropped his veil and Kimba jumped into his arms, "thanks dad, thank you, thank you", she said, "it's alright your safe now, quickly turn around and we'll get those restraints off you", Kamdar said, he removed the torniquet and as Kimba turned to face him, her expression turned into one of shock and panic, blood spilled from Kamdar's mouth.

          by Lore Casta Pendragon

Petricus had reformed himself and stuck his spear through Kamdar's stomach, Kimba screamed as Kamdar's blood splattered across her face, "did you really think it would be that easy to destroy the field commander of the vanguard!", Petricus grunted.

Kamdar fell to his knees, blood running down from his mouth, Petricus pulled the spear from Kamdar's body and let him fall, Kimba shook uncontrollably as she tried to form a seal with her fists.

Shock paralyzed her and she couldn't make her hands work properly, Petricus advanced forward, shield and spear in hand, Kimba tried to backstep but tripped and fell down as Petricus raised his spear to strike, in an instant Petricus was blown into a thousand pieces for a second time and Kimba was covered in bits of Petricus.

Kimba wiped the blood and tears from her eyes with shaking hands as Lore came into view, he helped her to her feet and took her on his shoulder, "I'm sorry my girl, there's nothing we can do", Lore said.

Kimba let out a wail of grief and tears and fought against him.

Lore knew they were fighting a losing battle and remembered Den saying something earlier about the caves having a back entrance, "I'm sorry my dear, but I cannot let this power fall into Guldamere's hands, we'll sneak out the back while they're distracted", he said turning into the caves.

Ailyn knelt down next to Den, sadness covered his face, "I'm sorry master, this was all my fault, I should never have brought them here", Ailyn said, "it's alright, Ailyn", Den coughed painfully.

"Sometimes we lose the way, the most important thing is that we take the correct path, the path of the Aikitai, promise me you won't let our way end here, that you'll teach the path to others and show them how to live in harmony as we did", Den asked.

"I will master", Ailyn replied tearfully, "then we'll train again someday, in the lands, beyond", Den smiled as his head lolled in Ailyn's arms.

Ailyn felt his heart break again just as it did when his family passed years ago, tears blurred his eyes.

No sooner had he opened them he was blindsided by Harram's gigantic boot, Den fell from the cliff and Ailyn narrowly held on by grabbing the ledge with one hand.

Harram was bleeding from a wound on his head and was holding his side where his ribs were visibly broken, Ailyn was dazed from the attack, but managed to pull himself up, no sooner had he found his feet Harram grabbed him by the face and lifted him with one arm just as he did when they had first met in the living forest.

by Lore Casta Pendragon

"This time your mummy isn't around to catch you", Harram said as he threw Ailyn from the cliff face, Ailyn remembered the falling technique Den had showed him as the ground rushed to meet him, he landed flat on his side with his arm extended out protecting his head on the stoney path below, Ailyn hit the ground hard knocking the wind from him but managed not to break anything.

He groaned and rolled to the side, slowly finding his feet, Harram jumped down using one meaty hand to tear down the face of the cliff landing firmly on his hugely muscular legs.

Ailyn scrambled to his feet, but Harram punched Ailyn so hard that he flew backward through the air and through a wall of vines under an overhang, he landed with a splash into a pool of water, blood trickled from cuts on his face.

Ailyn moaned and raised an arm to find his side had gone purple with bruising, it was hard to breathe, he looked into the water, his face was swelling up from where Harram had just hit him.

Harram ripped the vines out of his way and stepped into the overhang, "well ain't this perfect", he said with a smile, "you can go the same way as the rest of your family".

Harram walked over to him, Ailyn tried to swim away but Harram grabbed his foot and pulled him back.

Harram lifted Ailyn by the hair and dragged out him into the middle of the pool, he pushed Ailyn's head under the water and held him there, Ailyn struggled and tried to move but Harram was strong, too strong, his iron grip felt like a bear trap had grabbed his skull.

Ailyn felt himself losing consciousness, then he stopped struggling, "I'm sorry, mother, brother, father, I couldn't avenge you", he thought as visions of his family welcoming him home crossed his mind".

Ailyn felt a bright white light in front of his eyes.

"Ailyn", Asta's voice called again, "mother", he answered, "still think I'm your mother huh?", The wisp responded, "an unspeakable evil is corrupting the world, I can't stop them, but if you make a bargain with me, I can give you power", the wisp said, "I'll do whatever it takes and I'll destroy Guldamere if it's the last thing I do!", Ailyn said, "good, then here's the bargain, find the five shards of power and use them to seal the abyss once again", the wisp said, "as you wish", Ailyn said.

The pool glowed with a white light when Harram finally let go of Ailyn's lifeless body, he panicked and stumbled out of the pool.

Ailyn began to rise, the white light drew into him and increased in brightness, Harram shielded his eyes until the light faded.

  by Lore Casta Pendragon

Ailyn stood before him illuminated, Harram couldn't believe his eyes, he grunted and moved to grab Ailyn again, but Ailyn placed a hand on his chest and used Aethor's close range punching technique, he hit Harram so hard he bounced off the stone wall cracking the stone and landed on the floor face down, the overhang shook from the blow and the crack began to run up the wall.

Ailyn walked out from behind the vines, he drew back and punched the stone cliff face with such force that a larger crack appeared along it, the overhang broke off.

Harram got up and ran to the pool as the overhang began to come down, the stone above him broke loose from the cliff face coming down over him.

Harram put his hands up to stop it, but even his might couldn't hold the tremendous weight of stone, Harram cried out a throaty growl as the overhang slowly pushed him down into the pool.

Ailyn listened vengefully as he heard Harram choke in his watery grave, the light faded from him and he slumped exhausted and nursing his wounds.

"Besting Harram Halfborn is no easy feat, you certainly are impressive for one so young", Silus said behind him, Ailyn tried to turn but Silus struck him hard on the back of the head with the hilt of his blade, then everything went black.

by Lore Casta Pendragon

Chapter Eight

Iron halls

Silus threw Ailyn's unconscious body at Guldamere's feet and took a knee, "Pendragon and the Kindheart girl have escaped, Stratomancer is missing, presumably stuck in his own pocket dimension, Charon is at the bottom of the gorge deceased, Harram Halfborn was buried under the rubble below deceased, Petricus Postmortus is scattered all over the temple it will take some time for him to regenerate, but he can use parts from the clerk and the keeper of the temple to regenerate", Silus reported.

"Harram Halfborn is not lost, my forces will recover him, collect the bodies for Petricus and look for Charon's body, is this the Allheart boy?", Guldamere asked, "it is, Harram beat him mercilessly, but it's him, somehow he managed to defeat Harram in single combat", Silus said impressed.

"No easy task for a boy less than half his size", Guldamere croaked stroking his skeletal chin, "after you're done prying information from him, send him to the pit", Guldamere instructed.

"As you command my lord", Silus picked up Ailyn and tied him to the rear of a cart, Guldamere put his hand together in prayer and black fog began to make a bridge over the gorge, his forces began to make their way over to search the temple and pursue their targets, when Guldamere was done, he burned the temple leaving nothing but rubble behind.

Lore and Kimba made their way through a dark tunnel with many crossroads, many large tree roots ran through the cave reinforcing the walls.

"How long do these cave systems go for?", Kimba asked, "from what I can tell they probably stretch as far as the living forest itself; they look to have been made by the rotted root systems of the giant trees above, probably eaten away by termites over centuries", Lore said.

Kimba was quietly sobbing and sorrowful while they made their way through the cave, "I'm sorry I didn't make it in time to save Kamdar, believe me if there was something I could do to save him, I would have", Kimba wiped her eyes, "first my mother and now my father, I still can't believe he's gone, what do you think happened to Ailyn?", Kimba asked.

"I'm afraid he may have been captured or killed, going back for him now would be suicide", Lore said painfully, "I didn't expect a full assault, we cannot face Guldamere's forces directly at this time, not until we've found suitable support of our own, but where we could find such a force is beyond me", Lore said.

"There are kingdoms in Thalaria not under church control, if we could convince them to join our cause, we may be able to fight against Guldamere's forces", Kimba said, "there's Paladins

                              by Lore Casta Pendragon

Reach to the northeast, oh, or the elven forest to the east, they are both located in green zones", she said.

"Do any more people live in forests like these?", Lore asked, "the other green zones aren't like the living forest, I've never been to any city outside of Necropyre, but my father used to tell me stories and show pictures from the books he borrowed from the church, apparently Paladins Reach is a large castle surrounded by rolling hills of grassland and the ronin city is surrounded by a bamboo forest that is haunted by devils", Kimba explained.

"Well, since we have to visit the green zones anyway, it might be prudent for us to visit these cities as well", Lore said thoughtfully, "come along now, we have to find a way out of these caves first".

Lore and Kimba walked onward down the dark tunnels, but as the long hours past, they became increasingly lost, "summoning light is much like summoning fire, just in a purer form, light exists in everything, pull it like you pull on heat when making fire, infuse it with your own life energy and…", Lore explained as he illuminated his hand, Kimba nodded following his instruction, the effort was exhausting, though not as much as fire.

"We've been walking for half a day now, I'm exhausted, surely we can stop for a rest?", Kimba complained, Lore looked at her with pity, "I am sorry my dear, I forgot you don't hold a reserve of power like I do, I'm getting rather forgetful in my old age, let's take a break", Lore said, sitting down on the cave floor.

After a while they put some old rotted tree roots down to start a fire, Kimba's stomach rumbled.

"I haven't had a thing to eat all day", Kimba said grumpily, Lore reached into the sleeve of his silk robe and pulled out a healthy-looking apple, a loaf of bread and a canteen of water, handing them to Kimba, "where on earth were you hiding those?", She asked with a stunned expression.

"It's an enchantment on my robe that increases the size of the space inside a container, good for keeping things close at hand, but unfortunately it still keeps the weight of said items, so storage on your person is still limited to how much you want to carry", Lore explained.

"So that's how you didn't starve to death in that cave", Kimba said, "could you show me how to do it?", Kimba asked, "erm well I would but… I forgot how to do it", Lore grumbled, Kimba looked at Lore unimpressed.

"Well let's stick you in a cave for five hundred years and see how much you can remember!", Lore said to her grumpily, Kimba sighed, "forget about it", "all of my magic techniques were written in my books, you found one of them so if you could find the others, you could learn quite a bit more about chaos magic", Lore said.

                                    by Lore Casta Pendragon

"There were plenty of your books in the reliquary in the cathedral of the god feared where my father used to work, along with books written by Guldamere himself, but showing our faces there now would be suicide", Kimba said.

Lore raised a bushy eyebrow, "interesting, I'm surprised Guldamere kept such relics of the past, I bet he's kicking himself now considering one of them led to my release", Lore chuckled.

"I have a friend I left in Necropyre, his name is Felix Flight, I wonder what happened to him", Kimba said worryingly, "I'm sure you'll see your friend again before all of this is over", Lore consoled her.

"What is stopping Guldamere from creating another cataclysm?", Kimba asked, "the power", Lore responded, "while he seems all powerful, he's not, he only holds one third of the power, he would need all three parts if he wanted to create another cataclysm the likes of the one five hundred years ago", Lore said, Kimba shuddered at the thought of Guldamere with that much power, "we can't let that happen", Lore and Kimba said at the same time, they smiled, "at least we're on the same page", Lore said getting comfortable.

Later on, Kimba was sleeping next to the fire, Lore was smoking a pipe and nodding off himself when the light of the fire started to grow dim, Lore threw another rotted root onto it and it caught alight but didn't produce any additional light.

Lore's mouth opened agape and his pipe fell from his mouth, he reached over and shook Kimba awake, "on your feet my dear, something is coming", he whispered quietly.

Extending a hand to the fire, it died out, then swishing his finger up, the smoke formed into one column like a small tornado then faded out completely.

Kimba found her feet and the two moved to hide behind a large tree root staying perfectly quiet in the darkness, the darkness grew thick and dense around them like molasses.

"I know this scent", a shrill scratchy high-pitched voice rang in the darkness, Lore's eyes narrowed as he tried to remember where he heard that voice before, "the scent of winds from long past", the shrill voice echoed off the cave walls.

"The stink of old magic", it said, "what is it?", Kimba whispered, "I, I can't remember", Lore whispered back, "found you", the voice said.

Lore and Kimba felt like they were grabbed by the darkness itself, by many different clawed hands, Lore remembered the cave at mount Muse, he remembered Aram being pulled into the darkness, he remembered this creature.

Lore slammed his fists together and light began to build from his hands, the claws came into view they were gripping him from the dark, ripping at him to keep hold, fighting against the light, Kimba was pulled further into the dark lifting her high as she slammed her fists together, light building from her hands, she screamed as the claws dug into her skin, around her face and body.

 by Lore Casta Pendragon

Lore screamed out with the effort as the light from his hands burst outward illuminating the cave in iridescent brilliance, shredding the clawed hands, causing cuts on their flesh as they grasped desperately to them.

Kimba hit the floor, the darkness pressed in against them and Lore struggled to hold it back, his life energy visibly burning around him in the form of light.

"To your feet Kimba, we need to hold it back!", Lore shouted desperately, whatever this thing was, it was strong, too strong.

Kimba ran to his side, she slammed her fists together joining him as the darkness pushed in around them, clawed hands grabbed at the light, trying to pull their way toward their prey, "store the light in your body and when I say, let it rip", Lore said as they both begin to glow with a bright white light.

The creature began to press in on them, "Now!", Lore instructed and the light burst from them, a shrill screech filled the cave as the darkness shot backward, down the tunnel.

"Now's our chance, run!", Lore said and they held the light in their hands running the opposite direction to which the monster fled.

The darkness followed behind trying to push in toward them, they reached a large iron door covered in runes at the end of the cavern and tried to push it open but it wouldn't budge.

Lore turned and extended his hands toward the encroaching darkness, hands of shadow reaching out from it at blistering speed, it was one with the dark itself.

His light burned away at him, Kimba's light dropped and she placed a hand at her elbow summoning a fireball, she let it rip at the door with a loud clang, but the door did not budge, "it won't open!", She yelled as Lore struggled to keep the darkness at bay, "I can't keep this up much longer!", Lore growled, Kimba turned to help him reinforcing the light but they were both exhausted and nearing their limits the darkness pushed in, clawed hands reaching toward them inch by inch growing closer, until it was almost close enough to grab them.

Suddenly from behind them two slots in the Iron door opened and two dwarves threw out two bombs, they flashed and glowed intensely with a white light pushing the darkness back, a stone wall opened up further back down the cavern and five dwarves in full iron armor threw more bombs behind.

"C'mon lads, we've got it trapped, it's time for revenge!", One of the dwarves said.

The darkness pushed back into itself, shrieking at the light, the dwarves press forward throwing more bombs, as each one exploded in light it pressed the darkness back further toward the door, Lore and Kimba press forward from the other side assisted by the two dwarves throwing bombs from the door until there is just a ball of clawed hands and swirling inky black darkness between them and the dwarves.

            by Lore Casta Pendragon

The ball of darkness shrieked then sprouted eyes in all directions, they squinted against the light, the dwarves threw more bombs, the wicks burning down, the creature pressed against a wall and slowly disappeared into a crack in the stone.

"Blast!", A dwarf grumbled and began shouting colorful language at the crack in the wall, Kimba dropped to the cave floor unconscious as Lore fell to a knee, his vision blurred as the dwarves approached, with a smile he fell to his side and passed out.

Ailyn woke to a bucket of water thrown in his face, he was tied almost naked to a chair in a small and mostly empty room that smelled of blood, a table sat to one side covered in instruments of torture.

Ailyn struggled against his restraints, a figure cloaked in the shadows dropped a bucket to the floor, his eyes gained focus and he noticed his fingers were separated by finger holsters built into the chair.

"Where am I?" Ailyn asked, his face still puffy and swollen from his fight against Harram, he felt a slap across his face, but the swelling had already made it mostly numb, "don't ask questions, just answer me and you might leave here alive", the figure lifted his chin.

Silan Silus stood before Ailyn, knife in hand, "you!", Ailyn scowled at Silus, which was returned with another hard slap, Silus grinned wide, "your strong, but everyone has a breaking point, Ailyn", Silus said, "you killed my father you bastard!", Ailyn spat at him, Silus just smirked then squished Ailyn's cheeks hard with one hand, "that's nothing compared to what I'm going to do to you Ailyn, you're going to tell me everything you know about your little temple home, the living forest, your family, Pendragon, hell you're going to tell me what you had for breakfast five days ago, if I want to know it and if you don't I'm going to make you suffer", Silus said throwing Ailyn's head back.

It hit the back of the wooden chair, Ailyn stared at him with contempt, "first things first brat, where is Pendragon heading?", Silus said pulling up a stool in front of Ailyn, playing with his knife and waiting for an answer.

"I don't know and even if I did, I wouldn't tell you", Ailyn said defiantly, "very well boy, but this is not going to be fun for you", Silus placed his knife under Ailyn's little fingernail and began to push it underneath.

Ailyn clenched his teeth trying not to scream so Silus pushed further, the nail bled and ripped, then he twisted the knife and the nail ripped up entirely, Ailyn let out a little whimper and Silus smiled at him.

"Oh, what a brave boy you are, let's see how many of these little piggies I can remove before you start to howl", Silus taunted, moving to the ring finger.

by Lore Casta Pendragon

Ailyn tensed up as the knife slipped under, Silus slowly pushed the knife in making sure Ailyn felt every nerve as the nail was removed from his finger.

Ailyn tried to be strong but as Silus continued to slice off his fingernails one after another.

He tried hard not to but he started to cry, tears rolled down his face, "such a big man you are, blubbering like a baby", Silus taunted as he started on Ailyn's other hand.

"Tell me why Pendragon was at the temple?", Silus said, Ailyn bit his lip, tears streamed down his face as Silus placed his knife under his fingernail.

"I don't know, I only just met him, please stop!", Ailyn pleaded, "begging already Ailyn?", Silus said, even Harram Halfblood had more constitution than that, Silus said playing on Ailyn's hatred.

"You should at least make it interesting for me Ailyn, I thought you were a fighter", Silus said as he removed another fingernail, Ailyn grunted with the pain as Silus continued to remove the last of Ailyn's fingernails.

"It seems I'm out of nails, time for the toes", Silus said in a mocking tone, he pulled a lever on the chair and it pushed Ailyn's feet up on a rest, his feet were braced into it.

"I'm sorry, please, don't!", Ailyn begged but Silus ignored his pleading and removed the nail from his big toe, Ailyn screamed in pain and Silus asked him again, "what was Pendragon looking for?", "He said the forest might be enchanted by some sort of power, that's all he said about it", Ailyn blubbered. Silus's grin got larger and he got more excited.
"Now we are getting somewhere Ailyn, you have no idea how happy you have made me", "where did he say it was located, was it at the temple?", Silus asked.

"I don't know, I never understood what he meant, he said the power might be a catalyst for the forests growth", Ailyn said.

Silus got up, "thanks Ailyn, but I can't stand leaving a job undone", Silus continued to remove Ailyn's toenails, "you bastard!", "Stop!", Ailyn screamed, "just a reminder of what happens when you disobey me boy", Silus said, after removing all Ailyn's toenails, Silus left the room.

Ailyn's head drooped tears rolling down his face, he thought of his father, mother and brother, "am I going to die here?", He thought to himself as he looked over to see a rat eating someone's rotted finger in the corner of the room.

An hour later Silus returned, he removed the back of the chair and took a lash from a hook on the wall.

"I was going to let you go since you so graciously gave me the information I sort, but my lord Guldamere wasn't satisfied with your answers, so now", Silus whipped Ailyn in the back with a loud crack, the skin flaying from the force of the blow, Ailyn screamed in agony.

        by Lore Casta Pendragon

"Tell me what the petroglyphs at the temple refer to?", Silus asked, Ailyn whimpered then responded.

"They're pictures of aikitai, the martial form the monks of the temple use", Ailyn stammered sobbing.

"But there are others too aren't there?", Silus said, "what are they depicting?", Ailyn coughed out blood and snot from his face, whatever dignity he had, Silus had taken it away.

"They show the monks living in harmony with the forest", Ailyn responded, "our soldiers found more, below the temple near where you killed Harram", Silus said angrily, he whipped Ailyn again.

"I never liked Harram Halfborn, the man was a pig, but he was one of ours", Silus said, Ailyn gurgled out a scream, his back dripped blood, "I saw one, covered in vines below the temple, they seem to worship some goddess maybe", Ailyn said.

"Did you help Pendragon escape his prison!", Silus asked, "no", Ailyn said which was immediately followed up by a crack of the whip, Ailyn screamed out in pain.

"No, no, I had nothing to do with it!", He cried, Silus cracked him again and his head fell unconscious from the pain, Silus placed the whip back on the wall and untied Ailyn from the chair, he threw a rope above a beam then tied Ailyn standing upright, blood dripping to the floor, "can't have you being eaten alive by the rats before I'm done, can we?", Silus said as he exited the room.

Lore awoke on a very comfortable stone bed, it was made of small round river pebbles, it was warm and contoured to the shape of his body, he'd never known such comfort.

Looking over he saw Kimba asleep on a similar bed on the other side of the room, the room had no door but it was surprisingly warm and quiet.

A dwarfess walked in, carrying a mug of liquid, she placed it on a table next to Lore and he groggily asked, "where are we?", The dwarfess smiled and whispered, "best to keep your voice down, the youngen is still resting, drink up, it's good for what ails ye, lord Ironhammer will be along once your both fully rested", she smiled again and left the room.

Lore felt a peace in this place, the air was still and silent, the sound of a distant clanging could be heard far away, he picked up the mug and gave it a sniff, "it's alcohol?", He thought then gave it a try.

"It's good", he smiled, then gulped it down wiping froth from his beard, he laid back down on the river pebble bed and put his hands behind his head, "I never knew the dwarves lived such luxurious lives", he thought as he closed his eyes.

101

Hours later, the king of the Iron halls was growing impatient, "they are awake", queen Navi said to her husband, Farin Ironhammer, he was stout as dwarves are, with a long-braided beard adored with gold and brass jewels, he wore an armored helm with a crown adorned on it and silver mithril armor, the best in the land.

"Well, it's about time, lazy over worlders", he grumbles as he picked up a bright silver hammer covered in dwarven runes and stepped down from his throne, he made his way down a hall carved intricately from the stone itself, other dwarves bowed their heads as he passed.

Fire lamps burned white with natural gas illuminating the halls and keeping the place warm, several of his guards began to walk with him adorned in fabulous armors, he made his way to the infirmary to see Lore and Kimba sitting on the edge of their beds conversing.

"They don't seem to be hostile", Kimba said as Farin entered the room, "I can assure you lass, we are not", Farin said.

Kimba and Lore noticed the crown adorned on Farin's helmet and stood from their beds bowing respectfully, "I'm Lord Farin Ironhammer, welcome to the Iron halls, tis a good thing you found us here, you just about got eaten by the creeping dark", Farin said.

"Thank you for your hospitality, Lord Ironhammer, I'm Kimba Kindheart", Kimba said bowing low.

"No need for such formality lass, call me Farin, there's no better place in the world than the Iron halls, we very rarely accept over worlders here, consider yourselves fortunate", Farin said, the dwarven guards around him laughed and nodded at his comment.

"Would you mind telling me how you came to be here?", Farin asked, "we got lost in the caves beneath the living forest, then we were chased here by the creeping dark", Kimba responded, "I see, you must have come across one of our tunnels that connects to the living forest underground, your pretty far from their now, you've wondered quite a way underground", Farin explained.

"We were happy that you helped lure that monster to us though, we almost had it that time, so who's your stoic friend in the fancy robe lass?", Farin said looking over at Lore.

"This is Lore Casta Pendragon", she said, the dwarves all laughed heartily, "yeah and I'm Thor Thunderfist", Farin laughed, "who are ye really?", Farin said sternly to Lore.

With a sigh, Lore responded, "I am Lore Casta Pendragon, this young lady found me in the valley of Muse and set me free from Guldamere's prison, no word of a lie", a silence gripped the room, Farin cocked his eyebrow toward Lore, "that's one hell of a tall tale, lucky for you we'll have plenty of time to find out if it's true when your full of ale at the feast", Farin said and his guard cheered, "feast?", Kimba and Lore both said together confused.

by Lore Casta Pendragon

They were escorted to a dining hall with a long wooden table full of every kind of food one could imagine.

Giant mugs of dwarven ale lined the table, Farin seated himself at the far end and introduced them.

"This is Lore Casta Pendragon and Kimba Kindheart, wizards from the overworld, they helped in the near capture of the creeping dark this evening", Farin proclaimed.

There were whispers mixed with cheers as they took their seat near Farin and Navi, "this here is queen Navi Ironhammer, the loveliest of dwarfess", Farin said as he rubbed noses with Navi, "tis a pleasure to meet ye", Navi said, she was beautiful with very long thick red braided hair that reached her ankles.

"So, tell us Pendragon, we are all dying to know why you decided to break the world", Farin asked and the room fell silent except the sound of mugs hitting the table.

All eyes were fixed on Lore, Lore knew how to turn the crowd, so he stood with a flash of his colorful silk robe and began the tale of how he and Aram found out about Guldamere's plot and how they fought their way up Mount Muse to battle Guldamere.

At the end of the tale the dwarves were mesmerized, "that's when I burst free from my prison in an explosion of light, next minute I met lady Kindheart here and that's how I escaped Guldamere's time prison", Lore finished and the dwarves cheered and beat their mugs on the table.

Farin looked at him skeptically and raised a hand, the cheering dulled down.

"Quite the incredible tale master Pendragon, I especially like how you changed it up to make Guldamere out to be the big bad, he's long since found the dwarves to be a thorn in his side, we don't accept his claim over the Iron Halls and we learned to burn our dead long ago, so Guldamere has found his forces lacking down here", Farin said.

"It's no tale lord Farin, I can attest that every word is true", Kimba interjected, "we also hold your apprehension towards Guldamere's claim over Thalaria", she said, "in fact, we are looking for men who are sympathetic toward our fight against Guldamere to join us in fighting his forces", Lore added.

Farin stroked his long thick beard and considered Lore's offer, "I'm afraid the dwarves aren't really fond of fighting their own", Farin said, "what do you mean?", Kimba asked, "lord Guldamere controls the risen, meaning any of our fallen brothers who fight with us, end up fighting against us, he also sent that monster down here to keep us trapped and stop us from interfering, which has made it difficult to trade with overworlders above", Farin explained.

"We are safe down here because we very rarely lose dwarves in battle underground, although the creeping dark has consumed many of our brothers who strayed too far from home", Farin said, many of the dwarves raised a cup to the memory of their slain kin.

                         by Lore Casta Pendragon

"Meaning his men and our friends that were defeated in the living forest are probably all risen by now?", Lore asked.

"Maybe not", Farin said, "Guldamere is a powerful necromancer, but even he has his limits", "that means Ailyn, Den and my father could also come to fight against us?", Kimba asked, "sadly that might be a possibility", Lore responded, Navi leaned over and whispered into Farin's ear, he nodded his head with a grin and looked to Lore and Kimba.

"Tell you what Pendragon, if you can use ye magic to rid us of the nightmare that haunts these harrowed halls, you'll have the full support of the dwarves of the Iron Hall, what do ya say to that?".

Lore thought for a moment then smiled, "you've got yourself a deal, king of dwarves", Lore heartily agreed and the dwarves cheered, bashed their mugs on the table and took a long drink, sloshing ale down their long beards, Kimba looked at Lore concerned.

Later they were shown to their rooms, they were beautifully adorned with artwork chiseled into the stonework, greenery overlooked a natural hot water spring, surrounded by limestone pillars.

"I don't think I ever want to leave this place Kimba", Lore chuckled as he looked out the window of their room.

"How do you plan on killing that thing, it almost killed us the first time", Kimba said frustrated, "that's the second time that thing has attacked me, it has an obvious weakness to light, although it's marginally stronger now than it was five hundred years ago", Lore explained.

"You fought that thing five hundred years ago?", Kimba asked, "Aram and I fought it off before we battled Guldamere on Mount Muse, I stayed behind to recover and asked Aram to scout ahead, had we attacked together we may have been able to defeat Guldamere before he caused the cataclysm, you could say that the creeping dark was an imperative part of Guldamere's plan, killing it will weaken his forces significantly and give us a better chance of defeating him", Lore explained.

"We also need to find the missing power before he does, so time is really against us", Kimba reminded him, "indeed, we are in a race against time and we are already far behind our enemy, we'll rest our wounds then be on our way, I have a plan, but it requires some dwarven assistance, let us hope they're feeling generous".

Lore and Kimba made their way to the throne room where Farin was arguing over architectural blueprints with another dwarf.

"Ahh, Pendragon, why don't you come and enlighten my fool of an associate", Farin said angrily.

                                by Lore Casta Pendragon

"I was only trying to come up with a solution to the problem of waste gasses from the underground, they aren't going to last forever as fuel you know and venting them to the surface has been difficult with that thing lurking about", the dwarf said in a nasally high-pitched voice.

Lore looked at the dwarf, he was wearing some sort of mechanical exoskeleton with magnifying glasses attached to his helmet, they moved into place as he turned to look at Lore, making his eyes look three times the size.

"I don't believe we've met, I'm Lore Casta Pendragon", Lore introduced himself, "yes, yes, I'm well aware, your somewhat of a celebrity here of late", he responded, "I'm Mech Mholnir, I'm the royal engineer of the Iron Halls", Mech said, "and a royal pain in the ass", Farin muttered under his breathe.

Mech's magnifying glasses lined up in rows and he gave Farin a magnified stink eye, "an interested helmet you have", Lore said, Mech turned to look at Lore big eyes protruding from the lenses, "would you mind if I took a look", Lore asked.

"It's more than just a helmet, I'm blind as a mole without it", Mech responded, "oh is that so", Farin said with a grin as he snatched the helmet from his head and threw it to Lore, "hay, Farin, that's so undignified, give it back, I can't see a thing", Mech whined as he fumbled around, Lore lined up the lenses and put them on a nearby table, he slammed his fists together then extended a finger.

It lit up in a bright white light, he placed his finger behind the lenses and they focused the light into a super bright beam, "it seems you're just the person I was looking for Mr. Mholnir", Lore said, he picked the helmet up and placed it back on Mech's head, "thanks", he said as he straightened it up.

"I have a plan to defeat the creeping dark, but I'm going to need your expertise", Lore asked, "Mech will be happy to assist you", Farin interrupted trying to get rid of him, Mech grumbles at him then turned to Lore, "how can I assist?", Mech asked, "the lenses on your helmet, how big can you make them?", Lore said, Mech smiled wryly, "as big as you need them".

Several days later Farin came to Lore and Kimba's rooms, "it's done", he said, Lore smiled at him and the three of them went to Mech's workshop.

In the middle was a large apparatus covered in a white sheet, "welcome, welcome", Mech said, "let me introduce you to my latest invention, the rotating elevated telescopic and reduction device", he lifted the sheet revealing a large multi layered glass tube connected to a rotating base.

                                           by Lore Casta Pendragon

Lore, Farin and Kimba tried to hold back their laughter and Mech looked at them confused, "what?", "Is it the color?", "Because I thought the brass rings made it look nice while also being structurally sound", he tried to explain.

They burst into laughter then Farin perked up, "you called it retard, you fool", "oh, oh no, that won't do at all", Mech said, he looked around then added, "well we can just call it the telescope then, please stand here master Pendragon", he showed Lore to a platform at the back of the telescope.

"From here you can use your magic and the lenses will amplify the beam, the lenses can telescope forward and backward using these levers here and rotate by turning this crank left or right", Mech explained.

"I'll handle the controls while you focus on the light", Kimba said.

"It's perfect, you have really outdone yourself Mech", Lore said and Farin patted him on the back, "the only thing now is to set the trap, we need to lure the creeping dark to a space with only a single entrance, no windows or escape routes of any kind", Lore said.

"Leave that to me", Farin said, "we'll use one of the material storage rooms closer to the mines and rig the door to close, only problem is, once we're inside, we'll be trapped in with it", Mech added, the group went silent.

The thought of being trapped in a room with the creeping dark terrified them all, a chill ran down their spines as the realization of the plan came to light, Farin broke the silence first, "so be it", he said loudly.

"I won't allow that foul thing to eat any more of my kin, come what may", "so it's all or nothing", Kimba added.

"It seems to have a fondness for my scent, so I'll be the bait, make sure I have a clear path to the storage room, we'll situate some dwarves with flash bombs along the trail in case it discovers what we're up to and tries to flee", Lore said.

"There's a break area in the mines that we closed off a few years ago, seems to be a favored hunting ground for the creeping dark", Farin said, "that's where we'll set the trap", Mech added.

As night fell or the approximation of night, it was hard to tell underground but for the dwarven clocks which Lore had no idea how to read.

He wandered out with only a torch, Kimba and Farin moved to their positions with the dwarven bombardiers, while Mech readied the telescope in the storage room, Lore eventually made it down a wide bending tunnel and past warning signs with poorly illustrated pictures of a dark cloud with comical looking hands and sharp teeth, he reached the break area and sat

by Lore Casta Pendragon

down to light his pipe, Farin turned a small red valve on a gas line and the torch lights that were lining the mine walls died down to a dim light.

A few hours passed, Lore became increasingly worried, a fatal flaw in their plan came to his mind, the creeping dark must have anticipated their trap, his eyes grew wide and he put his pipe away, rushing back down the wide tunnel, at the first spot where a bombardier unit was stationed the walls were covered in blood, body parts and bones were strewn around the tunnel, Lore covered his mouth at the horror.

"Kimba!", he said in a panic, then rushed down the hall, his torch light getting dimmer as the light squeezed in around it, Lore made a small circle between his middle finger and his thumb and the tip of his index finger began to glow with light, he pointed his finger forward like a torch to illuminate his way as best he could against the pushing darkness, he didn't want to use too much of his life force before he encountered the creeping dark again.

Lore heard a loud bang down the tunnel and light flashed in the distance, Lore covered his eyes then ran to the location of the second bombardier unit where Kimba was stationed, the darkness pressed in from the walls either side of Lore and he stopped looking around for any sign of movement, his eyes not adjusting as fast as he would have liked.

Dark claws reached out of the darkness from his side and placed a cloth over Lore's torch causing it to go out, Lore slammed his fists together and summoned a tremendous burst of light just as the clawed hands reach out for him from every direction.

They stopped in their tracks being repelled by the light; he was absolutely surrounded by the creeping dark.

Lore growled with the effort and the light increased in potency pushing the claws back, he trudged down the tunnel one step after another while maintaining the shield of light, the dark claws pressed him from every side.

It felt like he was walking under water, another loud bang and a burst of light and the dark opened revealing Kimba pushing back against the darkness ahead huddled against one wall with the dwarven bombardiers nearby.

Lore ran to meet them, opening his palms and facing them toward one another, he formed a ball of light between his hands, it grew in size as Lore growled to build the power of his spell, as he got close to them, he threw the ball of light and an explosion of luminescence lit up the tunnel burning clawed hands into black smoke, the creeping dark disintegrated around Kimba and the dwarves and Kimba dropped to the floor panting.

"It knew, somehow it knew, we don't know how", Kimba said exhausted, Lore helped her to her feet, "that won't hold it back for long, we have to get to Farin", Lore said motioning to the dwarves to move, they took Kimba by the arms and ran down the tunnel, the creeping dark reassembled itself, its shadowy claws forming a new, it continued its pursuit, rushing down the tunnel towards them shrieking out a bone curdling cry.

by Lore Casta Pendragon

They reached another bend in the tunnel, one side lit up by gas lamps, the other side devoid of light, they moved down the darkened path and the creeping dark followed sticking to the shadows where it could move faster.

"Now Farin!", Lore yelled as the creeping dark passed the bend, Farin and a group of bombardiers popped out from behind the bend, the bombardiers threw their blinding light bombs in the tunnel illuminating the path behind the creeping dark, the creature shrieked as it was cut off from the darkness behind it.

"We've got you now, you wicked thing", Farin said, he turned a valve letting gas leak into the tunnel, he threw a torch and the gas ignited, sending a torrent of flames into the tunnel, the creeping dark recoiled back into the darkness of an adjoining tunnel and continued chasing after Lore and the others, who baited it toward their goal.

"The storage room is just up ahead to the right, Mech is waiting for us", Lore said as they ducked to the right into the storage room, the torchlight from the dwarven bombardiers shined brighter, as they backed into the room, Lore took his position, they waited silently hoping for signs of the creeping dark.

"C'mon, you horrid thing, come get us", one of the dwarves said, a bomb in hand, the torchlight began to press inward and clawed hands formed all around the door and spread into the dark corners of the room, a single large eye appeared in front of them and in a shrill high voice it said, "I've cornered some little mice, some tasty little mice", it giggled to itself as it moved in slowly from all sides.

Several bombs went off with a flash from outside the storage room door and the eye squinted then disappeared with a shriek, Mech appeared in the light at the door and said, "we've got it trapped now finish it!".

He threw a lever and a large stone door fell into place sealing the room shut, the creeping dark let out a wicked shriek and everyone in the room covered their ears at the deafening sound.

Kimba slammed her fists together and formed a radiant light, pushing against the dark, the beast could finally be seen for what it was, it looked like a void of black miasma with black clawed hands protruding out from all over it and a large bloodshot eye at its center.

The eye squinted at the light then widened as it realized it was trapped, it fought against them light in the room, the room grew darker, clawed hands snuffed out the torchlight around the room then grabbed a dwarf, his scream echoed through the small room as it grabbed another, sharp, dark claws ripping them into pieces, steely teeth appeared in the blackness and devoured them.

One dwarf pulled the pin on a bomb dropping it to the ground exploding in a final coup de grace of light, the beast shrieked as it repelled backward.

                              by Lore Casta Pendragon

Another dwarf scampered backward lighting a bomb in hand, he threw it toward the beast, and it exploded forcing it back into one corner of the room, as more light filled the room the creature seemed to get smaller and denser.

Now out of bombs the dwarves ran back toward Lore and Kimba, Lore ripped the cloth off the telescope at the other end of the room and Kimba winded a valve turning the telescope into position.

Lore slammed his fists together and grabbed his elbow, circulating his life force, "if I ever needed this power, now is the time", Lore said to himself extending his fingers wide aiming at the lens of the telescope, his hand glowed with a bright light, he focused it toward the lens, then the beam it formed struck the creeping dark.

The beast hissed and it was pushed into the corner, it tried to extend itself in either direction to move around the directed light but every time it extended itself more of it was burned away.

It shrieked a horrible blood curdling sound that pierced the ear.

Kimba saw that Lore was struggling against the pain in his ears, so she took her hands off her own ears and covered Lores, Lore concentrated all of his power into the beam, growling with the effort as he summoned all of the power he could handle.

The horrid shriek began to lessen as the creature grew smaller, darker, clawed hands disintegrating before they could form against the light, Lore couldn't see what was happening, the light was so bright and hot it burned at his skin, he fell completely exhausted taking a knee as the light drained from his hand.

Kimba slammed her fist together and started channeling light in her hands but Lore held up a hand to her, the creeping dark was still now, just a tiny ball of black in the corner of the room, a seething eye at its center, the dark edges disintegrating away, Kimba put Lore's arm around her shoulder and helped him up, they moved in to see the creature.

"Well done, Lore Casta Pendragon", it said in a high shrill voice, "you've beaten me, but I'll be back, death holds no sway over the abyss, as long as the contract holds, I'll keep returning to life, the path back will remain open and we'll meet again", it giggled as it disintegrated into black smoke.

"So that's how the nightmare creatures got here?", Kimba asked, "Guldamere made a contract with the abyss itself and has been opening the way for them by returning the dead to life", Lore said.

One of the dwarves took out a pickaxe and smacked out a tune against the stone door, on the other side they could hear loud cheers and the smacking of pickaxes against the door, after a

while they smashed the stone door down and Farin and Navi came through and embraced them as a procession of dwarves followed him cheering their praises.

Farin placed a hand on Lore and Kimba's shoulders with a great grin of appreciation, he turned to his men, "Lore!", Farin yelled, "Lore!", he yelled again, Mech picked up the chant, "Lore!", "Lore!", "Lore!", Other dwarves also picked up the chant as they made their way down the tunnel.

"Who is the man with no fear", Farin sang,

"Lore", "Lore", the dwarves responded,

"Who kicks the ass of beasties near", Mech sang after him,

"Lore", "Lore", the dwarves sang,

"Who took the dark and made it light", Navi sang

"Lore", "Lore", the dwarves chanted,

"Who gave the creeping dark a fright", Kimba sang chuckling,

"Lore", "Lore", the dwarves chanted,

"Who's the man with balls of steel, you can hear them clap like thunders peel",

The dwarves continued chanting and singing as they headed back home.

They were met with cheers and ale as they entered the large iron doors of the underground city, Lore and Kimba were hoisted up on the dwarves' shoulders as they celebrated the defeat of the creeping dark and their newfound freedom.

They were carried to the throne room, and placed down before the throne, dwarves poured into the hall, Farin stood between them and raised their hands in a sign of victory, a loud cheer went up, Lore and Kimba were smiling ear to ear as the dwarves celebrated.

Kimba let out a happy laugh and looked at Lore, Lore nodded back at her glad to see her smile once again.

Farin let them soak in the glory of their victory before raising a hand to silence the dwarves in the chamber.

"Lore Casta Pendragon and Kimba Kindheart have stayed true to their word, the creeping dark will no longer haunt the iron halls", he proclaimed, another cheer went up and Farin held his hand out to show that he was not finished and the cheer died down.

by Lore Casta Pendragon

"We'll be telling their story in the iron halls for centuries to come, they've lived up to their end of the bargain and so shall I", Farin said turning to Lore and Kimba taking off his helm and holding it to his chest, "when the time comes, the Iron halls stand with you against the dark as you stood with us", he said as a loud cheer filled the Iron Halls, that night they celebrated until dawn.

by Lore Casta Pendragon

Chapter Nine

The pits

Ailyn found himself plunged into a dark river, it wasn't wet, it wasn't liquid, but it pulled on him, it pulled on his soul.

Not far ahead he could see a drop off, every now and then he'd see someone float past and fall, some struggled, some accepted their fate, a dark figure reached down with dark black claws and pulled him from the ethereal river, before he reached the precipice.

Waking up Ailyn hung in Silus's torture room, hands tied to a support beam above him, blood and drool ran down his chin, he couldn't find the strength to hold himself upright anymore, the tearing pain in his shoulders kept him awake most of the time.

Silus had deprived him of everything, light, food, water, even a toilet, his own excrement piled at his feet and stuck on his legs, it stung.

The rats had chewed at him while he slept and the unsanitary conditions made the bites infected, the ripped off toenails would certainly be infected now, if he could see them.

Every now and then an especially fearless rat came to nibble on his feet, Ailyn swore that one day he'd get revenge on that rat.

He would have died from his wounds days ago, but something kept pulling him back from the abyss and each time and he would awake to a new nightmare, worse than the last.

He knew when Silus came back more pain would follow, more questions that he couldn't answer, Ailyn was resigned to the fact that he was going to die, there was nowhere to run, nowhere to hide, no one left to save him.

He heard voices from outside and two men came into the room, they threw a bucket of water over him.

"Gawd, he stinks", one of them said, "you'd stink too if you were brought back from the brink of death covered in your own filth", the other responded, "poor fool, but that's what you get for defying Silan Silus", they bantered back and forth.

"We should just finish him off, ya know, put him out of his misery", said one, "not a chance, you mess with him and Silus will have you take his place", the man shuddered visibly.

They scrubbed him down and swept the filth from the floor and away from his legs with a broom, they left carrying out the buckets full of excrement and rotten pieces of human that was strewn around.

by Lore Casta Pendragon

Silus walked in with his red scarf covering his mouth and nose, the smell was even starting to get to him.

"It seems our little game is at its end Ailyn, if you had any more information, you would have given it to us by now, my lord has grown tired of raising someone with your weak constitution over and over, this isn't even fun anymore, with you just hanging there like a lifeless corpse", Silus remarked prodding at Ailyn's limp weakened body, "time to go to the pit, just know that those who don't pull their weight in the pit, don't eat and looking at you, you won't last more than a day in there", Silus said as he cut Ailyn's restraints with a single slash of his knife.

Ailyn dropped to the floor, Silus took his knife and carved a symbol into the back of Ailyn's hand, the letter 'S', with what looked to be a wide brimmed hat.

"This way everyone will know your one of mine, so they won't kill you straight away, take him to the pit warden", Silus ordered, the two men from earlier entered and grabbed Ailyn under both arms dragging him out, Ailyn groaned as they placed a black bag over his head.

He gave a sigh of utter relief and collapsed almost immediately, he drifted in and out of consciousness. Ailyn briefly remembered being thrown into the back of a carriage designed for transporting prisoners, then being thrown down a steep embankment, he rolled for some time his body dragging against gravel on the steep downward slope.

Ailyn's life began to flash before his eyes, the time he spent with his family, his mother's smile, his brother's friendship, his father's lessons, his time with master Den in the living forest and his meeting with Lore Casta Pendragon and his pretty apprentice Kimba.

Then he free fell for what seemed to be a long time, Ailyn wondered if he had finally fallen from the falls and into the abyss of death.

Darkness gripped him as he fell, it grew darker until he hit cold water hard, it shocked him awake, he flailed his arms trying to swim to the surface but couldn't conjure the strength, someone pulled him from the water.

"It's alright lad, we've got you", he heard a familiar voice say, they placed Ailyn down and he coughed up a lot of water, he couldn't see who was talking, his eyes were blurred and he couldn't keep them open.

"They really did a number on him", someone said, "another one of Silus's victims, look at his hand", another said, "bastard", said another.

Ailyn closed his eyes, he waited for death to embrace him but it wouldn't come, the unknown men took him somewhere and laid him down, "here, it's not much but it's the only food we get, so if you bring it back up, you'll be eating it", someone said as they spooned food into Ailyn's mouth.

It was disgusting, but he was happy to finally have something to eat, he was laid down and was gripped by a deep dreamless sleep.

He woke briefly to eat and drink over the course of the next few weeks, someone was nursing him back to health, but he was in and out of consciousness for so long that he couldn't make out who it was, one day he woke to hear fighting.

"Did you think you could hide him from me", a disturbingly deep voice echoed through the tunnel, Ailyn heard a crash and a groan of pain, he could hear someone say, "let us go you bastard", echoing off down the hall as they were dragged away, Ailyn was too weak to investigate, instead he laid himself back down and fell into sleep.

Later Ailyn was reefed from his makeshift bed, he was dressed in prison rags, a pickaxe was thrust into his hands and he was pushed down the hall by two guards, he could hear screaming mixed with the sound of people bashing on stone with pickaxes.

He stumbled along, still he hadn't found his strength, they pushed him to his place between two other prisoners and stood back.

Ailyn just looked around not knowing what to do, the man to his left was shorter than him with black hair and looked to be from the southeast, he was surprisingly healthy looking compared to the rest of the men around him, the man to his right was very tall, dark skinned and heavy set, taller than Ailyn, he looked like he could lift a house, he grunted with every swing of his pickaxe.

Ailyn could tell he had an accent from the tone in his voice, "you'd best start working if you want to eat today", said the smaller man to his left, "they don't take too kindly to slackers down here and neither do we", said the taller man to his right, both men had strangely exotic accents.

Ailyn raised the pickaxe, but dropped it behind him as he raised it, he was still too weak from torture and weeks of inactivity.

"Find your feet man, the men watching you will report you to the pit warden, you don't want that", said the man to his left, Ailyn grabbed the pickaxe once more, he tried to remember what master Den taught him about breathing with your exercises.

He took in a deep breath and raised the pickaxe above his head, he let out the breath as he swung the pickaxe into the stone wall, bits of rock shattered away and Ailyn smiled, "there you are, but you might want to hold the axe at the end, it will give you a bit more leverage", the man on his left advised.

Ailyn did as the man said and tried again, this time more stone chipped away from the wall, he continued the exercise until the two men watching Ailyn walked off, Ailyn turned to face the man on his left, "thanks for the tip, I'm Ailyn Allheart".

Ailyn offered a limp skinny hand and the man took it firmly, his grip felt like iron, "I'm Shin, people call me Shin-son, this here is Brawn", Shin said happily.

                                    by Lore Casta Pendragon

"Welcome to the pit", Brawn said, "you'd best keep chipping away at that stone Ailyn if you want us to stay friends", Brawn gave him a threatening smile as he bashed into the rock wall with the pickaxe, his face was sprayed with dirt and rock.

"Don't mind Brawn", Shin said, "he's rather fond of his food and gets a bit upset if he misses out on his rations", Shin explained, "I see", Ailyn said.

"You see that cart over there?", Shin pointed to a cart half full of rock, Ailyn nodded, "if that's not full by days end, you don't get to eat, you don't want to see what Brawn did to the last guy that cost him a meal, you're standing in his spot now", Shin said as he drew a thumb along his throat.

Brawn threw a rock and hit Shin in his chest, Shin stumbled back and said, "ouch, careful Brawn, you could have hurt me", Brawn laughed heartily, a guard shouted down the hall, "get back to work if you want to eat, heretic scum".

Brawn put his hand on Ailyn's shoulder and said quietly, "I didn't kill him I just threw him down the pit, besides he was a snitch and didn't pull his weight", Brawn explained, he then began swinging his pickaxe again.

"Best get to it, we're already behind and we don't want to put up with a hangry Brawn", Shin said as he swung his pickaxe, they quietly exchanged small talk as they worked, Shin was from the Ronin city and was caught stealing, so they sent him to the pit.

Brawn was from a remote village on top of a mountain in what used to be the Thalarian ocean, he defied the church of the god feared when they sent missionaries to convert his people.

Ailyn and his new friends were sweating from every pore, Ailyn's body ached all over as they filled the cart to the brim, "what now?", Ailyn asked, "now we have to pull the cart up to the lifting area at the top of the pit", Shin said.

Ailyn and Shin took the front of the cart while Brawn and a few others working close by worked as the anchor behind it bracing the weight.

They made their way out of the tunnel to the central area, Ailyn looked up astonished to find a gigantic sinkhole, with a spiraling path around the outside lined with tunnels, there were ropes and pulleys toward the top and a giant body of water at the bottom.

Ailyn realized he had been thrown in here from all the way up the top, he was fortunate to be alive after falling into the pit from that height.

"We have to push this thing all the way up there?", Ailyn said horrified, "we do, not only that, we have to fight off the other groups or we'll lose everything we have", Brawn explained.

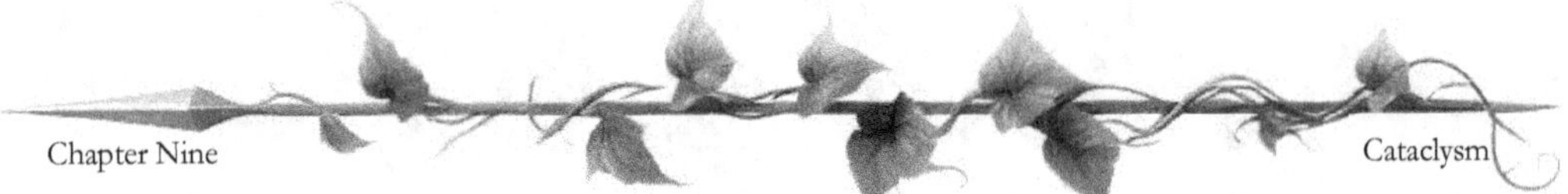

"The more carts you can deliver to the lifting area in one day, the higher tunnel you get promoted to, each tunnel represents a ranking of sorts within the pit, we're in the fifteenth tunnel, so we are ranked fifteenth in the pecking order", Shin explained.

"Needless to say, that being ranked higher makes the job significantly easier, the pit warden usually only puts the prisoners he likes into the higher tunnels", Brawn added.

They didn't encounter any trouble until about half way to the top, the cart began to creak as they tried to push it up a small bump in the path, the rickety carts wooden axel support snapped and the cart fell to its side, rocks spilled over the side of the cart and toppled over the edge falling down into the water below.

"No!", Brawn fell to his knees at the ledge gripping his head in disbelief, Shin just sighed deeply and sat down, Ailyn inspected the damage to the cart, he helped Aethor repair the cart-boat on several occasions when he came back from Dawnshire.

"I can fix this", Ailyn said, "with what tools lad?", a dwarf said to him, "they don't even give you tools to use?", Ailyn asked, "only this one", the dwarf replied holding up a pickaxe, "then we'll have to make our own", Ailyn said.

He picked up a sharp rock and bashed it against the broken axel support until it fell out with the nails used to secure it intact but slightly bent, he used the rock to straighten them out, which broke into two halves, then tore a thin piece of cloth from the arm of his ragged prison clothes and tied the sharp stone to one side of the broken wooden plank, making a makeshift hammer.

Brawn caught on and moved over to a nearby wooden railing, he ripped off the top of it with one mighty jerk, the dwarf was watching them inspired, "hold on a minute, that just might work, c'mon lads, it's gunna require all of ye to lift this cart back up", the dwarf said, the prisoners crowded around the cart.

Brawn gave Ailyn the piece of railing then took the front, "one…two…lift!", They shouted, lifting the heavy cart up.

Brawn was obviously taking most of the weight, Ailyn was impressed by the man's raw strength, he crawled underneath the cart then hammered the makeshift spare part into place with the nails he recovered while Shin and Brawn positioned the metal axel and wheel back into position, Ailyn crawled out blackened from the gravel and dirt.

"Well done lad", the dwarf patted Ailyn on the back, dirt and dust flying off his clothed.

"I'm a little embarrassed I didn't think of it myself, I'm Fyorn Finechisel, it's a pleasure to meet another artisan such as myself", Fyorn said.

                                    by Lore Casta Pendragon

"I'm Ailyn Allheart", Ailyn said but was interrupted by Shin, "c'mon boys we got work to do, get this cart moving, we can throw some loose stones into the cart as we go to make up for what we lost".

They all got back into position and pushed the cart up to the lifting area, several guardsmen in full armor were controlling the lift as they pushed the cart into position.

"Why don't we just use that to escape", Ailyn whispered to Shin, "forget about it Ailyn and keep your voice down, you see that guy in there," Shin said pointing to an imposingly large man sitting at a desk, his lower half seemingly blended into the darkness around him, a tentacle of black shadow picked up a pencil while he sat doing paper work.

"That's the pit warden, one of Guldamere's top generals, he can move in shadow, the last time someone tried to escape, he appeared above the lift and cut the ropes, no one survived the fall", Shin said.

Ailyn took a good measure of the man, he was also dark skinned, bald and dressed in a dirty black suit.

The prisoners walked back down to the fifteenth tunnel, a horn rang out, "that's all for today", Brawn said, they lined up outside the tunnel, after a while a group of soldiers came past with small cart and handed out an abysmally small amount of food to each of them, "is that all we get?", Ailyn said disappointed, the soldier turned to him, "you're lucky we gave you any at all", he jeered as they made their way to the next group further down the pit.

"Best not to complain Ailyn, that's just the way it is here", Shin said as he moved back toward the tunnel.

As they ate it grew darker, there was very little light in the pit, bar the torches held by the soldiers.

"Where are we going now?", Ailyn asked, "we're going to sleep", Brawn replied, they hunkered down in the dusty tunnel they spent all day working in, some people had makeshift hammocks others makeshift bedding.

Some just laid down in the dirt too tired to care, Shin climbed into a hammock made from sewn together prison rags.

"Where can I find one of those?", Ailyn asked, Shin looked at him sadly, "you stay alive long enough and you might be able to steal enough rags from the dead to make one", Shin said turning his back to Ailyn to go to sleep.

Fyorn laid down on what looked like a bed made of gravel while Brawn just laid down on a curved stone with a prison rag pillow.

by Lore Casta Pendragon

Ailyn sat down with his back against the stone wall, it was cold, damp, dirty and dusty, the stone was hard against his body and it made him hurt, but at least he wasn't strung up in Silus's torture room, Ailyn was exhausted and a light sleep soon found him.

He woke to the sound of a horn and groggily lifted his head, his neck, back and hips were aching from sleeping on the stone floor, they immediately got to work.

Ailyn was given the job of packing stones into the cart, he was sore, tired and weak and moved slowly, the rocks piled up from the other prisoners chipping away with their pickaxes, a prisoner threw a large rock which hit Ailyn in the shoulder with a thud, "hurry up useless!", He shouted at him and the prisoners around him looked at him with anger in their eyes.

Ailyn went as fast as he could, trying not to fall behind, it wasn't long before the cart was full and they began to push it up the spiral path toward the lifting area, they only made half a rotation around the pit when another tunnel of prisoners started throwing stones down at them.

One hit Fyorn on the side of the head and he fell down bleeding from the wound, Ailyn and Shin dragged him back away from the cart down the slope, Brawn batted some stones away but couldn't advance on his assailants from all the rocks being thrown his way and was forced back away from the cart.

Others also sustained injuries and started running back down the slope away from the onslaught, stones rolling after them.

Their attackers took control of their cart and began wheeling it up the slope, "damn it all", Shin said bashing his fist into the wall, "we've lost it", Fyorn said disappointed, "does this happen a lot?", Aylin asked, "yeah it does", Brawn replied, "if we just take one cart at a time they usually wont target such a small hoard, they usually target someone else, we were just unlucky this time", Shin said, "how do we get the cart back?", Ailyn asked.

"The soldiers will lower it down the pit when they are done with it", Shin answered, "all we can do now is wait", "why don't we fight back?", Ailyn asked.

The prisoners just looked down without answering, "It's not that we're cowards Ailyn, we just don't want to die for a pile of rocks", Fyorn replied, blood covering the side of his face, "that's understandable, I guess", Ailyn said, but in his heart he thought differently.

The prisoners went to the bottom of the pit and collected an empty cart, Ailyn was standing next to Shin at the front, pulling the cart as the others pushed from behind.

"Shin, when I first got here, I was looked after by someone, who was it?", Shin stayed silent for a while then answered, "it was a shaggy man and his fat friend from one of the higher tunnels, the pit warden doesn't like him, rumors say that he almost escaped", Shin said.

"Why were they helping me?", Ailyn asked, "how should I know?", Shin replied.

As they walked along Ailyn thought about what happened earlier that day, "why don't we modify the cart to provide us with some protection", Ailyn said, "no", Brawn said, "we can't waste any more time, I will not starve today Ailyn", "well if we manage to get a cart to the top, can we use one of the empty cards at the bottom for supplies?", Aylin asked, "that's a pretty tall order young one, it's taken us most of the day already and we're currently empty handed", a tall man in a prison rag hat replied in a calmly almost melodic tone, Ailyn raised an eyebrow at his strange way of speaking.

They made their way back to the fifteenth tunnel and began their work over, this time Ailyn's job was to smash the larger stones into smaller pieces, the cart was half full by the time the guards came around with food.

"Pathetic, not even a single cart delivered, you mustn't be hungry at all then", they went to move on, the tall prisoner in the prison rag hat walked up and threw himself at their feet, "please have mercy, our cart was stolen from us, we are weak already, please give us some food", he said in his melodic tone.

The guard threw a bowl of food over him then knocked his prison rag hat to the ground, two large pointy ears popped out and he quickly grabbed the hat scooping what food he could scavenge off his person and from the ground.

"Piss off elven scum", the guard said as they moved down the slope, the elf walked over to a water barrel and washed dirt from what seemed to be rice and some sort of hard bread, he tore it up into small pieces and offered a pinch of food to each of the prisoners.

"What is he?", Ailyn asked Shin, "he's an elf, apparently the world used to be full of elves before the cataclysm, they lived in the forests and were adept hunters, the cataclysm wiped out their forest homes", Shin replied.

The elf tried to hand Ailyn a small portion of bread but immediately his hand retracted from Ailyn, the bread dropped to the ground.

"I'm sorry young one, for a minute there I could sense the forest in you, here you can have mine", he said in a melodic tone, picking the bread up from the ground.

"Thank you, I'm Ailyn", Ailyn introduced himself, the elf stood straight with his legs together his feet pointed slightly outwards, he bowed with one arm across his mid-section the other out wide, he was tall long and lanky looking with sharp features.

by Lore Casta Pendragon

"I am Éoviel", he said melodically as he bowed, "I'd get that hat back on if I were you", Brawn warned, Éoviel shook the crumbs from his hat and placed it back over his head covering his ears.

"Why do you hide your ears?", Ailyn asked, "not everybody is friendly towards elves", Shin said, "the church of the god feared banned elves from entering the cities, placing a stigma on us, some elves possess a natural ability to understand magic, that which the church tries hard to keep hidden from public view", Éoviel explained.

"I see, is that why you ended up here?", Ailyn asked, Éoviel nodded, "I was only trying to buy supplies for my kin and they stuck me in the pit for it", Éoviel said, "well, let today be a lesson for all of us", Fyorn perked up, he had a makeshift rag bandage wrapped around his head, "if we are going to survive in this place for much longer, we are going to have to work harder than ever before, we've already got half a cart, if we work through the night and fill it up, we can race the cart to the top before the other prisoners can organize a raid in the morning, then do as Ailyn suggested and fortify the cart against further attacks".

The prisoners nodded and got to work, when the cart was full Ailyn collapsed to the ground, his toes were beginning to rot and the pain and exhaustion overwhelmed him, the other prisoners mostly ignored him, too tired and exhausted themselves.

He woke up later on the cold stone ground, a wet rag covering his forehead, "he's come down with fever, by the looks of it, his feet are infected, if the guards find him unable to work, they'll finish him off", Éoviel said.

"The weak ones never last long in the pit, let's get this cart moving", Brawn said as Ailyn fell unconscious again.

When he woke, he felt nauseous and vomited what little food and water was left to him, delirious he got up and wandered to a water barrel, soaking his face, excruciating pain shot through his entire body.

Ailyn couldn't take it anymore, it was night again, he must have slept through the whole day, he stumbled passed the cart in the tunnel, it had new wooden shields attached to the front and sides.

He limped over to the ledge which overlooked the filthy water below him, he could see broken wooden beams sticking out of the water below where a bridge must have once stood.

"A far quicker death, then suffering here any longer", Ailyn said to himself, he took one final breath and stuck his hands out wide, he raised his foot to take a step off, but just before he took the final step, he heard a voice from behind him.

"Wait, Ailyn", it was Shin-son, Ailyn put his foot back on the ledge, "let me go Shin, you know as well as I, I'm not going to survive another day in here", Aylin said, tears ran down his cheeks.

by Lore Casta Pendragon

"I asked around about the man who nursed you back to health, some people I know in the upper tunnels worked in the same tunnel, said he worked with big guy, by the name of Wynn", Shin said.

Ailyn took a step back from the ledge, confusion crossed his brow, "what was the other man's name?", Ailyn asked, his eyes darted back and forth, his heart pounded, had he dared to hope that after all this time he might still be alive.

Shin tried to remember the name he heard from earlier that day, "I can't remember, it was a strange name, it was, Aethor, I think", Ailyn's eyes went wide, tears started streaming down his face, Aethor, his father, was still alive.

Ailyn backed away from the ledge, "Aethor Allheart is my father, I thought my family were all killed by the church years ago", Ailyn explained, "I have to go to him, show me which tunnel he's in", Ailyn pleaded.

Shin gave him a look of pity, "well you see, it seems he was caught trying to escape to get you medicine by the pit warden, which got him thrown into the solitary cells by the wardens office up top, no one but the pit warden himself goes in there", Shin explained.

"I have to save him, there has to be a way in", Ailyn said.

"I'll let you in on a little secret, once a week the pit warden sits down to dinner with his favorite little prison snitch from the first tunnel, if we can make our way up the ranks here, we might find his favor and get an audience with the pit warden".

"He keeps the key to the solitary cells in his office, that might be the only way you're going to be able to see Aethor", Shin said.

"Will you help me?", Ailyn asked meekly, "what do I get in return", Shin said devilishly, "anything, I'll do anything you want", Ailyn said, "when the time comes, I'll name the price", Shin said.

Shin let Ailyn use his hammock and helped to clean him up, over the next few days Shin kept an eye out for passing guards, while Éoviel found some herbs growing on a far side cliff of the pit to help reduce the infection in Ailyn's feet, his body grew healthier and stronger each day, the crew increased their daily yield from one cart, to two, which doubled the amount of food they received at the end of the day.

Ailyn eventually recovered enough to join in and was even able to reinforce what now was referred to as the 'war cart'.

Ailyn filled the cart with the last of the days yield, this was their third cart for the day, "if we leave right now, we should be able to make it to the lift before the guards leave for the night", Ailyn called down the tunnel and everyone placed their pickaxes into several slots of the sides on the cart.

"Let's do this", Fyorn said, they began pushing the cart up the slope at pace, as they neared the fourteenth tunnel, they were bombarded with rocks again, the shielding in front of each man protected them from the assault and they pressed on soon passing safely.

Some other prisoners in the tunnels just watched as they passed while some threw stones and jeered, as they came to the tenth tunnel, they were ambushed by the other prisoners trying to take the cart from them, throwing stones and advancing toward them with pickaxes in hand.

Fyorn, Shin, Brawn, Éoviel and Ailyn all grabbed their pickaxes and moved to intercept them while the other prisoners kept pushing the cart up the slope, one man ran down and tried to bury his pickaxe into Éoviel's head, but Éoviel grabbed the weapon by the handle and smacked him in the face with the end of his own pickaxe, knocking him down.

Brawn grabbed a stone the size of a potato and hurled it with all his strength, it slammed into the chest of one prisoner and he crumpled where he stood clutching his chest.

Ailyn took the attention of three prisoners, weaving between them, showing his mastery over his taisabaki footwork, his feet moved in fast entering and spinning motions, his assailants got more disheartened with every failed attempt to strike at him.

Fyorn knocked out a wooden support beam holding up some loose rocks causing a small cave in at the tunnel entrance, stopping the prisoners inside tunnel ten from reinforcing those already fighting outside, he gave a chuckle and moved to help with the cart.

Ailyn was now in front of his three assailants his back to the tunnel, a prisoner with a makeshift sling whirled a rock and let it go, it whizzed just past Ailyn's head and he scoffed loading up another shot.

Shin moved toward the man and pulled out a sharp rock resembling a blade, he threw it in an underhand motion letting it fly loose from his hand, it flew straight, stabbing into the rock slingers hand, he dropped the sling and cried out holding his hand.

Ailyn nodded his thanks to Shin, his assailants tried to take advantage of the distraction to rush him but Ailyn threw the first over his hip, he switched his hips one eighty degrees and threw the next one over his other hip directly on top of the first as the third came in with an overhead strike of a pickaxe.

Ailyn moved with the weapon catching his opponent's arm over his chest and rotated with it in a sacrifice throw, the man rotated with Ailyn landing onto the pile of prisoners before they could get up.

122

Brawn came over with a large boulder and placed it on top of all three, they groaned from the weight stuck underneath it.

Ailyn, Brawn, Fyorn, Éoviel and Shin all laughed heartily as the men flailed helplessly, "funs over lads, there is little time left, heave ho", Fyorn said.

They took their positions on the war cart and continued moving it up the slope, they reached the lifting area just as the guards were starting to ascend, "wait", Ailyn shouted, "take this one with you", he pleaded to them.

"Piss off", one of the guards called down to him as they continued to rise, suddenly the lift stopped and the guards looked around confused.

"My lord will be happy with today's yields, be sure to take the cart with you", a deep voice echoed around them, the guards looked petrified and immediately reversed the lift to bring it back down.

"Impressive work tunnel fifteen", the deep voice said, out of the shadows on the ground near them the pit warden emerged rising out of it in a pool of black miasma.

"If you can manage to make three carts again tomorrow, I'll promote you to replace tunnel ten, they've been slacking of late", Warden said, "keep up the good work", the pit warden said, then sunk back into the darkness and disappeared.

"So we'll finally be moving up", Shin said, as they made their way back down the slope, some men who were watching from tunnel one watched as they past, "three carts well done, maybe one day you'll make it up here", a tall man said sarcastically adding a slow clap for emphasis, they continued down the slope and Ailyn asked, "who was that?", "His name is Wren, but people just call him the snitch, the pit wardens pet, the man beside him is Mole", Shin replied.

The snitch was a tall and lean man, long limbed and thin with a gaunt face, while Mole wore a gas mask that resembled a mole, with two large headed metal hammers that looked to be made from the bent remnants of broken pickaxes melted together.

"So, they're the team to beat?", Ailyn asked, "that's them, apparently they average about seven carts a day", Shin replied, "seven!", Ailyn gawked, "we don't know how they do it, they won't let anyone into tunnel one to sneak a peek, from the rumbling in the tunnel, I suspect one of them knows how to use chaos magic", Shin said thoughtfully.

"If they can use chaos magic, why don't they just escape?", Ailyn asked, "because the pit warden's office is right there, any attempt at escape would result in solitary confinement if he doesn't kill you first, trust me you don't want to be sent there", Shin answered, Ailyn looked down thinking about Aethor, "I'm sorry Ailyn, we'll get him out of there somehow", Shin said.

 by Lore Casta Pendragon

The next day Ailyn and his new friends pushed three carts to the top of the slope, surprisingly the other tunnels didn't attack them today and they made it with plenty of time to spare.

When the cart came around to hand out food, the guardsmen just stood out the front of the tunnel, when they approached a shadow grew long and a black miasma floated up from it, the pit warden rose from it slowly.

"Good evening gentleman, you look tired", he said in a deep baritone, "you've been working so hard lately, this pleases me, you've been pushing your limits it would seem, everyone is working a little bit harder to keep their places thanks to you, might I ask who the mastermind is behind this 'war cart' of yours?".

The prisoners looked to each other not sure what might happen to the person responsible, "I made the modifications", Ailyn said stepping forward, "most impressive young one, you are…", the pit warden pondered for a moment tapping his chin and trying to remember his name, "Ailyn Allheart, is that correct", "yes sire", Ailyn replied, the pit warden just laughed, "I'm not a lord Ailyn, just call me Warden", Warden eyed Ailyn up and down.

"You'll all be moved up to tunnel ten tomorrow morning, they've been lacking in productivity of late and causing me trouble, have your things packed and ready to go, my guards and I will be there to make sure things go smoothly", Warden said with a wicked smile, Ailyn smiled back, "thank you, Warden", he said with a bow, "keep up the good work boys", he said as he disappeared into the shadows black smoke trialing behind him.

"We did it", Shin shouted and the rest of the prisoner's cheered, "good for us but what about tunnel ten, they already hate us and I'm not too keen on a shiv in the back for our promotion", Fyorn said.

"Then we'll leave them a house warming gift and hope they see it as a peace offering", Ailyn recommended, "what were you thinking?", Brawn asked, "we can leave them a cart full of stone, I'm sure the extra food will help smooth things over", Éoviel added.

The next morning, they were woken by guards before the morning horn sounded to begin work, they worked through the night to fill another cart of stone to leave behind then were escorted to tunnel ten.

On the way there they were met with the jeering faces of tunnel tens former occupants but chose to ignore them, they made themselves at home, hanging their hammock beds and settling in.

"This should make the trips between about thirty percent faster, which should allow us to increase our efficiency and output, with any luck we might get close to four carts now", Fyorn said, "that's if we aren't attacked on our way there", Brawn added.

by Lore Casta Pendragon

"This is just the beginning, with each step we'll improve and sometime soon the top spot will be ours", Ailyn said, his eyes showed a new found determination that he hadn't felt in a long time.

Chapter Ten

Emancipation

Several months in the pit had passed, Ailyn and the prisoners he shared his days with continued to work the pit, the work strengthened them and they began to rely on one another, keeping each other's spirits up, giving each other words of encouragement and the occasional ladle full of water.

Ailyn let the other prisoners in tunnel ten in on his plan to save Aethor and a new plan began to form, they were all determined to leave the pit or die trying, with every promotion they were given, they increased their output and grew closer to the top, until the day came when they were promoted to tunnel two.

The prisoners finished their day hauling six carts to the lifting area each one of them now well fed and had grown fit with conditioned muscular frames from days of hard labor.

As they moved past tunnel one, the Snitch, Mole and several other prisoners of tunnel one, were waiting out front for them.

"Seems you've caught up to us with pure grit alone, I can respect that, but you'll never surpass us, we might actually have to start working again and I personally don't like the idea of that", the Snitch said.

"How about you fellas give it a rest or we might just have to show you what makes us number one", the Snitch, the prisoners of tunnel one chuckled with him.

"Listen to them, they're trying to intimidate us because they know that someday soon, they'll be getting evicted from the top spot", Ailyn said mockingly, making sure Wren heard him, "we'll see about that", the Snitch said, he nodded to Mole, Mole nodded back and they strolled back into tunnel one.

Ailyn and his prison crew returned to tunnel two and were soon greeted by the guardsmen with the food cart, they were all given a hefty plate of food each, the guardsman then returned to the cart and pulled out a small barrel of ale.

"A gift from the pit warden, he's eager to see you square off against tunnel one tomorrow", the guard handed the barrel to Brawn and they all stood there, mouths agape.

Never in the history of their time in the pit, did they receive thanks or reward for their hours of labor.

Shin was standing next to Ailyn dumbstruck; Ailyn slowly lifted his finger under Shin's open mouth and closed it, Shin snapped out of his disbelief as the guards rolled away the food cart.

Brawn lifted the keg with a mighty victory cry and an almighty cheer erupted from the prisoners, the Warden looked on from his office with a smile, on his desk was a letter from Guldamere himself expressing his appreciation for the increased profits the pits had given to Necropyre in recent times.

That night for the first time since Ailyn fell into the pit, he saw his friends smile, dance and chant merry tunes around a makeshift coal fire, they drank all of the ale that night and had a brief rest from the hardships of their labor.

The morning horn reverberated through the tunnels, with groans of protest each prisoner in tunnel two groggily made their way to their cart, no sooner had they all got into position the tunnel began to tremor, "cave in!", Fyorn cried out.

They pushed the cart out to the tunnel entrance, the rumbling was short lived, no structural damage had been done to the tunnel, further up the slope they noticed dust bellowing out from tunnel one and not long after the prisoners from tunnel one led by Wren the snitch pushed their first cart out to the lifting area.

The race was on and the prisoners of tunnel two pushed their cart up the slope to the lifting area, the Snitch was leaving the lifting area as Ailyn and his fellow prisoners approached.

"That's two carts already, you're falling behind so soon", the Snitch jeered at them, they all growled at him, pushing the heavy cart into position on the lift, as they moved back down the slope past tunnel one as another tremor rocked them.

They almost lost their footing, a huge cloud of dust poured out from tunnel one covering them, the Snitch and his crew came out again pushing a full cart of stone, "impossible", Éoviel said watching them with disbelief, "how can they?", Éoviel started.

"It's chaos magic, it has to be", Shin interrupted patting the dust from his clothes, "I often wondered how they managed to keep their position at the top and still seem so relaxed, I suspect Mole is the one causing these tremors".

"No point standing around like Etten-folk we've got to move if we want to keep pace with that", Brawn said and they returned to tunnel two.

As the day drew long Ailyn and his friends loaded up their last cart, the tremors had not ceased that day and the Snitch's crew never stopped hauling carts to the lifting area.

Ailyn's crew made a total of seven carts that day, a new personal best and in line with what tunnel one would usually produce, but as they approached the lifting area, they were greeted by the pit warden, the Snitch and Mole stood close by.

A tally was carved into a wooden beam, it said tunnel one had twelve, tunnel two had seven, tunnel three had five and so on.

by Lore Casta Pendragon

"Quite the feat wouldn't you say boys", the pit warden smirked at them, taunting them, "you'll have to do much better if you're going to dethrone tunnel one", he said, his deep voice echoed off the stone walls.

"We didn't know chaos magic was allowed", Shin muttered, "I'll be interested to see how you manage now that you've seen tunnel one in action", the pit warden said as he walked into a shadow on the wall disappearing from sight.

"I told you, I don't like all this effort", the Snitch said, "you can't beat us, so you might as well just give up trying", Mole added, his voice muffled behind his gas mask, dual hammers in hand.

"You might have won the battle, but we'll win the war", Ailyn said in a challenging tone, "oh really?", "Well, if you're not going to give up, then we'll have to make it harder for you", the Snitch said looking over at Mole who slammed the hammers on the ground.

The pit began to shake violently and sharp bits of rock began to jut out along the slope just below tunnel one all the way down to tunnel two, Mole panted from the effort under his mask, "that's enough you've done too much for one day", the Snitch said putting his hand on Mole's shoulder.

"You cheating bastards", Ailyn yelled, the Snitch just smirked at him, "good luck traversing that mess tomorrow, hope you don't trip", the Snitch chuckled as his crew moved back into tunnel one.

Ailyn and his crew made their way back to tunnel two, avoiding the now treacherous spikes between them and the lifting area, they sat around moping about their defeat.

"If this is what we have to overcome then we will just have to double our efforts", Ailyn tried to motivate his crew, but they remained silent.

"It's over boy, we can't compete with that, they don't even need to use their tools to mine the stone", Fyorn said as he kicked a rock against the wall.

"There must be something we can do to bridge the gap", Éoviel said.

"If Mole wasn't with them, it'd be an easy task", Brawn said, Shin was sitting their pondering silently but as soon as he heard those words come from Brawn's mouth, he lifted his head.

"That's it", Shin said, "what is?", Ailyn asked, "if we kill the Mole, we win", Shin said as he looked around the group, "are you for real?", Ailyn said.

"It's the only way we can beat them", Shin said, "I agree with Shin, once Mole is out of the picture, we'll be a shoe in for the top spot", Brawn agreed, "we can't just murder him, there has to be another way", Ailyn protested.

    by Lore Casta Pendragon

"Then we'll take a vote, all in favor of killing, Mole say I", all of the prisoners except Ailyn chanted, 'I' in unison, Ailyn threw his hands in the air and shook his head in disbelief, "count me out, I'm not murdering an innocent man", Ailyn responded.

"Mole is the only thing standing between you and a dinner date with the pit warden", Shin looked Ailyn in the eye and grabbed him by the shoulder, "you're so close now Ailyn, it's just one sacrifice for all our sakes".

"I'm sorry Shin, I can't do it, sure Mole is a problem, but that doesn't mean we should kill him, he's a prisoner just like us", Ailyn said trying to make them reconsider, "sorry Ailyn, you saw what he did today, he's just another lowly crook like the rest of tunnel one, Mole has to go, we'll raid tunnel

one tonight once the guards change their shift", Shin said.

Ailyn slumped, sadness covered his face, "when the night guard goes up from the lifting area at midnight, they'll be changing shifts, that's when we'll have a short window to do the deed and get back here before anyone notices what happened", Shin said as he explained his plan.

At Midnight Shin, Brawn, Éoviel and Fyorn smeared themselves with coal dust and left tunnel two, Ailyn watched as they left, concerned for his friends, he felt ashamed that he didn't go with them, but he couldn't bring himself to murder an innocent man.

Ailyn couldn't sleep a wink, so he made a small coal fire, he sat there poking at it watching the embers as they danced up like fireflies.

Fyorn, Brawn and Shin came stumbling in carrying Éoviel, he was wounded in the stomach.

"What happened?", Ailyn asked as they laid Éoviel down near the fire, "Ailyn, I drove my pickaxe into his chest, I got him, Mole won't be causing us any more trouble", Éoviel said, he coughed and blood dribbled from his mouth, his hand covered the wound on his stomach.

"Thank you, you gave me hope Ailyn, before you came, I never thought I'd ever see the elven forest again, you gave me hope", Éoviel groaned in pain and pointed toward a makeshift bag by his hammock.

"Grab my things will you", he said in a melodic tone, Ailyn grabbed the bag and gave it to Éoviel, Brawn lifted Éoviel's head and tried to get him to drink a bit of water, but he immediately coughed and spat up more blood.

Éoviel reached into the bag and pulled out a silver insignia resembling a leaf pattern, "give me your arm Ailyn", he said, Ailyn obeyed as Éoviel placed the insignia on the underside of Ailyn's forearm he cupped his hand over it then chanted something in elvish.

129

"When you make it free from this place, this insignia will grant you passage to see those you've lost", Éoviel said as he removed his hand, the silver insignia was embedded into Ailyn's skin.

"Journey well, Ailyn", Éoviel said as the strength left him, his body went limp in Ailyn's arms, tears formed in Ailyn's eyes and his chin dropped to his chest, he held Éoviel close and mourned the death of his friend, everyone stared, not knowing what to say as Ailyn laid Éoviel down then walked out of the tunnel.

"I hope it was worth it", Ailyn shouted back at them, his words stung, Fyorn beat his fist on Brawn's shoulder, "ay, the cost was too great", Fyorn said, "let's get this cleaned up, we got a big day tomorrow", Shin said turning away to go make preparations.

Ailyn and his friends carried Éoviel down the slope on a makeshift stretcher made of scrap, Ailyn on the front and Brawn on the back, they carried him down to the water at the base of the pit.

They covered the stretcher in as much rag, wood and coal as they could find then set the stretcher adrift pushing it outward on the water after setting it ablaze using a pickaxe and flint.

The fire burned Éoviel's body as his friends watched sullenly, Shin placed his hand on Ailyn's shoulder, then turned back to tunnel two, sleep was scarce that night and in the morning the guards pulled all of the prisoners out from their respective tunnels.

They were all made to line up single file, a large sphere of darkness appeared outside of tunnel two, the pit warden stepped out of it with a look of utter hatred on his face.

"Last night Mole of tunnel one was murdered in his sleep", he addressed them, his deep voice booming, enhanced by chaos magic, "as such I'm taking measures to prevent such wanton murder, any prisoner caught outside of their allocated tunnel after dark will be sent to solitary confinement for the rest of their days, however short that may be", he chuckled the last part.

"Now get back to work", no sooner had he said the words, the prisoners retreated to their tunnels, "not you", he said to the prisoners of tunnel two, pointing his large finger toward them.

"Who's going to tell me what happened to the elf?", Warden asked leaning over them, "we don't know, he stumbled in drunk and wounded late last night", Shin explained looking straight ahead as the pit warden leaned inches away from his face.

"Is that so?", Warden said raising an eyebrow, "he passed away from his wound last night, we took it upon ourselves to do the burial rites", Shin said sweating, breathing heavily through his nose, Warden stood up to his opposing full height, black miasma draped from him like a coat, he started pacing up and down the line of prisoners.

by Lore Casta Pendragon

"So, you're saying this elf took it upon himself to sneak into tunnel one and assassinate Mole, all by himself, even though Mole was the only thing between you and a promotion to the first tunnel", he stopped walking, eyeing them, they shuffled nervously, no one responded until Shin spoke up.

"It would seem so sir, we're just as shocked as you", Shin replied bowing his head and averting his gaze from the pit warden.

"I'll be keeping a close eye on you, any more funny business and you'll be drinking piss from a hole in the ground in solitary", Warden said, he turned his back and black miasma rose about him as he walked into a shadow disappearing.

Shin let out a breath, he must have been holding it out of fear, Aylin patted him on the back as they were pushed by the guards back to tunnel two.

Éoviel's death took a toll on Ailyn and the crew, they worked sluggishly over the next few days, moral was low, but their cart numbers remained decent, tunnel one had dropped off severely only producing three-four carts each day, now that Mole wasn't around to use his chaos magic infused hammers to fill their carts, they had to resort to the same backbreaking labor as the rest of them and they were bad at it.

Wren the snitch snarled at them whenever they passed, he looked exhausted to the point of breaking, in his desperation he started giving false information to the warden, Ailyn and his crew were loading a cart into the lift when they saw him arguing with the pit warden in his office.

Wardens deep voice boomed at him, he got up from his chair and wrapped a shadowy tentacle around Wren's throat.

Wren struggled against it, but the warden just walked outside and held him over the edge of the pit.

"Your usefulness has run its course", the warden said in a cold uncaring voice as the shadow tentacle ripped Wren's head from his body, Warden still had hold of Wren's head while his body dropped to the water below, he sneered at him as the light left Wren's eyes then threw the head into the water below.

Ailyn looked at Shin horrified, the display of sheer brute power was like nothing they'd ever seen, the pit warden was a fearsome foe, he looked over to them begrudgingly, "congratulations on your new promotion, this is the fate of those who disappoint me", then slid back into his office and took his seat dabbing an ink quill into a pot.

Ailyn looked at the barred door behind his office desk, somewhere in that place, his father Aethor might still be alive.

Ailyn and his crew were moved into tunnel one, it ran much deeper than the other tunnels, Mole had done a lot of excavation there, Ailyn set up his hammock near a bunch of draping sheets which made up a room of sorts and offered a small amount of privacy.

"This must have been Mole's room", Ailyn thought to himself, tallies were kept on the wall, uncountable in number, he must have been here for a long time.

Blood still stained the floor where Éoviel and Mole had wounded each other, Ailyn would have to clean it away lest he be accosted by the smell of blood each night.

Two large war hammers rested against the wall made from the twisted parts of broken pickaxes.

Ailyn laid in his hammock, reaching up to stretch his arms he noticed they were twice the size they used to be, "my arms have gotten pretty beefy", he said to himself and he closed his eyes trying to sleep.

Ailyn could feel a cold breeze, he opened his eyes and noticed the sheet tied up against the wall was moving slightly, he frowned then walked over to it, holding his hand out feeling a breeze coming from the corner of the sheet, he pulled on it and it fell down.

A boulder the size of his torso, was against the wall, Ailyn felt the breeze coming from the small gaps around it, he grabbed his pickaxe and pried the boulder away from the wall, behind it was a small tunnel.

Ailyn crawled his way into it, there was barely enough room to wriggle through, but he continued onwards, "Mole must have made this", Ailyn said to himself as he crawled through.

He eventually came to a large crack leading to another series of tunnels, Ailyn closed his eyes and listened, he could hear the breeze howling through one tunnel, he followed it along following the slight breeze and the cave widened enough for him to stand up.

Ailyn came to an underground creek surrounded by limestone, he tasted the water, it was clean and clear, he hadn't had clean water in so long he'd forgotten what it tasted like.

He followed the creek along until he eventually came to a pool, the cave continued under the water, so he dropped his torch and stripped off, diving in under the rock.

Ailyn knew that if he swam too far, he would die in the water but he came out the other side and was greeted by the night sky in a small gorge, "Mole tunneled his way out of the pit", Ailyn thought, the thought of leaving then and there, just abandoning everyone and making his escape crossed his mind.

                    by Lore Casta Pendragon

 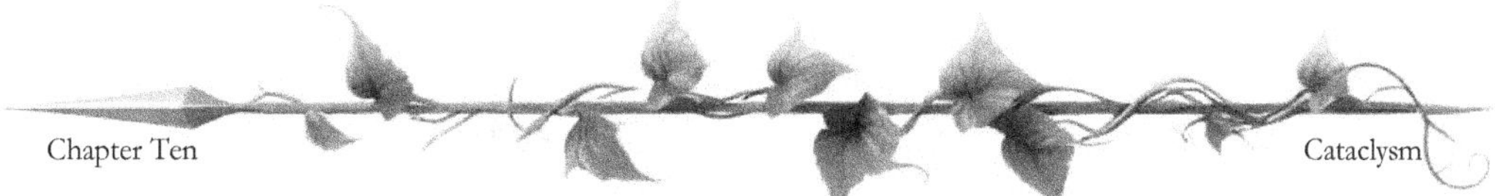

But if the soldiers of Necropyre didn't find him, the nightmare creatures certainly would, he also couldn't abandon his father or his friends, so he swam to shore, breathed in his freedom, then reluctantly he headed back.

When he got back Shin had already found the entrance to the tunnel and informed the crew, as Ailyn squeezed back through the tunnel, they pulled him out.

"Ye mad crawling in there, ye could have died, well, what did you find boy?", Fyorn asked, "it leads outside", Ailyn replied, "you found a way out?", Shin said astonished, "well, what are we waiting for, let's get out of here!", Brawn said excited.

"I can't leave yet", Ailyn said, "my father is still here in solitary, I can't leave without him", "if we leave now, you'll lose the opportunity to save him", Shin said.

"I've been here for longer than I can remember, I can wait just a little bit longer", Brawn added, putting a hand on Ailyn's shoulder, "but you'd better not mess this up for us", he warned, smacking Ailyn on the back hard making him stumble forward, they placed the boulder back and began making plans for their escape.

Brawn came to visit Ailyn in the morning, Ailyn was tying his sandal laces as he came in holding a dirty big rat, "I got this for you, thought the protein might help you stop being so scrawny", Brawn said laughing, Ailyn wasn't sure if he was serious or not and grabbed the carcass by the tails looking over it with a sour expression, "ahh, thanks, Brawn", Ailyn said sarcastically.

They continued working through the day as they always did, the pit warden nodded happily at the end of the day, approving of their work, as they turned to leave the lifting area the pit wardens deep voice boomed, "Ailyn, come to my office".

The rest of the crew look to Ailyn smiling and wishing him luck, Ailyn took a deep breath and stepped over a small bridge and into the small wooden building, "take a seat prisoner", Warden commanded.

Ailyn sat down in front of the Warden's desk, there was a plate of food in front of him, nothing like the scraps they were usually fed, cooked meats with vegetables and a mug of ale, right of the rear door he could see a set of keys to the solitary cells hung on a hook.

"You've done for well for yourself, Ailyn, I've kept an eye on your rise to power here and I have to say I am impressed", Warden eyed him waiting for an answer expectantly, Ailyn looked at him and snapped back to attention.

"Yes sir, I'm very fortunate to have such a hard-working crew", he said nervously, "I have a proposition for you Ailyn, if you can keep up the good work and squash any attempt by the other prisoners to overthrow you and keep me informed of their movements, you can reap the

 by Lore Casta Pendragon

rewards, I can make your life here comfortable", Warden said, holding his large hand out before the food in front of him.

Ailyn put on his best fake smile and said, "I would be honored to help you sir", Warden sat back in his chair relaxing, "then we have an accord Ailyn, needless to say that you know what happens if you fail me", Warden said gesturing to the edge of the pit where he beheaded Wren.

"Of course, sir", Ailyn replied bowing his head, "excellent, please help yourself to this fine meal", Warden said, "thank you sir", Ailyn said as he began eating, he took a drink of ale when the warden asked.

"Aethor is your father is he not", Ailyn spat ale and choked on his food at the sudden questioning, he looked at the pit warden and wiped the food from his mouth, "Aethor is my father yes and I'd do anything to see him again, is he still alive?", Ailyn asked.

"He is, for now", Warden said indignantly looking over at the barred door, "he's a trouble maker and far too strong to be left with the rest of the rabble, he tried to escape and almost succeeded, so now he rots in a solitary cell, I may allow you to see him, should you do what I have asked".

Ailyn looked at him hopefully, "yes sir, thank you sir, I'll do everything you ask of me", Ailyn said knowing that was the exact answer the pit warden wanted to hear, "that's a good boy, now leave me, you can take your meal with you", Warden said.

Ailyn thanked him again and left quickly, upon returning to the tunnel he told his friends what had transpired and they quickly hatched a plan for Ailyn's next meeting with the pit warden.

A week past and Ailyn was summoned again to the Warden's office, "come in Ailyn, tell me, what has been happening amongst our inmates", Warden asked, already starting on the food.

Ailyn took a seat and started rattling off a list of minor events and fighting that occurred that week in the pit, when shouting erupted from one of the lower tunnels, guards were fighting prisoners who were shouting something about the food.

"Excuse me, while I deal with this", Warden said, wiping his mouth with a handkerchief as he stood from his desk, the light in his office faded almost entirely and he disappeared from sight.

Ailyn wasted no time grabbing the food, he ran to the barred door and grabbed the keys, he opened the door and ran into the solitary confinement quarters, it was just a long corridor with barred cells built into the floor.

Running down the hall he found a now much thinner Wynn, chained up sitting in one corner of a cell, "Wynn, it's me Ailyn, Ailyn Allheart", Wynn responded in a low croaky voice, "Ailyn?", "Gods boy, if your caught here you'll be executed, leave us here", Wynn said, he showed no hope in his voice, like a man waiting for death.

by Lore Casta Pendragon

"Have you seen my father?", Ailyn asked, "Aethor?", "He's in the next cell down", Wynn said, "here catch", Ailyn said tossing some bread and meat down to Wynn, Wynn caught it and a bit of life came back into his face, "thank ya boy, there might be some hope yet", he called to Ailyn as he scampered off to the next cell.

Aethor was sitting against the wall looking disheveled and gaunt, "father?", Ailyn asked, no sooner had the words left his lips Aethor was on his feet, "Ailyn?", "Praise be your alive, I thought for sure I'd lost you, tell me boy, where is your mother and brother?", Ailyn looked at him remorsefully.

"They were killed, years ago, Harram Halfborn drowned them in the river", Ailyn said sadly, Aethor slumped down to his knees, pain covered his face.

"When I found you alive at the bottom of the pit, I dared to hope, they survived as well, how did you escape?", Aethor asked fighting back his grief.

"After Harram killed them, he came after me, the only reason I escaped was because of the injuries you gave him, I ran deep into the living forest and survived there on my own for a while until I met master Den, it's a long story and I'll catch you up fully once we get you out of here, catch".

Ailyn threw Aethor the rest of the food and fumbled to find the right key, he unlocked a latch on the cell and lifted it, he sat on the edge and hung upside down hooking his feet into the bars, he couldn't quite reach Aethor, but that was no problem, even weakened Aethor was a force to be reckoned with.

Aethor stuck the food in his teeth then ran at the cell wall, jumped away from it and launched himself up enough to grab Ailyn's hand, he pulled himself up with Ailyn's help and they both climbed out of the cell.

"Ok, now we should free Wynn and make our way out", Ailyn started to say when Aethor embraced him in his arms, Ailyn stiffened, his eyes went wide, he relaxed then put his arms around Aethor, tears burned at his eyes.

"I'll never let them take you, I'll never fail you again", Aethor promised.

Ailyn felt just like the small boy he was in Riverside before anything had happened, before Dawnshire, before the living forest and before he was tortured and thrown in the pit.

"What's the plan?", Aethor asked, "first we free Wynn, we found a tunnel that leads to the surface, if we can get back to tunnel one without the pit warden noticing us, we'll be free", Ailyn explained, "well done boy", Aethor said rubbing Ailyn's hair and smiling.

They undid the latch on Wynn's cell and both helped to get him out, which took both of them a considerable amount of effort to help lift the large man, they quickly explained the plan and Wynn nodded.

They hurried to the barred door and they entered Warden's office, Ailyn could hear the fighting below had already stopped, "shit, we're out of time", Ailyn said.

He crouched down and snuck to the front door of the office, two guards were standing out front with five more guarding the lifting area, the guard's quarters were through a door next to the lifting area, "we can't get through here without a fight, if the pit warden comes back, we're done for", Wynn said.

"There's only one thing left to do then", Aethor said standing up and ripping away the ragged cloth he wore, he was weakened but his body was still muscular and formidable to behold.

"What are you doing, get down", Ailyn said to Aethor, but Aethor looked at him, no sign of fear crossed his face, "this time we won't lose", Aethor said, Wynn stood up beside him, "then we fight our way out", he said.

With a mighty kick the door was ripped from its hinges, the two guards out front ducked down covering their heads as Wynn and Aethor walked out.

Wynn grabbed the guard on the left and threw him over the edge of the pit like a sack of potatoes, while Aethor knocked the other out with a blisteringly fast straight punch to the jaw, the five guards at the lifting area saw them and moved to sound the horn.

Aethor, Ailyn and Wynn moved to intercept them, two moved on Ailyn drawing swords, Ailyn used his taisabaki footwork to move around a downward strike, he took the guards wrist and slid under his arm, turning again he overextended the guard's arm, forcing him to swing around plunging the sword into the second guard as he advanced, he released the sword out of panic.

Ailyn moved back in front twisting the guard's wrist around his hip, the guard flipped upside down and Ailyn placed his palms together, he slammed the guard in the chest, sending him flying over the edge of the pit.

A guard wielding a spear advanced on Aethor trying to stick him in the mid-section, Aethor used his keinohenka technique, moving around it and dropping to one knee, his back heel spun around with incredible speed and he took the guard off his feet, he grabbed the spear from him as he fell to the ground then speared the guard through the chest.

A guard advanced on Wynn wielding a claymore, he swung the five-foot longsword around violently showcasing his strength, Wynn picked up a large boulder and hurled it at the guard it smashed an indent into his steel body armor and the guard fell unconscious.

Wynn picked up the claymore resting it against his shoulder, "this is a nice sword, just my style", Wynn said with a smile.

by Lore Casta Pendragon

Guards started running back up the slope toward the fighting, Shin was keeping a look out from tunnel one and saw the guards coming up the slope, "looks like the plans gone sideways boys, arm yourselves, it's do or die now!".

Fyorn, Brawn, Shin and the rest of the prisoners moved out from tunnel one to intercept the guards moving up the slope, they clashed together, Brawn sunk his pickaxe deep into an armored guard's breastplate, Shin ducked a mace and slammed his pickaxe into a guard's knee breaking it, he followed it up by burying the pickaxe in the man's face.

Fyorn ran out from the tunnel wielding Mole's dual war hammers, he swung them one after another in large arcing overhead strikes, slamming one guard into the ground and then another with the other hammer, Fyorn let out a mighty battle cry and the guards around him backed off fearing the dwarf's strength.

Some of the prisoners from tunnel one made their way up hill toward the lifting area and engaged the guards coming from the guard's quarters as Ailyn, Aethor and Wynn engaged more guards.

"Don't let them get to that horn", Ailyn said, fighting off a couple of guards with swords, Aethor leaped onto a wooden rail blocking the path of two young guards heading for the horn.

Two more were coming up from the other direction, Wynn swung his claymore finishing off another guard, then swung the sword with both hands over his head and flung it at the horn, the sword smashed into the head of the horn and pinned it against the stone wall, the two guards struggled to free it, so one of them just pressed his lips to the horn and blew.

"Ah, shit", Wynn said, shoulders slumping, unfortunately the horn was still able to make a sound and the alarm horn rang throughout the pit.

Having quelled the riot below the pit warden stood in front of the lined-up prisoners, he heard an alarm horn sound, then gritted his teeth and looked up to see more fighting above near the lifting area, "you dare betray me!", "Fool", he said.

The prisoners in front of him showed clear signs of discontent, one of them punched a guard too busy looking up and the fighting began again, the pit warden turned as a prisoner tried to stab him with a makeshift knife made from the sharp end of a broken pickaxe.

A shadow tentacle wrapped around the man's arm before he got close, breaking it in multiple places.

The knife dropped to the floor and Warden wrapped another shadow tentacle around his other arm, he pulled them in either direction, then wrapped another around the man's waste, he tore the man's arms off and threw the remains at the other fighting prisoners.

    by Lore Casta Pendragon

Warden picked up the next prisoner fighting one of his guards and tore the man in half, the prisoners saw this happening and turned to run for their lives.

Warden sunk into the shadow on the floor and rose again in front of the men running away, they stopped in their tracks and watched with horror as the pit warden's imposing form rose above them.

Tentacles turned into sharp black blades and he sliced them to pieces, tentacles whipping about slicing flesh from every direction, Warden finished his onslaught then looked upward, he growled then walked into a shadow on the wall.

Prisoners from the other tunnels caught on to what was happening and rushed out of their tunnels heading up the slope toward the lifting area, they caught the guards that Shin, Fyorn and Brawn were fighting from behind forcing them back against the cliff face.

The crowd of prisoners outnumbered them and advanced forward, the guards started pushing each other from the ledge trying to back away from pickaxes being swung at them, the prisoners forced them back bit by bit until one by one the guards fell from the ledge and plunged into the water below, their heavy metal armor drowning them beneath the surface.

The prisoners then moved up to the lifting area toward the guard quarters, before they made it, they heard ropes snap from above, a lift with a cart full of stone fell down crushing a dozen prisoners underneath it.

More ropes where cut and the lifts crashed down the side of the slope and into the water below, a large shadow grew from the wall as the pit warden stepped out from it, the prisoners moved back in fear.

With one horizontal slash of his shadow tentacle, ten prisoners were dismembered and killed, screaming in pain as they clutched at a severed hand, arm or leg, one got caught across the throat and died instantly.

The prisoners turned and ran back down the slope unable to fight against the pit warden's dark magic.

Ailyn, Aethor, Wynn, Shin, Fyorn and Brawn all stepped forward from the fleeing crowd, Ailyn took his Aikitai stance, while Aethor bounced, shifting the weight on his feet front to back.

Wynn let the tip of the claymore fall to the floor with a clang, Shin held his pickaxe in hand, Fyorn lifted up both war hammers from his sides and Brawn picked up a large boulder and rested it on his shoulder, they stood side of side defiantly in front of the pit warden.

Warden looked over them with pity, "Lord Guldamere himself tasked me with holding this prison, four centuries have passed and I've held it, not a single prisoner has ever escaped me,

but I must say, this is the best effort I've seen so far, too bad you've already failed", Warden said as the shadows drew long around him.

A shadow tentacle wrapped around Ailyn's leg, Ailyn yelled out in pain and shock as the tentacle squeezed, threatening to break his leg, Wynn ran over and with a single swing of the claymore he chopped the shadow tentacle off from the ground it was rooted from, it vanished into a puff of acrid black smoke.

Aethor charged at Warden, he jumped to deliver a flying kick, but Warden moved backward into the shadow on the wall and Aethor kicked the solid wall instead.

"Fight me you coward!", Aethor shouted, Warden's deep imposing laugh echoed from the shadows all around them, they looked around unable to determine which direction it was coming from.

Warden appeared behind Fyorn and a shadow tentacle whipped around his legs, it pulled him upside down while another tentacle whipped across looking as sharp as a sword ready to decapitate him.

Fyorn lifted the hammers and blocked it, he swung one hammer up to the tentacle that held him and it disappeared into smoke, he fell holding the hammers as he fell, they hit the ground and the earth beneath him shattered, sending out a wave of earth in every direction.

Warden got hit by debris and was sent flying backward disappearing into a shadow on the wall.

The others who were running to help also got caught in the crossfire and were sent across the room, Brawn and Shin were blown to the edge of the pit.

Brawn grabbed part of a railing and caught Shin's hand as he was falling, they swung precariously from the ledge, "thanks Brawn", Shin said nervously.

Ailyn avoided most of the damage by dive rolling away, while Aethor did a backward handspring to avoid a large piece of rock knocking his head off, Wynn put his claymore up to block some smaller debris but was knocked back into the wall.

"What was that?", Ailyn asked Fyorn, "these hammers must be enchanted!", he said happily, "don't do that again, you almost killed us all!", Brawn said pulling Shin-son back up from the ledge.

"Where did the pit warden go?", Aethor said, "he's still here somewhere", Wynn said as Warden appeared at the wall behind him, a large jagged dagger in his hand, "look out!", They all said at once.

Wynn spun around throwing all of his weight with the claymore, Warden sunk back into the wall as the claymore sparked against the stone wall, "slippery bastard!", Wynn said, before he could recover for another swing, warden came back out of the shadow and stabbed him with the long-jagged dagger in the middle.

139

Aethor came flying in from the side, he ran up the wall and kicked the warden in the side of the head, knocking him away.

Wynn dropped to his knee's placing a hand on his wound, Aethor landed on his feet and advanced on Warden, Warden landed on a shadow and sunk into the floor then rose again on his feet.

As Aethor advanced, Warden slashed at him with the dagger, Aethor frog leaped onto his back then straight back to his feet following it up with a straight punch to Warden's stomach, Ailyn and Shin came in behind kicking out the back of Warden's knees, he started to fall backwards as Brawn threw Fyorn into the air toward him, Fyorn let out a mighty war cry as he brought down both hammers.

Everyone jumped back as the hammers hit Warden with tremendous force, he disappeared into the floor and a plume of black smoke filled the air.

"Is it over?", Brawn whispered, unable to see through the smoke, they looked around, no one made a sound, the smoke made it hard to see, a deep laugh filled the pit, "now you've made me mad", Warden said.

The first thing they heard was Shin's scream as a tentacle snatched him and he was thrown from the edge of the pit.

The next was Brawn's, then Fyorn, Ailyn found Aethor in the smoke, "stand with me, back-to-back", Aethor said, Ailyn nodded, they stood ready as Warden stabbed at them through the fog from the left, they parted avoided the blade as both threw backfists at Warden hitting him either side of the head.

Warden took the hit and slashed Aethor across the chest, Ailyn grabbed Warden's arm and twisted it at the elbow joint, he turned one hundred and eighty degrees twisting the arm and locking out the joint in a shihonage hold, Warden grunted and dropped the dagger to the floor, it disappeared into smoke.

Ailyn struggled to keep hold of the large man, he dropped his weight and Warden was thrown to the floor, his shoulder dislocating.

Warden growled and tried to fall into the shadow on the floor but Ailyn held on, Aethor grabbed Warden's arm as well and they pulled him out of the floor only for Ailyn be greeted by a giant fist uppercutting him from the dark into his genitals, he released Warden's arm as he was thrown upward by the blow, Aethor connected with a powerful somersault kick onto the top of Warden's head, he growled in pain as he disappeared into the floor once again.

Aethor grabbed Ailyn, "are you alright boy?", "I'm fine, just took me by surprise, he fights dirty", Ailyn replied, "how's your chest", Ailyn said concerned, "don't worry, what doesn't kill me makes me stronger", Aethor replied.

by Lore Casta Pendragon

"Remember, there are no rules when it comes to survival", Aethor said.

The black fog began to clear as Warden appeared from a shadow behind them, launching a powerful kick to Aethor's back, Aethor flew off into the far wall smacking his head against the stone.

"Father!", Ailyn yelled, as the warden threw a barrage of punches at Ailyn, Ailyn couldn't believe the speed the large man moved at for his size, he moved his feet using his taisabaki technique, each hit narrowly missing him by millimeters.

Warden got increasingly agitated not being able to connect and his punches got even faster each punch trailed by a black miasma which made them hard to track.

Ailyn tried to counter attack but a punch made contact with his jaw staggering him, then another to his mid-section followed up by an uppercut.

Warden grabbed Ailyn by the shoulder and punched him in the face, Ailyn's legs went limp, blood ran down from a cut above his eye, Aethor came to and saw the onslaught through blurred vision.

Aethor got to his feet, wiped the blood from the gash on his chest and licked it, his eyes shone a bright red, Aethor sprinted at Warden with incredible speed and delivered a devastating flying kick to his side.

An audibly loud crack could be heard as Warden's ribs broke, he shot across the stone floor stopping only when he smacked into the wall, Warden gasped for breath, grabbing at his shattered ribs, he crawled and writhed in pain, utter hatred shown in his eyes as he looked back towards Aethor who had Ailyn in his arms.

"Wake up Ailyn!", Aethor shouted, Ailyn lifted his head groggily and gave a faint smile blood in his teeth, Aethor helped him to his feet.

Warden got to his feet as well, his face a mask of fury, he ran toward them.

"I got this", Aethor said as he lined up to finish him off with a dragon kick, Aethor leaped, his back leg going behind his front as his foot shot out at Warden, Warden exploded into black smoke and Aethor's eyes went wide, "it's a fake!", Aethor cried out as the real warden burst through the fake made of black miasma.

He grabbed Aethor by the leg spinning him as he ran forward and hurled him with all his strength off the edge of the pit.

Aethor reached a hand toward Ailyn as he disappeared over the edge, Ailyn saw Aethor falling, his father who he risked everything to save and his eyes flashed red for a moment, then a white aura surrounded him illuminating everything, Ailyn felt a well of power he hadn't felt since he fought Harram Halfborn and he leaped to the edge of the pit.

by Lore Casta Pendragon

He pushed from the ledge and shot out like a missile, he caught Aethor and landed on the slope on the other side of the pit, he placed Aethor down who looked at him confused, then wasted no time running at blistering speed up the slope, then along the vertical wall.

Warden saw him coming in fast and tried to sink into the shadow on the wall but as he got to it, the aura surrounding Ailyn illuminated the wall, blocking his escape.

Warden turned as Ailyn hit him with an almighty punch to the face.

Warden flew into the stone wall and went limp.

"How?", Warden said unable to breath properly or see straight, Ailyn walked toward him, the shadow miasma surrounding the Warden faded away.

Warden began to chuckle, "I get it, he kept you alive, a terrible mistake, this power, your power, you found it, the missing, piece", Warden said struggling between each breathe.

"Lord Guldamere, must have, that power, with it, he can grant, life eternal", he said.

"You think I'll let you live after what you did to us!", Ailyn said, his fury boiling over.

Warden looked at Ailyn, his eyes turned pure black, the black miasma lifted from his skin, the shadows fought the light on the wall behind him, shadow tentacles wrapped around the warden lifting him to his feet, a dozen tentacles exploded out behind him each one as sharp as a sword.

They whipped out toward Ailyn from all directions, Ailyn moved, jumped, turned, weaved, somersaulted and cartwheeled out of their way in a matter of seconds, he remembered his training with Den, remembered the bamboo flumes and the tegatana, a knife hand technique Den had once shown him by putting a log in half with his bare hands.

Ailyn pointed his fingers to resemble a blade, the white aura surrounded his hand and became razor sharp, he sliced off the tentacles as they attacked dodging just like he did the water at the temple each one bursting into black smoke, he finished the last of them then cut straight down, the tentacles holding Warden burst into smoke and a line of blood ran down from his scalp.

Warden looked at Ailyn in disbelief as his life force burned out completely, he used everything he had with his last assault.

The shadow around Warden returned to normal as he took his last breath, the light faded from Ailyn too, a cheer erupted from the prisoners watching around the pit, Ailyn hadn't noticed the scores of prisoners who were watching the battle, Shin stood holding Brawn upright, Fyorn wounded but safe, stood beside them.

Aethor made his way back up the slope and helped Wynn with his wound, Ailyn moved to the edge of the pit and looked out over the prisoners.

by Lore Casta Pendragon

"Men of the pit, you no longer have to fight each other to survive or toil and die for the church of the god feared, follow me to the surface!", Ailyn shouted, the prisons and his friends all let out a mighty cheer.

Shin, Fyorn and Brawn all started to chant, "Ailyn", "Ailyn", "Ailyn", as the prisoners joined them, Aethor walked up behind Ailyn, "I'm so proud of you my son", Aethor said as he put his arm over Ailyn's shoulder, Ailyn smiled wide blood still covered his teeth.

Soon the prisoners made their way up the slope raiding the guard's quarters for food, ale, armor, weapons and supplies.

"There's a tunnel in tunnel one that leads to the surface, you can get out through there", Ailyn said to the prisoners who stood around pondering how they were going to get up without the lifts.

Ailyn stayed behind to rest with his father and his friends before they made their way to the surface, they had to widen some of the tunnel to get Wynn and Brawn's large bodies through, but eventually they made their way out.

To their surprise the prisoners were waiting for them on the outside, an older prisoner walked up to Ailyn and took a knee before him.

"I'm Gear, thanks to you, we were able to leave that terrible place, but I'm afraid now that we're free, the dark one will be looking for us, alone we are weak and vulnerable, but together we can be strong", Gear said looking up at him.

"Some of us have spent most of our lives at the mercy of that monster, we won't ever let that happen again", Gear bowed deeply before Ailyn.

"Ailyn Allheart, I am your man, from this day onward, will you lead us?", Gear said, some of the prisoners behind him took a knee and the prisoners behind them followed suit until all the prisoners had taken a knee before him.

Ailyn looked to his friends and they bowed also, Aethor was standing behind him and pushed Ailyn forward.

"You got an army at your back now son", Aethor said smiling, Ailyn stepped forward and held his head high.

"From this day, we won't fight each other for scraps, we stand together, against the dark!", Ailyn cried out for all to hear, his words met with cheers as he basked in the admiration of his newly found comrades, he turned to his friends and asked, "what now?".

                              by Lore Casta Pendragon

Chapter Eleven

The Paladin's Reach

Lore and Kimba were escorted by Farin and a dozen of his dwarven guard topside, "where to now?", Kimba asked Lore, "we continue to look for the missing power, I can imagine Guldamere and his forces have already pillaged the living forest and found the power there, so the gap between us is already widening, we need to find the other shards of power before he does, where is the nearest green zone from this side of the living forest?", Lore asked.

Kimba tapped her finger on her nose then said, "the fields of Paladins Reach to the east, past the scar of the world, the gorges cut in the land by the cataclysm, though passing it might be trouble, there are giant nightmare creatures that prey in there", Kimba explained.

"Well then we'd better get you up to scratch with your spells between here and there", Lore put on a grumpy face and waved a finger at her, Kimba chuckled.

"I have something for you", Lore said reaching into his sleeve, he pulled out a folded silk cloth.

"What is it?", Kimba asked, "take a look", Lore said, Kimba unfolded it revealing a magnificent red robe similar in fashion to Lore's own, "it's enchanted like mine, a spare of mine, but it's enchanted with added durability and has an almost infinite amount of room for supplies", Lore said.

"Thank you master Pendragon", Kimba said embracing him, "oh, that's alright", Lore said mumbling bashfully, "well, try it on", Lore said putting his fists together, Kimba became veiled then changed into the robe, it seems to shrink to fit her, "it's perfect", she said excited, "it's time we make our leave", Lore said.

"Before ye go", Farin said, "take this to the king of Paladins Reach, thanks to the creeping dark we haven't been able to send any messages out for some time, the king of Paladins Reach should know what has been happening here on the western front", Farin said handing a parchment to Kimba, Kimba placed it inside the sleeve of her new robe and they said their farewells to Farin and the dwarves.

Travelling eastward they set out, Lore taught Kimba the finer points of chaos magic that he could remember while Kimba caught Lore up on what she knew of recent history and geography.

Kimba honed her skills against lesser nightmare creatures in the blasted lands, fighting side by side with Lore, she still mourned the death of her father Kamdar, but training under Lore

by Lore Casta Pendragon

Casta Pendragon himself gave her a sense of pride she'd never known and everyday seemed like a grand adventure.

Walking down the path, they crested a hill and finally reached the scar of the world, Kimba's eyes widened at what she saw, it was bigger than she imagined, so big she couldn't see the bottom, the huge canyon cut the land.

There were five such scars originating from the crater of Mount Muse that stretched over most of the known world, within them contained the remnants of what used to be the world's oceans, the hot rock at the bottom heated the sea water making clouds condense inside of it, it often rained for days inside a scar.

Lore showed Kimba a handy trick for deflecting the rain, but they would have to stop and rest occasionally as they moved southward back toward the Mt. Muse crater, it wasn't possible to cross a scar on foot but the closer you got to the Mt. Muse crater, the shallower and closer the scar got, passing via the crater was much easier as it was much higher in elevation.

As they approached the scar, they looked down at the drop in awe, "it's incredible, I've never actually seen it in person", Kimba said.

She glanced at Lore who looked at it in horror, he looked away in shame, Kimba noticed his pained expression.

"It wasn't your fault, you tried to stop it", she placed a hand on his shoulder, "everyone believes I did, this", Lore extended a hand toward the scar.

"I failed them all", Lore's said, his chin dropping to his chest, the shame and anger he felt was eating him up inside.

"We'll make it right, the people will know it was Guldamere who caused the cataclysm and we'll clear your name", Kimba said trying to comfort him.

"We'll camp here for tonight, then move off in the morning", Lore said walking off to be alone, Kimba looked at him wondering how she could make him feel better.

She decided to cook them a nice meal by campfire, she took some supplies out of the sleeve of her robe, summoned a fire and began to cook, the smell of food was intoxicating after the long day of travelling and Kimba's mouth started to water.

Lore sat downwind of the camp smoking his pipe, he couldn't smell the food over the smoke, he finished his pipe and decided to head back to camp, the sun had just disappeared below the horizon.

Kimba stopped stirring a pot of stew, it smelled so good she couldn't wait to try some, she pulled out a spoon and went in for a scoop when she felt a small rumble on the ground, the water in the stew pot rippled from the noise and she stood there silently listening.

        by Lore Casta Pendragon

Thinking it might have just been a storm cloud from below she went to take a spoonful when it happened again, this time louder, the ripple in the stew was getting larger, then another, then the sound was coming from the edge of the scar and getting closer, more rapid.

Kimba stood up straight and backed away, a large crab-like leg appeared over the edge of the cliff, Kimba backed off further as another leg twice the size of her came over the ledge.

A giant scorpion-like nightmare creature covered in hard exoskeleton crawled over the ledge, it grabbed the pot of stew in its mandibles and ate it pot and all, "that was my dinner you gluttonous cretin", Kimba yelled at it.

Still not satiated the scorpion creature came at Kimba, she slammed her fists together and grabbed her elbow just as Lore had shown her, she sent a fireball directly into the oncoming creatures face knocking it back but not really hurting it much despite the charred mark on its face.

It shook it off and continued forward, a big barbed tail extended over its body and tried to squash Kimba, she summoned a ward of magic which cracked with the impact of the beast's tail.

The ward shattered like glass, she veiled herself blurring out of focus as Lore came over a rocky ledge to see the beast looking around for Kimba, it's keen sense of smell sniffed her out, Kimba walked silently over to Lore and dropped the veil appearing next to him startling him.

"Ah, you'd best not creep up on a wizard like that lest you get turned to ashes", Lore said firmly, the creature heard him and advanced on them.

Lore slammed his fists together and growled with the effort as several large pieces of rock broke off from the ledge around them, the beast came in fast and Lore launched the rocks at the creature hitting it several times smashing pieces of carapace from its armored body, driving it back.

Kimba followed his lead and they both hurled boulders toward the creature, they forced it back to the edge of the scar then standing back-to-back Lore extended his left hand while Kimba extended her right, they both summoned a powerful gust of wind and the creature was blown off the edge falling into the scar, several moments later they heard a loud thud as the creature finally hit the bottom.

Lore looked around suspiciously then nodded to Kimba to let her know it was safe to drop the seal.

"Judging by how long it took that thing to fall, I'd say we aren't far from a place to cross", he said.

They sat by the fire, Lore placed a magic ward around the camp which would wake him should anything wander too close, they slept around the fire that night, Lore slept upright his back against a boulder, every now and then a nightmare creature would trip his ward and he'd open one eye grumpily and raise a hand out from under his coat, blowing it away with a fireball, Kimba must have been exhausted because she didn't wake at all to the explosions.

They woke in the morning to a damp cold fog; shoe slugs were sucking on Kimba's clothes which she picked off with a stick.

"Bleh", Kimba complained as she picking the slugs from her cloak.

Lore left the camp and condensed the fog over his head, taking off his robe he pulled in the warm air and took a hot shower, he left the spell channeling when he returned to the camp.

"You should clean up too before we head off, it's quite refreshing", he said, Kimba agreed and pressed her fists together raising a wall of stone for privacy.

"Ahh that feels good after all the walking", Kimba said happily after she was done.

"Today we'll descend into the scar", Kimba said.

They made their way down into the gorge, large insects scurried around under foot.

Kimba noticed a centipede half her height crawling along the cliff face, the scar was eerily quiet and seemed to support its own ecosystem, there was even a small amount of greenery here, something not usually seen outside the green zones in Thalaria.

After about an hour they reached the valley floor, the fog thickened and Kimba lost her sense of direction.

"Master Pendragon, I think we just walked around in a circle", Kimba said, Lore stopped and looked around.

"Indeed, we must have taken a wrong turn somewhere", Lore replied, "when trapped in a maze, stick to one side and you'll eventually find the way out", Lore said as he continued onward, "we turned left here last time, so we'll go right this time", Lore said.

Kimba followed his lead but after a short period of time they ended back at the same spot, "hmm, must have taken another wrong turn", Lore said confused as he stood stroking his beard.

"There's another path here to the right", Kimba said pointing in another direction.

"Well, it's the only path we haven't tried yet, so it must be the way", Lore replied chuckling as he walked past her down the path, Kimba was getting increasingly concerned, Lore found himself getting more and more confused.

by Lore Casta Pendragon

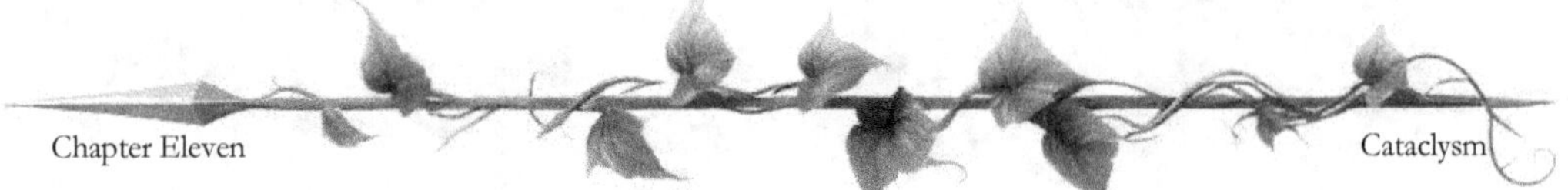

After a while they again found themselves back at the same place, Lore's mind felt just like the thick fog around them, Kimba was also starting to feel the confusion.

"Something isn't right here, this fog isn't natural, it's heavy and wrong", Lore muttered, grabbing his head trying to retain some focus, the fog got thicker again and Lore didn't know which way was up, he stumbled through it, Kimba followed close behind.

"Maybe we should head back the way we came", Kimba suggested but Lore didn't listen, he kept moving forward, he stood on something soft and wet, pushing down on it with his foot, it felt fleshy and a pinky white in color, Kimba was behind him on the path and saw him frown as he looked back at her.

"Look out!", Kimba shouted, slamming her fists together, she extending both hands as she blasted wind towards him in a wide upward arc, the fog blasted past him and dissipated enough for them to see Lore standing in giant toad's mouth.

It tried to clamp down on Lore, but Kimba pulled Lore out of the way just in time as the toad snapped its wide mouth shut.

Lore shook his head regaining his senses and slammed his fists together extending one hand and grabbing it at the elbow, he shot a fireball at the beast, it took the hit in the mid-section leaving a large charred mark on its belly, the toad looked unphased but turned and jumped away into the fog, the path opened up behind it and as it got further away the fog dissipated.

"That creature almost had me for breakfast, thank you Kimba", Lore said, "it seems to be using that fog to disorient its prey enough to eat it, what a terrifying monster", Kimba said, "we'd best leave before it comes back", Lore said.

They continued until they reached the slope to the other side of the scar, then rested a bit before heading back up the other side, when they reached half way the fog began to clear, after a day's hike they, reached the top and were greeted by a vision in the distance.

The rolling grass hills of Paladins Reach, "now that's a familiar sight", Lore said, "you know this place?", Kimba asked, "most of Thalaria used to look like this, rolling hills of green", Lore said.

They made their way down the trail which turned into dirt road, they saw farmers toiling and fisherman fishing in ponds, they crested a hill and Paladins Reach came into view, a large fortified castle of white stone topped with blue roofing.

The king of Paladins Reach's standard draped down from the watch towers.

"I remember this place, this city was here, before the cataclysm", Lore said astonished, "it seems not everything was destroyed after all", Kimba said skipping out in front of him.

"Paladin's Reach has stood for thousands of years, but unfortunately the people who inhabit it are not the same, most of them were wiped out by Guldamere's forces centuries ago, the Paladian's retook the city and have held it ever since", she explained.

They saw peddlers hocking wares on the roadside as they reached the giant white stone walls of the city.

An extremely large and imposing wooden gate stood before them, eight sentinel guards stood four each side along the path, they wore shining suits of steel armor holding seven-foot-tall spears with blue ribbons attached to the spear tips which flapped with the wind.

Two men in bulky paladian armor of white and gold were at a desk, one had large shoulder pauldrons making the armor look even bigger.

Paperwork piled about the desk with an ink pot slightly spilled to one side, one man had a large red feather quill and was writing something down talking to a peddler, the other man stood just behind him holding a large tower shield which was also white with gold trim.

Lore looked to Kimba concerned then approached the desk as the man addressed them in a heralding voice.

"Halt, what brings you to Paladins Reach?", he said, the man was handsome with a wide chin and chiseled featured, his blue eyes contrasted with his white skin and short light hair, he looked at Kimba and she blushed turning away.

"I'm Lore Cast Pendragon, and this is Kimba Kindheart, we just came from the Iron halls where we slayed the creeping dark, after battling with Guldamere's forces in the living forest, I humbly request to speak with the king of Paladins Reach, I'm afraid it's of utmost importance", Lore said.

The handsome Paladin looked at him with his mouth open and one eyebrow cocked, the paladin replied in a drawn-out tone, "right", looking Lore up and down.

"You must be another one of the theatre troop then", he said as he wrote their names down and pointed them back toward a door in the stone next to the larger gate behind them.

"You can find the theatre in the upper region to the right of the keep", he said dismissively.

Kimba began to correct him but Lore just raised a hand, "thank you ah, I didn't catch your name sir knight", Lore said.

"He is his royal highness prince Link Lionheart", his companion answered, "I apologize, most people who travel to Paladins Reach know him", he said.

"Why is the prince of Paladins Reach taking names at the gate?", Kimba asked, the prince waved a hand at his companion before he could speak for him again, "it's ok Vince, I'm perfectly capable of answering the lady", Link said.

Vince gave a little bow and a stepped back.

"I am the prince, but I am also castellan of the city guard, a man needs work to keep him occupied lest he grow weak and weary", Link explained.

"This is my second in command and close friend Vincent Vanguard", Vincent was a head taller than link, he had brown hair and rounder features, though still had the same chiseled face and broad chin.

"It's a pleasure to meet one so beautiful miss Kindheart", Vince said with a slight bow, taking Kimba's hand, he kissed it then looked up at her with a cheeky smile, Kimba forget to retract her hand looking like a stunned fish, her face went beet red and all she could do was make slight murmuring sounds.

"Come on Vincent, you've petrified the poor girl, how many times have I told you not to come on so boldly", Link said.

Lore breathed a sigh and took Kimba's hand pulling her toward the door, "thank you gentleman, I'm sure we'll be seeing you again soon", Lore said as he dragged Kimba through the door.

Paladins Reach was lit by sunlight, a stark difference to the badlands which surrounded the rest of the continent, they walked into the city to see parade flags crossing a cobblestoned street, the city was clean and bright.

The people bustled around between buildings, shops lined the main throughfare, leading to the gates of the keep which towered over the rest of the city, to the right of the keep was a large building that resembled a church organ.

An angelic choir echoed out from it radiating over the city in soothing melodic tones.

"That must be the theatre", Kimba said grabbing Lore's hand and pulling him, "can we please visit it?", Kimba said jumping up and down in excitement.

"I don't see why not, I'm actually curious how this city looks so, and not, well", Lore said trying to find the words to describe the rest of the Thalaria.

"Dark", Kimba said helping him find his words, "yes, dark", Lore responded, "but first we have to visit the keep and introduce ourselves to whichever lord resigns over this place", Lore said as they made their way up the thoroughfare.

They passed shops and friendly locals; Sentinel guards patrolled the city as they clanged past in silver armor.

Paladins Reach seemed to be the safest place in all Thalaria with its monumental high walls and well armored troops.

Lore and Kimba found themselves in front of a large white marble staircase leading to a bridge that spanned a moat surrounding the central keep, the keep stood almost as tall as the front gate of the city with its own large wooden door, there was a smaller door carved into it guarded by two sentinels with pikes and silver suits of armor, they crossed the pikes over the door as they approached.

"We request an audience to see the king of Paladins Reach, it is a matter of grave importance", Lore said in a commanding tone slightly enhanced by magic.

The two sentinel guards looked at each other than one of them responded, "typically you would write a letter to the city speaker who would make a request on your behalf to see his majesty, you're not from around here are you", the guards voice was heavily muffled by his helm.

Lore raised a bushy eyebrow at him, "if you could tell him Lore Casta Pendragon requests an audience at his soonest convenience, I would be quite appreciative".

The guard stayed silent for a few moments, his face was hidden in his helm but Lore could tell he was trying to figure out if Lore was making a joke or not, the other guard huffed, "if your Lore Casta Pendragon, then show us some magic", he said sarcastically, "yeah, show us what you can do, all mighty wizard".

Lore looked at Kimba then shrugged taking a few steps back, with a flourish of his robe he put his fists together, "very well, how's this", Lore said raising an arm to the sky extending his fingers wide, he grabbed his elbow with his other hand and planted his legs firmly, sparks began to shoot from his palm five meters high then bounced off the ground before disappearing.

The guards began to clap their armored hands together, "that's a nice trick, please wait here", the guard tapped on the wooden door and a small boy in formal dress took a message from him, the door closed and the guard retook his position at the door without saying a word.

They waited for what seemed to be a long time until the boy returned, "the king will see you now", he said and the guards opened the door, "good luck wizard", the guard said sarcastically as Lore passed.

The keep was made of white marble with gold trim, the kings blue and gold standard lined the halls with the gold lion symbol of his house on it, Kimba's mouth was wide looking around,

by Lore Casta Pendragon

she'd never seen extravagance like this, they walked on a red carpet leading to the throne passing lines of sentinel guards.

Six paladins stood on the stairs leading up to the throne, Link and Vince were standing either side of the king, the red carpet stopped at the bottom of the stairs so they stopped there.

The king of Paladins Reach sat on his throne, his bulky paladian armor adorned with the golden lion, a helm the shape of a lion's head also made of gold sat on a stool beside him, he had short silver hair, indicating his advanced age, but he had chiseled features which made him look strong and youthful despite the grey in his short cut hair and goatee.

"Follow my lead", Lore whispered to Kimba, she nodded as a caller announced them in a posh voice, "the lady Kimba Kindheart", Kimba gave a slight curtsy to the king.

"The honored…", the caller trailed off unenthusiastically and rolled his eyes, "Lore Casta Pendragon", Lore gave a slight bow never taking his eyes away from the king, "his royal majesty, the king of Paladins Reach, Locke Lionheart", the caller said.

The king waved the caller away and drummed his fingers on the arm of his throne, "so master Pendragon, what's this matter that was so urgent that it couldn't wait", the king said loudly, a tone of command in his voice that could only be acquired from years of rule.

"Nothing less than the very fate of all Thalaria", Lore replied, Locke learned forward in his chair and the people in his court began to whisper, Lore noted that he now had the attention of the entire court so he went on.

"The lich Guldamere is hunting for a source of great power, should he succeed, there will be no power left capable of stopping him, I believe this land may contain a fragment of that power, there is no doubt in my mind that he will stop at nothing to obtain it and that his ambition will eventually bring his forces here", Lore explained, murmurs could be heard throughout the court.

"I can assure you lord Pendragon, Paladins Reach is safe, Guldamere and his religious soldiers are not welcome in Paladin's reach, any attempts he has ever made have resulted in failure, nor do I see any reason to take the word of man claiming to be a wizard who's blatant use of chaos magic decimated the population of the world in the last age, in fact this is the most foolhardy attempt on my life yet and it shows the desperation our enemy must feel, if he hired such a bumbling idiot to make an attempt on my life", Locke began to shout as he signaled to his men.

They dropped their pikes horizontally toward them marching in, they surrounded Lore and Kimba, Lore calmly placed his fists together under his robe, Kimba saw what he was doing and shook her head speaking up.

by Lore Casta Pendragon

"A fabrication made up by Guldamere himself to frame Lore Casta Pendragon for the cataclysm he himself initiated, after which he imprisoned him behind a magic seal for five hundred years!", She shouted, which was followed by more murmurs throughout the court.

"What proof do you have of these claims", the king shouted, Kimba's head went to her feet, "I don't have much, just a tale to tell, but I have travelled from Necropyre to the crater of Mount Muse, where I freed Master Pendragon, to the living forest where we battled Guldamere's forces at the temple of the Aikitai, where my father Kamdar and our friends were slain in battle, we managed to escape to the Iron halls, where we fought and defeated a nightmare creature called the creeping dark which held them hostage underground, a creature sent to them by Guldamere himself, there they gave me, this", Kimba said pulling the parchment from her enchanted sleeve and holding it out to the king.

Locke signaled the boy from the door earlier and he took the parchment from Kimba and give it to Locke, bowing low and he backed away.

Locke read the parchment then handed it to Link who also read through it.

"Stand down", Link ordered his men, they raised their pikes and marched back in formation, "so what you say is true, you truly are the legendary wizard Pendragon?", Locke said.

"The very same", Lore responded, "I apologize Master Pendragon, Guldamere and his inner circle have been relentless in their attempts on my life, I took your meeting as another assassination plot, even if you were telling the truth, a man of your reputation could have very well destroyed my entire kingdom with chaos magic", Locke said.

"I am not the herald of doom who destroyed the world in the stories, I'm afraid I'm just a humble conjurer", Lore replied with a chuckle.

The king signaled to some ladies in waiting, "please make our guests welcome, they may stay here in the keep for as long as they need", Locke said, they bowed then scurried off quickly.

"Thank you, lord Lionheart,", Kimba said, "you must be weary from your long journey, enjoy some time to rest, I'll summon you to the hall later once I'm done here", Locke said waving the next person forward to address his court.

Lore and Kimba were escorted by two sentinel knights to their rooms in the castle tower, Kimba's room was extravagant with large tapestries, expensive rugs and furniture, the bed was the size of a small house and a large balcony extended around it overlooking the city, after checking out the view she laid down on the bed, it was so soft, she couldn't remember the last time she had rested in a bed, as she drifted off to sleep she thought about Felix and Ailyn and wondered if they were still alive.

Lore's room was located at the top of the tower, it had windows on all four sides and a bookcase full of books, mostly histories of Paladins Reach, he pulled down a book and laid

down, the book recounted the many battles against Guldamere's forces and an object they called the paladins heart, an artifact of chaos magic which erected a barrier over the lands around Paladins Reach.

It was most potent around the town and was instrumental in the defense of Paladins Reach.

"It nullified the dark magic Guldamere used to revive dead soldiers, it has to be the missing power, what else could it be", Lore thought to himself, he yawned and rest soon found him.

Guldamere sat at his throne, Silus came into the cathedral, his boot heals echoes on the floor as he approached, he kneeled before Guldamere as a raven flew in carrying a message, it landed on Guldamere's shoulder, he raised a boney skeletal hand and the bird spoke.

"The prisoners of the pit have revolted, the pit warden was defeated by Ailyn Allheart and his father Aethor, they've formed an alliance under the Allheart's and raised their own standard, they are in open rebellion against the church of the god feared, Ailyn Allheart possesses the power shard from the living forest".

Guldamere stood clenching his boney fingers around the bird strangling it, the raven dissolved into black smoke.

He calmed himself then placed his hands together and the black miasma reformed back into the raven.

"It seems your talents are needed, collect the shard for me", the lich said in a scratchy dead voice, the raven flew off, Silus looked up as the bird flew from the cathedral window.

"Torturing the boy wasn't enough to activate the latent power within him, fortunately we know where it is now, I will lead my forces toward their last know location and squash this rebellion before it gains strength", the lich said.

"My lord", Silus interrupted, Guldamere looked down at Silus, "what is it?", he croaked.

"Messages have been coming out from the Iron Halls, it seems the creeping dark was defeated by none other than Lore Casta Pendragon with the help of the Kindheart girl and the dwarves, they were last seen headed east", Silus said.

The lich cackles in response, "the creeping dark is eternal, they may have defeated it temporarily but it will crawl out of the abyss again in due time", Guldamere said.

Silus shuddered at the thought, he was not afraid of anything, in fact most people feared him more than any nightmare creature, but the thought of the creeping dark sent chills down his spine.

                                                    by Lore Casta Pendragon

"As for Lore Casta Pendragon and his new pet, they'll no doubt seek shelter at Paladins Reach, Petricus and my forces will accompany you, take a few phylacteries to Paladins Reach and make sure Lore Casta Pendragon does not obtain the power before we do", the lich commanded.

"Yes, my lord", Silus bowed and then turned to leave.

Petricus Postmortus was waiting just outside, "our orders?", He asked, "we're marching on Paladin's reach", Silus said, "it's about time", Petricus replied with a smile kicking up his spear with his foot.

Chapter Twelve

The Battle of Torins well

Aylin and his friends decided to head northeast, it seemed the best direction to head as none of them wanted to be anywhere near Necropyre or the pit, their heading, Paladins Reach.

As they were walking, Wynn moved up beside Ailyn and Aethor, "the nightmare creatures have been following us, they're growing in number", Wynn said concerned.

"It's eerie, usually they just attack blindly, I've not seen them fear away from anything", Aethor added, Shin moved up beside them.

"It's because we are numbered in the hundreds, they're staying back to pick off the weak and elderly first like predators, it would be best to have them travel closer to the middle of the line", Shin suggested.

Ailyn dropped back and gave the command, they stopped and waited for the old, young and the feeble to make their way to the center of the line, then continued onward, Fyorn was moving slowly, dwarves had amazing endurance but due to their short legs, they weren't overly fast.

A few other dwarves ended up at the rear of the line and started to fall behind, Fyorn stayed back with them, he looked around and noticed a long-barbed tail moving behind a rock.

"Did ye see that, did anybody see that", Fyorn said, he lifted the dual war hammers, nobody else took any notice until a barghast climbed over a rock, its toothy protruding jaw was dripping with drool, it let out a roar and Fyorn almost jumped out of his skin.

The dwarves around him brandished their weapons and started yelling at the beast, "yar, ye beast begone wit ye", "Begone foul creature", they shouted.

The barghast started to shy away, until another two showed up on the other side of them, the dwarves turned to face them and the beasts roared loudly, Fyorn and the dwarves backed into each other, they were surrounded and had fallen too far behind.

The first barghast which was clearly the alpha due to it being slightly larger than the others, pounced at Fyorn, he brought both hammers to bear and hit the creature on the side knocking it away, it roared as it tumbled across the ground.

The other two barghast took the first ones lead and both leaped in to attack, two dwarves sunk pickaxes into the first beast to reach them felling it, the second grabbed hold of one dwarf's leg and began dragging him away.

                              by Lore Casta Pendragon

Ailyn and his companions heard the dwarf's cry and started running back to help them, the large barghast got up and ran at Fyorn, Fyorn tried an overhead strike with one hammer to squash the beast flat, but it leaped behind him, its barbed tail hooked into his shoulder as he turned.

Fyorn cried out in pain as the barb stuck, the beast tried to run pulling Fyorn off his feet, but he held onto his heavy iron war hammers dragging them behind, grunting at the tearing barb in his shoulder.

The beast was slow to move with the added weight, the other dwarves grabbed onto the dwarf being dragged by the leg and pulled back, the beast pulled hard, like playing a game of tug-o-war.

Ailyn's men caught up to them and stabbed at the barghast killing it, the alpha barghast pulled Fyorn uphill, its muscular frame bulging with the effort, Brawn came running down, a longsword in hand and severed its tail with one swing.

Its tailed flipped around like some kind of serpent as it growled in pain, it turned and slashed at Brawn with its front claws, Brawn swung the longsword and connected slashing a gash between a front claw.

The longsword was knocked from Brawn's hand and clanged to the ground, the barghast was bleeding heavily, it's breaths rapid, a look of visceral hatred in its eyes as it let out a mighty roar.

Fyorn found his feet as the barghast leaped on top of Brawn, it thrashed and snapped almost taking off his arm, Brawn took a handful of dirt and rubbed it into the beasts four eyes then kicked into its stomach with both legs.

He jumped on its back and wrapped his arms around its neck, the beast fell down on its side thrashing wildly.

Brawn got a gash from the creatures back legs kicking and winced in pain, but he wouldn't let go, Fyorn walked up hammers in hand.

"Ye thought ye had me beasty, but it takes more than that to fell a dwarf!", he yelled.

Brawn's eyes went wide as Fyorn raised the hammers, Brawn released the beast and rolled away as Fyorn brought the hammers down, they smashed into the beast's prone side with earth shattering force, blood and viscera exploded out in every direction covering Fyorn and Brawn in blood and gore.

They heard the sound of hooves feet running as the nightmare creatures observing the battle hoping for an easy meal retreated.

                              by Lore Casta Pendragon

Brawn got to his feet, holding his wounds, he looked at Fyorn who looked back at him picking guts from his clothing, they both pointed and laughed heartily at each other as Ailyn and the others caught up only to be greeted by a vision of bloody gore.

"What happened?", Ailyn said astonished, "it's alright lad, we took care of it, I don't think the nightmare creatures will be attacking again any time soon", Fyorn chuckled flicking guts from his hammer.

Cresting a hill, a small town came into view surrounded by a deep fast running river, as Ailyn approached, he noticed the villagers had set up makeshift barricades, they were shabby and looked to have been erected in a hurry, a man stuck a pitch fork through a gap and addressed him.

"Bandits!", He shouted, "leave us be, we're just a small village, not worth the plundering", the man said.

Ailyn addressed the man in turn, "we're not bandits, we're refugees from Necropyre, we escaped the warden of the pit and need a place to rest and tend to our wounded", Ailyn explained.

"Then look somewhere else", the stubborn old man snapped at him, "come now Eldar, we should welcome them, they've already suffered enough", a voice sang out from behind the barrier, it was soft and feminine.

After some time arguing behind the wall the barrier was dragged back, "err, but only for the day, we ain't got the food to feed them all", Eldar said.

Ailyn walked up and was greeted by the most beautiful woman he'd ever seen, she was tall and thin, her long black hair was slightly curled and looked to be made of silk, she wore a black dress that clung to her figure, her lips were painted red, her eyes were light blue and resembled a cat's eyes.

Ailyn's mouth hung open as she approached him, "I'm Violet Valentine, I can help tend to your wounded if you like", she said, "yeah, yes, please", Ailyn said mouth agape.

Violet giggled and linked her arm with his as she walked him into the town, "we'll get your wounded set up at Torins Well inn, it's the big building over there on the right", Violet said, Ailyn didn't know what to say, he was intoxicated by her, the smell of her perfume, the way she walked as if she glided with her feet slightly crossing over with each step, her hips moving from side to side.

"Seems your boy, lost his tongue", Wynn jabbed at Aethor who look at Ailyn with concern, "can you blame him", Shin replied bumping into the back of their shoulders as he pushed through them, Gear waved for the rest of their men to follow as they entered the gate.

        by Lore Casta Pendragon

They filled the town erecting makeshift tents, bedding, hammocks and shelters, the night was warm, so most just set up to sleep on the street.

The bottom floor of the Inn was packed with people, so much so that you couldn't walk without jostling someone, the loft made into a makeshift hospital where violet and a few of the older women of the village tended to their wounded.

Violet finished bandaging Fyorn's shoulder and he took her hand in his, "thank ye kindly miss Valentine, you sure are a welcomed site for tired eyes", he said smiling at her with a big grin.

Ailyn watched her sitting on a makeshift bed opposite him and rolled his eyes, a pang of jealousy hit him, though he knew it was illogical.

Violet walked over to him and placed a tray of medical supplies directly in front of him at his feet, she gave him a clear line of sight down the front of her dress and she bent down, her breasts were full with a nice amount of cleavage.

Violet looked him dead in the eye as she rose, a cheeky smile on her face, "she did that deliberately", Ailyn thought to himself, he made an audible gulping sound and was immediately embarrassed by it.

Violet grabbed a rag and soaked it in alcohol, wiping the cut above his eye, Ailyn could not stop staring at her, until he realized he hadn't said anything since he saw her, then cleared his throat.

"I'm Ailyn Allheart, it's a pleasure to meet you miss Valentine", he said, "oh, so he does speak", she teased looking him in the eye for a brief moment, "I was beginning to think you were a mute", her voice was breathy and sweet, Ailyn felt his whole body relax listening to her.

"I have to admit, you caught me off guard, I didn't expect to see someone like you in a small village like this, it's dangerous out here", Ailyn explained, "I didn't expect to find such a handsome man out here either", she said grabbing onto his arm, "mmm you have nice arms Ailyn", "oh th-thank you, you're not too bad yourself", Ailyn stammered out awkwardly.

Violet leaned in closer to his face padding at the cut above his eye, she looked directly into his eyes as she did this and Ailyn went weak all over, the smell of her perfume hit him again and the entire world vanished.

All he could see was her face smiling at him mischievously, "okay all done", violet said as she stood up, Ailyn was violently shaken from his trance as she turned to go to tend to Wynn, Ailyn stared at her behind as she walked away, she looked back at him and shot him a smirk and shrugged one arm.

Aethor came up and sat beside him, "have you finished being seen to", Aethor asked, he was covered in bandages, "a woman like that can make or break a man Ailyn", Aethor said.

Ailyn looked at him embarrassed, "I wasn't", Ailyn started, but Aethor stopped him, "have your fun with her, but remember she isn't yours until she's said the words herself, come take a walk with me", Aethor said with an amused smile.

They walked outside through the crowded inn, "there are things you should know about women, son", Aethor said awkwardly, he then discussed in great detail what is expected of a man as they walked around the village.

Ailyn's face went beet red and he didn't say a word the entire time, when they got back to the inn Aethor placed a hand on Ailyn's shoulder, "I wish your mother was here to see how much you've grown", Aethor said as he walked inside, he was greeted by the cheering drunken crowd, he threw his hands up and joined the fray.

Ailyn stood there soaking in everything his father had just told him then started walking down toward the river to wash his face, it was hot and flushed, he got on his knees and bent down swooping the water in his hands, washing his face clean.

As he got up, he felt a caress on the back of his shoulders, "I was looking for you", Violet's breathy voice said from behind him, Ailyn's heart skipped a few beats as he turned to her, she gave a slight giggle as she drew a finger across his jawline, Ailyn took a step backward, his heart was racing.

"Care to join me?", Ailyn said offering her his arm, she gave him a playful look that said sounds like fun without having to say a word.

They walked down by the river bank until they found a spot in the moonlight beneath a wisteria tree, she tucked her dress beneath her as she sat down.

"So, how'd you end up in Torins Well?", Ailyn asked, Violet looked down, her smile faded.

"My family was attacked by nightmare creatures on the road when I was younger, I was left all alone, I found work here at the Torins well Inn and I've been here ever since", she said smiling at him.

"I'm sorry, I lost my family too, I only just reunited with my father when I found him in the pit, I had no idea he was still alive until recently", Ailyn explained, when he looked back at her she was staring at him intently.

"Your friends told me about how you defeated the pit warden", she said moving closer to him, "well it wasn't just me, my father, Aethor, helped a lot", Ailyn said moving backward and trailing off.

Violet advanced on him like some kind of predator, she crawled on top of him and kissed him letting out a whimper as their lips came together, it was then that Ailyn lost all control, taking her in his arms.

by Lore Casta Pendragon

Several hours later, they laid semi naked by the river bank, the moonlight shined over the water as they watched the fish jumping to reach it.

Violet drew circles on Ailyn's chest with her finger, "not too bad for a first timer", Violet giggled at him.

"Well, I had a very long and awkward pep talk beforehand", Ailyn laughed, she cuddled in closer to him and he sat up.

"Hold on I need to use the bathroom", he said as he got up and walked upstream a bit until he could no longer see her and the branches of a wisteria tree acted as a natural curtain.

He finished relieving himself, when he heard the sound of steel hitting steel, he turned to see two soldiers sneaking up behind him swords drawn, when they saw him turn, they ran at him.

Realizing how vulnerable he was unarmed and half naked he dived into the water, it carried him downstream faster than the soldiers could run, he scrambled back up the river bank and grabbed his clothes, Violet was nowhere to be seen and he saw smoke rising from the village.

He ran toward the village both soldiers in pursuit, "Violet!", He called over and over but he couldn't find her, as he approached the village, he saw his men were fighting.

Three soldiers set fire to a building with the two just behind him catching up, he dropped his clothes and focused, he knew they were in for a fight.

The soldiers came at him wielding short swords, he moved toward the first as the soldier slashed from the right, Ailyn grabbed him at the wrist, he slid his feet under the arm then ducked his hips below him, the soldier rolled over Ailyn's back and landed on the ground with a thud.

Ailyn turned the blade back toward the soldier and stabbed it into his throat, another soldier joined in and Ailyn skipped backward luring in and narrowly avoiding their attacks.

He used his sugiashi entering step to dash between them, they missed and almost struck each other when Ailyn kicked one in the chest plate, making him stumble backward.

Ailyn grabbed the soldier's sword arm at the wrist, he moved underneath it in a spinning motion disappearing behind as the sword of the other soldier almost stabbed him in the back.

He pulled the soldiers arm low and grabbed him by the back of the neck, Ailyn sprung back up and pulled the arm up over the soldiers back disarming him while throwing the soldier forward into his companion.

　　　　　　　by Lore Casta Pendragon

Ailyn directed the sword straight at a chink in his opponent's armor and it pierced through, he stomped on the other soldier's face crimping the men's helmet over his eyes as he dashed toward the town, his men might have been fighting in rags, but they were driving the Necropyrian soldiers back.

Years of working the pit had made Ailyn's men strong, stronger than the average soldier, a retreat horn sounded and the Necropyrian soldiers fell back into a lined formation, Wynn finished one off with a swing of his claymore knocking him from his feet as Ailyn approached.

The village was a haze of smoke and fire, "how did they find us so quickly?", Ailyn asked his friends, "might have been someone from the village", Brawn said, "we can't take on a fully armored army in rags", Aethor said, "then we'll need to retreat, get the slow and feeble out first, we'll hold them as long as we can", Ailyn said.

The Necropyrian line opened up and they started to move back as the fire light dimmed and turned green, the crackling of wood turned to silence as dark shadows grew out from the darkness, black smokey miasma crept in as Guldamere walked forward from the dark.

"So, Ailyn Allheart, we meet again", the lich said in a dead raspy voice, "it seems I underestimated just how much of a nuisance you were going to be", Ailyn froze to the spot it felt like ice was in his veins.

The lich's golden pupils fixed on him, the dark black of his eyes stared into him, half his face was missing giving him the look of a walking corpse, "you have something of mine Ailyn, something I will be taking from you", the lich croaked.

Ailyn couldn't breathe, he was terrified, Aethor stood in front of him, "you'll have to get through me first, you damned corpse", Aethor yelled defiantly, he bounced left to right in his martial stance, Fyorn, Brawn, Wynn and even old man Gear walked forward holding their weapons.

"Then I'll show you why they call me the god feared", Guldamere cackled, he put his hands together in prayer then extended his boney hand toward a cemetery just outside the village behind a small wooden fence by the ruins of a church.

The cemetery grounds erupted as the lich cackled shrouding himself and his forces in black smoke, the dead rose from the graves, ghouls and nightmare creatures ran out at them from the dark, a pickaxe was thrown into one of the ghouls and it exploded into a shower of flying bone and rotted flesh, piercing some of Ailyn's men with shards of bone.

They looked to Ailyn whose eyes went wide, "we can't fight this, retreat", Ailyn yelled and they turned to run as the ghouls pursued them, every now and then a ghoul would catch up to a slow man and began ripping at his flash with boney hands, some people would get the best of a ghoul only to be killed by exploding pieces of bone.

          by Lore Casta Pendragon

They reached the end of the village and crossed a small wooden bridge, Fyorn turned and waited for everyone to cross, "C'mon Fyorn we gotta go", Brawn called after him, "keep going lad, I've got this", Fyorn said, "Rancid bastards, be gone!", Fyorn cried out.

As the ghouls started running across, he brought the hammers down shattering the wood to splinters, the ghouls were dropped into the fast-running waters and washed downstream.

The ghouls quickly realized they were unable to cross after a few tried and were washed down river, "no time to stand on ceremony, let's move", Aethor called.

Ailyn realized he hadn't seen Shin with them, "has anybody seen Shin-son?", Ailyn said, he looked back over the village hoping to find signs of Violet as well.

Aethor grabbed him by the arm and dragged him away, they ran into the night as the village of Torins Well burned behind them, Ailyn saw Guldamere appearing out of the dark and smoke standing there on the other side of the river bank before he disappeared back into the dark.

Ailyn and his companions retreated northeast, eventually making their way to a cliff face overlooking the crater of Mount Muse, his men were exhausted having run through the night, several of his men fell behind and were lost, being too weak, wounded or drunk to continue.

The morning sun stung Ailyn's eyes at it rose over the horizon, the undead ghouls were relentless in their pursuit.

Brawn, Fyorn and Aethor held up the rear as best they could, pushing people forward and fighting off the undead as they fled from Guldamere's army on their heels.

Ailyn feared the worst, he slumped down exhausted at the edge of the cliff face overlooking the edge, he remembered looking down at the edge of the pit, when his despair felt too much to bear, when he first learned that Aethor was still alive.

"So, this is it then", Ailyn said.

Gear came up and sat beside him, he looked haggard, but just making it through that night for someone of his advanced age was nothing less than miraculous.

Gear looked out over the valley, the morning sun giving a gentle warmth, Ailyn was inspired by the man's resolve at overcoming all the odds and he felt a little stronger just being next to him.

"Lord Ailyn", Gear said quietly, "Gear", Ailyn responded, "my old bones can't take much more of this", Gear said, his eyes still looking over the valley, "don't say that, you didn't survive all those years in the pit to give up now", Ailyn said.

"Give up no, never give up, fight against the darkness, fight against the rising dawn, fight for every day, for every moment, fight with everything you have and fight for your people", Gear said, he paused then looked at Ailyn.

"Some of us have decided that we won't survive the retreat to Paladins Reach, it's a long journey, we'll stay behind and draw Guldamere's forces away", Gear said facing him.

"No, you can't, that'd be suicide", Ailyn said, "we thought as much, but better for us, instead of falling behind and dying anyway, we'll fight so that others can live, like how you fought for us against that monster in the pit, we had all resigned ourselves to thinking that we'd die there, at least you gave this old man one last look at the sun", Gear said looking back over the valley.

Ailyn tried to argue but Gear interrupted him.

"They'll be on us soon, take the ridge southeast and take the long way round, we'll take the shorter track to the north and lure them away, they won't know where you've gone, be careful of ravens, the dark one uses them as his eyes", Gear said, he stood up, Ailyn stood also, they held arms with a look of mutual admiration then Gear rallied the men.

The older men and women that were left stayed behind and waited for Guldamere's army to get closer while Ailyn and his companions moved off down the southeastern road, not long after they had left, Gear stood on the northeastern road waiting.

Black fog started to roll in, it coalesced into a shape, Guldamere himself walked out from it followed by lines of soldiers and acolytes.

"Finally ready to embrace your fate", the lich said, Gear retorted in turn as loud as his old lungs could yell, "it's about time you took your place in the abyss, Lord of the spurned".

Up on the ridge above several men pushed down on branches and leveraged a huge bounder, it fell down the cliff face and crumpled into thousands of smaller boulders, the lich puffed into black smoke, a large raven flew out of it, while a dozen men around him were knocked from the cliff face.

The raven flew fast in front of his remaining men and exploded into the ground in a cloud of black smoke.

The lich reappeared, giving them a wry smile, "wipe them out and find the boy", he ordered.

Gear smiled and gave the signal for his troops to run, Guldamere took the bait and chased after them.

The slight bit of rest they had gave them enough steam to keep a steady pace, but one after another they were picked off, one by a fireball, another by an arrow, some fell behind and the lich drained them of life leaving only a husk.

by Lore Casta Pendragon

Growing tired of chasing them, Guldamere held out a hand, thick black miasma curled into a small statue, a phylactery in the shape of a werewolf, he threw it in front of him and a cloud of black miasma formed, out of it a werewolf appeared running at full pace.

It pounced on an elderly woman crushing and slicing her before pouncing on another tearing into them.

Gear looked around but there was no one else with him, he ran for his life but the beast closed in, he ran into a clearing and stood on the edge of a cliff face, realizing there was nowhere else to go he turned to see the werewolf charging down the path at him, Gear walked back to the ledge and opened his arms wide closing his eyes, the beast pounced at him, taking them both off the edge.

Ailyn could hear the battle and the screams from the southeast road, he looked back concerned, he desperately wanted to go back and save them, but he knew if he did, his companions would follow and they would all perish, Aethor put a hand on his shoulder, "there's nothing you can do now, let's go", he said sadly pushing Ailyn onward.

They made their way around the outer edge of the crater of Mount Muse until they came to the eastern most edge, they took the road north crossing a large river bridge.

Over the next hill the landscape began to change, large tuffs of grass began to appear then over another hill, Paladins Reach came into view, rolling hills of grassland and at its center a large castle made of white stone.

Ailyn stopped in his tracks admiring the view, he'd never seen anything like this, it felt like this was the way things were supposed to be, not the plagued blasted lands he was used to, a feeling of relief washed over him, Aethor tapped Ailyn on the shoulder and pointed as he walked past, they pressed on to the castle gate.

As they approached a horn sounded, several men on horseback wearing bulky white and gold armor wielding lances followed by lines of sentinel guards in suits of silver armor marched toward them, Ailyn held up a fist and his men stopped, he extended his arm one way and the other and they lined up in formation as if they had already practiced the maneuver.

Ailyn felt pride that his companions trusted his judgements, the soldiers of Paladins Reach approached them and split into a lined formation, holding their weapons high, they looked to be duplicates of each other, a testament to their training.

One paladin wearing elaborate white and gold armor with large shoulder pauldrons climbed down from his horse and took off his helm, he was large and masculine, with chiseled features.

Ailyn walked out to meet him, "I am Link Lionheart, you and your army are trespassing on the Reach, turn back or else", Link shouted in a commanding tone.

Vince was not far behind him and his large war horse moved in anticipation of a fight.

"I'm Ailyn Allheart, we're fleeing pursuit of Guldamere's forces after escaping from the pit in Necropyre, I humbly beg you to allow us refuge in your city", Ailyn said dropping to a knee.

His men followed suit, bowing their heads before the Paladins of the reach, "send word to the king", Link said to Vince, Vince nodded and turned his horse, galloping back toward the Reach.

"If it were up to me, I'd not turn you away, but my father, my king, is a cautious man, he'll decide your fate", Link explained, "I understand, but please do so quickly, Guldamere's forces will not be far behind us", Ailyn said rising to his feet, his men also followed suit.

"Not to worry Ailyn, the church of the god feared will not march on Paladins Reach, at least they won't unless they want another ass kicking", Link said looking at his men, they all laughed and jeered.

"You look like you've been through hell already, I can't imagine what you've suffered in that pit, you're lucky to be alive, you're probably the first ones to ever escape and live to tell the tale", Link said.

"We were fortunate, we revolted and managed to defeat the pit warden", Ailyn explained, Link looked at him in utter shock, "you defeated that monster?", "Truly a feat in of itself, then you managed to make it all the way here on foot while being pursued by the forces of Necropyre?", "That is a story I have to hear", Link said impressed.

Vince made his way to the keep, he jumped off his horse and ran into the hall, "your highness", Vince said going to one knee before the king, "what is it, sir Vanguard", Locke said, "it's not an approaching army as we had suspected, they're refugees escaping the pit in Necropyre", Vince explained.

"Refugees?", Locke replied, "well this complicates things, bring their leader to me for an audience", Locke commanded, "yes my lord", Vince said bowing his head, he got to his feet and raced out to his horse, galloping back to the waiting armies outside.

"This is my father, Aethor and my friends, Fyorn, Brawn and Wynn", Ailyn introduced his friends.

by Lore Casta Pendragon

"They also fought against the pit warden", he said, "if by fight you mean got flung like fodder into the pit", Brawn laughed, "pleasure is mine, no need to be bashful, anyone who can stand up to one of Guldamere's generals is a hero to me", Link said.

They all stood a little straighter for the compliment.

Vince galloped back on his horse and addressed Ailyn directly, "the king requests an audience", he said offering his hand, Ailyn was hesitant at first, but Link gave him a reassuring smile so he took Vince's hand, he helped pull him up onto the large war horse, it was taller than Ailyn on four legs, with fur lining its feet, it was sweaty and muscular.

"Take good care of our guest Vincent, these men are quite fond of him", Link said with a wink as he turned back, conversing with Aethor, "Yar!", Vince said and the horse sprinted off, Ailyn jerked back from the acceleration almost falling off the back.

Ailyn had never seen anything so large or impressive, the castle stood taller than the living forest, the gates alone where just as tall as the trees he'd known as a child, he couldn't help but look up in wonder at the tall towers and buildings, when they reached the keep Ailyn's mouth fell open in awe.

Vince escorted Ailyn inside to the hall where the king was waiting, the hall was lined by sentinel guards, they reached the end of a red carpet before the king and Vince took a knee urging Ailyn to do the same, he followed Vince's lead and bowed his head.

"Welcome, Ailyn Allheart to Paladins Reach, tell me why have you've fled here of all places", the king said, Ailyn lifted his head, "my companions and I escaped the pit in Necropyre after staging a revolt, we were then chased by Guldamere's forces eastward, many of our friends died in the pursuit, I humbly beg for sanctuary behind your walls", Ailyn placed his head on the floor to emphasize his words.

"Many times, has Guldamere tried to infiltrate Paladins Reach and each time he has failed, this however, is the first time he's tried to play on my good nature as the paladian king", Locke said, signaling to Vince.

Vince drew a golden sword, grabbing Ailyn roughly and holding it against his throat, "I'm not spy, I swear it!", Ailyn said trying not to get cut by the blade.

"You wandered in from the badlands, claiming to come from Necropyre and you expect us to trust you?", Locke said standing from his throne, "Ailyn!", a familiar voice called from a side door entering the hall, Kimba came running over.

"You know this lad, miss Kindheart?", Locke questioned, "he fought with us at the Aikitai temple in the living forest, he was master Den's ward", Kimba explained.

                                                      by Lore Casta Pendragon

At that Locke gave a signal to Vince and he removed the blade letting Ailyn go, "it seems you've been exonerated Ailyn, I apologize, but we have to be ever vigilant, if we want to protect the kingdom from the church of the god feared", Locke said walking closer.

"It's fine", Ailyn began to say, but he was interrupted by Kimba crashing into him with a big hug, "your alive!".

"We thought you were dead", she said crushing Ailyn slightly, "I thought Guldamere had you too", Ailyn said slightly choking, she let him go.

"Where have you been all this time", Kimba asked, but Ailyn just gave her a pained look, "there will be time to catch up later, for now we have more pressing concerns", Ailyn said turning to Locke, "Guldamere chased us all the way here himself, I have something he wants and I don't think he'll stop until he gets it", Ailyn said.

Locke looked at him concerned, "so you found it before him?", Lore said walking into the hall, a serious look on his face, "Master Pendragon, it's good to see you alive and well", Ailyn said smiling, "did you find it Ailyn?", Lore said walking straight at him, "err, find what?", Ailyn said oblivious.

"The shard of power from the living forest", Lore said becoming impatient, "I found a wisp under the temple, it gave me some sort of power but it only seems to work when I'm in trouble, the pit warden said it was this 'missing power', though", Ailyn said.

Lore shook his head and let out a sigh, "I thought as much", he said turning away, "unfortunately your part of this now boy, the fate of Thalaria depends on the both of us", Lore said turning back.

"What do you mean, what is this power?", Ailyn asked, Kimba perked up and said, "before the cataclysm master Pendragon and Aram Allheart, your ancestor, fought Guldamere at Mount Muse, chaos magic was locked in equilibrium and sealed by three muses, they were living phylacteries of chaos magic that sealed the door between the abyss and the living world, when they were broken Guldamere gained the power of one, Master pendragon the other", she explained.

"Aram died in the cataclysm and without a host for the power to reside in, it shattered, casting shards of itself over the land, I speculated that these green zones were shielded from the cataclysm by shards of this power", Lore added.

"So, the wisp I found was a piece of this phylactery?", Ailyn said, "I assume so", Lore said, "and Guldamere wants the shard himself for power?", Ailyn said, "well, yes", Lore said nodding.

"Isn't he already immortal and all powerful, why does he want it so badly?", Ailyn asked.

"Because he's not completely immortal, he feeds on the living to extend his own life, he took my mother's life, then killed my father at the temple of Aikitai", Kimba said sadly.

                                        by Lore Casta Pendragon

"I'm sorry Kimba, Kamdar was a good man", Ailyn said lowering his head, "now that you have the power with you we cannot allow you to fall into the enemies hands, at the moment I'm at equal strength with Guldamere, which gives us the ability to fight back, should he obtain the shards, he'll gain an unfair advantage, if he takes the remaining power for himself, he'll become too powerful and I fear what will become of Thalaria should that happen", Lore said.

Ailyn then realized the importance and what this meant, between himself and Lore the balance of power stood in their favor, should one of them fall, all would be lost.

"Guldamere has the ability to raise those from the abyss and keep them living a while longer, but it's not permanent and comes at a great cost, every time he opens a portal to the abyss he brings part of it back with him, should he become more powerful, he'll be able to raise people from the abyss who were long dead and with them he'll open the gates to the abyss itself, unfathomable evils will spring forth from that opening and the world will be consumed by darkness", Lore explained.

Ailyn sat on the ground hard, his eyes lit up and he looked at Lore, "does that mean you also can bring back the dead", he asked Lore, Lore shook his head, "no, I cannot, the power I hold has preserved my life and is an extension of the magic that I already possess, I am ashamed to admit but I tried to bring Aram back to life long ago and I failed, there seems to be more to it, Guldamere made a blood pact with the abyss itself and may be helping the creatures of the abyss in exchange for powerful Necromantic power", Lore explained.

"I guess that's why the shard I possess increased my physical abilities, but didn't give me any magical power", Ailyn said.

"Well, this has certainly given me a lot to think about", Locke said, "your highness, we should bring the armies back to the castle, should Guldamere's forces advance on our position it would be good practice to have our troops ready and rested for battle", Vince advised, Locke nodded.

"See it done, you and your men are welcome here, Ailyn, you'll find no better sanctuary in all of Thalaria", Locke said, "thank you, my lord", Ailyn responded.

Vince marched out of the hall, "I should be seeing to my men", Ailyn said running after him, "his men?", Lore and Kimba said confused.

Chapter Thirteen

Safe at last

Link's men were sitting in a circle on the field with Ailyn's, when Ailyn and Vince rode up on the war horse.

"Ah, Ailyn, Aethor was just telling me how you got your ass kicked by a river fish", Link laughed, the men chuckled at his expense as Ailyn dropped down from the horse, Ailyn looked at Aethor who was grinning at him.

"You sure are chummy, having a good time?", Ailyn said pouting, "I'll take this over beating the life out of each other any day", Link said standing, "so what did my liege say", "all forces are to be escorted into the Reach and armed for battle", Vince said.

"This boy has some kind of power that Guldamere wants and his forces are sure to be on their way here to fetch it", Link's face went from smile to frown, "alright, let get moving", he said sternly mounting his horse, "follow me", he said.

The large front gate of the castle opened to let them through, Ailyn's men were sent to the armory for food, rest and were equipped with sentinel armor, a sentinel guard gave a suit of armor to Fyorn, he tried to place a boot on, only to realized it covered his entire leg then threw it away in frustration.

"Little good this will do", he said with a sour expression, "what we be needing is some dwarven armor, that's the good stuff", Fyorn said.

Brawn looked at him confused, "how do we even put this on?", He said getting frustrated, his armor was slightly skewed, his big chest and stomach bulging from the sides, he tried to put a helmet on but it wouldn't fit over his big head and he also threw it in frustration.

Aethor left his armor sitting on the bed, instead he went shirtless and donned some tied tanned pants and leather shoes, he jumped in place a few times then punched at the air, an audible crack sounded out and he smiled.

Link was attending his men on the outer castle wall, "my prince, two figures were seen stumbling toward the castle gate, one of them looks injured", the sentinel guard said, Link dismissed the man then turned toward the gate.

He marched out followed by Vince and a precession of sentinel guards, a stunningly beautiful woman in a black dress was helping a man who looked to be from the Ronin city with his arm over her shoulder, he was limping badly, they collapsed not far from them and Link ran over to them followed by Vince.

                                        by Lore Casta Pendragon

"Be careful Link, it could be a trap", Vince said, Link ignored the warning, he helped the woman to her feet first, "thank you my lord", she said in a breathy feminine voice.

"Please help my friend here, his leg is wounded", she said, "of course, but who are you?", "Why is a beautiful woman like you wandering out in the badlands", Link asked, "I'm Violet Valentine and this is Shin-Son", Violet said, Shin lifted his head to speak, "we were separated from Ailyn's army at Torin's well", Shin said.

"Any friend of Ailyn's is a friend of mine", Link said gesturing to his guards, "help them inside, bring Ailyn to us, Ailyn can vouch for them if their story rings true", Link told them.

Ailyn came into the armory, wearing an Aikitai Gi similar to the one he wore training under master Den.

"It seems someone finally got you to pay attention long enough to show you some of the martial arts", Aethor teased, Ailyn smiled, "you're looking stronger than ever father, your time in the pit hardly affected you at all", Ailyn said.

His admiration for Aethor hadn't faded at all after all that time, "well how about we catch up a little at the training ground", Aethor said with a wicked grin.

Ailyn gulped loudly while nodding his head, he had witnessed his father training when he was growing up and knew the kind of power he possessed, but he remembered master Den and his Aikitai training and was confident in his abilities.

"Do ye think that wise, we could be on the verge of a battle", Fyorn said, "it's been too long, I want to see how strong my son has grown, after seeing how he defeated Warden, my warrior's spirit is calling to be tested", Aethor replied.

He tightened the string on his pants then headed for the training ground just outside of the armory, Ailyn followed his lead stretching his arms as he walked.

"This I gotta see", Brawn said pulling Fyorn with him, they followed them and just like that the entire armory emptied outside, Ailyn and Aethor stood at either end of a circular arena lined with a wooden fence, there was a viewing area on the second floor of the armory which was filled with people.

"It seems I'm not the only one curious about your strength Ailyn, try not to hold back on my part", Aethor said, King Locke Lionheart walked up to the edge of the viewing balcony accompanied by Kimba and Lore, Ailyn took note that Kimba was watching him and he felt his nerves shoot through him adding to the already nervous tension that had built up in the training ground.

"Go Ailyn!", Kimba yelled from the balcony, Ailyn looked up and gave her an awkward thumbs up and a smile, "best not to keep the people waiting", Aethor said, bouncing on his heels, he took his martial form, the intercepting fist, Ailyn's stance closed up, his open palms

by Lore Casta Pendragon

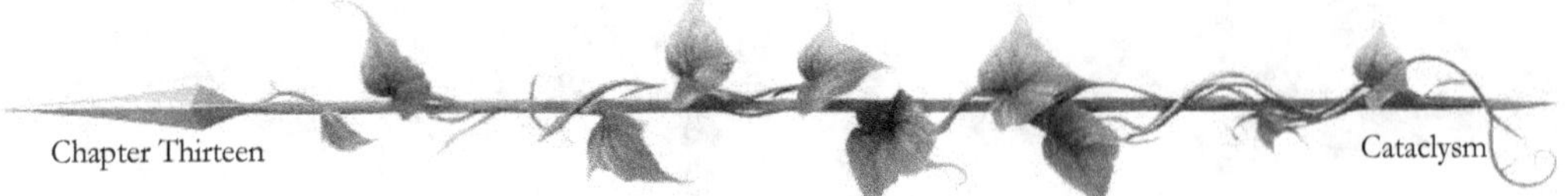

facing Aethor taking his Aikitai stance, the crowd went silent and the two stared at each other for a brief moment.

Aethor made the first move leaping forward with a side kick which Ailyn easily avoided by using his Irimi technique, an entering slide forward.

He placed a hand on Aethor's leg attempting to throw him off balance but Aethor quickly retracted it switching his hips and unleashing a backward kick at Ailyn, Ailyn used sugiashi, skipping backward from the forward foot narrowly avoiding the blow.

Aethor unleashed a barrage of jumping sidekicks from one side to the other, Ailyn mirrored his movements knocking away each kick, his back hit the outer fence as Aethor's kick came in.

Ailyn used his tenkan moving his back leg around as Aethor smashed the large wooden fence railing behind him.

Ailyn followed it up with a back elbow knocking Aethor forward off balance, Aethor used the momentum to jump forward onto a lower rail of the fence he just broke, jumping back toward him with a spinning tornado kick.

Ailyn wasn't expecting the sudden retort and the kick hit him hard on the side of the head, Ailyn rolled with the blow and regained his feet in an instant, the crowd cheered as the two danced around each other.

"Den must have been quite the teacher, he certainly made you good at running away", Aethor teased as he charged forward again.

Ailyn knew Aethor would continue the pressure with powerful ranged kicks, so he closed the distance, as Aethor moved in with a flying kick, Ailyn moved slightly out to the right, now they were face to face.

Aethor punched at Ailyn with such speed that an audible crack whipped past Ailyn's ear, Ailyn knew he couldn't survive a hit like that and dashed forward using Irimi, he raised his forward elbow and knocked Aethor's fist to the side, his elbow meeting Aethor under the jaw, while simultaneously sliding his forward leg behind Aethor's forward leg, Aethor's momentum carried him forward into Ailyn's awaiting elbow, Ailyn's feet planted and Aethor had nowhere to go but backward.

Ailyn was like a wall and Aethor hit his elbow then hit the ground hard, the crowd cheered again.

Aethor wiped blood from his lip and smiled at seeing the red fluid on his hand, Ailyn gasped as he realized his mistake in making his father bleed, Aethor threw his hand to the ground behind his head and frog leaped to his feet, he licked the blood from his lip, his eyes started to burn a familiar red.

"Whoa now, I thought this was a friendly bout?", Ailyn said nervously with his hand ups, Aethor smiled wickedly then leaped forward with incredible speed, he sunk his fist into Ailyn's mid-section knocking the wind out of him and blasting him backward through the railing into a nearby table and chairs, the wood splintered and dust enveloped him, the crowd let out an audible groan.

"Yup, that looked like it hurt", Lore said.

As the dust blew around Aethor's feet he looked straight ahead into the haze, his fist straight out in front of him, he panted heavily, waiting.

Link came up to Locke and whispered something to him, several guards escorted Violet and Shin in, "Ailyn is a little indisposed at this moment it would seem, you might as well stay and watch the show", Locke said to them.

They took a look over the arena to see Aethor standing in the middle, wood splinters and dust exploded out from the far wall of the training ground, Ailyn stood there not so impressed, the cut above his eye had reopened, he had a look of determination on his face.

"That's better, now at least you'll take me seriously", Aethor said, the red in his eyes, burned like a small flame, "your one to talk, you pulled that punch", Ailyn said grinning.

"I've seen you fell a tree in the living forest with that punch before", Ailyn said, Aethor just chuckled.

"I'm not trying to kill you Ailyn, but, I will if you don't take this seriously".

A small flash of red shone in Ailyn's eyes for a moment and Aethor smiled, "not long now", he said to himself.

Ailyn charged at him, he leaped forward, one hand passing over his head the other passing low, he switched his hips as he switched his hands, Aethor didn't know which direction the attack was coming from until it was too late.

Ailyn struck with an elbow high and a fist low, the iron vest technique, a perfect mixture of taisabaki body movement and defensive strikes.

Aethor tried to counter but was caught off guard by the attack, he felt Ailyn's elbow connect with his face as Ailyn's fist hit his mid-section at the same time.

Aethor staggered, then narrowly avoided another strike by using a backward handspringing kick, Ailyn blocked the kick with his lower hand, his body fully protected by the iron vest stance.

Aethor raised an eyebrow, "good technique", he grumbled, "but it can't block everything", Aethor said.

by Lore Casta Pendragon

He licked the blood once again and bounced back and forth on his heels with a smile, Ailyn knew this was Aethor's technique to threaten the enemy, much like how Den used Sagaan to threaten his opponents with fear.

Ailyn used his sugiashi to slide in then used tenkan from his back foot to close the distance, as he spun to deliver the elbow-punch combo, Aethor quickly leaped forward with his dragon kick, Ailyn crumpled in half then slid across the arena floor.

"Ailyn!", Kimba and Violet both shouted, Kimba looked over at the other woman, she was shockingly beautiful and a pang of jealousy hit her.

"Who is that?", Kimba said confused, Violet looked at her as if she was silently judging her, then turned back to Ailyn who was holding his back on the ground in pain.

"Ailyn, you don't want to lose in front of your girlfriend, do you?", Violet shouted and Ailyn's eyes shot in her direction, he got to his feet immediately embarrassed, "Violet your alive!", He said noticing Shin beside her, "Shin, praise be!", He said.

Kimba felt her heart sink a little, "did she just say she's, his girlfriend?", Kimba said pouting, "I didn't know he had one, but he didn't deny it", Wynn said amused, Kimba looked at Violet scornfully, Violet just shrugged one shoulder at her.

Aethor came in and took Ailyn from his feet with a sweeping kick, "you really shouldn't get so distracted during a dual", Aethor instructed.

Ailyn landed on his back as Aethor came round with a flipping overhead kick, Ailyn rolled backward, narrowly avoiding it, "once I've beaten you at our little match here, I might just take that girlfriend of yours on a date myself, so she can experience a real man", Aethor said.

Ailyn's brow turned down in anger, "that's right, take the bait kid", Aethor mumbled, "after everything I went through to save you, this is how you treat me", Ailyn said.

"You're not my son, you're half the man your brother was, no wonder you couldn't save Asta", Aethor goaded him.

Ailyn exploded with anger, another flash of red briefly flashed in his eyes, "that'll do it", Aethor said.

"If you want to beat me Ailyn, take that blood on your brow and taste it", Aethor instructed, "why would I take advice from you", Ailyn spat at him.

"Trust me Ailyn, taste the blood, taste your fate, taste your lineage, feel it mix with your rage and your hated, let it burn like fuel in a furnace", Aethor said.

Ailyn wiped the blood that was now dripping from his wound, he licked it from his hand and his eyes went red, his whole body began to burn, every part of him, his life force was burning like fuel in a fire.

                                        by Lore Casta Pendragon

"Now come at me", Aethor said, Ailyn shot off like a missile slamming Aethor with a spear tackle sending him through the wooden railing and through a barn door at the other side of the practice ground, they landed in the hay and Aethor groaned in pain as Ailyn raised a fist on top of him.

Aethor held up a hand, "Nice one son, it seems you got it down quickly", Aethor said pained but smiling.

Ailyn's anger faded and his eyes turned their normal blue, looking Aethor in each eye, "so that's what you were doing, you were teaching me how to use it, goading me into it", Ailyn questioned.

"Of course, fool, I didn't mean a word of it, the blood rage technique feeds on your fury, it's yours now Ailyn, now your enemies will fear your wrath", Aethor said ruffling Aylin's hair.

"Now if you don't mind, I think I need to go see a doctor then have a long soak in a tub", Aethor said.

Ailyn laughed and helped him to his feet, Aethor groaned in pain as he got up.

They walked outside and Aethor held up Ailyn's hand, the crowd cheered and applauded, Ailyn looked up to the balcony at Violet, she smiled at him, jumping and clapping her hands.

Kimba looked at her suspiciously then turned to leave, Link and Vince came down from the balcony to speak with them, "good show, I haven't seen a fight that intense since I saw someone steal Vince's lunch at prep school", Link said humorously, Vince nudged him and smiled.

"It's been too long since we trained together, would you train me, like you trained Aidem", Ailyn said.

Aethor's eyes were full of pride, "I would be honored son, you know, I've been waiting for you to ask since you took your first steps", Aethor said embracing his wrist.

"Hate to butt in on this touching moment but the king would like a word regarding those two", Link pointed toward Shin and Violet.

They headed up to the balcony, as soon as Ailyn was in sight Violet ran at him and embraced him at the stairs, sinking his face into her bosom.

"What an impressive display Ailyn", she said, she let go hearing Ailyn's muffled voice in her cleavage, he took a deep breath sarcastically and she giggled, "good to see your alive and well", Aethor said to Shin.

"Alive, but not so well", he said pointing to a wound on his leg, "nothing to worry about, Paladins Reach has the best healers in the world, come with me and we'll get you fixed up in no time", Link said.

"Before you go, tell us what happened at Torins Well", Ailyn asked, Shin paused for a moment.

"I stepped out to get some air, the inn was too crowded for my liking, I noticed a raven overhead, then saw the lights dim, I knew we were in for trouble when I saw miss Valentine running from some soldiers down by the river, I caught up and was able to dispatch them, but was injured in the battle, by the time I got back, Torins Well was on fire and an army stood between us and the rest of you, so we journeyed northward and eventually came by a road to pass the scar, we got lost and almost eaten by a hypnotic toad with a burn scar", Shin explained.

Just then Lore, Kimba and Locke joined them, "his story checks out, we also had a run in with a hypnotic toad", Lore said, Shin bowed his head to Lore, "that's proof enough for me that they aren't spies of Necropyre", Locke said, "go and get Shin-son seen to", Link and Vince bowed then escorted him to the infirmary.

"Tonight, there is a production by some travelling showmen at the theatre, our theatre is unlike anything you've ever seen, I'd like you to join me as my guests of honor", Locke said, "we would be honored lord Lionheart", Lore said with a bow.

Violet clapped excitedly, Kimba turned to Lore and whispered, "I'm not sure about her, there's something off about her", Kimba said, "ah, I understand your jealously miss Kindheart, but the heart is a fickle thing and so easily it corrupts as easily as it is corrupted, best to steer clear of matters of the heart", Lore advised moving on, Kimba stared at Violet contemplatively.

Guldamere Cursed, "the abyss will have that old fool!", He croaked as he made it to the bottom of the crater of Mount Muse, realizing he'd been juked, he looked even more decrepit than usual and he growled out in frustration then placed his hands together, two acolytes dragged one of the older men captured in the pursuit toward him.

Guldamere raised a skeletal hand as black miasma gripped the man and drained him of his life force until there was nothing left but a mummified husk.

"That's better", his voice gaining a bit of vigor, "they'll be at Paladins Reach by now, I wanted to avoid taking that fortress until I had secured more power, but it seems time has now run short, if Pendragon or that brat collects another shard, they might be strong enough to defeat me, this will not do", Guldamere said.

He led his forces to the center of the crater the same place Lore Casta Pendragon had been imprisoned.

An impossible looking waterfall flowed upwards from a pool, Guldamere stood by it.

                                        by Lore Casta Pendragon

"Prey with me and prey well", he said, acolytes lined up in a semi-circle behind him each one clasping their hands together as they joined the circle, smokey black miasma raised from them and reached out to Guldamere, each one raising his power.

Guldamere reached out a skeletal hand and black miasma made a smokey circular shape on the ground, it coalesced into the crushed, rotted and deformed body of Harram Halfborn.

It took four soldiers to drag the body into the pool after which they quickly retreated, Guldamere then held his skeletal hand over the pool, the water turned black as if someone had just poured black ink into it, it started to flow like a whirlpool, darkness spread from Guldamere as he extended his arms wide, the light around him grew dim and he chanted words of an unknown origin.

A nightmare creature the size of a house stomped out of the water, the head and horns of a bull emerged, followed by the hairy muscular body of a man with hoofed feet.

The black miasma stopped flowing from the acolytes and they all fell to their knees exhausted, Guldamere almost did the same but two soldiers came in to catch him and hold him upright.

The beast stood before him, it was massive in size and with its muscular frame it looked like it could crush them to dust easily, the soldiers moved back in fear and Guldamere straightened up.

The beast took a knee, still towering over them, "thank you for bringing me back my Lord, I will not fail you again", Harram said, "you'd best not, Harram Halfborn", Guldamere panted, "or it'll be, the last thing that you ever do".

Harram Halfborn was born four hundred and fifty years after the cataclysm, his mother was dying of an unknown sickness, she was brought to the cathedral of the god feared for healing, but there was little Guldamere was willing to do for her, she was a devout follower of the church of the god feared, but was poor and had little to offer the church.

Guldamere made a deal with her, in exchange for her life, he would make sure her unborn child live to see its first day, she took the deal and Harram Halfborn was born that day.

He was so small and practically lifeless, Guldamere had to reach into the abyss to revive him from death several times, each time it corrupted him, the abyss touched him, changed him, making him stronger but ever more twisted.

Guldamere grew fond of the boy as Harram gained the ability to fight the flows of the abyss himself.

Eventually Guldamere found he could find him in the abyss over longer periods of time, as if he could travel through the abyss much like nightmare creatures could, each time Harram died

by Lore Casta Pendragon

from illness, by accident or in the line of duty he was a little less human and much more of a nightmare creature.

He waited at the edge of the abyss, the black void around him, he could see the flows of the spirit river rushing past, not water, but life force being consumed.

Behind him the flow fell over a ledge into the black void below it, he knew if he fell over it, he could never return to the world of the living.

Guldamere had told him that if he gained more of the power he could reach further into the abyss, even enough to pull the long dead from it, but not those who had passed to the lands beyond, though what monsters he'd pull out with them he never knew, he'd never cared.

Guldamere had given him life for sixty years, a life he would have otherwise not have had, he pushed against the flow of the abyss, his incredible strength held him firm in the current from the brink of death and there he waited until Guldamere came for him.

"Has my lord abandoned me", Harram thought, "could he have been defeated?", He began to think to himself as endless time seemed to pass.

Eventually he lost hope and began to drift, he accepted his fate and over the ledge he fell, the abyss gripped him, but Guldamere appeared before him.

A shadowy apparition grabbed him in a smokey dark clawed hand, pulling him from the dark void of the abyss, his body changed, it morphed, it grew bigger, stronger and more twisted, he felt his body become more solid and he took his first steps back into the living world, raising himself from a pool of darkness, he took a knee before the lord of the damned.

"Thank you for bringing me back my lord, I will not fail you again", he said, determination burning in his eyes.

Ailyn was in his room at the keep, he sat on his bed with a sigh, he didn't own any clothing appropriate for such a hoity toity event and didn't want to embarrass himself, "maybe I shouldn't go", Ailyn thought when he heard a knock on the door.

Kimba came in holding some formal clothing, black trousers, a belt, a white formal shirt and a red and black tail coat with a floral design.

"I know you haven't had much time to yourself, so I got you these to wear, I even made a few modifications to the coat that I think you might like", she said with a smile.

Ailyn took the clothes looking over them happily, "thank you miss Kindheart", Ailyn said formally which got a frowned from Kimba, "Kimba is fine", she said sitting on the bed next to him.

by Lore Casta Pendragon

"They told me you were sent to the pit, that must have been awful", she said placing her hand on his leg, "it was", Ailyn said looking down at her hand.

"I would have died in there, but I found Aethor alive and I had to get him out, I didn't care what happened to me as long as I could protect him, like he protected me when I was a boy, if I hadn't gone there, I would have never met Shin, Brawn, Fyorn, Gear or Éoviel, he was killed in the pit and Gear sacrificed himself so we could get here safely", Ailyn said as his eyes began to tear up.

Kimba hugged him, "my father was killed as well, during the attack at the temple", she said sadly, "I'm sorry Kimba, I wish I had of been stronger, then I might have been able to", Ailyn was stopped short by Kimba turning his face to hers, she kissed him.

Ailyn was taken off guard and just stared at her in a state of shock, "I'm sorry, I shouldn't have done that", Kimba said standing up, just then Violet came walking into the room, she glared daggers at Kimba who also did the same in return.

"I should be going", Kimba said as she rushed past the other woman.

"Was I interrupting something", Violet asked as Kimba left, "no, nothing at all", Ailyn said unconvincingly.

Violet was wearing a purple skin tight dress, the dress was strapless ending at the arms and shoulders, fluffy purple and gray trim surrounded the top and showed an ample amount of bosom.

"You best not be sleeping around on me, Ailyn", she said pouting, pressing her breasts together to give him a good look, "no-no of course not, Kimba just came around to give me some clothes to wear", Ailyn stammered.

Violet glared at him for a brief moment then said "well, we best get you nice a relaxed before tonight, let me help you ease your nerves", she said pushing him back onto the bed.

Link was talking to his father in his quarters, "it's of no coincidence that these men showed up just as Guldamere's army marches on our doorstep", Locke said, "they did just escape from a famously inescapable pit", Link said.

"They have something he wants; he wouldn't risk a frontal assault on Paladins Reach unless he was desperate, he hasn't tried to take the Reach since his last defeat and I was a much younger man then", Locke said sitting down, he looked tired.

"Even if he was to attack, the purifying barrier would stop him from using his necromancy and he knows he can't stand against the paladins of the reach without that", Link said, "even so, double the guard around the theatre and keep an eye out from the wall", Locke commanded, "as you wish father", Link responded and turned to leave.

 by Lore Casta Pendragon

Lore was curious about the theatre, the music emanating from it seemed to carry chaos magic over the entire city, forming some sort of protective barrier, he entered Link's quarters as he was leaving.

"Come to see the king master Pendragon?", Link enquired, "yes, there was something I needed to ask him, perhaps you could enlighten me with the answer", Lore said stroking his beard, "I don't see why not, try me", Link replied.

"The theatre", Lore said, "yes, what about it?", Link said, "how does it work?", Links face went completely straight and he gave Lore a dumb look, "ahh well, umm, it, ahh, gee, hmm", Link stood there kicking at the ground holding his chin.

"That's a tough one, maybe you'd better go see the king after all, good luck", Link said as he disappeared quickly down the hall.

Lore just mumbled something about young people incoherently and went inside, "ahh, Lore Casta Pendragon, ready for the performance tonight?", Locke said excitedly, "yes, but I was hoping you might illuminate me on something about your city that has me rather perplexed", Lore responded.

"Of course there isn't a man alive who knows more about the rich histories of Paladins Reach, from the battles of old, to land rights to political policies and trade, I know it all", Locke said pacing while he boasted, "ahh, very good, very good", Lore said happily, he was finally going to get an answer to his question, "your theatre, the barrier, how does it work?", Locke stopped still in his tracks, a stupefied look pinned on his face, "well it, I think it might be, from the records it, maybe it's, you know what?", He turned to face Lore, "I haven't a clue", "this whole damn time, it's been protecting our city from evil and I never once questioned how it worked, after the show tonight I'll send my best scholars to figure it out", Locke said puzzled.

"Ahh, I see", Lore said, he thought as much, no one living knew why Paladins Reach was protected from dark chaos magic, "would you mind if I took a look too, I'm kind of an expert on all things magic related", Lore said boastfully.

"I don't see why not, you might even be able to improve it for us", Locke said with a chuckle, "now let's get a move on, before we're late for the show", Locke said putting an arm over Lore's shoulder and directing him out the door.

by Lore Casta Pendragon

<u>Chapter Fourteen</u>

<u>A show to remember</u>

Ailyn and Violet made their way across the marbled steps of the keep toward the amphitheater, large organ-like pipes rang out with choir music, which could be heard everywhere within the city, yet was soft on the ears.

Violet held Ailyn's arm as they walked, her smile dazzled him, dressed in his fine clothes with such a beautiful woman on his side, Ailyn couldn't believe how his fortunes had changed so drastically since he escaped the pit, from his utmost despair to the greatest high of his life, for the first time since he was a child, Ailyn was truly happy.

As they walked along the cobblestone road, they saw Fyorn, Brawn and Shin, all dressed in formal wear and surprisingly well groomed, Shin wore a formal Gi and Hakama with an iaito, a type of sword made only in the ronin city in the south.

Fyorn wore a pleated kilt while Brawn wore a brown and tan three-piece suit, Ailyn had to stop to admire them, he smiled and embraced his friends.

"Look at us, I never thought I'd live to see the day that we'd be attending a theatre production with a king", Ailyn said happily, "and dressed all fancy at that", Fyorn said, "we've come a long way in a short time", Brawn added in a slow drawl.

"Must be good leadership", Aethor called out heading toward them with Wynn by his side, Wynn wore a basic formal suit while Aethor was wearing a custom-made suit that also looked like running sweats at the same time, he never liked his clothes to be too tight fitting.

Aethor embraced Ailyn, Violet offered him a hand which he kissed politely.

People in extravagant formal clothing were making their way inside the theatre when two lines of men with long trumpets lined up outside the door, two white and gold horse drawn carriages with the livery of the king came trotting up to the front of the theatre, the soldiers' trumpets blew, announcing the king's arrival.

"Make way for his majesty King Lionheart of the Reach", said the crier, Locke Lionheart stepped out from the carriage dress in a white formal suit with gold plate mail adorned with filigree with a large white and gold cape which trailed behind him.

With a crown on his head Locke looked every bit the king, he waved to the crowd and turned as Kimba came out of the carriage behind him, she wore a shimmering red dress, her hair and makeup were done, her lips shined with glossy red lipstick and her high heeled red shoes matched the dress.

                              by Lore Casta Pendragon

She looked incredible, the crowd cheered as Locke took her hand to help her down, Ailyn and his companions mouths hung wide open as she took a few steps forward with the king, her smile radiated her beauty and her dress sparkled in the light.

Violet made an audible sound of jealousy and tugged on Ailyn's arm and he closed his mouth and straightened up to regain his composure.

As the king and Kimba passed them, Kimba shot Ailyn a wry smile, tucking the hair back behind her ear, Ailyn felt his heart melt and Violet scowled at her.

Lore stepped out from the carriage, he wore his usual silk robe but chose to leave his pointy behind in favor of a stylish woolen cap, his long grey hair and beard had been groomed, he put his fists together and floated down from the carriage.

Raising his hands, sparks of different colors flew from his fingertips and the crowd cheered and applauded, the horns blew again shortly thereafter.

"Prince Link Lionheart and sir Vincent Vanguard", the crier said, Link and Vince rode up in an open carriage and jumped out in one leap, landing with a loud clang.

They still wore their Paladian armor and waved to the crowd, "you could have saved some of the limelight for us", Link said to Lore, Lore just smiled and said, "had to give the people what they wanted", chuckling to himself as they made their way into the theatre.

"Ailyn with me", Vince waved and the group joined the precession heading into the theatre, the entrance to the theatre looked like a cave made of hollow silver pipes which projected sound, the noise coming from the theatre was a cacophony of voices and singing.

Rows of seats were lined before a stage, with several raised platforms around the outer edges, Locke took his place with Kimba, Lore, Link and Vince on their own personal platform to one side of the stage, Ailyn and his companions took their seats in the front row.

Violet squeezed his leg and shot him an excited smile as the house lights dimmed and the curtain drew back.

The music changed as the actors moved onto the stage and introduced themselves, preparing the mood for the show, two of the actors were hooded in black robes, possibly playing the part of church members and the crowd booed as they were introduced.

"Our story begins on a night not so different from this", a narrator off stage cried out, Violet turned to Ailyn, "I'm a little thirsty, I'll get you boys some drinks", she said quietly, they barely noticed her leaving enraptured by the show before them.

"I am quite pleased you decided to accompany me tonight miss Kindheart, you certainly made a showing of it, this old man hasn't had a woman on his arm since Link's mother died", Locke said to Kimba.

by Lore Casta Pendragon

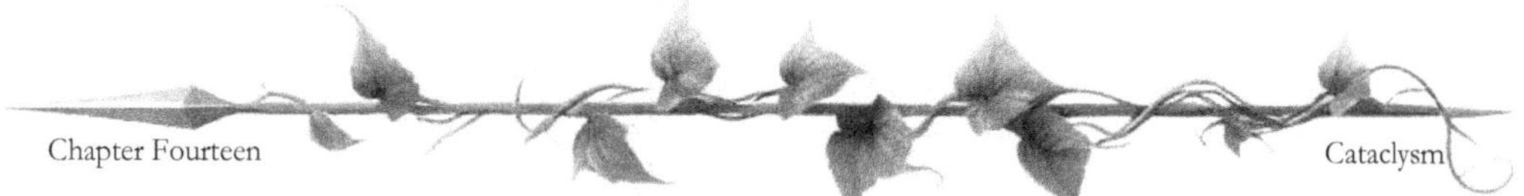

"Thank you for inviting us and giving me this beautiful dress", Kimba responded with a smile.

Kimba noticed Link looking at her, "you certainly did make quite the impression tonight, everyone in the kingdom will be talking about it for days", Link said which made Kimba blush.

Lore leaned over to Vince, "so what happened to the queen of Paladins Reach?", he asked quietly, "she was murdered, an assassin hired to kill the king, but instead found lady Lionheart, she raised the alarm only to be killed in his place, truly tragic, Link has never really stopped grieving for her", Vince explained, "it's partly the reason why he keeps such a close watch on the city", "by his chirpy demeanor I never would have guessed such pain resides within him", Lore said, "as the prince he cannot afford to lose the confidence of his people or his men, so he puts on a front of controlled confidence, but that is not who the prince truly is", Vince said.

Violet returned carrying six mugs of ale, giving Ailyn and his companions a mug each, which they mostly drank down in one, "they certainly make it taste better, but it doesn't quite have the kick of prison wine", bellowed Wynn, which was followed up by hushes of people in the nearby seats. "Sorry, sorry", Wynn tried to whisper.

Violet sat down next to Ailyn, who took a long drink of ale, Violet smiled at him wiping the froth from his upper lip with a handkerchief she pulled from her brassier, "enjoying the show?", Violet said, "I am, even more so having you by my side", he said taking her hand, she smirked amused and sat with her head on Ailyn's shoulder.

"I must admit I had an ulterior motive for having you as my guest of honor", Locke said, "oh?", Kimba said.

"My son is quite taken with you lady Kindheart, he won't admit it, but I can see it by the way he looks at you", Locke said.

"Oh, I hadn't noticed", Kimba said embarrassed, she looked over at Link who shot her a smile, she quickly looked away her face turning beat red, "what would you say to an arranged marriage with my son", Locke said quietly.

Kimba gasped audibly and Lore took notice, "I, uh, I, that is", Kimba said lost for words, Link leaned over, "you don't have to answer right away, take your time to think about it", Link said.

"Well, I-I would have to ask master Pendragon first and", Kimba started to say, but Lore interrupted her, "seems like a good match to me, but I'm afraid you can't have her", Lore said, "at least not yet".

"Would you care to explain why you would deny us", Link asked, "Kimba is in training and her talents are needed in the coming days, need I remind you that the fate of all Thalaria is at stake", Lore said, "I have to agree with master Pendragon, there are more important things I need to do, I'm not saying no, but I can't say yes either", Kimba tried to explain.

"I understand", Link said, "in order for our mutual goals to be realized I suggest an agreement, once Guldamere has been defeated, the lady Kindheart should return to Paladins Reach to

by Lore Casta Pendragon

marry my son prince Lionheart and in return, Paladins Reach will offer its support to your cause", Locke said, "give me time to think about it", Kimba said as she looked down at Ailyn from the balcony.

Just then the music stopped, the actors looked around confused as a black rat trailing black smoke wandered out to the stage, "excuse me, I need to use the powder room", Violet said, she got up and walked away, the two hooded actors walked out and one of them stepped on the rat, it puffed into acrid black smoke.

A shimmering wall of magic started to dissipate over the city and the guards of the city wall, pointed up at it, an alarm sounded from outside the city's main gate, the people in the theatre began to get nervous and restless, the two hooded figures on stage threw back their hoods, one of them had a face covered in scars, he pulled a large brimmed hat from behind the curtain and stuck it on his head.

"Silus?", Ailyn shouted as he got to his feet, the world began to spin as he stood, "Petricus!", Kimba shouted down, "now for the final act", Silus shouted back, he threw two knives and they sunk into the faces of two nearby sentinel guards, the people in the theatre panicked and begun to flee.

Petricus pointed his spear toward Kimba and Lore, "I've come to finish what I started with your father", he said menacingly.

Link turned to Vince, "gather our forces and secure the wall, I'll deal with this", Link leaped from the balcony and landed heavily on the stage below cracking the wooden floorboards.

Vince rushed to the door of the theatre as Ailyn, Fyorn, Brawn and Wynn all tried to move to join Link but all fell to their knees, all except for Shin and Aethor.

"What's wrong with us?", Ailyn said, he looked down at the mugs of ale, "poison?", he proclaimed as he looked around for Violet.

Shin turned to Aethor and blew powder in his face, Aethor moved back trying to avoid the powder but he breathed it in and collapsed to the floor.

"Shin?", "What are you doing?", Ailyn said struggling to stay upright in his chair, "it's not Shin, Ailyn, it never was, it's Sin, Sin Sonata, I've been tracking you since before we met in the pit, but I'm afraid this is as far as you go", Sin said place a hand on the scar of his iaito.

Violet came walking up next to Sin and laughed.

"Did you really think all this was about you, we needed a way past the barrier and thanks to you and your band of merry misfits our army has finally weakened the Paladian's protection", Violet said.

She held up a glowing white shard, it looked as if it were made from light itself, "once I give this and you over to lord Guldamere, we'll be even closer to achieving true immortality".

by Lore Casta Pendragon

A fireball exploded in front of Shin and Violet, Lore and Kimba came floating down from the balcony with a gale of wind, landing between them and Ailyn, several sentinel guards surrounded Locke and headed for the exit.

Link pulled a wide gold broadsword from under a plate in his armor and placed his helm on his head, "fiends of the lich, prepare to be smote!", Link shouted, Petricus pulled a spear hidden by some props from the stage while Silus had two daggers in hand with a flick of his wrists.

Link charged at Petricus who stabbed at him with the spear, it bounced off Link's thick armor with a spark and Link brought down the broadsword, Petricus sprang back raising the spear, the sword dented the spear shaft, buckling it in the middle, Petricus scoffed.

"He's going to be a problem", Petricus said standing next to Silus, "I'll take left, you take right", Silus said as they sprinted outward, arcing back toward Link they both attacked high.

Link raised his arms, the heavy pauldrons covered his head in amour, Silus and Petricus slammed into him, weapons sparking against the armor but they couldn't penetrate it.

Link punched both arms out and threw both assailants away, "that armor is impenetrable by weapons", Silus said grunting.

"Then we'll just have to burn him out of it", Petricus said pulling a vial of liquid from his pocket, Petricus threw the vail of liquid at Link, Link caught it and smiled at him, Silus threw a dagger at blistering speed shattering the vial in his hand, spilling liquid down Link's arm, "shit!", Link said as both Petricus and Silus moved in to attack.

Link raised his arms again, the noxious smell of fuel filled his nose, Petricus and Silus slammed into him again from either side, sparks ran from the tip of Petricus's spear igniting the fuel and engulfing Link's arm in flame, Silus and Petricus leaped back to avoid the flames.

Link dropped his sword and reached over his shoulder to a latch on his amour, the arm of the armor dropped to the floor with a thud, fire flaring up around it, Link kicked it away from him, he now had one arm bare and vulnerable.

Shin placed a hand on his Iaito, ready to draw, Violet put her hands together in prayer, as Kimba and Lore slammed their fists together.

Violet threw both hands forward and two large claws of black miasma reached out and grabbed Lore, Kimba grabbed her elbow and shot a fireball toward Violet as Shin drew the sword so fast it was barely visible.

A shockwave moved out knocking the fireball away from Violet, it exploded on the wall behind her, she smiled wickedly, but Lore started to glow with a bright white light, so bright that it eviscerated the shadow claws holding him, everyone shielded their eyes until the light faded.

by Lore Casta Pendragon

"You might be a powerful mage young lady, but you're not quite at my level", Lore said extending a hand toward Violet, Shin drew his sword, the shockwave passed through Lore's extended arm and blood splashed out from it, Lore's arm dropped to the floor and he screamed out in pain grabbing at the stump.

Kimba grabbed Lore's shoulder and they both faded from sight, Violet extended an arm toward Ailyn, a fireball burst into life in her palm.

Ailyn looked at her paralyzed from the poison, unable to move, "please, don't", Ailyn pleaded, but she let the fireball fly, Kimba and Lore appeared in front of him, raising a magic ward, a physical barrier appeared in front of them and the fireball exploded around them, flames spouting out from the barrier.

"She used you as bait so we'd reveal ourselves", Lore said, he placed his severed arm back on the bleeding stump and it immediately began to heal, "this may take a while", Lore said to Kimba and she nodded, "we need to take out Sin first, his skill with that sword is too dangerous", Lore said, "keep out of sight until you've healed your arm, I'll keep Violet distracted", Kimba said.

"Violet, why?", Ailyn said, Violet looked at him with a pitying look, "stupid boy, you're nothing to me, you were easy to manipulate and decent fun to play with, you served my purpose and when Guldamere flattens this city to the ground, he'll take the power from you and I'll be given life and beauty eternal", Violet said scornfully.

Ailyn felt his heart break, of all the terrible things he'd been through, the pain of losing his mother Asta and his brother Aidem, the death of master Den, Gear and Éoviel, being tortured and sent to the pit to die, of all of those things, this was by far the worst.

Rage built inside of him and he bit into his own cheek, blood filled his mouth and his eyes caught fire, a blaze of red and a faint white aura emanated from him.

Ailyn stood up, his entire body burned through his life force like a furnace, his vision was still blurred but his body obeyed his commands.

He ran at an arc around his friends and shot toward Sin like a missile, Sin drew again, so fast it was barely visible, but Ailyn leaped over him, the cut sliced through the chairs in front.

Ailyn landed behind him and pushed off one of the seats, he punched Sin in the back so hard he shot out and slammed into the bottom of the stage, breaking through the wooden supports.

Ailyn rushed at Sin, grabbed him by the shirt and lifted him, "after everything we've been through, you'd turn on us now!", Ailyn shouted.

"Compared to what Guldamere offered me, your friendship means very little", Sin said flicking a switch on his saya, a second blade shot out from the saya and stabbed into Ailyn's ribs, Ailyn dropped Sin to the ground grabbing at his side.

by Lore Casta Pendragon

Flicking the switch, the hidden blade retracted and Sin picked up his sword returning it to his saya, Sin readied himself to draw, aiming low so's not to kill Ailyn, he wanted him alive, he drew expecting to take Ailyn's legs from under him but Ailyn jumped, his hands grabbed onto Sin's shoulders and he vaulted behind him.

Ailyn wrapped his arms around Sin's neck for a chokehold but Sin reversed his sword and plunged it through his own body into Ailyn, "foolish, Guldamere can revive my body, your however cannot", Sin said as Ailyn pushed himself off the sword, both him and Sin fell to the ground, the red in Ailyn's eyes and the white glow faded.

"Sin, you, bastard", Ailyn said losing consciousness.

Lore retreated below one of the balconies behind a wall, reattaching an arm was no easy task, he needed time, he scolded himself for being so careless, the muscles and tendons moved back into position and he grunted with the intensity of the pain.

Violet's fingernails grew into pointed claws, she aimed at Kimba and shot one out like a bullet, it stuck through a seat near where Kimba was crouched almost hitting her, Kimba's eyes grew wide and she ran for cover.

Violet shot four more claws each one barely missing Kimba sticking into the seat beside her, she ducked behind a curtain and through a service door, Violet sighed with frustration and went after her, there were props and costumes stored back there and Kimba hid behind them.

Violet came in scanning the room, she walked carefully through the dark room, searching for any signs of the girl.

"You know, it was easy for me to seduce him", she said trying to provoke her, "he melted like butter in my hands, it wasn't hard considering my competition was a pathetic little mouse like you", Violet taunted.

Kimba snuck around her and back toward the door as Violet walked into the room, she poked her head out, Violet was faced in the opposite direction and she extended one arm grabbing her elbow with her other hand, the light of the flame made Violet turn suddenly.

Kimba shot a fireball at her, but Violet raised a hand and a ward of her own, the fireball struck her outstretched palm, plumes of fires exploded out around it, catching on the props and clothes around her, Violet slid backward from the force of the fire, then returned a fireball of her own.

Kimba dashed out from her hiding place as the fireball exploded, more of the room caught fire, smoke began to fill the room and Violet smiled, she raised a hand to the ceiling and the smoke turned darker, circling and coalescing around her until it formed into a smokey demonic figure, its eyes glowed like embers.

 by Lore Casta Pendragon

Violet clawed at the burning props and clothes in the room trying to find where Kimba was hiding, the powerful strikes produced gusts of wind that fed the flames tossing fiery objects around the room.

Kimba placed her legs up against a piano and kicked out as she summoned a powerful gust of wind, it flew out at Violet who held it off with bellowing black smoke from her hands, the piano caught fire and turned to ash.

Violet saw Kimba heading for an exit door and clawed at her, fiery objects being picked up by the bellowing smoke and smashing around the door as Kimba jumped through it.

Vince and Locke arrived at the city's main gate, Paladins and sentinel guards were fighting along the wall, firing large longbows and hand-held arbalests at nightmare creatures trying to climbed over the walls, a wraith floated through the wall grabbing a guard by the ankle and throwing him over the edge, the guard screamed as he fell and as he hit the ground several barghasts each grabbed a limb dismembering him.

A Fake scurried up the wall near a watch tower using its long limbs to dodge left and right avoiding incoming arrows.

It clambered up to a window narrowly avoiding being shot in the face by a crossbow, it grabbed the guards helm with its long thin clawed arm and screamed in his face as it sucked the life from his body, Pulling the leftover husk through the window and throwing it down to the ground to be devoured by the creatures lurking below.

Several more guards in another nearby watch tower aimed an arbalest toward the monster and fired, they skewered it with the large javelin and it fell from the wall being pinned to the ground below.

"Get a battalion of paladins to secure the gate, get Ailyn's army to evacuate the people to the keep and get my armor", Locke commanded, "yes, my king", Vince said quickly running for the armory.

Guldamere smirked or what could be insinuated as a smirk with half of his face missing as he walked toward the main gate of Paladins Reach, "Harram, bring that gate down", he commanded, pointing his boney finger at it, Harram walked up beside him, towering over the rest of Guldamere's forces.

He ran toward the gate at a full sprint, a guard on top of the wall saw him coming, "what is that thing?", the guard yelled, other guards started shooting at Harram hitting their mark, but not sinking deep enough into Harram's thick skin to deal any real damage.

They fired an arbalest into Harram's shoulder but he didn't even miss a step, he grabbed the javelin and pulled it out as he continued to run, Harram raised both of his gigantically muscular arms and lowered his horned head forward.

by Lore Casta Pendragon

Locke was standing back behind the front gate when he saw it explode into pieces as Harram ran through it, wood and iron flew out everywhere.

Harram shook the broken planks of wood from his horns and snorted, he looked down at Locke, several sentinel guards stepped in front to protect their king but in three stomps, they were all crushed like insects under his hooved feet.

Locke began to back away ready to flee, he had no chance of defeating Harram, especially without his weapons and armor.

As Harram reached out to crush the king is his massive hand a heavy golden Lance struck Harram in the mid-section, Vince's Warhorse neighed as Vince let out a war cry with the Lance in hand.

Four Paladins ran up, placing their heavy tower shields in a fortified line in front of the king, "we'll hold him off your highness, get your armor and head for the keep", Vince said, "well done Vanguard, I'll bring reinforcements, don't be fallen", Locke said, running back to the armory.

Harram snorted and pulled the Lance from his body, he stabbed it down at Vince who leaped away as the lance stabbed a massive hole into its back, spraying blood and gore out everywhere.

Harram kicked back twice with his hooved foot then ran at the line of paladins, they broke formation and formed stairs in front of Vince with their tower shields, Vince jumped up each one and leaped toward the charging Harram pulling a golden sword from his armor.

Vince raised it above his head blade down and plunged it into Harram's chest, sinking the sword deep but not deep enough to reach past the man's large pectoral muscles.

Harram roared grabbing Vince in both hands squeezing him like a tin can.

Vince's armor shattered, bits of it fell to the ground, Harram grabbed the helmet from his head in two fingers and threw it, he looked into Vince's eyes, "now you die", Harram gloated.

Vince glared at him teeth gritted, the other paladins raced forward stabbing at Harram's hugely muscular legs from behind their tower shields, Harram took a few steps back then swung Vince at them like a makeshift weapon, knocking them aside, he threw Vince straight down on the pavement with such force that the stones broke around him and what remained of his armor shattered into pieces on the stone.

Locke run up covered in armor with an ornate golden sword, "you want me beast, come get me", Locke shouted.

by Lore Casta Pendragon

Harram looked up from Vince and snorted, he charged at Locke, Locke ran toward Haram, he put his thick tower shield on his back then dived at Harram's foot slamming the shield with all his weight against his forward foot before Harram could place his foot completely on the ground, Harram tripped and fell forward, stumbling into a building, he crushed it under his immense weight, a cloud of dust blew up around the wreckage.

"Grab Vince and retreat to the keep", Locke ordered to the other paladin's who were just regaining their feet, one of them got knocked into the next street from Harram's onslaught, he was still dazed and shaking his head, but managed a groggy, "yes, my lord".

"Again, left and right attack formation", Petricus said, Silus nodded as both charged in arcing circles toward Link, "if I block one, I'll get hit by the other, so in that case", Link thought as they came in from both sides, he held up one arm for protection against Petricus and slashed at Silus with his sword.

Silus raised both knives and was deflected by the attack but Petricus threw another vail of fuel over Link's defending arm, Link turned to stab at him, but caught Petricus's spear tip instead and another gout of flame erupted over Link's armor, he pulled off the topmost part of the heavy armor dropping it to the floor with a clang, underneath was a figure that looked to be sculpted from stone and only slightly less imposing than the armor itself.

"Thanks, you did me a favor, now I won't be slowed down", Link said smiling at them, "now we can finish you fool", Petricus said as they moved to pincer attack him again, the tip of the spear flew at Link.

Silus saw a bright light coming from the side and leaped away, Petricus's eyes went wide as a lightning bolt cracked across the room and speared Petricus in an instant, sending him flying into the curtain to the side of the stage, it burst into flames with Petricus inside of it, thunder roared and a bright flash lit the theatre.

Link stood there with his hair standing on end wondering what had happened, Lore stood there with his index finger pointed like a gun, he blew on it and pretended to put it back in his pocket.

"Well shot, Pendragon", Link said, Silus snarled toward Lore, then reached into his pocket pulling out three black phylacteries and a paper ball, Silus threw them down at his feet and a cloud of white smoke exploded outwards concealing him.

Four different Silus's moved out in different directions from the cloud, Link moved toward one of them and attempted to slash it, but Silus dodged, following it up with several slashes cutting Link multiple times before he could bring his sword around again to fend him off.

The Silus copy took the hit and exploded into white smoke, Link felt a sharp stab in his lower back then swung his sword behind him, another stab struck him, looking down he saw a

by Lore Casta Pendragon

dagger sticking out of his chest, a third attempt saw Link deflect it with a swing of his blade, another Silus was smiling wickedly at him.

Link was finding it hard to breathe now, he coughed up blood, "shit, that must have pierced my lung", he thought.

Lore extended both hands and fired fireballs at both Silus's in rapid succession, the Silus's ran fast outpacing them as they exploded behind them, rapidly closing the distance from either direction.

Lore clapped his hands together as the two Silus's attacked in unison, Lore's body turned into water and they splashed into it, the water quickly froze into ice and Lore appeared close behind it.

Lore chuckled to himself as the two Silus's were trapped in the frozen spire, Lore walked up to finish them but they exploded into white smoke.

"So that must be the real one", Lore said looking toward the theatre stage, he saw Silus throw a knife into Link's unexpecting back, then his front and another to finish him off, but thankfully Link deflected it with his sword.

"So, you like stabbing people in the back", Lore grumbled as he grabbed his elbow, life force flowing like a river, he pointed his finger like a gun, electricity started to crack and flash, growing larger, Lore aimed straight and true and let the lightning go.

Silus heard the crackling sound from behind him, he felt a pang of sheer mortal fear run through him and began to turn, no sooner had his eye caught sight of Lore he saw a blinding white light and was struck by a lightning bolt that sent him flying across the stage, pinning him against the far wall, thunder cracked and he felt his whole-body tense with agony, then everything went black.

Kimba ran out of the theatre and down to a river bridge, she turned to see the smokey visage of Violet, bellowing through the door, the smoke rose around her like a demon, she glided quickly toward Kimba who slammed her fists together.

"Once I'm done with you, I think I'll make Ailyn my own personal toy", Violet said mockingly, "once I'm done with you, you won't be hurting anyone ever again", Kimba said.

She placed her index fingers together on her thumbs making what looked like a symbol of infinity, she circulated her life force there, she felt her life force drain from her body as two large water spouts rose from either side of the bridge, Kimba extended her hands toward each and they moved with her arms.

Violet came in fast and Kimba crossed her hands over, one water spout went high the other low, collecting Violet in a deluge flipping her sideways.

by Lore Casta Pendragon

Kimba made a circular motion with her hands and the water flowed like a vortex at high speed, washing away the smoke and ash, she tossed both hands down and the water crashed into the bridge, slamming Violet on the cobblestone road.

Violet laid there dazed and dizzied, she tried to stand but the world spun and she fell, she saw Kimba approaching her and shot fireballs, gusts of wind and sharp nail projectiles, but nothing she did was going in the right direction, Violet was so disheveled and confused she couldn't see straight.

"You know, Ailyn loved you, that was obvious by the way he looked at you, it hurt me knowing that, but at the same time it made me happy to see him happy, if you changed your ways, he might even forgive you in time", Kimba said, Violet's eyes seethed with hatred and she regained enough composure to see Kimba.

"Leave Guldamere's service and you might be able to set things right", Kimba said to her.

Violet scoffed, "you stupid child, this world was destroyed long before your birth and we will be here long after you have died, as long as Guldamere reigns he will bring us back to serve him", Violet said scornfully.

"Then I'll just have to make sure that next time you come back, it won't be for a long time", Kimba said raising a hand and grabbing onto Violet's face, she grabbed her elbow and fire sparked in her hand, Violet's eyes went wide through her fingers as Kimba released a torrent of flame directly into her face.

Violet screamed in agony as the fire burned her into dust, the flame from Kimba's hand died down and she collapsed burning through too much of her own life force, she fell to the cobblestoned ground on the bridge and looked over at Violet's remains as a gust of wind blew some of the ashes away revealing a glowing white shard sitting on the bridge as she lost consciousness.

by Lore Casta Pendragon

Chapter Fifteen

The Battle of Paladins Reach

Lore helped Link first, he sat him up and removed a knife from his body taking a bandage from his sleeve.

"I'm sorry, I wish I could do more, but I can only heal myself", Lore said, "no need", Link said pulling a vail of what seemed to be glowing white liquid from a hatch on his armor.

Lore looked at him curiously, "it's concentrated chaos magic, it has healing properties", Link said uncorking it with his teeth and sculling it down, his wounds began to heal on their own, "now that is something", Lore said astonished, "in five hundred years, I've never seen anything like it".

"If this city falls you never will again, it's notoriously difficult to make, only the paladins of the Reach know how it's done, here I have one left", Link passed the vial to Lore.

The glowing white liquid seemed to glow brighter in his hands, "this is a chaos magic catalyst", Lore said, as he uncorked it, he drank a small amount and his wounds healed immediately.

"I've not felt this strong in, centuries", Lore said smiling, he moved over to Ailyn and put some in his mouth, Ailyn coughed a few times while his gut wound stitched together.

Link helped him to his feet slowly, "what happened?", "How did you?", Ailyn said startled at the destruction to the burning theatre around him, "not much time to stand around now Ailyn, the city is under siege, give your friends some of that elixir and let's get to the keep", Link said.

Ailyn put a few drops of the elixir in everyone's mouth and they groggily got to their feet, Aethor looked at Sin lying on the ground, sword through his stomach, "bastard traitor", he snarled.

"I never knew, I was with him all this time and I never knew", Brawn said mournfully.

"Leave him, we have to go", Fyorn said sadly, "Kimba!", Lore shouted his voice magically enhanced, there was no reply, "is Kimba, ok?", Ailyn asked, "she was fighting with Violet and retreated backstage, last I saw her", Lore said.

"I'll find her", Ailyn said as he rushed off, "we better go, before this place comes down on our heads", Wynn bellowed, they raced out of the amphitheater and headed toward the keep.

Harram clambered out of the broken building and back out to the street, his prey was no longer there, he looked down the street to see them running toward the keep and he moved after them, his large legs smashed through stalls and cleared whole staircases in one stride.

by Lore Casta Pendragon

Guldamere's forces spread like ants into the city, the sound of distant screams could be heard as people fled or were consumed by nightmare creatures.

Guldamere walked through the main gate, the dead laid about his skeletal feet, his acolytes following closely behind, some soldiers approached dropping to a knee, "find Pendragon and the boy Ailyn, kill the rest", Guldamere ordered, they bowed and quickly ran to pass on their orders, Guldamere gave a satisfied grin, "finally after centuries of resistance, Paladins Reach is mine", he croaked.

Locke, Link and the other paladins made their way to the keep, frightened people were still retreating inside when Locke saw smoke coming from the amphitheater, he saw Lore, and the rest of Ailyn's companions running toward them, "what happened?", Link said looking at Vince.

"He fought that", Locke said pointing toward Harram, who was quickly approaching, "everyone inside, bar the doors with whatever you can find, we have to protect the people", Link said.

"Link", Vince coughed, "you certainly have seen better days Vince", Link said attempting to humor him, "put me down", Vince said, they placed him down on the steps outside the keep, "do you remember, when we were kids, we made that pact, to always have, each other's back", Vince was struggling to breathe, let alone talk.

"Of course I do, we haven't left each other's side since", Link said with a chuckle kneeling down, a tear streamed down his face, he looked at Vince's armor, it was crushed, shattered and leaking blood, "I won't be able, to, hold that promise, now, look after yourself, brother", Vince said as he took his final breath, "Vince?", Link said his eyes darting, he couldn't accept what he was seeing, tears and rage welled up in him, he let out a mournful rageful cry, then got up and turned toward the charging Harram, he drew his golden sword and held it at his side.

Standing there, his regal and muscular figure stood statuesque against the backdrop of the burning township, sword in hand his visage inspired everyone, Locke moved beside him and placed a hand on his shoulder, pride and grief showed in his eyes as he stood by his son.

Lore stood on his other side, Aethor and Wynn stood beside them, Fyorn and Brawn on the other side, the paladins lined up behind them followed by sentinel guards, the gate of the keep opened and Ailyn's forces marched out all dressed in suits of armor.

Harram saw the army before him and stopped charging, he smiled and let out a deafening roar, the shadows drew long and darkness pushed back the firelight, numerous horrific nightmare creatures walked out from the shadows.

Guldamere's forces charged up behind, the cacophony parted and the lich himself walked forward, black smokey miasma followed his every step, his boney feet clacked on the stone as he walked slowly to the front.

"Finally, all the pieces come together and the crows can come home to feed", Guldamere croaked.

"It's good to see you again Pendragon, I was beginning to think you too much the coward to face me", the lich provoked.

"I've done enough running Guldamere, today you're going to answer for the millions of lives you've destroyed, the families you've torn apart, you're going to answer for turning this world into a baron hellscape", Lore said.

"Me?", "I'm afraid the world remembers that story a little differently, it was you who caused the cataclysm in your mad pursuit of power and now you're collecting that power to do it all again, we are here to stop you", Guldamere laughed.

His forces cheered and jeered, vastly outnumbering the force in front of them, "there's nowhere left to go, we fight or we die", Locke said, slamming down his helm.

"We can't win, by numbers alone we're beat and that's the great lord of the damned down there, he'll just revive his dead soldiers even if we kill them", Link said.

"What if we offer a challenger, someone to fight on our behalf", Brawn said.

"Guldamere would never agree to terms like that", Wynn bellowed, "it'd be worth a try", Fyorn said, Link nodded.

"We offer a challenge lord of the damned, a champion from either army to settle this, the losing side lays down their arms", Link shouted across the square.

The lich cackled at the suggestion, then turned to Harram, "we will crush then however the worms may squirm, but crushing their spirits first will be even more delightful", Guldamere whispered.

Harram snorted with a big smile, "Harram will be your opponent", the lich called, the gigantic creature walked forward between the armies without hesitation or fear.

Guldamere's forces cheered, murmurs of doubt sprang up around Locke's army, no one man could possibly defeat something so imposing.

by Lore Casta Pendragon

Aethor walked forward, his face a mask of focus and fury, "did he just call that thing, Harram?", Aethor asked, "I thought Ailyn killed him in the living forest", Fyorn said, "Guldamere must have changed him into this monstrosity, I'll fight him, I'm probably the only one who can", Lore said rolling up his sleeves.

Aethor put up his hand in front of Lore, "you're the Harram who killed my Asta and my boy, Aidem, then ran my boy Ailyn into the wilderness to die, is that right?", Aethor called out.

Harram snorted, "It was a shame I didn't have time to have my way with your wife before I killed her, I still remember how she begged and how your boy squealed as I held their heads under the water", Harram taunted, his voice was loud and deep, it reverberated around them and his words penetrated sending fear through their men, they could feel his presence like a lion about to attack.

Aethor ripped off his shirt, he grabbed a dagger from his boot and carved three shallow lines into his chest.

"Have you gone mad, Aethor?", Link asked, the blood trickled down Aethor's body and he wiped it with his hand licking the blood from his fingers, his eyes caught fire and went red, "this guy's about wish he stayed dead", Aethor said glaring at Harram.

Without warning Aethor burst off from where he was standing kicking a cloud of dust from where he stood, everyone's mouths hung open in disbelief as Aethor charged the enemy front line, he leaped and punched Harram directly in the mid-section, sending him falling back onto several of his own men, a cheer went up as Aethor landed on his feet.

"How can a man move like that", Link said, "that's Aethor for you, he's Ailyn's father and a descendant or Aram", Wynn said, Lore gave a happy laugh at the mention of Aram memory.

Harram crushed even more of his men while he got back up, causing Guldamere's army to flee from around him.

"I remember that punch well Aethor, it's not something a man soon forgets", Harram said getting to his feet, kicking back with one foot, he charged at Aethor.

Extending a hand out he ripped a statue from nearby as he ran and swung it at him, Aethor bolted off to the side, running circles around Harram, Harram tried a downward strike to squash Aethor, but no sooner had the statue missed and hit the ground Aethor used it like a platform running straight up Harram's arm, he leaped delivering a flying kick toward Harram's face.

Harram ducked his head but didn't account for the horns, Aethor made contact with one of them and Harram's head whiplashed backward.

by Lore Casta Pendragon

The horn snapped and Harram fell to the side, stumbling into a building, Aethor again landed on his feet, the paladian army cheered with looks of disbelief.

Harram snorted, lifting himself away from the building, a balcony collapsed under his weight, rage consuming him.

He charged again, raising both arms and crashing down toward Aethor, Aethor jumped as Harram approached and as the attack slammed into the ground, Harram raised his head to look up at Aethor as he came down with an axe kick that hit with such force that Harram's head bounced off the cobbled pavement.

Harram let out a pained groan and Aethor stood in front of his prone body, he grabbed Harram's ugly bull face and looked him in the eye.

"If you come back again, I'll be here and I'll be waiting", Aethor said, Harram's eyes went wide as Aethor unleashed a barrage of kicks and punches into Harram's face crushing it into a mass of blood and viscera.

When there was no longer a sign of life from him, Aethor backed off covered in sticky hot blood, steam rose from his body as he turned to Guldamere, "bring him back so I can kill him again", Aethor's rage was all consuming, he was so intense that even Guldamere felt awed, a cheer went up.

"Aethor, Aethor, Aethor", the paladian army cheered.

Guldamere's face turned into one of utter disgust, his front line was still and silent, an acolyte spoke to him, "uh, my lord, your commands?", Guldamere raised a boney finger at Aethor.

"Kill them", he croaked, his army charged forward, Locke and Ailyn's men charged in turn, Aethor readied himself as the faster nightmare creatures reached him first, he leaped back to avoid the bite of a barghast then sprang back with a backfist, followed up with a spinning kick at another that leaped at him, knocking it away.

Link charged in beside him, slashing wildly and powerfully with his golden sword, a Fake avoided the slashes and grabbed his sword arm, it overpowered him with long powerful sinewy limbs, pinning him to the ground.

Wynn came in with his claymore and severed the Fakes front arms, it shrieked as Wynn cut its head off.

Fyorn and Brawn ran in, Fyorn nodded to Brawn and he hurled Fyorn into the air, he raised the magic infused war hammers and slammed them down behind the front line, the ground shook with a loud thud and splintered the stonework sending bodies flying in every direction.

The two armies collided and the ring of steel against steel rang out, Locke and Ailyn's men fought hard, holding the enemy army deadlocked as men fell to the sound of screams of pain and rallying cries.

Petricus crawled out from under the burning rubble in the temple, his body was in two pieces, he was burned all over, Silus was leaned against a wall on the other side of the theatre stage, he was breathing but clearly injured and not moving.

A wounded soldier came wandering in, "a deserter from the battle outside?", Petricus thought, clutching at a stomach wound he sat in one of the theatre chairs trying to tend to a heavily bleeding wound.

Petricus smiled and crawled toward him, the soldier didn't notice him until Petricus crawled up and grabbed him by the ankles, the man cried out with fear as Petricus pulled the life force from himself into the other man and forced the soldier out into his own dying body.

Petricus got up and stomped on his old body until the soldier died, he realized this man's body too was dying, he felt faint from blood loss and looked over at Silus who sat there panting, he smiled and stumbled toward him.

Silus awoke to a burning sensation, his clothes started to catch fire, he quickly patted out the flames, coughing and crawling away from the fire, he tried to stand several times but fell down each time, the lightning bolt that hit him had done something to his muscles, they weren't moving right.

"Damn that wizard", Silus thought stumbling into a wall, he slid down and sat against it, panting and struggling to breathe against the acrid smoke of the fire, he looked around and saw Petricus's dismembered body crawling toward an unaware soldier, the soldier stomped Petricus to death then looked toward Silus smiling and staggered toward him.

Silus noticed the blood gushing from the soldiers wound and his eyes widened, "stay away from me you foul thing", Silus warned, but Petricus kept stumbling forward, Silus pushed against the wall to his feet, his muscles strained to lift him.

He tried to throw a knife but he missed completely, "Silus, give yourself to me, give me your body", Petricus said angrily, getting closer, Silus walked a few steps then collapsed, "that's right don't struggle now, we can share", Petricus laughed.

Silus noticed a rope tied near him holding up a bundle of sand bags, with a flick of his wrist a knife was in his hand.

He waited for Petricus to get closer, then slashed the rope, Petricus tried to move out of the way, but the sand bags crashed into him, pinning him to the floor face down.

by Lore Casta Pendragon

Silus limped over to him, "you're a despicable creature, I doubt Guldamere will bring you back after I tell him you tried to kill me", Silus said turning to walk away.

Petricus chuckled at the words and Silus stopped, "Guldamere doesn't care if you live or die, you're merely a pawn for him to use and discard, you think the promises he made of bringing back your lost lover were genuine?", Petricus said, "he simply used that as a leash to tame you, he never had any intentions of bringing her back to you", his words cut deep, but Silus was too exhausted to fight and left Petricus alone in the burning theatre.

Ailyn ran through the theatre searching for Kimba, he followed the path of destruction outside a service door and found Silus limping toward her.

Kimba was collapsed on a bridge not too far away near a pile of embers, Ailyn felt a pang of fear, he sprinted down the path as Silus turned to face him.

"Oh, you're alive, that is truly a miracle if ever I saw one", Silus said, Ailyn saw that he was obviously injured as he was stooped, clutching at his chest.

"Silus, you tortured me and my father and now you're going to pay for what you've done", Ailyn said approaching him.

Silus sunk down to a knee unable to keep himself standing any longer, "do what you want Ailyn, I can't stop you, but remember, your father and you survived, I spared you both when I could have killed you, I'm not like Harram, I don't murder people on a whim", Silus said.

"Liar!", Ailyn shouted, "you killed my mother and my brother", Ailyn said.

"No Ailyn, Harram murdered them, I took your father away from you, because it's my job to extract information from people for lord Guldamere, we may be enemies, but I'm not the monster you think I am", Silus said.

"Then why work for Guldamere, why work for them", Ailyn said not caring much for the answer, "because he promised to bring back the only person I ever loved", Silus said, "there's nothing I wouldn't do to see her again", Silus said.

He tried standing again but failed, "if you think Guldamere would stay true to his word you're a bigger fool than I took you for", Ailyn said walking past him.

Silus gritted his teeth, Ailyn picked Kimba up, he looked at the pile of ashes near her, a breeze blew the ashes away revealing a glowing white shard.

Ailyn walked over to it and it began to glow brighter.

Ailyn put Kimba down, the shard filled his head with heavenly music, the beauty of it lured him and he reached out for it, the bright light cast beams through his fingers and a voice called out to him.

"Well done, Ailyn, you've found the two of five shards, hurry, take me to the front", the shard spoke to him in his mother's voice, Ailyn understood what he had to do and nodded.

He picked Kimba up and ran for the keep, Silus snarled as he watched him pass, unable to pursue him.

Acolytes began reigning fireballs onto Locke and Ailyn's men, Lore slammed his fists together, then extended his fist to the sky, it glowed with a penetrating light from behind the frontline of troops and blinded them, the nightmare creatures shrieked and ran as Locke and Ailyn's men took advantage of their weakness to press their attack.

Guldamere gave a signal and two groups of acolytes lined up into semi circles, they all extended an arm toward an acolyte at the center who aimed a hand at an angle over the battlefield.

A fireball the size of a barrel grew in the acolytes open palm and he fired, Locke was observing the battle field from the rear and saw the large ball of fire coming in.

"Take cover!", He called, Lore magically enhanced Locke's voice so it carried over the noise of battle, the fireball crashed in and exploded, sending bodies behind their front-line scattering.

"We've got to take out those mages", Locke said, "can you distract Guldamere?", He asked Lore, "I'll do my best", Lore said, "right, sentinels on me", Locke said marching off toward to the western flank.

The acolytes were readying for another volley, Brawn fought side by side with Fyorn, he held a pickaxe in each hand digging away at enemies in front of him, just like how he used to pick at the stone in the pit, each powerful blow pierced through armor.

Fyorn was slamming enemies left and right with those devastating war hammers, carving a path through the enemy's defenses, the enemy parted and back off as Guldamere walked toward them, both men raised their weapons and faced him.

"It seems death himself has come for us", Fyorn said, "let's not make it easy for him", Brawn replied.

Guldamere raised a hand to his rotten mouth and made a circle with his fingers, he blew through it and a black-green smokey miasma poured out and bellowed toward them, the cloud of acrid rot swept over them and they began to choke and cough, falling to their knees grabbing at their throats.

A gust of wind kicked up and blew the smoke away violently, Guldamere and the enemy soldiers shielded themselves trying to keep their footing as Lore dropped his veil and appeared beside them.

by Lore Casta Pendragon

"On your feet", Lore said as he moved between them and Guldamere, "keep the fodder away, I'll keep him busy", Lore said.

Fyorn and Brawn got to their feet, they darted left and right as the enemy army collapsed in on them.

Lore shot fireballs toward Guldamere, black miasma rose from behind him, a demonic shadow rose around him like dark hands, encasing Guldamere as the fireballs collided.

They opened, then arced around either side of Lore and attempted to crush him, Lore slammed his fist together raising magic wards to either side as the clawed hands slammed into them.

Lore extended a hand forward and blew a gust of wind at Guldamere, launching himself backward as the demon claws shattered the wards like glass, then slapped together like an iron maiden of sharp spikes, he landed in between Brawn and Fyorn.

Lore slammed his fists together again, electricity started crackling around him, he raised both hands to the sky as enemy soldiers ran toward them from every direction, clouds circled in like a tornado in the air above them.

It crackled as it built charge, Lore's robe rose from the static as he brought his hands down, lightning exploded all around them, blasting enemy troops and nightmare creatures away, several bolts struck at Guldamere, but he raised a demonic hand shielding himself.

The acolytes in the rear summoned another fireball and let it go, it exploded into the rear line of sentinels, felling many.

Locke and Ailyn's men had begun to thin, fighting desperately for their lives, the acolytes heard a sound coming from the left, the unmistakable thud of horse hooves as Locke and Link came riding around a block of houses from the left with a dozen of his paladins on horseback, they crashed into the Acolytes before they could react, spearing them with lances and trampling them under foot.

Guldamere saw his men dwindling and smiled wickedly, black miasma rose around him into a demon with Guldamere encased at its heart, smoke curled up as it grew, Guldamere opened his arms wide, looking toward the sky, the form around him copied his movements, the darkness spread from him.

Trails of black smoke rose from the ground under foot as the dead that littered the ground on both sides opened their eyes.

Aethor and Wynn were fighting on the frontline, bodies piled up around them.

                                        by Lore Casta Pendragon

The risen started to get up and they backed into each other back-to-back, both of them were tired to the point of collapsing, "we're done for", Wynn said, "even if you put them down, Guldamere will just bring em back again", "keep fighting, we have to, keep fighting", Aethor responded.

Fyorn and Brawn were over-run, the men they felled got up and surrounded them, inching closer, spears and swords pointing in at them, the dead snarled at them and the nightmare creatures became eager for the feast to come.

Locke and Link finished off the last of the acolytes in the backline as Lore aimed his fingers at Guldamere, electricity crackled from him, it grew in intensity until he fired a powerful bolt of lightning at Guldamere which caught him in the chest, both Guldamere and his demonic apparition flew backward, but his gambit left him wide open, Guldamere's army leaped on him, cutting and biting at him, he was completely overwhelmed.

The sound of a horn came from behind the enemy forces, Gear ran through the gate followed by Farin and the dwarves of the Iron halls, a war balloon floated over the wall, Mech and Felix flight were piloting it.

"Keep her steady", Felix said, "looks like we're late to the party", Gear said, "let's show them the might of the Iron Halls!", Farin cried as the dwarven army charged in, crashing into the rear line, they smashed away at the undead men, hacking them to pieces, but every time a man fell, he rose again, some dwarves turned on kin but they kept on fighting.

Farin's men smashed at the enemies forces again and again with war hammers and mauls, the risen continued to fight even with bodies so broken, they looked unrecognizable.

An undead soldier grabbed at Farin's ankle, Farin took a solid hit to his helm from a broadsword and fell back, "fall back and regroup", Farin ordered as the dwarves fell back into line.

Farin shot a flare into the air and Mech waved down from the war balloon, they positioned themselves over the enemy troops and a battalion of dwarven grenadiers threw down their bombs, they exploded sending the enemy forces scattering.

A group of acolytes on the wall saw them and shot a fireball at the war balloon.

"Incoming!", Felix yelled as the fireball shot a hole through the fabric lining, the balloon began to sink as it lost air pressure, Mech pulled on a lever and a parachute deployed, "we're going down", Mech said as the balloon fell toward the river near the keep.

"It doesn't matter how many we fell, if they keep being risen, we can't win, we need to take out the lich", Locke said swinging his sword at a soldier with an arm missing.

by Lore Casta Pendragon

Ailyn ran up the stairs in front of the keep, he placed Kimba down in front of the gate, then turned to see his friends being overrun.

"Hold the shard high Ailyn, pour your life force into it", he heard Asta's voice say from the shard, Ailyn held the glowing shard above his head and a white light poured out from it, a barrier of white light extended out in an expanding dome, accompanied by a heavenly choir of music.

It travelled fast and as it encompassed the battlefield.

The undead dropped, nightmare creatures saw it coming and attempted to flee only to be obliterated upon its touch, the men surrounding Ailyn's friends mostly fell away leaving only a tenth of Guldamere's forces remaining, the dome contracted again as Ailyn absorbed the power of the shard.

Aethor slammed his fist into one of the remaining men, sending him flying, the men around him ran which began a cascade of enemy troops fleeing, the enemy had broken.

Link, Locke, Fyorn and Brawn all noticed Lore on the ground and heavily wounded, they dispatched the last of the enemies around them as they ran to help him.

Link got there first and lifted Lore from the ground, "Pendragon, speak to me", Link said.

Lore was covered in wounds and was bleeding heavily, "I don't have the power left to heal", Lore said faintly, his hands shook uncontrollably, his body went limp and his eyes closed, Link turned to Locke, "do we have any Elixir left?", He asked, "no I'm afraid not", Locke said sadly.

Aethor and Wynn walked up their faces sullen under a cover of dirt and blood.

"Let me see him", Ailyn said walking up from behind them, he knelt down and placed a hand on Lore's shoulder, a white glow emanated from Ailyn and Lore opened his eyes, he placed his fists together and hummed in a low pitch, his wounds slowly began to stitch together.

"How did you do that?", Locke asked, "I thought mages couldn't heal each other", Aethor added, "I didn't heal him, I merely woke him up and gave him the power to heal himself", Ailyn responded.

A house exploded into shrapnel as Guldamere's demonic shadow burst from it, acrid black smoke bellowed out around him, more of his flesh had been burned away from Lore's attack, a few wounded soldiers were still attempting to retreat past Guldamere, black miasma rose around their feet and grabbed them, they screamed as he drained the life from them.

"I will not tolerate deserters, turn or die", Guldamere said, his voice enhanced by chaos magic, "he's alone, we can end this here and now", Ailyn said.

                                                by Lore Casta Pendragon

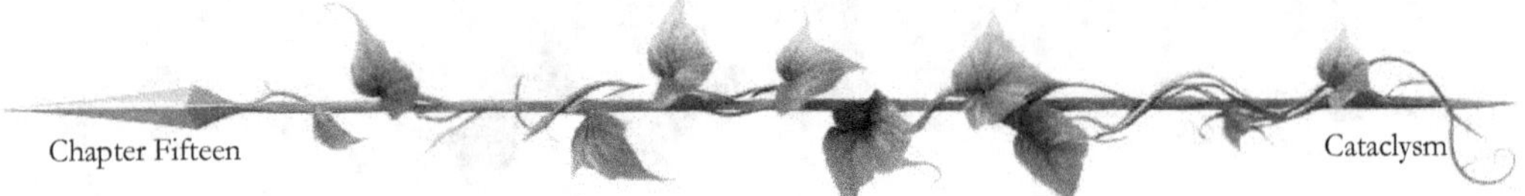

He got up and walked toward Guldamere, "even with your power, your still just a man", Ailyn said.

"A man?", Guldamere smirked, "I am so much stronger than a man", he cackled, standing to the full height of the demonic apparition that surrounded him.

A white glowing mist rose from Ailyn's body, he ran at Guldamere, his friends watched him charge completely fearless of the evil before them, their backs straightened and they looked upon him with a hope they never felt before.

"What are we waiting for, lets end this!", Fyorn said running after him, one by one, Aethor, Brawn, Link, Locke, Wynn, Farin and even Gear, charged after him.

Guldamere's large shadow claws formed a fist and smashed down toward Ailyn, he dashed to the side narrowly avoiding it as it shattered stone beneath it.

Guldamere followed up with an attack with his other clawed hand, using his momentum Ailyn slid under it then leaped in the air kicking Guldamere in the chest, he stumbled backward a few steps, he looked up to see Aethor was right behind Ailyn slamming him again.

Guldamere tried to crush them bringing the large shadow claws together, but Link, Locke and a company of paladins stood to either side shields up, the hands slammed into them driving them together, but they held.

Brawn threw Fyorn right up the middle and the war hammers came down, Guldamere took the full brunt of the magically infused hammers and the demonic apparition slammed down into the ground face down.

Guldamere had a look of shock on his face as he looked at his skeletal hands, the bones were starting to crack and splinter, Guldamere was reaching his limit, the shadow claws pushed him back to his feet.

"You, you can't do this to me, I am the god feared, I will destroy you all", Guldamere croaked, but no sooner had the words left his mouth, Wynn raised his claymore high and threw it with all his strength it turned end over end and slammed into Guldamere's ribcage, the claymore stuck right through the demonic apparition and skewered him.

Guldamere went limp his head dropped to his chest, the demonic shadow around him still held him in the air.

Felix and Mech ran by Kimba, "Miss Kindheart", Felix said rushing over to her, she opened her eyes to see destruction and death splayed out in front of her, "Felix?", she said confused.

"Are you ok?", Felix asked, "I'm fine, I'm just so tired", Kimba responded, "a battlefield is no place to take a nap", Mech said.

                              by Lore Casta Pendragon

"Is it over, did we win?", Kimba asked, her eyes came back into focus, she saw Guldamere's huge demonic form looming over her friends, "not yet but it looks like we got him backed into a corner", Felix said.

Ailyn and his friends just stood there wondering if Guldamere was finished.

Guldamere started to laugh, quietly at first, then louder until it became a full maniacal cackle.

"You insignificant worms, you can't defeat me", the lich said, his golden eyes a blaze of black miasma, "I control death, I control who lives and who dies, I raised you all from the dead after I destroyed the world and when I'm done, I'll do it again and I'll feast on you all, lacrimosa is coming, the great reaping", Guldamere cackled again.

Silus moved out from the shadows, "you never had any intentions of bringing her back, did you", he addressed the lich, the lich looked down at him with a pitying look.

"The chains that bind Silus, I think a clean slate is best", he smirked.

Silus felt his heart break, everything he'd done, he'd done holding onto the hope of bringing Cinder Crowler back, he snarled whipping his coat back, he launched a dozen daggers at the lich, a black claw moved to impede their path but Silus stretched his hands out like he was controlling a marionette puppet, the daggers darted around it, he clapped his hands together and the knives stuck into Guldamere from both sides.

Guldamere didn't even make a sound, he turned toward Silus and snatched him up in a claw, Silus grunted in pain as Guldamere squeezed him tightly looking him in the eye.

"I think your usefulness has run its course", he said, throwing Silus like he was nothing, Silus flew through the air and smacked heavily against the stone wall of the keep right near Kimba and the others, they backed away with a fright as Silus landed face first into the marble stone.

 by Lore Casta Pendragon

Chapter Sixteen

The ultimate sacrifice

The lich extended both arms and the shadows grew long, extending below their feet, Aethor walked up beside Ailyn.

"Let's end this", Aethor said, swiping the blood from his chest wound and licking it from his fingers, Ailyn followed suit and bit into his thumb drawing blood, their eyes went red and a white aura emanated from Ailyn pushing the shadows back from around him.

Guldamere smirked and raised his hands above his head, small dark claws extended from the shadows grabbing everyone by the legs, Lore raised his fist and grabbed his elbow, it glowed with a bright light then exploded outward in a small radius, the shadow claws around him were burning away.

Men screamed and bashed at the claws trying to get free, the lich extended both hands to his sides and the black miasma demon slowly formed a scythe in its hands, the dark claws reached for Ailyn and Aethor but were unable to permeate the white aura surrounding him, "I'll stick with you", Aethor said, "try to keep up old man", Ailyn smirked.

They shot off like a bullet, moving around to one side and running up the side of a building, they leaped together punching at the lich, but Guldamere swung the scythe toward them, they punched into the thick handle of the scythe making Guldamere slide backward, he grunted and swung at them again.

Ailyn and Aethor both placed their feet on the scythe handle and backflipped away.

Guldamere tried to slice at them again as they fell but they kicked off one another avoiding the blade, they landed on the ground and another slash came at them, they leaped up avoiding the blade again by inches, landed the sprung off punching at the lich.

Shadow claws stretched out around Guldamere, forming into a clamshell like shield as the fingers linked, they slammed into it, the demonic form slid back again.

The shell opened and Guldamere swung low, they both dashed forwards with a dragon kick aiming at the scythe, they made contact with the rigid handle and it cracked, the blade burst into smoke, the clawed fingers snapped shut linking together around Guldamere once more.

"It's not impenetrable, we can break through", Aethor said, Ailyn and Aethor charged forward pummeling the hard black shell protecting the lich, it began to crack and Guldamere cried out in anger.

by Lore Casta Pendragon

The black miasma form shattered and fell away, revealing the lich, he had both hands extended toward them fireballs in each hand, Ailyn and Aethor were caught unaware and raised their hands to guard as the fireballs blew them away.

They flew across the battlefield leaving smoking trails across the sky, Ailyn landed nearby to the keep while Aethor flew into Lore, who caught him with a gust of wind, suffocating the fire smoldering on his pants.

"Ailyn!", Kimba said getting to her feet, she moved over to him, padding the fire from his clothes, Ailyn smiled at her the red fading from his eyes and the white aura growing dim.

Aethor looked up at lore, "he got me", Aethor chuckled, his eyes going from red to brown, "you've taken out his defenses, I'll take it from here", Lore said, the wind picked up around him and he rose up with it.

Petricus managed to free himself from under the sand bags, his newly stolen body was badly burned, wounded and broken.

"I must find new flesh", he thought, he could hear the battle raging outside and slowly he crawled out of the theatre while his enemy was distracted.

He crawled across the battlefield, searching around until he found severed body parts that would serve his purpose, he assimilated them to his body until he had a functional form, he came across the body of Harram and smiled wickedly, "this will do nicely", he said squeezing himself into Harram's broken eye socket like a maggot.

Guldamere was panting, he was losing strength quickly and he knew it, "I won't be defeated, not by mere mortals and not by you", Guldamere said pointing at Lore.

He clasped his hands together, Lore came floating down on the wind, "I've been waiting for this moment for over five hundred years", Lore said walking toward him and raising a hand toward the lich, fire began to flicker in his palm, people began to scream out in pain behind him and Lore turned to see the men still being held by their legs begin to be drained of their life force.

Lore turned back to Guldamere his face one of hatred and disgust, Guldamere used the life force he stole to summon a shadow claw and grabbed Lore dragging him close.

"Be gone you vile thing", Lore said as a gout of fire spread out from his hand, burning at Guldamere's mid-section, first his tatted black robe, then his rotted flesh, until all that was left was a blackened charred spine, men began to drop behind Lore as Guldamere drained the life from his victims to give himself strength.

by Lore Casta Pendragon

"Just die you fiend!", Lore shouted, a white aura sprung out from around him, Guldamere's gold pupils fixated on it, the flame got larger and hotter than before, encasing all of Guldamere's body in fire, the knifes and broadsword that were previously penetrating him dropped to the ground as the lich slumped into a pile of charred bone, the black miasma faded off, the golden light in the liches dark eyes faded and the black miasma that made them swirled away leaving only an empty skull, the dark claws faded off into smoke and everyone fell down exhausted.

Link got up and helped Locke to his feet, "we did it!", "The lich is defeated!", Locke shouted and a grand cheer went up.

Ailyn slowly rose to his feet, "Ailyn, are you ok", Kimba asked, "somethings not right", Ailyn said concerned, "what do you mean?", Kimba asked, "I can still feel him, that cold feeling you get in your spine when nightmare creatures are near", Ailyn explained, "I feel it too", Kimba said.

Lore kicked at the smoldering bones by his feet, "was the power destroyed with him?", He wondered.

Black miasma condensed behind him forming into a dark robed figure, the only tangible feature was the glowing golden pupils showing inside the cloak.

"Behind you!", Fyorn called out, but it was too late, the figure plunged a black dagger made of black miasma into Lore's back it stuck through him then burst and disappeared, Lore gave out a breathy cry of pain, then turned.

"Did you think you had won Pendragon", Guldamere's ethereal body grabbed Lore by the shoulder, "I control death, I control darkness, if I could bring the dead back to life, did you not think I could bring myself back also, fool!", the lich said scornfully.

His voice wasn't the raspy dead voice of a lich anymore, but the echoing voice of a bodyless wraith, he plunged another dagger into Lore whose eyes went wide with horror, Lore threw his arms around the lich's body, his face sullen, blood dripped from his mouth, "if I have to go, I'm taking you with me", Lore said as he clasped his hands behind the lich firmly, Guldamere tried to pull away but some magical force held him.

Ailyn got to his feet and charged as fast as he could toward Lore, "be careful Ailyn", Kimba called after him, "let me go fool", Guldamere said a dagger appearing in his hand, he stabbed Lore again in the side and Lore grunted in pain, "let us see what the lands beyond have in store for us old friend", Lore said as a blinding light began to emanate from Lore consuming him.

Ailyn couldn't see them anymore, the light exploded outward and men were consumed by it as it travelled outwards, Ailyn rushed through to reach Lore.

by Lore Casta Pendragon

Guldamere cackled maniacally, the power flowed into him as the entire city was engulfed by light.

Lore and the lich disappeared, consumed by whatever spell Lore had used.

Ailyn felt his body become lighter, his whole world became an empty void of whiteness, after a short time, he felt himself drop, he fell hard and landed on a large sand dune, he rolled down unable to find his feet and tumbled off a cliff face, he grabbed the ledge and hung from it.

Wind and sand blew all around him and he couldn't see the bottom, he tried to pull himself up but the sandy ledge crumbled away and he almost fell.

Holding on by his fingers, he began to slip but a heavily scarred hand reached out and grabbed his arm, he looked up squinting to see who it was.

Silus had him by the arm and his eyes went wide, to his surprise Silus pulled him up, he looked at him cautiously, "why help me?", Ailyn asked, Silus just nodded towards a nearby rock face and started walking toward it.

Ailyn tore the sleeves from his burned Gi and wrapped it around his head to shield his eyes from the dust and sand, they made their way over to the cliff face, Silus walked into a narrow slit in the cliff which opened into a small cave, Ailyn followed.

Kimba was already seated by a fire inside, once she saw Ailyn coming, she got to her feet and embraced him, "Ailyn, I'm so glad you're alive", she said relieved.

"You too, but where are we, how did we end up here?", Ailyn asked.

"From what I can tell, we're in the blasted lands of the eastern desert", Silus replied, Ailyn frowned at him, "why are you here and why are you helping us?", Ailyn said standing in front of Kimba.

"I'm not your enemy Ailyn, I only followed Guldamere's orders so he'd bring back Cinder Crowler for me", Silus said looking down, "I was wrong, he betrayed me".

"That doesn't excuse all the people you've hurt", Kimba said, "I know that, but if the shoe was on the other foot and someone offered to bring back your family, you'd have done the same", Silus said.

"Of course not!", Kimba shouted at him, "I might have", Ailyn said, lowering his guard.

"So how do we get out of here", Ailyn asked, "we have to wait out the sand storm, I don't suppose either of you have any supplies", Silus said. Kimba sighed and reached into a pocket in her now ruined dress, she pulled out her robe, then moved outside to change.

Ailyn and Silus stood there silently not saying a word until Kimba came back in, she pulled out a loaf of bread, some cheese and a canter of water from the sleeve of her robe.

                                             by Lore Casta Pendragon

"How did you fit all that in there", Ailyn asked, "a girl has her secrets", Kimba shrugged at him.

"What happened back there?", "All I saw was that light and I ended up here", Kimba said, Ailyn looked at her sadly, "you might want to sit down Kimba", Ailyn said sullenly.

"Lore Casta Pendragon is gone, he used the last of his power to take Guldamere with him to the lands beyond, but not before Guldamere took Lore's power for himself", Ailyn explained.

Kimba looked at him with tears in her eyes, Ailyn had to look away, "that's not good", Silus said, "Guldamere always said that if he obtained more of the power, he could revive anyone, not just from the abyss but from the lands beyond as well, that probably includes himself".

"So, your saying Lore's sacrifice was in vain?", Kimba said tearfully.

"We don't know the extent of his power now, but there is a chance he could come back", Ailyn added.

All three of them sat there thinking about what horror might await them if Guldamere was to return, "what do you think happened to everyone else", Ailyn said, "if we ended up here, it's possible that the others got transported away as well, there might be more of us out in that storm, we should go look for them", Kimba said, "don't be a fool", Silus replied, "I couldn't see anything out there, it was only by chance that I found the two of you".

"He's right, if we go out there now, we'd be buried alive in that storm", Ailyn said, "we'd best get some rest and search in the morning", Silus added.

He walked over to a sandy spot by the cave wall and laid down, Kimba wrapped her robe around her and laid down by the fire, Ailyn looked over at Silus, he didn't trust that Silus wouldn't try to kill them in their sleep, so he sat by the fire and tried to stay awake.

Ailyn opened his eyes, the morning sun shone hot through the cave entrance, he didn't mean to fall to sleep, Kimba and Silus were gone.

Ailyn began to panic, he dashed out of the cave to find Kimba using chaos magic to draw moisture from a singular white cloud high above them, a tiny trickle of water was coming down from the sky and she held up her canteen, the cloud slowly faded from sight as the last of it trickled into the canteen.

Kimba shook the canteen, it was only half full and she pouted, Ailyn stood next to her, "we can't stay here, even with your magic, there isn't any food", Ailyn said.

Kimba smiled, happy to see him and offered him the canteen, he drank sparingly and returned it to her, "I know, but it's hot, I don't know if I'll last long in this heat", she responded, "I heard there was an oasis in the middle eastern part of the desert", Kimba said.

                                        by Lore Casta Pendragon

"Well, if the sun rises in the east, then we'll need to go that way", Ailyn said pointing toward the sun.

"Where did Silus go?", he asked, "he was gone when I woke", Kimba said, "it's fine, we don't need him, if he perishes here, it'll be better for everyone", Ailyn said.

Silus threw down an animal from the rockface above them, it was covered in scale armor plating from head to toe, he jumped down from the ledge, Ailyn had to move out of the way so Silus didn't land on him.

Silus stared Ailyn in the eye then walked past to collect the creature, he grabbed it by the leg and dragged it over to the cliff face rolling it onto its stomach, with a flash a knife was in his hand and he gutted the animal right there in front of them without flinching.

Kimba gagged and had to walk away, Ailyn walked up to Silus, "why'd you come back", Ailyn said, Silus just continued on the animal and didn't say a word, "if we're going to get out of this place it'd be best if we worked together", Ailyn said.

Silus stopped and lifted his head, "and what exactly can you do to help", Silus said, "there's a green zone, an oasis, to the east, the sun rises in the east, so if we follow the sun in the mornings, we could reach it", Ailyn said, "do you know how large the eastern desert is boy?", Silus said.

Ailyn shook his head, "not only that, the nightmare creatures here aren't afraid of the light, there are sand stalkers, dune mines and sand pirates here, not to mention these things", Silus held up the animal he was slaughtering.

"This is only an infant, the adults are much, much larger and their armor is so thick it can't be penetrated by steel, the armor is soft when they're young and the meat is tender", Silus explained.

"The creatures here prey on the merchants that trade between the oasis to the east, the elven forest to the north and the ronin city to the southwest, if we try to cross the desert, we'll be swallowed whole by sand stalkers, eaten alive by dune mines or murdered by pirates", he added.

"Then how are we going to get back", Kimba asked, "the trade merchants use giant ships with cannons and hire mages from the cities to maneuver the sands, they cross quickly, the pirates though, are always a problem", Silus explained.

"So, we need to find a trade route close by and try to hail a ship?", Kimba said, Silus winked at her.

by Lore Casta Pendragon

"But that runs the risk of hailing pirates", Ailyn added which got another nod from Silus.

"So, no matter what we do, there is a risk we might die", Kimba said, "now you're catching on", Silus replied, ripping the armored hide from the animal, he threw the offal over the edge of the cliff face and stood up and thrust the carcass toward Kimba.

"I'll need fire to cook this, I'll find us some salt", Kimba gagged again while trying to nod, Ailyn chuckled which gained Silus's attention, he looked him dead in the eye.

"You can fight, make yourself useful and go look for tracks in the sand, look for long lines carved into the crest of the dunes, but be careful, the sand stalkers leave very similar trails", Silus instructed, Ailyn nodded and turned to go, "oh, don't fall into any sand mine pits or you'll never be seen again", Silus added and Ailyn gulped and began stepping much more carefully.

Silus dug a hole in the cave and Kimba summoned fire to heat the sand, Silus threw the carcass in and buried it in the hot sand, "that should insulate it enough for a few hours of cooking, I'll dig it up again and you can heat it up as we need it", Silus said.

"Brilliant", Kimba said, "come with me, we need salt to preserve the meat", Silus said and Kimba followed him outside.

The sun was glaringly hot, it burned at any skin they left uncovered, they wandered out for a while until Silus found a flat of hard sand, "here, now shift the sand like you're trying to loosen the earth beneath", he requested.

Kimba put her fists together then placed her hand on the sand flat, it vibrated and the heavier sand began to fall while the lighter salts rose to the top, "how do you know how to do all of this", Kimba said impressed, Silus looked at her then looked away.

"I trained Guldamere's forces along with Petricus, we were planning an operation to overtake the oasis and needed our army to be able to survive the desert environment", Silus said sullenly.

"Why did you follow him?", Kimba said abruptly, Silus sighed, "when I was young, I was abandoned and sold to a workhouse for children in Ravenhill, I grew up there with a girl, her name was Cinder Crowler, we got into some trouble and were sold into the service of a man named Malacore who tortured me relentlessly while he trained us to be assassins for the church of the god feared", Silus felt the scars on his face.

"That's horrible, is that where you got those?", Kimba said trying to comfort him.

"Malacore tricked me into killing Cinder, I took my revenge, but that was exactly what Malacore wanted, he wanted to be free of Guldamere and for me to take his place, I died in the battle and my life should have ended then and there, but Lord Guldamere revived me with a promise that if I served him and helped him to obtain more power, he would bring Cinder back to life", Silus explained.

                                              by Lore Casta Pendragon

"So that's why you did all those terrible things, for her?", Kimba asked, "I don't know anymore, I realize now how foolish I was, merely a dog on a leash, I did things, terrible and horrible things and in my mind, it was all justified because there is nothing, I wouldn't do to bring her back, to make amends to her for what I did", Silus said as a single tear ran down his cheek.

Kimba reached up and wiped it away, "he's gone, you don't have to do what he tells you anymore", Kimba assured him, but Silus looked at her with knowing eyes, "he'll find a way back, he always does", Silus said disheartened, "If you think you were the first people to rise against him or defeat him, you're sorely mistaken".

Ailyn looked out over the barren sandy dunes, after the sandstorm had blown through, he doubted there would be any tracks to speak of, but he trudged on regardless, the sun burned on his skin and the heat of the sand was hot through his shoes.

Ailyn crested a dune, the highest one he could see, he peered out at the horizon, he saw nothing but sand in every direction, he looked closely at a dune to the northeast, it had a triangular split in the top like something large had moved through it, he headed in that direction.

After a while the heat started to get too much and he thought of turning back, there was an explosion of sand behind him and it piled on top of him, he ducked and slipped down on the sandy slope which started him sliding down the steep dune.

He came to a stop and tried to free his feet when another explosion of sand happened in front of him, this time he saw it coming, he closed his eyes to avoid being blinded as the sand piled up around him pushing him further down.

The sand shifted, he noticed the dune was a pit-like shape and remembered what Silus had told him, "Oh, don't fall into any sand mine pits or you'll never be seen again", Silus's voice echoed in his memory and Ailyn began to panic.

Another explosion of sand and he was almost at the bottom of the pit, two very large pincers came up out of the sand and snapped at his legs, he retracted them just in time and narrowly avoided being dismembered, another explosion of sand and in the brief moment as the sand went up before crashing down, Ailyn saw the thing that was trying to devour him, it had four black beading eyes and pincers that were the same height as a man, "that looks like it could be a sand mine", Ailyn said.

The sand came down and buried him at the bottom of the pit waist deep, he felt the cold chill of realization run through him, he knew the next thing would be the pincers pulling him beneath the sand.

"You're not going to eat me!", Ailyn said, he bit into his thumb, the blood made his eyes go red and a white aura surrounded him, the pincers came up around him and clamped.

Ailyn grabbed onto them straining against the strength of the beast, its head came up out of the sand, its mouth biting at his feet.

Ailyn kicked its face and it ducked back beneath the sand, it pressed tighter with the pincers and Ailyn pushed back, he forced the pincers apart then put his legs against them pushing outward, with a loud crack, they broke apart, Ailyn ripped the pincers from the beast.

The monster howled a muffled cry and buried itself further below the sands, Ailyn grabbed the pincers like climbing poles and dug them into the sand to pull himself out of the pit, once he reached the top, he threw the pincers back in the hole and looked around, the pits were much more obvious to him now and he made a mental note to avoid those parts of the sand.

In the distance he saw a flag rising over a dune, the flag got taller and taller, then sails appeared, a ship came over the dune floating on the sand as if it were water, it headed off to the east and over the dune with the triangular crevasse, "that must be the merchants trade route", Ailyn thought, he turned and headed back, following his footsteps in the sand.

Silus was resting with his wide brimmed hat covering his face, he was snoring loudly and Kimba went outside to get some fresh air, she wandered around the cliff face which housed their cave and around to a dune which led up to the top of the rocky cliff face above, she looked out over the land, a scar was seen cutting the land in half, too large, too steep and too deep to cross from here, the desert met the edge of it and stopped as if the world ended right there.

"If master Pendragon had stopped Guldamere in the last age, none of this would have happened, I wonder what the world would have been like then", she thought, after a while she got up and turned around to see Silus was standing right behind her and she screamed.

"Silus!", "You scared me", Kimba said startled, "my nickname at the workhouse was silent Silus", Silus said smirking.

Kimba elbowed him as she walked past and Silus pretended to be hurt while chuckling, Kimba stopped in her tracks and Silus ran into her still chuckling to himself, he looked up and the smirk drained from his face.

Silus grabbed Kimba and leaped off the edge of the dune, they crashed hard into the sand below as an armored creature like the one Silus had killed earlier but about tenfold the size, rolled over where they were previously standing curled into a ball of armor.

Silus pulled Kimba to her feet and dove forward, sand crashed down around them as the beast rolled over the top of them.

by Lore Casta Pendragon

"We need to go, go", he said, part of the cliff face broke off burying the entrance to the cave in rock and sand.

Unfurling itself to see where they had gone, the creature saw them running off into the desert and ran forward on all fours after them, it gained momentum then curled up into a ball of armor plating rolling at speed down the dune, catching them quickly.

Silus pulled Kimba to the side as the creature rolled past almost flattening them, it unfurled again changing directions and running after them, again rolling into a ball of armor.

Kimba slammed her fists together and pulled a bridge of sandstone over the top of her and Silus, the creature rolled over the top of it, they changed directions, this time running up the steep sand dune.

The creature reoriented itself running after them, the creatures was faster than them and it was right on their heels as they crested the dune.

Kimba extended a hand and blasted the thing with a fireball, it just put its armored head down and shrugged it off, "that's not going to work against that armor", Silus said.

It reared up on its back legs attempting to trample them with its front legs, but Kimba extended both hands and summoned a powerful gust of wind.

The sand blew around them, the wind caught the wide flat underside of the creature and it lost its balance falling on its back, curling into a ball and rolling back down the dune.

"Time to go", Kimba said as they turned to run, Ailyn saw them running and joined them, "what's going on?", Ailyn asked, Kimba tried to reply though she was panting heavily, "Rolly, creature, chasing, us", Kimba said and Ailyn looked behind them, "I don't see anything", he said looking around, Silus and Kimba looked back relieved to see the creature was no longer chasing them.

"I'm guessing that was the mother", Silus said panting, "oh, yeah, I was almost eaten by a sand mine back there, but I found the trade route you were talking about", Ailyn said with a smile, Kimba looked up at him looking disheveled, "good, let's get out of here", she said walking past Ailyn.

Silus walked past, Ailyn shrugged and followed remembering his run in with the sand mine, "ah, better let me lead", he said, running to catch up.

Chapter Seventeen

Dune Dancer

Ailyn, Kimba and Silus trudged through endless steep sand dunes, the path of the ship that past earlier could be seen clearly, but the sun beamed down hot and heavy, there was no wind to cool them and the sand was scorching and bright to look at.

"How often do the sand ships pass this way?", Kimba asked as they crested a dune, "usually a few times a day", Silus said, "if a merchant reports pirates in the area though, no merchant will chance a crossing", he added.

"We're going to die out here", Ailyn said sitting on the sand, Kimba put her hands together and the sand began to shake, Ailyn and Silus starting to sink down into it, "what are you doing!", Silus shouted as a wall of sandstone rose out of the sand.

Kimba stopped and gestured towards it, "ta-da!", she said with a happy smile, "you certainly are useful", Silus said snickering, they sat with their backs to the wall, which provided some shade and rested, Kimba tried to summon water from the air but there was none to be found, she drank the last of her canteen and sat back down, "not a single damned cloud", Kimba sighed squinting at the sky.

A few hours later she was sitting down playing a game in the sand using chaos magic, Silus was resting against the wall, his large brimmed hat covered his face, Ailyn stared at the horizon in a daze, half asleep, half awake, a black flag popped over the horizon, Ailyn thought it was just a trick of the light and continued staring until it was followed by a mast.

Ailyn woke up a bit in surprised, then jumped to his feet, "here is comes!", He shouted, Silus lifted his brimmed hat and Kimba stopped playing around, they got to their feet and watched as the ship made its way toward them, "Kimba get their attention", Ailyn said frantically.

Kimba slammed her fists together, extending one arm directly up and holding her elbow, she fired a small fireball into the air and it exploded like fireworks.

The ship slowed as it approached them, then stopped far short of where they were, "who might ye be wandering the desert at high noon, ye have a death wish?", A gnarled man in a brown brimmed hat and brown coat called down to them.

"I'm Ailyn Allheart, this is miss Kindheart and err, Silus", Ailyn said not knowing Silus's actual name, "I'm Silan Silus, pleasure to make your acquaintance", Silus said sweeping his large hat in a grandiose bow, we've been marooned out here for a day and a night, may we come aboard captain?", Silus asked.

                     by Lore Casta Pendragon

"I be Captain Villias Schmidt of the Dune Dancer, come portside, there be a ladder and be quick about it, sand stalkers aren't far off", the captain said looking at something on the horizon.

They climbed a ladder reaching the deck of the ship, the captain took Kimba's hand and helped her step down onto the deck, Silus leaped over the rail as Ailyn climbed up in awe, he'd never been on a ship before.

"Welcome aboard, there be no free passage on this ship, so I'll be putting ye to work right away", Villias eyed them grabbing each of them by the arm one after the other to take their measure, as he walked, he made a loud thudding sound, Ailyn looked down to see the captain's leg was amputated and in its place was what looked to be a cannon barrel.

"Ye look strong enough, ye can help with the lines", Villias said to Silus and Ailyn, "young lady, you look to be a mage of some such, I have a couple mages on board who could use ye help, with you on board we'll reach Oasis in no time and possibly save me some coin, come I'll introduce ye", Villias offered his arm and took Kimba to meet with the other mages, a couple of burly men grabbed Silus and Ailyn and began showing them the ropes.

Kimba walked up the stairs to the flybridge, two mages were stationed there in flowing robes, their faces were masked by hajibs to shield them from the desert sun.

"The las here is Kimba, she be helping ye with the moving of me ship, I trust ye be ok with showing her what to do", Villias said, he seemed a little bit nervous talking to them, the first mage turned to face Villias, obviously female, her figure was slim and the long robe she wore was tight against her figure.

When she spoke, it was slow and drawn, but feminine, "this is fine, but you will compensate us for the extra workload", she said, "err, yes, yes of course", Villias responded casting his eyes down, "well I'll leave ye to it", Villias walked off, his false leg clunking on the deck as he walked.

"Ahoy and make headway!", Villias shouted, the crew began prepping the ship to sail, "we will have to see your control over chaos magic, we will soften the sands from beneath, summon the wind for the sails", the other veiled mage said, his voice and figure marked him as male.

Kimba slammed her fists together and extended both hands toward the sails, a gale blew up and the sails blew forward filling with air, the ship creaked and lunged forward, the two mages grabbed her arms, Kimba looked over at the girl, "not too much, you'll break the ship before we get moving", she said amused looking over at the other mage, her eyes showed surprise.

"Let the wind pick up gradually, or you'll snap the riggings", the male mage said, his voice was also a slow drawl with the same accent, Kimba followed their directions as they joined her.

The ship sank slightly down and the sand around them began to level out and bubble, the ship started sliding forward as Villias came back to take the wheel, "I get it now", Kimba said,

                                                    by Lore Casta Pendragon

"you're pushing air through the sand to lower the surface tension, which allows the ship to sail the sands", "indeed, you are very wise to catch on so quickly, I am Inaya, this is my brother Rayan", Inaya said.

"It's a pleasure to meet you both, I'm Kimba Kindheart, how long have you been on the ship?", Kimba asked, "the good captain hired us from the grand Ger in Oasis, our job is to move the ship but also, to provide protection", Rayan replied.

"I see, what is Oasis like, are there many mages there?", Kimba asked, "a few, we are trained to provide services to the merchants, this provides Oasis with supplies and wealth from the outside world, though the eastern desert is a dangerous place and not all mages make the return journey", Inaya said, Kimba nodded having spent the last two days just trying to survive.

Ailyn climbed up the crow's nest to take a look at the view from the top, once up there he peered out at the endless stretch of sand, he could see several wrecks of ships in the distance, some large armored creatures, craters where sand mines awaited prey dotted the sand and, in the distance, he saw massive waves of sand bellowing out with a large fin pointing out, it seemed to be heading in their direction.

Ailyn watched it squinting as it got closer, it was far off by the look of the sand it was kicking up, it was big, really big, and moving very fast, Ailyn leaped down to a lower mast and jumped off, landing right near Villias who jumped back with a fright.

"Ay boy, ye nearly made me capsize the ship!", He said angrily, "sorry captain, but I saw a large wave of sand heading our direction at speed", Ailyn said, Silus was fixing a rope nearby on the deck and lifted his brimmed hat and looked at Ailyn with concern.

The rest of the men on board stopped what they were doing, one of them climbed up the crow's nest as fast as he could, "ye be sure of what ye saw boy?", Villias asked, "I am", Ailyn said confused.

Villias looked up to the man in the nest, "what do ye see", he called, "sand stalker, closing in fast to starboard captain", the man called down.

"Festering sand fleas", murmured Villias, "miss Kindheart we got company, give the sails more push, we got to move", Villias shouted, "Ay, ay, captain", Kimba said with a smile and the wind picked up.

The ship jolted forward and the crew all lost their footing giving out a collective groan, the ship slid slightly sideways in the sand until Villias got up and grabbed hold of the wheel, "for shit's sake, ye trying to send us overboard girl!", Villias said, Kimba giggled, she was having too much fun with this.

"Glad you're enjoying yourself", Ailyn said, Kimba just shrugged, "I'm not going to act like this isn't fun, because it is".

                    by Lore Casta Pendragon

They crested a sand dune and started down the other side, they made it half way down when the dune exploded out from behind them, a wall of sand falling just behind the ship, from behind the wall of sand a massive worm appeared, four angular beaks opened up showing a mouth lined in teeth and tentacles.

It closed the beaks and air blew sand from holes in its head, it speared itself back into the sand, a large fin trailing like a shark, it was almost as thick as the ship itself and probably tenfold the length.

"What do we do?", Ailyn asked, "we run, we run and hope it finds something else it wants to eat", Villias said, the worm burst out from behind the ship spraying a wall of sand over the deck, it snaked over the back of the ship to the right-hand side, the crew looked up to see the worm's massive size and braced for impact.

Kimba thrust both hands forward and the wind pushed the ship forward avoiding being squashed by the monster, it caught up and moved along beside the ship, "if that thing lands on us, the ship will be nothing more than splinters", Silus said.

The worm exploded out of the sand next to the ship, Silus threw daggers at it and it blew them away with a snort of wind from the holes on its back.

Inaya looked at Rayan, "I got this, go help them", she said, Rayan ran to the side of the ship, some men were preparing a cannon to fire, Rayan placed his hand on the rear of the cannon, the sand stalker exploded out from the sand again aiming toward the ship.

Rayan summoned fire and a cannonball fired out of the cannon, the sand stalker gave a roar as the cannonball knocked it back slamming into it, denting the thick hide, the worm thrashed and crashed back into the sand, even a cannonball couldn't penetrate its thick skin.

The massive fin came up alongside the ship again, Ailyn saw it breathing through holes at the back of the fin, he bit into his thumb, his eyes went red and the white aura surrounded him, he grabbed a keg of gunpowder next to a cannon and ran up the mast tying a rope around his waist then, watched as the hole behind the fin closed.

As the worm took another breath Ailyn backflipped away from the ship, he threw the keg into one of the sand stalkers fin holes and as it closed it got wedged inside of it.

Ailyn swung back to the ship as the fin disappeared under the sand, Silus caught onto what Ailyn was doing and grabbed a rag from a bucket and an oil lamp from a wall, he soaked the rag in lamp oil, pulled out a dagger with a looped hole in the hilt and tied the rag to it.

"Light this!", Silus yelled to Rayan who extended his hand shooting a small flame toward it, the rag ignited and Silus leaped up the main mast, a wall of sand exploded from right next to the ship and the sand stalked threw itself over the top casting a shadow over the entire ship.

 by Lore Casta Pendragon

Silus leaped from the crow's nest as the sand stalker snapped the main mast, he soared over its back narrowly avoiding the fin as he past, he saw the keg and threw the burning knife, it hit true and split the keg, it detonated.

Everyone on the ship dived to the deck as the sand stalker exploded into two halves landing either side of the ship, wriggling and showering the ship and the crew in a rain of gooey worm ichor and viscera.

The explosion sent Silus flying overboard, but Ailyn leaped out and caught him by the arm, they swung back to the ship and some of the crew members helped pull them back up to safety.

The ship came to a stop, as Inaya, Kimba and Villias stood their arms wide covered in sticky hot worm goo, Kimba gagged and ran to the side of the ship, Villias wiped the goo from his eyes then flicked it onto the deck, some of the crew started removing their clothes to get the stuff off of them, one man rang the goo from his shirt which stuck like a giant glob of snot.

Inaya summoned the wind blowing most of the goo off herself and back onto the crew who were already half cleaned, they looked at her none too impressed with a collective groan.

Later on, they helped to clear the mess from the ship and prepared what was left of it for sailing, Villias walked up to where Ailyn and Silus were working.

"Impressive work back there, ye saved me ship as well as our lives, I'm in your debt it would seem", he said with a smile shaking the goo from his hat which splattered on the deck.

"Just get us out of this desert and we'll call it even", Ailyn replied, "right ye are, we aren't far from Oasis now, from there I be travelling to the other side of the desert, the Elven Forest to drop spices to the elves, I can take you there if you wish", Villias offered a hand and Ailyn took it.

"Thanks captain", Ailyn said, "no thank you Ailyn, it's a dangerous business and I'm glad to have men of your fine caliber aboard me ship", Villias said also addressing Silus, Silus threw a pale of viscera overboard and wiped some of it from his coat, Kimba blew some viscera overboard with a gust of wind then walked up still covered in goo, "I don't suppose you have a bath on board?", she asked suppressing a gag reflex.

Once the ship began to sail, they made their way through the desert, Ailyn was amazed at the speed they travelled at despite losing the main mast and soon enough the Oasis came into view as the sun began to set, it was located in a huge rock formation of four spires that protected it from the wind and moving sands of the desert, they passed between two of them and into a valley inside, there were large palm trees surrounding a mass of yurts and a gigantic multi story

                         by Lore Casta Pendragon

Ger, a circular building made of felt, which was located around a large Oasis of sparkling blue water.

At the center of the water was a spout of gushing water that tapered off the closer it got to the shore; the ship followed a path of deep sand which led directly to the large grand Ger.

A man in white robe with a curled goatee, wearing gold chains and golden rings adorned with large gemstones met them as the crew lowered a gang plank, Villias walked down to meet the man arms wide.

"Emir Azir!", Villias called, "Captain Shmidt!", Ezir responded as they moved to embrace each other.

Azir was a short man, he wore a white cap called a keffiyeh on his head, "what have you brought us today captain?", Azir asked, "produce mostly, but I also brought steel and textiles from the Ronin city", Villias added.

"It seems you found a bit of trouble out there on the sands", Azir said his voice slow and drawled much like Inaya and Rayan.

Ailyn, Silus and Kimba walked down the gang plank, "ye wouldn't believe my luck, I found this lot roaming the desert and they managed to defeat a sand stalker, if not for them we'd be worm food", Villias explained.

"Truly, that is some feat, only in stories have I heard of such a thing", Azir said disbelievingly, he looked over the ship, the mast missing and the ship still covered in bits of sand stalker were proof enough.

"Truly", he said astonished, "we will see to repairing the damage to your ship, at a price of course, please make yourselves at home until then, welcome to the Oasis", Azir said to them, he placed a hand on Villias's back and walked him inside the grand Ger to talk business.

Ailyn peered out over the city, night began to fall and the lights from the yurts made the whole place glow with a soft light.

Ailyn heard a rumble which increased in intensity, the building beneath him began to vibrate, Silus whipped out his knives in a flash, "another sand stalker?", he questioned as the rumbling and shaking increased.

"No", Inaya said walking down the gang plank, "look at the cliffs surrounding the valley", she said.

They looked out to see the cliffs had begun to move closer, "the cliff faces that surround Oasis are actually a living creature, each night it closes the valley off from the desert outside", Rayan added.

by Lore Casta Pendragon

"It acts like a natural barrier to invaders and keeps the city safe", Inaya explained, "this valley is actually the mouth of Amanth, a giant sand stalker", Rayan said.

"You built a city inside the mouth of a giant monster, that's madness", Kimba said, "not to worry, Amanth has been asleep since the cataclysm over five hundred years ago, it was said that there used to be a green zone here and that Amanth devoured it, after which he fell into a deep sleep".

Kimba looked over at Ailyn concerned, Ailyn nodded back at her knowingly, "it is well known in Oasis that when Amanth reawakens he will devour the world and it will be the end of all things", Inaya said, "that seems to be an even bigger threat than lord Guldamere", Silus muttered.

Some men came out to collect the ships freight and Villias came to collect them, "Ezir Amir has provided us with lodgings in the city, follow me", he said.

They were escorted to a few luxurious yurts by the waterfront, each one contained beautiful rugs and comfortable furniture, but more importantly each one had a bath and a bed.

Silus walked into his yurt without a word, "I think I'll need to soak for a few hours", Kimba said to Ailyn, "same here", Ailyn added, "can't remember the last time I actually had time to clean up", he said, "oh, I can believe it", Kimba said holding her nose, Ailyn sniffed himself, a look of disgust washed over him, Kimba waved goodbye with her fingers daintily as she disappeared into her yurt.

Ailyn found his yurt and walked inside, he began to strip off, he was happy to find his bath had already been filled and he hopped in, he cleaned off and couldn't remember the last time he had felt clean water, it was warm and comforting and his eyes drew heavy, sleep found him without notice.

Ailyn found himself in his home in Riverside, Asta was cooking in a big cauldron by the fire, Aethor was repairing his boots at the table and Aidem was laying in his bed, there was a knock on the door and Aethor got up to see who it was, as he opened the door to a figure covered in a black cloak, black miasma trailed him as he walked in, Ailyn took a step back as Guldamere walked in as if he was an old friend and sat at the table.

Aidem and Aethor joined him and Asta served them a bowl of soup, Ailyn saw this as surreal, "what's going on?", Ailyn said confused, Guldamere looked at him his pupils were golden light, his eyes made from slowly swirling black miasma, his bony hand gestured for Ailyn to come and sit.

Ailyn cautiously made his way over to the table, "this must be a dream, this isn't real", Ailyn said joining them, his family starting eating not saying a word, Ailyn looked down at the bowl of soup, there were dead insects and pieces of viscera, there was a severed finger in it, he saw

by Lore Casta Pendragon

an eyeball come up on Asta's spoon and she ate it without flinching, Ailyn felt sick to his stomach.

"This is a nightmare, I have to wake up", Ailyn said closing his eyes, after a while he opened them, Guldamere just sat, fingers joined under his skeletal chin with his elbows on the table, his eyes were fixed on Ailyn.

"You're dead, Lore took you to the lands beyond himself", Ailyn said, Guldamere didn't respond, his family took another mouthful of gore, "why are you here?", Ailyn shouted.

Guldamere stared at him, then replied, "you have the power in you, the power I greatly desire", Guldamere's ethereal voice echoed around him, "I have the power to bring them back Ailyn, all I need in return is the power you currently possess", Guldamere said, his gold eyes never left Ailyn's, he never even shifted at all, the black smoke curled around him, his family kept on eating without speaking, ignore the two of them.

Ailyn thought about it, he could have it all back, everything he had lost, but he remembered what Guldamere said when they last met, about his plan, his 'lacrimosa', as he called it.

"No", Ailyn said bluntly, "no, Ailyn?", Guldamere straightened slightly, an air of agitation seemed to wash over him, "you would rather your family dead?", Guldamere asked.

Black miasma rose from under the table, it formed into tentacles and gripped them all by the throat choking them, Ailyn reached out to his family members, "one way or another Ailyn, I will have the power, there is nothing that can stop me now, not distance, nor time, nor death", Guldamere said.

Ailyn's family members began to rot before his eyes, they turned to dust as Ailyn was lifted from his seat by the throat, his feet dangled from the floor, the table disintegrated into black smoke as Guldamere stood before him, he couldn't breathe, "I'm coming back Ailyn and when I do, it will be the end for all of you", Guldamere said.

Ailyn closed his eyes then sat up in the bath, he must have slipped under the water while he slept, he gasped for air turning to grab a towel nearby, he got out of the bath and wrapped the towel around his waist.

Kimba came in wearing a thin white robe, Ailyn could see straight through it, so he diverted his eyes.

"Are you ok?", "I thought I heard something", she said, "I'm fine", Ailyn said, "just fell asleep in the bath", Ailyn replied, "yeah, me too, I had the strangest dream", Kimba said.

Ailyn looked at her confused, "I was visited by Guldamere, he said that if I bring you to him, he'd revive my father, Kamdar", she admitted, walking toward him.

by Lore Casta Pendragon

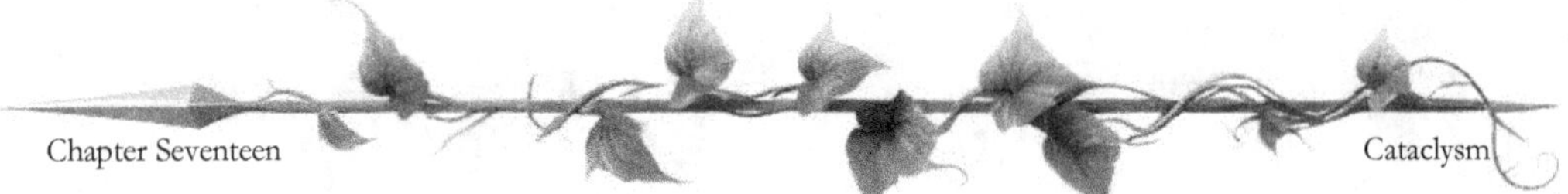

Ailyn took a few steps back, Kimba walked right up to him and looked him dead in the eyes, "when I refused him, he tried to kill me, he said that he would being me back to torture me forever if I didn't give him what he wanted", she said looking at his lips, her big brown eyes penetrated him, she looked so innocent, Ailyn was tense, he wouldn't bare it if Kimba betrayed him, not her, not like Violet had, she moved forward and kissed him.

Ailyn stepped back tripping over his towel, he grabbed onto Kimba and they fell back onto the bed, Kimba landed on top of him, the towel had come loose and he laid bear with her on top of him.

She looked deeply into his eyes, he only then realized that he could see down the thin white robe and she wasn't wearing anything at all beneath it, she kissed him again and he embraced her as she straddled his hips.

Sleep would not come for Silus, he sat against the headboard of his bed sharpening his knives, he heard some chatter outside his yurt and stopped what he was doing, "tonight's fighters are pretty tough, especially the one from Dawnshire", he heard one say as they passed.

"Fighters?", Silus said curiously, he grabbed his coat and hat, then followed the two men who were talking amongst themselves oblivious, they disappeared into a yurt and Silus snuck in behind them.

The yurt was deceivingly spacious inside with a large circular balcony overlooking a fighting pit that was dug into the ground, two men were fighting bare handed to the cheers and jeers of the crowd.

Money was being bet on the fighters and Silus pushed his way to the balcony edge to see who was fighting, one of the men lifted the other smaller man over his head then slammed him down onto his knee, raising his arms to the cheers of the crowd.

A man walked out and raised the fighter's hand in victory, "another flawless victory to our reigning champion Jaleel!", He said to the cheers of the crowd, the other fighter was dragged off leaving a trail of blood behind him by two men.

"Is there any here who would like to challenge the mighty Jaleel for the title?", The announcer said and cheers went up, several fighters looked to be ready to jump into the pit, but Silus leaped down from the balcony and landed close to the announcer and Jaleel first, his coat bellowed out behind him as he landed, he rose slowly to his feet holding the tip of his wide brimmed hat covering most of his scarred face.

"Looks like we have a challenger", the announcer said moving closer to Silus, "you sure you want to fight him, he's twice your size", the announcer muttered unsure of Silus's metal.

"Yeah, I'm sure", Silus said, confidently smirking, the crowd cheered, "fighters to your corners!", The announcer yelled.

by Lore Casta Pendragon

Silus leaped back to his corner with a single jump, coat ruffling, Jaleel swung his large arms and went to his corner, he took a knee, both hands facing toward Silus, obviously he meant to charge Silus and finish it quickly.

A bell rang out and the crowd went wild, Silus stuck his hands in his pockets as Jaleel ran at him, his large rounded shoulders would have made his attack deadly to anyone in his way, little did he realize Silus was a master assassin, Silus leaped over him and stepped on Jaleel's back making him stumble to the floor, Jaleel got to his feet more cautiously now, Silus hadn't even taken his hands out of his pockets.

Jaleel raised his fists and closed the distance; he threw wide arcing punches at Silus who avoided them easily ducking under his arm and leaping backward.

Silus was so light on his feet that he seemed to float around him, Jaleel tried to grab Silus to stop him from moving but Silus launched a kick straight up under the big man's jaw, Jaleel's head snapped back like a whip and Silus leaped off to the side as Jaleel fell face first into the floor, Silus never removed his hands from his pockets.

The crowd went wild and the announcer came back in to raise his hand, Silus smiled soaking in the applause, the crowd hushed as several men cleared space, Azir walked up to Silus.

"Very impressive, you're one of Villias's crew, aren't you?", Azir said, "since you're fighting anyway, why not fight for me, we could make a pretty penny together, you and I", Azir offered, Silus smirked and just nodded his approval.

by Lore Casta Pendragon

Chapter Eighteen

Rivals

Ailyn awakened in the morning with Kimba resting her head on his chest, the smell of her intoxicated his senses and he didn't want to move, but he desperately needed to use the bathroom, he kissed her forehead and managed to slide over and out of the bed, Kimba gave a sleepy groan but did not wake.

He moved to a portioned off section of the yurt to do his business.

When he was done, he quietly tried putting his clothes back on, Kimba woke and smiled at him mischievously, the bed sheet barely covered her naked body, Ailyn smiled at her and she threw the bed sheet at him, he brushed it aside but not before Kimba had disappeared, he looked around confused, not knowing where she had gone, "Kimba?", Ailyn called.

He went to the door to look outside for her and he felt an ice-cold chill waft up his back from behind that startled him, he turned to see Kimba fully dressed with a very cheesy grin on her face.

"How did you?", He said confused, "just a bit of hocus pocus", Kimba said playfully as she threw his clothes at him.

They walked over to the shoreline and peered out at the gout of water which made up the lake at the center of the Oasis, "there's a shard here, I can feel it calling to me", Ailyn said.

"We can't exactly take it from them, I get the feeling it's providing this place with more than just a steady supply of water", Kimba said, "maybe we can make a deal with the Azir for it", Ailyn suggested.

"But what could we possibly offer him that could match an infinite supply of fresh water in a desert?", Ailyn added, "the power to create water from the air itself", Kimba said, pulling out a copy of Lore Casta Pendragons magic tome from her sleeve.

"This book contains some of the knowledge of Lore Casta Pandragon's magic, including the manipulation of water, it's been invaluable to me in my training and it's worth is far beyond anything else that we could offer", Kimba said.

"No Kimba, I couldn't possibly ask you to trade something so valuable", Ailyn said, "it's ok Ailyn I've read through it hundreds of times, I could rewrite it from scratch and even improve on it, if I wanted to", Kimba assured him.

"Alright, but I'll pay you back for it, let's ask Captain Schmidt to set up a meeting with Azir", Ailyn said as they headed for the Dune Dancer.

Villias was standing on the Dune Dancer yelling directions to his crew, a large wooden scaffold was erected with a crane at the top, it was heaving a large wooden mast in place which had a wedge shape to it, the old mast had been cut off and hollowed out to fit the replacement mast inside of it.

Ailyn and Kimba walked up behind him as they lined up the mast, it slotted into the old mast shaft and they fitted a large iron ring full of nails around it and two pins to secure it in place, the crew began hammering it in, with rhythmic coordination.

"Job well done", Kimba said surprised, Villias turned to them, "the Dune Dancer be good as new", he said, "now all that's left to do is to get the ropes and sails back on and clean her up a bit", Villias said, a foul smell had started to emanate from the rotting pieces of sand stalker now solidly stuck to the ship.

"Captain", Ailyn said, "there is something I needed to ask", "ay boy, after ye saved my ship, least I can do is a small favor", Villias said raising an eyebrow putting an emphasis on the word 'small'.

"We need you to organize a meeting for us with Azir", Ailyn said, "a meeting with Azir?", "I'll see what I can arrange, I was going to see him anyway, you should be able to join me", Villias said, "really?", "That was easy", Kimba added, "thanks Captain", Ailyn said.

Villias left the crew to continue their work and walked to the grand Ger with Ailyn and Kimba, they were greeted at the entrance by Azir's guards who wore long curved swords at their sides, one held a ledger in his hands and hurried off to find Azir, not long after, Azir came into the room which was adorned with large pillows of different colors.

"Captain Schmidt, I hope the repair work is coming along to your liking", Azir said in his slow drawl, "ye be fast as ever Emir Azir, I do appreciate it, before we talk trade though, the lad needed to ask ye something", Villias said, Amir looked over at Ailyn and Kimba.

"Oasis contains a valuable artifact, one that supplies it with fresh water, an artefact we mean to procure", Kimba said, Azir shook his head, "I've no idea what you're talking about", he said, playing dumb.

"The water comes from underground water tables, the pressure pushes the water to the surface", Azir turned as he explained, looking over a balcony at the city, Ailyn walked over and stood beside him, a white aura emanated from his body.

"I can feel the power, its calling to me", Ailyn said, Azir looked at him as the white glow faded, Azir turned back and rested his elbows over the balcony, "we've kept it hidden for centuries", Azir said, "without the power, Oasis will cease to exist, I cannot allow you to take it from us", Azir said slamming his hand down.

by Lore Casta Pendragon

"We don't intend to take it from you, but rather trade it for something even more valuable", Kimba said, "something more valuable?", Azir scoffed, "what could be more valuable in the sands than an endless supply of water?".

"This", Kimba said softly pulling the tome from her sleeve, "a book?", Azir said puzzled, "not just a book, this book contains the spells devised by Lore Casta Pendragon about the control of chaos magic, within these pages you will find not only the ability to learn spells long forgotten, but also the ability to summon water from the air, the ground, anything, amongst many other things, it's the only one of its kind", Kimba explained.

Azir's eyes went wide at the possibilities, then returned to normal.

"Surely you do not believe that is enough", Azir said turning to hide his insidious grin, "sounds a good deal to me Azir, what else could you ask for", Villias said, he knew all too well when a trader was trying to hustle for more coin.

"How about a wager, if you can beat my fighter in the pit tonight, I'll take your deal, pay for your repairs and supply you with Inaya and Rayan for free, however, if you lose, you'll hand me the book and get nothing", Azir said.

"That hardly seems like a fair wager", Villias said, Azir turned to him, "take it or take your leave, I don't have time for idle chatter", Azir said, he started walking off.

"I'll do it!", Ailyn called after him, "I'll fight", Azir smiled and turned to him, "very well Ailyn, be at the central yurt tonight at sun down and don't be late", Azir said offering Ailyn his hand to shake, Ailyn took it, Azir smiled wide, then turned and left.

"I hope ye know what you're doing boy, you should not have agreed so quickly to his terms, he played you for a fool", Villias said, Ailyn looked to the door where Azir had left, "we'll see who fools who", Ailyn said determined.

Later that night Ailyn and Kimba were in his yurt, Ailyn was feeling nervous but confident, "be careful out there tonight Ailyn", Kimba said obviously worried, "don't worry about me, I'm stronger than I look", Ailyn said smiling.

Kimba gave him a concerned look like he was doing something stupid, "ye be ready boy?", Villias said entering the yurt, "it's time", Ailyn said standing, his hands were wrapped and his Gi repaired and ready, his long hair was tied in a braid behind him, "let's go", Ailyn said.

They headed for the central yurt in the city, it was larger than the rest, drum beats pounded as they grew closer, some men cheered him on which only grew louder as he entered the yurt, the men eyed him down and placed their bets.

                    by Lore Casta Pendragon

Kimba looked over at a ledger containing tallies of each person's bets, most of the men were betting against Ailyn, so she took a few gold coins from her sleeve and bet in Ailyn's favor, Villias saw her and did the same giving her a wink.

From across the way on the other side of the balcony they saw Azir sitting in a chair, beautiful women in see through fabric dresses sat either side of him feeding him fruits and wine, Azir raised his glass to Ailyn, Ailyn nodded to him then leaped into the pit.

The crowd cheered, it was so loud inside the pit, the noise seemed to reverberate around him and he began to feel slightly overwhelmed.

Azir put up a hand and the crowd dulled to a murmur, "tonight we have Ailyn Allheart, son of Aethor, Descendant of Aram, versus", Azir extended his hand out and Silus leaped into the pit, he smirked at Ailyn.

"Silan Silus, master of the assassin's guild of Ravenhill", he said smirking, "wait, Silus?", "What are you doing here?", Ailyn said, "I've been curious which one of us would win in a one-on-one bout, I guess now we get to find out", Silus said as the bell rang out.

Silus leaped forward, closing the distance he unleashed a volley of punches, Ailyn took a few quick steps back, slapping each one to the side but being driven backward.

Silus turned his body with each punch, hiding his fists behind his body so Ailyn had little time to react and counter, he managed to step to Silus's dead side, his fist came up under Silus's leading hand and Silus took the hit on the chin, he stumbled back, reset his posture raising a hand to cover Ailyn's line of sight.

Ailyn stepped forward to reach for Silus's extended hand, Silus used it as bait and drew Ailyn's hand as he stepped in launching a knee to Ailyn's mid-section following it up with a heavy elbow to Ailyn's back, the crowds cheer erupted through the yurt as Ailyn hit the floor, wind knocked out of him.

Ailyn realized he was in danger and rolled away from Silus as he kicked him in the ribs, Ailyn rolled to his feet grabbing at his mid-section, Silus wasted no time unleashing another volley of short and sharp rolling punches.

Ailyn slapped the first few away, then dashed forward, he stomped on Silus's foot and rotated his knee around Silus's leading leg, his pushed his knee on the back of Silus's knee then grabbed Silus around the throat with one arm and held Silus's wrist with the other, he forced his weight down and Silus was forced to bend backward.

"We need to win this Silus, we made a deal with the Ezir", Ailyn tried to explain, "I don't care!", Silus responded headbutting Ailyn hard in the nose with the back of his head, Ailyn stumbled backward and Silus launched a backward kick into him, Ailyn hit the wall of the pit hard, his vision blurred with tears as Silus unleashed a series of punches to Ailyn's face and body.

							by Lore Casta Pendragon

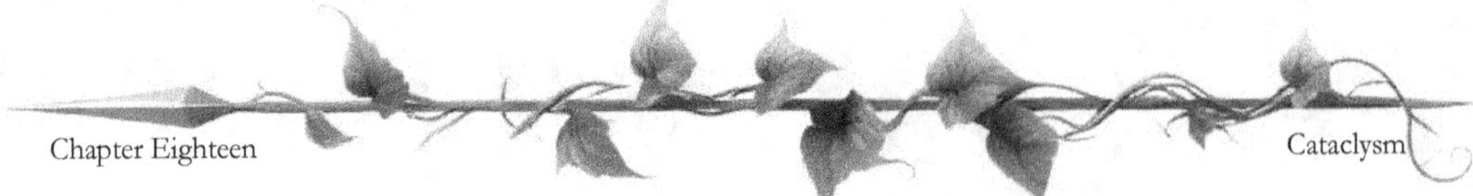

Ailyn managed to roll out with one punch to the side of his face and counter balanced back onto his feet, Silus was relentless in his pursuit until the white aura began to rise around Ailyn, he caught Silus's next punch in his hand, placing his fingers at Silus's diaphragm, Silus looked down as Ailyn let it rip.

The short-ranged punch hit hard and Silus bounced off the floor and into the far wall, Ailyn licked the blood from his mouth and his eyes went red, the white aura glowing around him, the crowd gasped and murmured.

Silus got up panting for air, "so that's how you defeated the pit warden, it makes sense now", Silus said, "it's an interesting technique, but I can tell your burning through your lifeforce like a wild fire, all I have to do is outlast you", Silus said.

Ailyn rushed at Silus like a bullet, but Silus pulled a phylactery shaped like himself from his coat and clapped his hand together in front of himself, a black miasma cloud billowed outward, Ailyn leaped back unable to see Silus as the black fog encompassed the pit, the crowd jeered unable to see the action.

Ailyn was looking around frantically trying to locate Silus, "Ailyn can't hit, what Ailyn can't see", Silus's voice seemed to be everywhere at once taunting him, Ailyn took a hit to his back, then his front, then his side as he turned, he couldn't locate Silus through the blackness, he seemed to be everywhere at once.

Ailyn sprinted toward the edge of the pit like a missile, he ran along the circular wall of the pit at such speed he created a vortex of air, the black fog began to curl and dissipate, he saw Silus trying to conceal himself and jumped off the wall, he hit Silus in the back and heard a loud crack.

That Silus exploded into black miasma, "shit, it's a diversion", Ailyn said as Silus took advantage of his mistake, leaping out of the fog and kicking Ailyn into the wall before backward handspringing back into the fog.

Ailyn pursued him, the fog was merely a black haze now, Ailyn tried a direct entry attack but Silus used the wall to his advantage, he grabbed Ailyn's arm and leaped off the wall landing behind Ailyn, he used a shoulder throw and Ailyn got pulled over Silus's back, he tucked and landed on his feet but got a kick to his chest, Ailyn stumbled back then tried to advance only to have Silus throw sand in his eyes.

"You dirty", Ailyn tried to say, but was tripped by a sweeping kick, "all's fair Allheart", Silus said as he leaped up for a decisive blow while Ailyn was prone, Silus came down with a punch into Ailyn's chest that shook the ground with a thud, the crowd cheered and Ailyn went limp.

"Ailyn!", Kimba cried out, "we have to stop the fight", she said to Villias, "afraid we can't do that, it seems our boy is finished anyway".

by Lore Casta Pendragon

Ailyn felt the last of his life force drain and the red color in his eyes burned out, "no", Ailyn coughed.

Silus bowed to the cheering crowd, removing his wide brimmed hat and bowing deeply like he was putting on a show, water started seeping into the pit, first a trickle from the wall and then then a torrent, it picked Ailyn up and placed him down on his feet, then condensed into a glowing white shard in front of him.

"I can hear your pain Ailyn", Asta's voice said, "take the shard", it commanded.

Azir got out of his chair, "stop him!", He shouted, but it was too late, Ailyn reached out and grabbed the shard, an explosion of white light emanated from him blasting away what remained of the black miasma.

The crowd shielded their eyes and Silus sneered covering his face with his hat, the light died away and Ailyn stood there, the white aura glowed around him brighter than before, Silus looked at him curiously, "what is this?", "No matter, I'll just have to put you down again", Silus said leaping at Ailyn.

Ailyn saw him coming and kicked him to the side like he was nothing, Silus slammed into the pit wall and fell down unconscious, the crowd was silent unsure how to proceed until Villias and Kimba cheered in unison, the crowd picked up on the spectacle and cheered along with them.

Azir tried to silence the crowd to no avail, Ailyn walked over to Silus.

"Hay", he said, offering him a hand, Silus woke up grabbing at his ribs, he looked at Ailyn disappointed then took Ailyn's hand and Ailyn pulled him to his feet, "you almost had me there", Ailyn said.

"I had you beat", Silus said, "next time you won't be so lucky", he said leaping out of the pit and disappearing into the crowd, the announcer came running into the raising Ailyn's arm.

"Ailyn Allheart is the new reigning champion", he said and the crowd gave a final cheer, most of them had sullen faces having bet against him.

Ailyn climbed out of the pit, Kimba embraced him and Villias ruffled his hair, Azir walked up to them with a sour look on his face, "you cheated me", he said to Ailyn, "you're a thief, I'll have you locked up", Azir said, "the shard came to me and I won the fight, fair and square", Ailyn said defensively.

Two men came up and handed two large bags of gold to Kimba and Villias, no one expected Silus to be defeated so the odds were in their favor, the winnings were quite the hoard, they look at each other and Villias threw his bag at Azir's feet.

"This should pay for the repairs of me ship and to hire Inaya and Rayan for the foreseeable future", Villias said smiling, Azir's eyes went wide.

by Lore Casta Pendragon

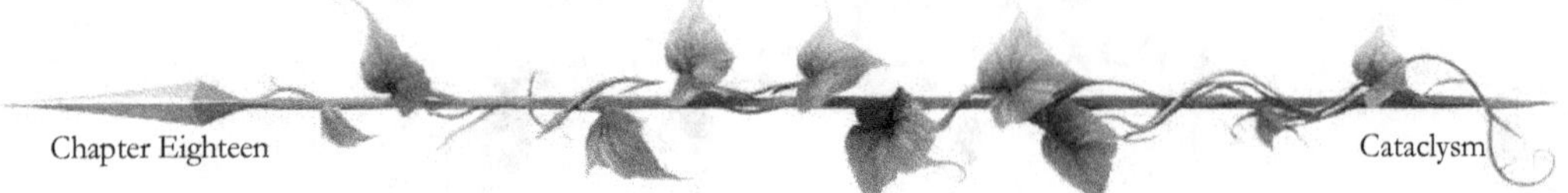

Kimba walked up to him and handed him the bag of gold, "this will help pay for anything you need until you can train some mages to summon water for you", she said, reaching into her sleeve she handed Azir, Lore Casta Pendragons tome, "a deal is a deal after all", she said flashing him a smile.

"Ah, lady Kindheart, you certainly do live up to your namesake", Azir said humbled, "was a hell of a fight Ailyn, would you consider fighting for me, I can make it worth your while", Azir said smiling wryly, "not a chance", Ailyn said as he left the yurt heading back for some much-needed rest.

The next morning just before sunrise Ailyn was resting over the rail of the Dune Dancer when the rest of the crew came aboard, he made eye contact with Silus who was looking a little rough, he must have been drinking all night, Silus scowled at him and sat on the rail at the other end of the ship.

Kimba walked over to Ailyn and took his arm, "we'll be heading for the Elven Forest to the north of the eastern desert, I've heard it's very beautiful, I've always wanted to see it", Kimba said excitedly.

"We need to get there first", Villias said, "the desert is a dangerous place, ye best be on guard, go on and help Inaya and Rayan get this ship moving", Villias ordered.

"As you wish captain", Kimba said teasingly, Ailyn and Villias watched her leave, "ye be a lucky man to have such a beauty on your arm Ailyn, I can remember a time when I too had one such as her", Villias said as he stroked his beard reminiscing, Ailyn just smiled.

"Look", Inaya said as the mountains surrounding Oasis started to move back and open the passageway outside.

Silus was still sitting on the rail on his own when Kimba walked over to him, "so, what will you do now?", Kimba asked as she leaned against the rail beside him, "I haven't decided yet", Silus said still pouting over his loss in the pit.

"Might go back to the assassin's guild in Ravenhill, but no doubt Guldamere would have his spies there already and all I'll find is a knife in the back", Silus replied.

"You know if you stick around, you and Ailyn could have a rematch", she said, "we don't exactly have an agreeable past, I was charged with, *'extracting,'* information from him before I threw him into the pit to die", Silus said using air quotations to emphasize his words.

"I know you've done things in the past you regret, but you also helped us escape the desert and saved us all from a sand stalker, there is good in you Silus and Ailyn can see that too, you should try apologizing to him, even if he doesn't accept it, it'll be a start to mending the rift between you", Kimba said.

Silus nodded and hopped down from the rail, he approached Ailyn, both men looked tense and the whole ship stopped to look at what seemed to be a fight brewing, they met in the middle of the ship.

"You looking for a rematch?", "Here?", Ailyn said looking at him cautiously, "not here to fight Ailyn, but we'll fight again and soon", Silus said, "then what do you want?", Ailyn replied.

"I'm", Silus growled trying to get the words out, "I'm sorry, about what I did, to you, and, to your family", Silus mumbled.

Ailyn frowned, "you tortured my father, then you tortured me, you helped that monster Harram kill my mother and my brother", Ailyn began to shout, "now you want forgiveness?", "Unbelievable!", Ailyn said.

Silus gritted his teeth, "I was tasked with tracking down the power shards for Guldamere, your father is very unique and powerful, we figured he may have information about the shards, Harram was tasked with murdering your family", Silus explained.

"Why should I believe you?", Ailyn asked, "all the things I've done, all of it, was so that Guldamere would bring back the only person I ever loved, I would have done anything to keep her safe, these scars are a testament to that and I am truly sorry for what I've done to you and I will make amends", Silus said walking away.

Ailyn clenched his fist with rage, tears welled in his eyes, the white aura surrounded him, Kimba walked up to him and placed a hand on his chest, "let it go, Ailyn", Kimba said and Ailyn let his hands go loose, the white aura faded and tears ran down his face, "after everything he's done, how could I forgive him", Ailyn said walking off in the other direction tears falling from his eyes.

Kimba dropped her hands to her sides seeing the crew all looking their way, then looked up at Villias on the flight deck, "what are ye all gawking at", Villias shouted, "get back to work, we got goods to haul", the crew scattered and went back to work, soon after the ship was heading back out into the eastern desert, toward the Elven Forest in the north.

The day was long and hot, Ailyn walked over to a water barrel and picked up a ladle dumping it over his head, he looked up at the sun glaring overhead, the breeze of the ship's movement cooled him, looking over to the flight deck he saw Kimba struggling to keep standing under the heat, sweat beaded on her brow, he wondered how Inaya and Rayan remained so cool under their full body of robes, they seemed unperturbed by the heat.

Ailyn filled a ladle with water and went up to the flight deck, Kimba had both hands extended and looked like she was about to drop.

by Lore Casta Pendragon

Ailyn lifted the ladle to her mouth and she drank the water down greedily, Inaya put a hand on her shoulder, "I think it's time you took a break, before you drop dead", Inaya said and Kimba knelt down, she looked exhausted.

The ship slowed as Inaya took Kimba's place but was still moving at a decent pace, Silus leaped down from the crow's nest, flipping around a cross mast and sliding down a sail, he landed next to Villias giving him a start.

"By the five moons man, what is wrong with you", Villias said agitated, Silus snickered at him, "sand stalkers, half a league to the east", Silus said, "swing west", Villias called turning the wheel, as the sail turned, the ship swung to the left, "keep an eye on them", Villias said to Silus as he leaped his way back up to the crow's nest.

"I don't suppose you know how to use a ladder", Villias grumbled, another crew mate pointed dead ahead, "Captain, there's a strange dust cloud ahead", Villias took out a telescope and honed in to see a Felinine running for his life, a large dust cloud following behind him, "too small to be a stalker", Villias said, "get the rope ladder ready, we'll swing past", Villias said.

As they got closer everyone looked overboard to see who it might be, "it can't be", Kimba said as she ran to grab the telescope from Villias, "hay!", Villias protested, but Kimba ran to the front of the ship, she peered into the telescope to see, "Felix!", Kimba said.

As he topped a sand dune he was waving at the ship, "turr rouw", she heard him say, "what?", Kimba shouted back at him, "turn around!", Felix said waving frantically, "turn around?", Kimba replied, "turn around!", Felix shouted as the hill revealed what was making the dust cloud.

A dozen rolling armored creatures were chasing after him, "dust devils", Villias said, "everyone hold on", he shouted, he turned the ship and the sail swung hard, the ship tilted heavily to the side and the crew let out a collected groan as they tried to hold on.

"We can't leave him here", Kimba said as she slammed her fists together, the sand under Felix began to shake and he sunk down a little, then a smooth formation of limestone pushed out from under him, he slid down the dune on its smooth surface picking up speed as Kimba made the end of it into a ramp.

Kimba launched him through the air, Felix screamed like a girl as Silus grabbed a rope swinging in a large arc around as the ship turned kicking him out wide, he grabbed Felix from the air, swinging back around to the ship.

The dust devils were like rolling cannon balls, they launched off a nearby dune and slammed into the ship's hull, sending wood splintering, leaving huge holes in the ship then sank beneath the aerated sands.

                                        by Lore Casta Pendragon

Rayan stopped his magic and the dust devils were buried beneath the ship, they stopped quickly and some of the crew tumbled over the ships deck, Silus dropped the screaming Felix on the deck and he landed hard on all fours, Silus gracefully landed next to him.

Kimba ran up to him, "I can't believe you're here, are you alright?", she said concerned, "I'm fine miss Kindheart, thank Astariel I found you", Felix said as Kimba helped him to his feet, "how did you know we were here?", Kimba asked, "oh I didn't", Felix said.

"Mech and I were searching for lost survivors in the air balloon, when the biggest creature I've ever seen came up out of the earth and just about swallowed us whole, luckily, we dropped a fire bomb down its gullet and blew ourselves free, unfortunately the balloon was damaged and we were stranded in this horrid desert.

Mech stayed with the wreckage and I went in search of help, only to find myself being sport for those rollie poly thingmajigs, I must have been running for hours", Felix explained.

Silus couldn't help but let out a little chuckle, Felix straightened his tailcoat trying to regain some semblance of dignity.

Villias walked over, "ye know this Felinine lady Kindheart", he questioned.

"This is Felix Flight, inventor extraordinaire", Kimba said with a flourish and a bow, Felix caught on and bowed along with her jerkily, "an engineer then, good you can earn your passage by fixing the holes your friends left in me ship", Villias said sternly.

No sooner had he finished the dozen dust devil's burst out of the sands landing on the ships deck, the crew backed off grabbing whatever weapons they could find.

Ailyn sprinted forward and dragon kicked one so hard it flew off the deck bounced off the sand and disappeared over a sand dune, "my word", Felix said astonished looking at Ailyn, "sorry I'm still getting used to my own strength", Ailyn shrugged.

With a flash Silus had his knives in hand, he ran at one and slid underneath it, he jammed six knives into the soft underbelly joints of the creature and it collapsed as he slid out behind it and sprang to his feet.

A dust devil lunged at Villias and he fell backward narrowly avoiding its beaked mouth, he threw back his coat and grabbed his false cannon leg, he pulled a pin at the knee and a fuse fizzled, with a loud boom it fired a small cannonball into the creature sending it overboard.

Another leaped at Kimba and she slammed her fist together, "hold onto me", she said to Felix and he crouched behind her, she focused a gust of wind that blew around them, the creature slowed then landed before her, it tried to run against the torrent, but lost its footing and crashed through the railing at the other side of the ship.

Inaya and Rayan moved as if they were dancing, three of the dust devils were charging them and they moved together in unison the wind pushing the dust devils away as they moved.

 by Lore Casta Pendragon

The crew were swinging at dust devils trying desperately to keep the creatures back, a creature leaped at Inaya's back, Ailyn took two steps up the main mast, he leaped and shot out like a missile toward her kicking the dust devil away it hit the sand like a cannonball.

Inaya and Rayan parted as another jumped between them, Ailyn kicked it high in the air, then leaped up after it, it curled into a ball and he bicycle kicked it off the ship, "Voilà", the crew cheered as Ailyn landed back on the deck.

Silus grew jealous and wouldn't be outdone, he tied a rope to a barbed knife, he dodged as one of the dust devils rolled at him, it crashed over the siderail as another leaped at him, trying to tear at him with its beaked mouth, he dodged right, and jammed the knife between its armored plating, it turned to have another go at him as he tied the rope to a cannon.

Silus pushed the cannon over the deck and the creature let out a little whimper as the weight pulled it overboard.

Inaya and Rayan stood back-to-back, summoning a powerful gust of wind they blew a creature off the ship.

The crew threw a cargo net down and one of the creatures charged then rolled up, "now!", They yelled and the net rose, capturing the dust devil inside, Ailyn looked around and smiled thinking the creatures were defeated.

One last creature snuck up behind Kimba over the rail behind, Felix saw it coming at the last second and drew a flintlock pistol, he blasted it at point blank range, the creatures armor plating shattered and it fell dead, Felix put the flintlock pistol away at his side and turned to the rest of the crew, "well, that's that then", he said, and the crew gave a celebratory cheer.

Looking around at the devastation to his ship Villias sat there miserable, he had a bottle of liquor in hand and was getting very drunk, "now what do we do", Ailyn asked.

"We have to send a party for supplies to Oasis", Rayan said, "Rayan and I will go, we are no strangers to the desert", Inaya offered, "Mech isn't far from here, we could use the parts from our air balloon to repair the ship", Felix said.

"Do you know the way", Kimba questioned him, "of course, those things left an easy trail to follow", Felix replied, "well, what are ye waiting for", Villias said in a drunken stupor falling on his back with a hiccup, "Felix, go with Inaya and Rayan, they can help you bring your balloon back to us", Kimba said, "as you wish miss Kindheart, we'll return promptly", Felix said with a curt bow.

A few hours later, they came back over the dunes, riding on a makeshift raft made of and carrying parts of the war balloon,

by Lore Casta Pendragon

Kimba took Mech's hand and helped him on board, "tis good to see you again lass, I was afraid we lost you", he said, "I am sorry about master Pendragon", Mech said, Kimba smiled at him, "he sacrificed everything to save us from Guldamere, do you know what happened to everyone else?", Kimba asked.

"We were scattered all over the lands of Thalaria, we found Farin and a fella named Fyorn to the west they said they were headed back to the Iron Halls, Paladin's reach was all but abandoned, the king and his son were among the few people who made their way back there after the battle.

We made our way here after that", Mech explained, "I see, so master Pendragon probably feared that Guldamere might cause another cataclysm and teleported the entire city away before he dragged Guldamere to the lands beyond with him", Kimba theorized.

"Guldamere is dead?", Felix asked, "no", Silus interrupted, "he always finds a way back and now that he's stronger, I'm afraid the worst is yet to come when he does return", everybody's faces took on a serious look but not another word was spoken.

Villias was sobering up drinking water, "so how about we get to fixing the ship before we get into any more trouble", he slurred.

"You got the best engineers in the world with you, we'll make it better than ever", Mech said winking towards Felix, a wry smile came across Felix's face, "I think I know what you mean", he said.

Chapter Nineteen

The Elven Forest

Villias was sobbing to himself and drinking again, Inaya and Rayan were trying to comfort him as Felix and Mech tore the ship apart fitting it with bits and pieces, they tore down masts for wood and rope for supplies and used the sails with the air balloon to make a giant envelope.

They got Kimba to heat and fill a boiler to make steam which powered large rotating fans, "okay hit it!", Mech shouted to Felix as he turned a valve, the balloon envelope inflated, the ropes holding it snapped tight as it rose, "purrfect", Felix exclaimed as the ship began to rise from the sand.

Mech turned some more valves and the fans increased in speed, "take the wheel captain", Felix said.

Villias stumbled into position on the flight deck, "maybe, we should get someone who isn't drunk to fly the ship", Kimba said.

"He'll be fine", Mech said as he explained the controls for Villias, "now this one controls the pitch, it will make it go up and down, the wheel controls the yaw, left and right, the balloon will keep her steady, so all you have to do is turn the valve to vent pressure and pull this lever to release it", Mech explained.

Villias immediately pulled the leaver the whole way back and the airship accelerated forward, everyone on board let out a collective groan having to grab to hold onto something, "Inaya, keep the water level topped, Rayan keep the boiler temperature here", Felix said pointing to a gauge.

"If the ships boiler goes out, we'll lose power", Felix explained strapping some goggles to his face, Villias smiled wide, "with this kind of ship we could deliver cargo to anywhere in Thalaria", he said excitedly.

Ailyn and the crew were watching the desert sand rushing beneath them, sand kicked up and swirled in a vortex as they flew over the top of a large dune, sand stalkers raised up from the desert sands looking at the ship, they didn't bother to pursue, they couldn't match its speed or reach its height.

"Dune Dancer isn't a proper name for this ship anymore, now she's the Sky Dancer", Villias proclaimed with a laugh, the crew nodded their approval.

by Lore Casta Pendragon

"You've really outdone yourselves, why don't ye all join me as part of me crew, I can't run this contraption on my own you know", Villias said, "we would be honored captain", Inaya said in her drawn accent, "never did I imagined I'd be soaring through the sky like a bird", Rayan said happily.

"I'd be happy to come on board", Felix said, "I might even be able to make some improvement once we find our way to my workshop in Necropyre", Felix said.

"Ay, I'd love to, but my king needs me in the Iron Halls", Mech said, "we've got to find the remaining power shards before Guldamere does", Kimba declined politely, walking up and putting a hand on Ailyn's shoulder, "I've also got to find my father, my men and my friends", Ailyn said.

"I'm going to search for a way to revive Cinder, if Guldamere can do it, there must be a way", Silus added.

"Looks like we've made it to the deserts edge, I can see the scar already", Villias said pointing forward, the gigantic rip in the land separated the eastern desert from the badlands near the elven forest.

The scar was full of dark fog, the airship flew right over the edge and an eerie silence gripped them, the air ship rose up in the air, the air currents pushing them higher, Kimba began to shiver as the temperature got colder, Ailyn held her close.

"The balloon will drop us lower as the temperature drops so keep the heat coming", Felix said to Rayan, they began to sink back down toward the other side, there was a spot not too far to the northeast, the green of the elven forest came into view.

They continued onward looking down at the land below, as the sun began to set as they passed the scar and found their way to the edge of the forest.

Flying above the canopy, a large tree dwarfed the rest of the forest, it was covered in rope bridges, platforms and tree houses in elven architecture made from the white wood the elven forest provided.

"The elven city of Eldamar, means elf home in the elvish tongue", Villias said, the crew looked at it in awe as they approached, the ship closed in on a wooden balcony.

The Elves had large Arbalests pointed at them like they were expecting an aerial assault, Villias waved a white flag and the crew threw some ropes to the Elves that were gawking at the ship as they approached, the ropes were tied off and the airship docked.

Elves donned in intricately carved wooden armor armed with bladed bows made their way through the crowd, an elven woman came forward dressed in clothes made from leaves and vines, the clothing seemed so natural that it was as if it grew onto her.

by Lore Casta Pendragon

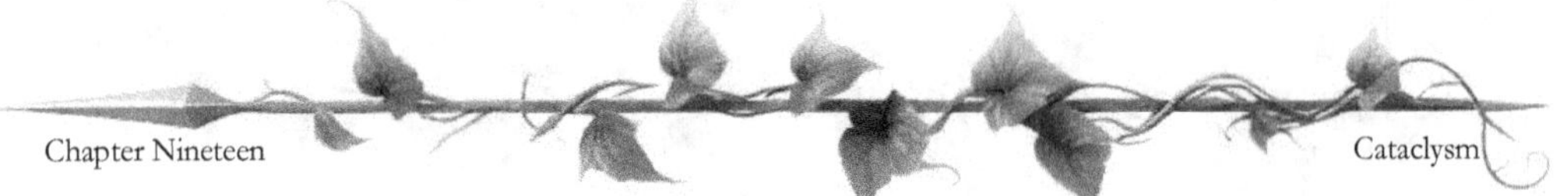

She was beautiful as all elves were with sharp pointed features, her ears were long and pointed and her skin was a strange shade of olive, her bright green eyes were large and round and seemed to glow with an earthy vibrance.

"Captain Villias, we were not expecting you for some time or for you to arrive flying through the sky", she said as the crew placed a gang plank down for her to cross, her guards took her hand as she walked across.

The way she moved was enchanting, like a deer in the forest, her legs were toned and obviously used to leaping through the trees.

"Welcome aboard the sky dancer, lady Ilutha, I bring spices, produce and textiles from Oasis", Villias began to list off his wares but Ilutha ignored him fascinated by the ship.

She moved her hand over it in wonderment, "who made this?", She asked, Mech perked up and stepped forward taking a breath only to have Felix step in front of him, "I did my lady, me and my cohort Mech, it's a pleasure to make your acquaintance", Felix said, she offered him a hand and he kissed it purring softly, "A Felinine, the honor is mine, I've only heard stories of you're kind", Ilutha said with a curt bow.

Mech groaned and rolled his eyes, Ilutha giggled then continued looking over the ship, "truly wonderous", she said, "this might be of great use to us", she said.

"What do you mean", Felix said, "we've been troubled by a creature most foul of late, it crawled from the well in the north, just after a massive flash of light in the west a few weeks ago", Ilutha said.

"Ay, I saw it too, few weeks back, strangest thing I ever saw", Villias said puzzled, "that flash, could it have been the magic master pendragon used to transport us here", Kimba asked, "it couldn't have been, we're too far away from Paladins Reach for it to be seen from here", Ailyn said.

"There were flashes in more than one direction", Villias said, "there's a chance that when we were transported, we also gave off a flash of light, meaning some of your friends could have been transported nearby", Silus said.

"What is this, well?", Kimba asked, everyone turned to Ilutha curiously, "the well is like a mirror between this world and the lands beyond, within it you can communicate with those who've passed through the abyss and ended up there", Ilutha explained.

"It's a sacred place, one that we have protected for as long as my people have lived", Ilutha explained, Silus raised his head from where he sat on the railing, then got up and leaped in front of Ilutha, she looked at his scarred face and backed away from him in fear.

"Silus?", Ailyn said cautiously, Silus dropped to a knee, "I am Silan Silus, master assassin of the guild of Ravenhill, I will help rid you of your foe, in return I ask that you lead me to this well, there is someone there I need to speak to", Silus offered.

by Lore Casta Pendragon

"That is quite gracious of you", Ilutha said nervously, "but I fear you are underestimating the enemy we face, to fight him head on, would be suicide", Ilutha said.

"What kind of creature is it?", Kimba asked.

"A dragon", Ilutha said.

"A dragon?", Kimba said, "like in the old paladin tales?", one of the crew asked, "it started off smaller, but it's grown immeasurably since it came from the well, it's been hunting and eating my people, growing bigger, its fast and brutal, sweeping down from the sky without a sound, it used the sun to hide its path and retreats before we can attack", Ilutha said, a tear formed in her big eyes, "I'll help you", Ailyn said, "I'll help too", Kimba agreed.

"We better get some rest, in the morning, we hunt for a dragon", Silus said.

"I'll have my people make up some quarters for you", Ilutha said waving to some elves nearby who left to carry out her instructions, she looked Ailyn up and down with a wry knowing smile then led them to an elevator platform held by ropes and pulleys, it led up to a large fork in the branches which was the heart of the city.

Eldamar was beautiful, intricately designed homes were carved into the tree itself and built to complement it, they were given rooms at a place called the all the way inn, which they all found quite amusing since it was carved into the massive trunk of the Eldamar tree.

Ailyn laid down to rest, the bed felt like heaven, his eyes were heavy, the soreness in his muscles ached and he drifted to sleep without a second thought.

The next morning, he woke to the chirping of birds and the smell of food, he opened his eyes and reeled backward in his bed, Kimba was before him strung up above the floor with metal beams pierced through her hands, her hair and body was soaked in blood, "Kimba, Kimba, no!", Ailyn cried out.

She caught fire and began to scream as she burned into ash, acrid black smoke bellowed from her, the smoke turned into a whirling column then condensed and dissipated.

Guldamere stepped out from it, he was no longer the skeletal lich from before, he was darker, a more complete version of himself, yet still he looked like a dead thing, a dark thing.

"Did you enjoy that, Ailyn?", "I certainly enjoyed giving you this little horror, I'm going to give you all such terrors, terrors until you can no longer take it, terrors until you beg me for the sweet release of death and then I'll bring you back and do it again until I am satisfied", Guldamere said.

His voice echoed through the room, "your dead, I watched you die, I watched Lore gut you with fire and drag you to the lands beyond", Ailyn said.

Guldamere smiled at him wickedly, "I mastered death well before you were born, the only reason you exist at all is because I brought your ancestors back from the abyss, had I known that Aram had progeny, I would never have revived them, you and your family were an oversight that has proven to be a thorn in my side", Guldamere said calmly.

"How are you here, why do you keep appearing in my dreams?", Ailyn said, "you still hold my power Ailyn, release it to me and I will release you from your nightmares", Guldamere offered his hand.

"Never!", Ailyn said reeling back, "did you truly think that death could hold me Ailyn, I am immortal, I am a god feared by gods and you will face my wrath and face it soon", Guldamere said raising his hands.

The room heated rapidly, the bed Ailyn was on caught fire and Ailyn began to scream as the fire burned him, he woke up screaming and the pain stopped instantly, Kimba jumped out of the bed terrified and dripping in sweat.

She must have snuck in during the night but Ailyn was too exhausted to notice, he grabbed his chest, his heart was beating like a drum, "Ailyn, what was that, are you ok?", Kimba said concerned, "I'm ok, it's just, the last two nights I've been having these nightmares, about Guldamere, he keeps threatening to kill me and everyone else, the dreams, they feel so real, so real that I can feel the pain, like here's there with me", Ailyn explained.

Kimba held him to her, "has what Silus said gotten to you?", "Guldamere is dead, master Pendragon sacrificed his own life to see it done, it was just a dream", Kimba said trying to calm him, but Ailyn knew that something wasn't right, he could feel it.

Villias and his crew were loading and unloading wares from the ship, Ailyn and Kimba decided to go for a walk, "so far we've had luck on our side, the shards seem to be drawn to you", Kimba said quietly so the elves walking past wouldn't hear.

"The shard is here, I can feel it, but I can't pinpoint it exactly, it's like it's everywhere here, not just in one location", Ailyn said, Ilutha walked up behind them.

"So, you're searching for the power", she said startling them, "how did you hear us?", Ailyn said panicking, "did you think these ears were for show?", Elves can hear a twig snap a mile away, it's what makes us such adept hunters", Ilutha explained with a smile.

Ailyn and Kimba looked at each other with the stunned realization that even though they kept their voices low that all of the elves had heard their conversations and probably more of what they did that morning, Kimba blushed embarrassed.

by Lore Casta Pendragon

"I've already obtained three of the shards, only two remain, one is here and the other is somewhere to the southwest, probably in the Ronin city, I'm trying to stop Guldamere from obtaining them, so he can't invoke his plan to kill us all in a second cataclysm, his 'lacrimosa' as he called it", Ailyn explained.

"I understand your urgency, we've faced off against Guldamere's forces before, his rot still stains parts of the forest, be careful if you wander, the nightmare creatures here are cunning, I felt the power call for you as soon as you arrived", Ilutha said pulling a leaf wrapped item from a vine wrapped bag.

Ailyn felt the object pulsating through his arm as he took it, he slowly unwrapped it and beams of light shot out from it, it floating up from his hand.

"Ailyn, you haven't got much time left, he's coming back and he's strong, too strong, you have to hurry, collect the final shard!", Ailyn heard Asta's voice again in his head, the shard moved into his chest in a blinding flash of light then it was gone.

Ailyn turned to Ilutha, "thank you, but why did you offer it to me so freely?", Ailyn said taking her hands, "I can tell that you're strong Ailyn, you didn't hesitate to offer your help even when facing off against a dragon and I know you're going to need all of your strength to defeat it", Ilutha said, "it's in our best interest that you be at full strength", she winked at him.

"Ailyn, did the shard talk to you again?", Kimba asked, "it did, it told me that I need to hurry, Guldamere is coming back and stronger than before so we have to be ready", Ailyn said, determination flashed in his eyes.

"So, we should get to the ronin city as fast as we can, I'll tell the captain", Kimba said.

"No, not yet", Ailyn said, "I can't leave without repaying your kindness", Ailyn said to Ilutha, "I'll make sure that the dragon won't come after you or your people again".

"Thank you, Ailyn, I'll organize an assault party to accompany us", Ilutha said, "us?", Ailyn said, "did you think we'd make you face it alone, your strong Ailyn, but not that strong", Ilutha said raising an eyebrow looking him up and down.

She gestured them to come to a balcony on the north eastern side of Eldamar overlooking the forest, "you see that rocky mountain in the distance", Ilutha said pointing toward the north, a mountain gutted out over the canopy of trees.

"Yeah, I see it", Ailyn nodded, "the well is located in a large sinkhole between those cliffs, the beast usually slumbers there", Ilutha said, "then that's where we'll go", Ailyn said smiling at her, she smiled back at him warmly.

"Collect your people and meet me at the All the way Inn", Ilutha said as she walked away, Ailyn watched her go, her outfit was revealing in the back and Ailyn stared a bit too long, "it's like you just attract trouble", Kimba said jabbing Ailyn in the ribs as she walked past.

They were seated at a table at the All the way Inn, Villias, Inaya, Rayan, Felix and Mech were pondering over a blueprint Mech had spread on the table, he was pointing at it and explaining the details while Ailyn and Kimba were reading up on reports of the recent dragon attacks that they received from Ilutha.

Ilutha came into the inn accompanied by elven troops with large bladed longbows, she wore a type of armor that looked to be made from some sort of tree bark, she peered over the papers all over the table, "so, what's our plan?", Ilutha asked.

Mech took a deep breath to begin explaining but Felix stepped in front of him, "we are going to install one of the Arbalest you've installed on the tree on the bow of the ship and use it as a weapon against the dragon, but first we're going to need a team to bait the dragon from the cavern, our ground team will consist of yourself, Ailyn and Silus", Felix said.

Mech let out an annoyed sigh behind him, Felix spread out a poorly illustrated map on the table, "you'll enter the forest near to the cavern here", he pointed to the map, "we'll hide the airship down here", he pointed again, "you'll bait the dragon out and we'll attack it here", he pointed to a funny picture that slightly resembled a dragon, Kimba snickered at the poorly drawn illustrations.

"We shouldn't risk a frontal assault, we'll walk by foot to the cliff face, while you take the air ship round from the east", Ilutha added, "this way we'll be covered by the forests foliage until we get close, the dragon likes to sneak up on you and this way we'll take that advantage away from him if he wakes before we get there", Ilutha said.

"Sounds like a good plan", Villias said, "this is going to be dangerous, the dragon is agile and deadly, the fire from its mouth can melt steel, so avoid a frontal assault at all costs", the crew nodded in acknowledgement.

"Are we ready then?", Ilutha yelled and everyone cheered, gulping down the last dregs of their drinks.

Ailyn grabbed Villias's hand, "we're counting on you, see you there", he said, "Ay boy, I won't be letting ye down, just do whatever you did to that sand stalker and it'll be smooth sailing", Villias replied.

Ailyn gave the rest of them a nod and turned to Silus, "I got your back, do you have mine?", He said looking him in the eye, "try not to get in my way", Silus said smirking taking him by the cuff.

by Lore Casta Pendragon

Villias, Kimba, Mech, Felix and the crew headed off for the sky dancer whilst Ailyn, Silus, Ilutha and the elves headed down a long staircase which came to a rope lift, they descended the tree into the forest below, "follow me", Ilutha said softly, her bare footsteps barely audible on the forest floor, Silus was also very light of foot and Ailyn couldn't help but feel out of place every time a twig snapped under step.

Ilutha turned to them as they crested a hill, she crouched down, hiding behind a short plant and waved them over, Ailyn tried his best to stay quiet as both him and Silus crouched beside her.

She moved the plant revealing a pond with grassy green banks, a white stag with large impressive antlers was drinking there, ever cautious, its ears flicked forward and backward trying to pick up on any sound.

"It's beautiful", Ailyn whispered, "it's dinner", Silus responded a knife appearing in his hand with a flick of his wrist, "no, not this one", Ilutha said sternly placing her hand on his arm, "this pond is sacred to all the creatures of the forest, an unspoken law abides here that no harm comes to those who come to drink here", Ilutha explained.

A dire wolf came into view panting heavily, it lapped at the pond and the stag did not run, "you see", Ilutha said, "waste of a good pelt", Silus said walking off, "is he always like this?", Ilutha asked.

"Unfortunately, he's the gruff and unfriendly type, Silus has a lot to work out, he was one of Guldamere's officers until recently, he's trying to make amends for what he's done", Ailyn said.

"Are you sure you can trust a man like him?", Ilutha asked, "he's saved our lives more than once, he has a lot to answer for, but if we're going to defeat Guldamere once and for all, I have a feeling we are going to need him", Ailyn said turning back to the pond, the stag and wolf were gone, "let's get moving", Ilutha said.

As they closed in on the rocky mountainside they came across a small valley, large cobwebs covered the trees casting shadows on the ground, black spiders large and small were making webs and falling from the trees on silken webs.

"We'd best go around, nightmare creatures' nest here", Ilutha said and they turned to start back up the hill, when they heard a man screaming.

Ailyn ran down into the valley ducking under the webs, brushing them off with his hands, they stuck to his arms, he tried to rip the webs off as he ran only for them to stick to his hands, "stop you fool", Ilutha called to him, but he kept on going.

                                    by Lore Casta Pendragon

With a flash, knives were in Silus's hands, "damnit Ailyn", he said going in after him, "don't go in there it's a trap", Ilutha called but Silus didn't care.

"No, get away", Ailyn heard a familiar voice call, a thick matte of webbing now covered him and it got increasingly harder to move as the web clung to other webs around him ensnaring him, he came into a circular clearing.

Clutches of spider eggs were hung up all around him, large black spiders were climbing toward, "Brawn!", Ailyn shouted, "Aylin?", "Praise be, get me out of here!", Brawn shouted, he was covered in webbing.

Ailyn raced toward him and tried to pulled him out, as his cobweb covered hands grasped onto the cobwebs covering Brawn, he tried to pull back against it only to realize that his hands were now stuck.

He tried to place a foot against the web to pull an arm free, only to have his foot become stuck as well, a disgusting black spider crawled up his now stuck leg and tried to sink its fangs into him.

A knife came flying out and skewered it, spider ichor splattered over the wall, Silus came up beside him, "thanks for making a path", Silus smirked, relatively free of cobwebs.

He brushed a small spider from his shoulder and shuddered, with a flick of his wrist two knives were in his hands and he began slashing at the webbing so quickly that Ailyn could barely keep up.

Ailyn and Brawn fell to the ground stuck together in a heap, the black spiders didn't like that and they reared up hissing at them, one of them spun down to the ground and reared up, its two front legs raised.

Silus threw a knife and stuck it to the ground, he cut Ailyn's hands free and gave him the knife, with a flick of his wrist two more knives appeared in hand, the spiders leaped at him, he moved around slashing spiders left and right, when Ailyn was finally free, he released Brawn, there were bits of spider everywhere, other spiders started dragging off and eating the dismembered ones.

"It's good to see you Brawn", Ailyn said embracing him, brawn embraced him to, "It's good to see you again scrawny, I got you a gift", Brawn said, he attempted to reach for his pocket but realized they were stuck together and Silus had to help cut them loose again.

"Thanks Ailyn, what's he doing here?", Brawn said looking over at Silus, "Silus has turned over a new leaf, he has been saving our lives ever since", Ailyn said.

"True enough, Brawn said as he moved to embrace him, Silus put his hand on Brawn's chest, "I think you'd be best served if you stopped hugging people", Silus said walking away.

by Lore Casta Pendragon

"Oh yeah, before I forget", Brawn said, reaching into his pocket and handing Ailyn a dead rabbit, "eh, thanks, Brawn", Ailyn replied disturbingly.

"How did you end up here?", Ailyn asked, we were camped nearby, heading toward Eldamar, when we were attacked by giant spiders, they dragged us here", Brawn said, "us?", "Who else was with you?", Ailyn asked.

"Aethor and Wynn, they were dragged further down to the burrow, not too long ago, we should probably go save them", Brawn said nonchalantly, "you don't seem very concerned about your friends", Silus said, raising an eyebrow.

"Have you seen Aethor fight?", Brawn chuckled, "let's go", he said and walked toward a cobweb funnel leading further down.

"Stop!", Ilutha said catching up to them and muttering something harshly in elvish, the elves behind her carried torches, burning their way through the webbing, "allow me", she said burning away the cobwebs revealing a cavern entrance, they moved down the cavern and disappeared into the tunnel.

Aethor awoke with his entire body encased with thick spider web, he tried to move but the flexible spider web held him like glue.

He pulled with all his strength to no avail, his hands were stuck were he laid the night before, one by his side and the other next to his head, Aethor chewed into his cheek hard, blood trickled into his mouth and his eyes felt like they caught fire turning red.

He punched forward ripping at the cobwebs which snapped his arm back into place like elastic, a few more times and the cobwebs tore enough to loosen his arms, he ripped at the webs with all his heightened strength until his legs were free, then he kicked out tearing the cobwebs apart, this gave him enough room to move and he grabbed a hand full of web pulling himself along, it tore out behind him as he slowly tore his way through, his clothes tore leaving him bare, but Aethor didn't care.

There was a bundle of web with a long claymore sticking out of it, it could only have been Wynn.

Aethor pulled himself along, web sticking him everywhere, clumping on top and tearing away, small spiders crawled over him but he tried to not take notice of them.

He got to Wynn who was closer to the cavern wall enough so that Aethor could place his feet on the wall, he grabbed the bundle of cobwebs that held Wynn and braced his feet on the sticky cavern wall, with a mighty leap, Aethor and the cobweb bundle ripped free of the wall and crashed to the cavern floor, the claymore tore into the cobwebs and Wynn reached a hand through the gap, grasping frantically for something to hold.

Aethor placed both hands in the gap and tore it outward, the web stretched and snapped as Aethor strained to break it open, Wynn's face broke free and he gasped for air, Wynn screamed out in panic.

"What the hell is going on?", Wynn bellowed, "we were taken in the night by some horror of the forest", Aethor said.

"Once we rid ourselves of our burden, we'll find Brawn and get out of here", Aethor said, "we should find you something to put on as well", Wynn said awkwardly, Aethor stood unashamed,

Wynn didn't blame him with a body that looked like it was chiseled from stone.

The cavern was dark, only minimal light shined through the webbed holes in the ceiling, they spent a long time trying to free themselves from the sticky webbing enough to be able to move freely.

"Did you hear that", Wynn said his deep voice echoing through the cavern, a chittering sound was drawing closer, large thin legs climbed over a tunnel heading further down to their left, a massive eight eyed spider's head peeped up, followed by a gigantic red striped abdomen, another popped up to the right next to them.

Wynn freed the claymore from the webbing and rested it on his shoulder, "I'll take this one, if you got the other", Aethor said, Wynn gave an approving grunt, they rushed out toward the creatures and the creatures rushed toward them.

Wynn swung the claymore collecting a front leg and severing it, the spider backed off shrieking then quickly retaliated with its other front leg, knocking Wynn backward.

Aethor charged out with a dragon kick straight into the spider's face, the impact left the creature with a foot mark permanently imbedded in its head, but it clamped down with its mandibles on Aethor's foot, it reared up and Aethor hit the ground, it released him attacking with six legs and two mandibles.

Aethor managed to dodge the first five attacks but got pummeled three times and kicked away, Aethor and Wynn hit the ground at the same time landing with their faces next to each other.

"How's yours going?", Wynn said lying next to him, "could be better", Aethor said, both men quickly got to their feet as the spiders came back in.

"Ready?", Aethor said, "for what", Wynn said, Aethor ran grabbing their attention, "attack now!", Aethor yelled, Wynn swung the claymore taking out the remaining three legs on the spider's right side, it crashed down with a shriek.

The other spider crawled over its fallen kin to get at him, Wynn swung the claymore wildly cutting off a mandible before being knocked to the side.

                                        by Lore Casta Pendragon

Aethor leaped over the top and axe kicked the spider to the top of the head driving it into the ground, its face exploded into a pile of ichor, it danced around, back stepping without its head until it finally came to rest against a wall.

The spider crawled toward them still trying to walk on the nubs of its missing appendages, Wynn ran up to it dragging the heavy claymore behind him, he used his forward momentum to launch the claymore over his body and down into the spider's head splitting it in half, Ichor splattered everywhere and the creature fell down twitching.

Aethor's eyes returned to normal, they panted with the effort of battle and chuckled to each other, another three large spiders came up from the lower passage, "c'mon then!", Wynn bellowed.

These ones had learned from the mistakes of the others, they reared up and squirted hot sticky liquid at them, Aethor tried to run but he was already spent, his foot got caught as the liquid hardened into webbing, the spiders covered the rest of him as Wynn tried to hide behind his claymore, the liquid whipped around it covering him, he struggled to move as it grew harder.

The spiders came in to claim their prize as Ailyn rushed in white aura surrounding him, he punched a spider in the side so hard it shot out and splattered against the far wall.

Silus ran in, with a flicker of his wrists another spider was hit by a barrage of knives, it rocked back and reared up only to have more knives stuck into its underbelly, Brawn threw a large boulder and crushed it flat as Ilutha and the elves came in chopping at the third with curved elven blades until it was nothing more than pieces.

They cut Aethor and Wynn free, Ailyn and Aethor grabbed wrists, "it's good to see you father", Ailyn said, "you've gotten stronger Ailyn", Aethor said proudly looking at the splattered remains of spider on the wall, "eh, thanks, where are your clothes?", Ailyn said embarrassed, Ilutha looked at Aethor with a her head tilted and smiled, "no rush", she said, Aethor smiled at her and an elven warrior handed Aethor some armored pants to put on, "aww", Ilutha said.

"This tunnel may be connected to the cavern where the well of ascension lies, we should follow this tunnel upward", Ilutha said, the elves helped her to burn away the cobwebs leading up the tunnel, Aethor noticed Silus.

"You!", Aethor growled, his pupils flashing red and he moved like a blur, he kicked Silus in the stomach, Silus buckled under the power of the kick flying into the far wall.

Ailyn ran in front of Aethor, "father please stop!", "I know he hurt you, he hurt me too, but Silus had his reasons, he's one of us now", Ailyn tried to explain.

"He's responsible for all of this, he's the reason Asta and Aidem are gone, how can you stand there while he's still breathing", Aethor growled, the pain and anger welled up in him, Silus

by Lore Casta Pendragon

picked himself up from the floor holding his stomach, "that brings back some memories", Silus groaned.

"Please father, he may have done some things in the past he's not proud of, but Silus spared us, it was Harram who killed them, not Silus", Ailyn explained, Aethor sneered at Silus, then turned away, "let's go", Aethor said walking into the tunnel.

Chapter Twenty

Abyssal Dragon

They entered into a large cavern, above them was a large opening where they could see the sky, the cavern was lined with the bones of elves, men and other creatures.

A black dragon laid curled around itself like a snake, its head resting on top, it had blue hair lining it's back, an altar of stone was behind it, water trickled down refracting many different colors as it fell.

"Quiet, if we take it by surprise, it'll be much easier", Ilutha whispered sneaking toward the creature, Ailyn moved to join her and Silus placed a hand on his chest shaking his head, "you move like a boulder falling, leave this to her, all we have to do is bait it outside", Silus said.

Ailyn nodded only a little insulted, Ilutha got closer and pulled a curved elven short sword from a scabbard at her waist, it made a slight ring when she drew it and she quickly grabbed the steel to make it stop, the dragon sniffed outwards, burning hot air blew over them and Ilutha tried not to yell out as the heat stung her skin, she wasn't far from it when Ailyn noticed the dragons mouth curl back like it was trying to hold back a smile.

"Ilutha look out!", Ailyn called and Ilutha's eyes went wide, the dragon quickly raised a giant clawed foot, the talons were the size of short spears and they pierced the ground as Ilutha rolled to the side to avoid it.

The dragon couldn't contain itself any longer and a smile curled from its jaw as it raised itself up.

"Fools!", The dragon bellowed, its voice like rolling thunder, "you thought I couldn't hear you coming, now you die", the dragon's wings spread wide and its thin body rolled out like a snake behind it.

Ilutha ran back toward them but the dragon was on her in an instant, it was fast, its wings flickering like a dragonfly and its tail whipped around behind it.

It snatched Ilutha in its claws so quickly that her head whipped around like a ragdoll, it brought her toward its face and she screamed as burning hot air cascaded over her.

"So weak, so pathetic, how dare you stand before me", the dragon said disgusted.

Ailyn came rushing in, white aura burning like flame around him, he leaped toward the dragon and kicked it under its snout, its head whipped back and it threw Ilutha in the air, Silus rushed in and leaped catching her then sliding across the dirt covered stone floor.

"Thanks", Ilutha said as he put her down, Ailyn landed before the dragon, it was no longer smiling, it bared sharp pointed teeth as it looked at Ailyn, "you dare", the dragon bellowed,

flames began curling up from its mouth as it spoke, Ailyn ran around behind it so the flames wouldn't take his friend behind him.

The dragon turned and shot a gout of fire that burned so hot and so intensely that it leaped up the cavern wall and the stone cracked and melted, Ailyn leaped out to the side and the dragon turned to follow, fire still spitting from its mouth.

Ailyn ran up the wall as the flames followed him, he pushed off and tried to backflip over the dragon, but it was fast and its reflexes were like nothing he'd ever seen.

The dragon grabbed him midair; its powerful wings blew gusts of wind and dust around the cavern; it was a calamity in itself.

The dragon opened its mouth, the hot air scolding Ailyn as it breathed out, he screamed out in pain pushing against the dragons' clawed hands and managing to pry them open, the dragon reinforced its grip with its other claw and Ailyn struggled to push back against its strength, the hands began to close in on him.

Aethor flew out eyes red and kicked the dragon in the back between the wings, it let out a painful growl, it swung around with a flick of its wings then threw Ailyn at Aethor, Aethor tried to catch Ailyn but the dragon threw him so fast they collided and skipped off the cavern floor hitting the wall behind.

Silus made his way behind the dragon and threw a dozen knifes at its wings, the knives ripped holes through the thinner skin, black miasma kicked up around Silus and he held his hands out like he was controlling a marionette puppet.

The knives obeyed his commands flying in and out of the dragon's wings, piercing small holes through them.

"That'll slow you down", Silus said, the dragon roared and raised itself into the air, powerful gusts of wind made Silus and his knives fly back, Silus hit hard against the cavern wall and slumped down, the elven warriors began launching arrows but none of them could hit the mark, the gale was too strong.

The dragon came down fire began to build up in its mouth yet again.

Wynn ran toward it and threw the claymore over his head, it spun through the air end over end, the heavy steel unaffected by the gale pushing against it and it stuck into the dragon's belly, it lifted its head and roared with rage spitting fire toward the sky.

"Shut up", Brawn said picking up a large boulder and throwing it up into the air, it sailed directly into the dragon's mouth causing it to choke.

It chomped down and fire spewed out melting the boulder to liquid, which dripped down from the dragon's sharp teeth.

                                                     by Lore Casta Pendragon

Ailyn looked over at Aethor who was unconscious on the stone floor, he rushed out as fast as he could and tackled Brawn and Wynn out of the way as the dragon spat fire at them.

Ailyn looked back to see the elven warriors nearby, one minute they were there and the next they were gone, completely burned to dust.

"We gotta go!", Ilutha said at the cave entrance, she had Aethor by her side.

"You won't escape me", the dragon raged, it flew toward the cave entrance and reached it just as Ilutha ducked through, very nearly missing them with its long spear like talons.

"I'll distract him get Silus to the exit", Ailyn said to Brawn and Wynn.

"Get my sword too will you", Wynn said sarcastically, "I'd ask you to get my boulder but he melted it", Brawn said as they moved to get Silus, the dragon whirled around.

Ailyn ran out in front of it, it tried to snatch him up again, but Ailyn leaped up and kicked it under the chin so hard that the dragon head bounced off the overhanging cavern roof above it.

Ailyn landed beneath it as its head fell back down and he uppercut it in the throat, the dragon made a gurgling sound and gasped for air, thrashing around like a worm in the sun.

The dragons tail collected Ailyn unexpectedly and he flew toward the cave entrance, he hit the ground and rolled to his feet, going straight into a run then dashed back through the cave.

Ailyn could hear the dragons rageful cries, anger filled its face as it looked to the sky then took off at speed, its body moving like a ribbon in the wind.

Villias was looking through his telescope on the sky dancer, he saw the dragon appear from the atop the cliff face.

"There she blows!", Villias said and the ship took off after it, Felix's pupils dilated following its movements, "it's fast", he said astonished.

"Just get us close, I'll take care of it", Kimba said to Rayan and Inaya, they nodded and extended both arms forward, the wind picked up and propelled the airship faster.

The dragon saw the air ship coming up from behind it as the crew loaded a ballista bolt into the arbalest, Mech sat behind the mechanism, he turned a valve and the Arbalest turned with him, he lined up a crosshair in front of his seat with the dragon centered in the middle.

"Fire!", he said, the bolt shot out toward the dragon, the dragon whipped itself in a circle like a spring avoiding the bolt then slithered through the air like a snake picking up speed as it flew.

It disappeared below them, "turn the ship to port!", Villias cried out to the crew but the dragon came up behind them slashing at the bottom part of the flight deck, wood shattered and splintered and the crew lost their footing.

by Lore Casta Pendragon

"The sky is my domain", the dragon shouted, its voice thundering over them, the crew felt their knees weaken at the sound of it, but Kimba, Inaya and Rayan stood in front of it.

Kimba slammed her fists together, Inaya and Rayan placed their hands on her back and Kimba felt the increase to her own power, she extended one arm and grabbed her elbow pointing her finger at the dragon.

The dragon lifted its head back fire building in its mouth, "this one's for you, Lore", Kimba said, electricity crackled around her, a bolt of lightning cracked from Kimba's extended finger, her arm recoiling with the blast.

The dragon's wings fluttered awkwardly and sporadically, it grasped at a smoldering wound where the lightning struck and it gasped for air.

"You, you puny, little", the dragon said trying to catch its breath, Villias turned the ship to face the beast head on, Felix helped the crew load up another Ballista and Mech lined up the Arbalest, "Fire!", He said, the Ballista fired out and pierced the dragon right where Kimba had struck it with the lightning, the weakened armor shattered.

The dragon roared a sorrowful cry as it fell from the sky, it bounced off the mountainside below and fell back into the cavern hole, its claws leaving deep gouges in the rock as it desperately tried to save itself.

It disappeared into the hole and landed with a loud thud, dust flew up from the cavern and the beast let out a weak growl which echoed from the hole.

Ailyn and his companions walked back to the cavern looking a little worse for wear, the dragon was still breathing but heavily labored.

Ailyn walked up to it, it tried to spit fire at him but choked on it coughing hot blood over itself, the liquid burned through its own flesh like acid.

"You're done", Ailyn said, "you have no idea what's coming for you", the dragon gargled and it seemed to smile at him as it took its last breath, its eyes blurring over then growing still.

The sky dancer came in from the large hole in the ceiling, it floated down and the crew threw bags of sand tied to ropes from the deck, it hovered just off the ground and a rope ladder was thrown overboard.

Kimba was the first one off the ship, she rushed down to Ailyn and embraced him, "thank goodness your alive, that creature was terrifying", she said looking over his wounds.

"It certainly gave us trouble", Ailyn said.

They looked to the stone alter where Ilutha was climbing the steps, she reached the peak to see a pool that shimmered silver like a mirror, the light caught on it and refracted into multiple colors.

                             by Lore Casta Pendragon

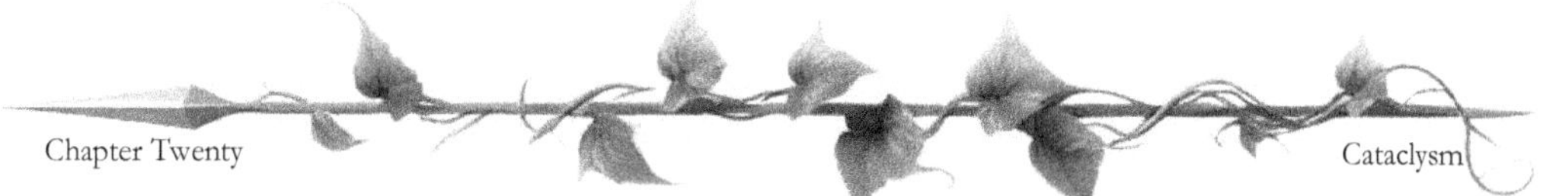

"It's ok, the well is untainted", she called down to them, with a sigh of relief as she waved for them to join her, Ailyn and his companions made their way up the stone alter and stood around the well.

"This place is special to the elves, it's a great honor to be here, as a reward for slaying the dragon, you can be the first to use its mystic power, who wants to go first?", Ilutha asked.

"I will", Silus said, Ilutha hadn't noticed him approach her and jump back startled, "You never make a sound do you", Ilutha said, Silus just smirked at her.

"Look into the waters, visualize the person you wish to see, remember them", Ilutha instructed.

Silus looked into the well, the water swirled then changed color from a mirrored silver to a clear shimmer, Cinder Crowler came into view below the surface, she looked around confused.

"Silus?", "Is that you?", Cinder said, "it's me Cinder, I'm sorry, for everything, I didn't know it was you, I tried so hard to bring you back, but, I failed, I'm, I'm sorry Cinder, for everything", Silus said painfully.

Cinder smiled, her voice echoed out from the water, "I never asked you to bring me back Silus, I had my time and fell to Malacore's plot, I should have known better than to trust his words, don't waste your life trying to change the past, don't be a slave to the whims of nefarious men, forge your own path and remember me for the time we had, not the time we lost", she said.

Silus's head dropped, his chin hit his chest and a tear ran down his face, "I will, I will bring you back, if Guldamere can do it, then I can too, I'll make it right", Silus said, Cinder just smiled.

"If anybody could, it would be you, but try to move on with your life, our times running short, so I'll make this quick, I'll see you again Silus, in this world or in the lands beyond", Cinder said as the pool changed back to the mirrored silver surface.

"What happened?", "Where did she go?", Silus asked, Ilutha took him by the arm to comfort him, "there isn't much of her energy left in the world, the longer it's been since her passing, the harder it is to communicate with her, the life force only lingers in the world for a time", Ilutha explained.

"So, I can't talk to her again?", Silus asked, "no I'm afraid not", Ilutha said, Silus huffed then walked over to a ledge and sat hiding his face beneath his brimmed hat.

"Who's next?", Ilutha said, both Ailyn and Aethor stepped up either side of her, they nodded to each other and looked into the pool.

"Mother, brother", Ailyn said and the water swirled, then cleared, Asta and Aidem appeared looking just the way they did before they had passed.

by Lore Casta Pendragon

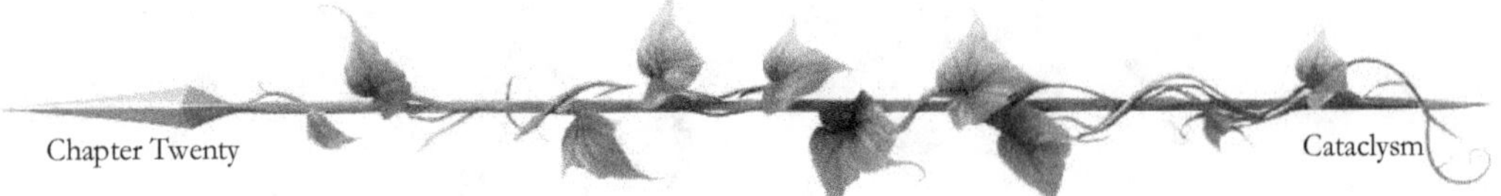

"Father?", Aidem said, Asta's hand went to her mouth in shock, "Aethor?".

"Asta my dear, Aidem my boy, it's good to see you, we've missed you", Aethor said.

"Aethor, tell me, what became of Ailyn", Asta asked.

"You're looking at him", Aethor said gesturing to Ailyn with a proud smile, "you've grown so big", Asta said tearing up.

"He's bigger but I bet the fish would still win", Aidem said teasingly, Aethor and Asta chuckled, Ailyn smirked, "it's good to see you brother, not even death could stifle your sense of humor", Ailyn said.

"I'm sorry I failed to protect us, all those years ago", Aethor said, "you did everything you could, to be honest I was surprised you survived, your wounds looked fatal", Asta said.

"Guldamere revived me several times during my torture", Aethor said looking over at Silus with a sneer.

"I was sent to the pits in Necropyre, I toiled there for years thinking you had all died, only to find out Ailyn had survived and not only that, he freed us all", Aethor explained.

"I'm happy you found each other again, we don't have much time, I just want you to know that I love you both very much, we'll be reunited again someday in the lands beyond", Asta said fading off,

"Father", Aidem said bowing deeply to Aethor, "see ya fish face", Aidem said with a wave to Ailyn disappearing from sight, Ailyn's companions had a chuckle at that.

Aethor put an arm around Ailyn, "that was heartwarming", Wynn said wiping a tear from his face, "wait, something isn't right", Ilutha said, "the well hasn't changed back yet".

Ailyn turned to look into the well, a man appeared before him, he had a bald head and wore Aikitai robes just like Ailyn, he held a steel staff almost as tall as he was.

"Ailyn Allheart", the man said, Ailyn looked at him confused, "who are you?", he said, the tattoo Éoviel placed on Ailyn's arm began to glow.

"I am Aram, disciple of Lore Casta Pendragon, you are my descendant, take hold of the staff", Aram said, he thrusted his staff forward it glowed with gold runes along it, the tip penetrated the surface of the water glowing with a soft golden light, Ilutha was stunned, "that's not possible", she said shocked.

Ailyn reached forward and grabbed the tip of the staff, Aram pulled forcefully, Ailyn tried pulling back and letting go but he couldn't, he was pulled into the well.

                                                  by Lore Casta Pendragon

"Ailyn!", He heard Aethor call, but it was distant, Ailyn fell through darkness, the world disappeared from him and he fell through a void of darkness, he remembered this place from when he was tortured.

Colors began to form and blur around him until he landed on his feet next to Aram, they stood on a rolling hill, the grass was green and short, the trees were shades of pink, orange and purple, a red bridge arced over a creek nearby, with mountains cascading with waterfalls, a temple was nearby which looked exactly like the temple of Aikitai in the living forest.

"Where am I?", Ailyn said, "you're in the lands beyond Ailyn", Aram said, "how did you bring me here?", Ailyn said, "it took quite a lot of cultivation of energy on my part and I'm afraid explaining it all would take longer than our time permits", Aram said.

"Lore told me what Guldamere has been up to, I have a gift for you, I think it might help", Aram said holding out his staff, golden runes appeared along the shaft.

"I've instilled all of my knowledge into that staff, touch the runes and it will show you the techniques I used in my time in Thalaria", Aram said.

Ailyn took the staff from Aram and it flooded his mind with memories, Aram's memories, Ailyn put his hands on his knees panting like he'd just ran a marathon, he turned his head to Aram.

"Thank you", he said, Aram nodded his head in a short bow, then he was enveloped by a golden light, Aram smiled at him as the world turned to whiteness.

Ailyn shot out of the well over the heads of his friends, he planted the staff down as he landed and used it to turn himself upright landing on his feet, he held the staff out in front of him, the golden runes moved along the staff.

Ailyn's head was bombarded with Aram's memories, then the golden runes then faded, "what happened?", Kimba asked him.

"I was transported to the lands beyond, I met Aram Allheart, he gave me this", Ailyn said hold out the staff.

"That staff, he used that to amplify his attacks with chaos magic, or so the story goes", Aethor said.

Ailyn took a good look at the staff, the white aura burned around him and the staff glowed with the golden runes, then seemed to burn away into the air and the staff was gone.

"Where did it go?", Felix said, "I can bring it back when I need it", Ailyn said.

"Oh, that's, that's quite handy", Felix replied, "I had a staff that was similar", "I don't think they were quite the same", Kimba said patting Felix on the back.

"Who's next?", Ilutha said, Kimba walked up to the well and looked into the silver waters, "Kamdar", she said.

The water swirled changing colors but nothing happened, "what's going on?", Kimba asked, "the person you asked for probably isn't dead", Ilutha said.

"Kamdar is alive?", "But where is he?", Kimba said, "he's part of Petricus now", Silus said, Kimba turned to him, "my father is part of that monster?", Kimba said shocked.

"Not only him, but that master of yours as well Ailyn, he consumed them both to make himself stronger", Silus explained, "that's what makes him so dangerous".

"How long have you known about this?", Ailyn said angrily, "I didn't tell you because it's better, you didn't know", Silus said, "when he comes for you, I didn't want you to hold back because they are a part of him", he explained.

"You dirty bastard", Kimba said angrily, Ailyn held out a hand to calm her, "can we free them?", He asked, "you can't bring them back, but you can kill them, by killing him", Silus said, "what kind of horrid creature would make you kill the people you love", Felix said, "he does", Silus said.

The waters began to swirl again, Lore Casta Pendragon appeared before them, "Kimba, I don't have much time, I held Guldamere here in the abyss for as long as I could, but he's broken free, he's looking for a way back, a physical form to incorporate, I can't stop him, he's too strong, whatever you do, don't let anyone near the well, if he gets free", Lore's voice echoed and faded before he finished his sentence.

"What's going on?", "Lore?", Kimba said kneeling by the well confused, a creaking sound came from behind them, ghouls started pouring out of the cavern entrance.

"Everyone back to the ship!", Villias shouted and the crew ran for it, "Lore told us not to let them near the well, we can't abandon it", Kimba said, Ailyn nodded to her.

"Subdue them, don't pierce their skin", Ailyn shouted.

"Allheart!", a voice shouted from the opening above the cavern, a huge figure leaped down and crashed into the floor, dust kicked up as he landed, the white aura began to burn like fire around Ailyn.

Aethor, Silus, Brawn, Wynn, Ilutha and Kimba stood by his side, while Villias and Felix got everyone else to the ship, Mech, Inaya and Rayan started prepping the ship for a fast retreat.

The dust cleared and before them stood Petricus Postmortus in Harram's tainted body, he held a large wooden club the size of a tree, and a makeshift iron reinforced shield made from a wooden gate door.

							by Lore Casta Pendragon

His face was a mixture of Harram's and his own, "Harram!", Aethor shouted, "I told you not to come back, now I'm going to show you why you should have stayed dead".

Aethor bit into his thumb the blood trickled down his hand, his eyes went red, he crouched down then burst off from his mark with incredible speed.

Aethor tried a flying kick, but Petricus moved as if he knew what was coming and swatted Aethor away with the shield, Aethor tumbled over the stonework but flipped to his feet.

Ailyn took note of his footwork, "It couldn't be, that looks like Aikitai", he thought to himself, the ghouls came running in, Ailyn dodged the first few hands that swiped at him then started throwing the ghouls around like ragdolls, moving in circles avoiding them.

Brawn ran up and clotheslined a ghoul at Ailyn's back.

"Thanks", Ailyn said, turning back he avoided a ghoul's hand grabbing it by the wrist and twisting is around his hip, the ghoul flew sideways toward the other ghouls knocking them down.

Kimba slammed her fists together, she redirected the waterfall falling into the well and condensed it into a water gun, spraying it over the ghouls as they came in, knocking them down and saturating the floor with water, the ghouls began to slip and fall on the muddy surface slowing them down.

Aethor shook the dust off with a flex of his firmly toned muscles then ran toward Petricus, Petricus put his fists together then extended a hand taking his elbow with his other hand, a massive fireball erupted from his massive hand and he shot it toward Aethor.

Aethor's eyes went wide, he couldn't dodge it at this range, it hit the ground in front of him, the force of the explosion kicked dust up everywhere.

Aethor shot back out of the dust, he bounced from the stone floor and slammed into the far wall, his head collided with the stone and it left a blood splatter on the wall, Aethor fell slumped to the ground.

Wynn ran up and swung his claymore at the back of Petricus's hooved foot, it sliced through the tendon and Petricus roared with the pain, he stumbled unable to keep the foot stable, but managed to stay upright.

Petricus swung the club and knocked Wynn flying, Silus threw three knives into Petricus's leg, Petricus turned and blocked several more with the gate shield, as Silus came in Petricus swung the club.

"Traitor!", Petricus roared at him, Silus just smirked and slid underneath it narrowly avoiding the tip, he leaped up from the ground grabbing onto the knives he threw like handholds.

by Lore Casta Pendragon

He pulled them out and stuck them into Petricus's body as he climbed, Petricus roared and spun, he swung the club in an attempt to get Silus off him, but his damaged foot was making it hard for him to move.

Silus kept stabbing as he climbed up onto Petricus's hairy back, Silus pulled a larger jagged dagger from his coat and jammed it into Petricus's neck, Petricus dropped the club, it hit the ground with a crash.

He thrashed around, Silus lost his footing and Petricus grabbed him from over his shoulder, he took him by both hands and squeezed him furiously, Silus screamed out in pain as his bones snapped and crushed, he felt his insides rupture and felt like his eyeballs were about to pop out of his skull, "fitting end, traitor", Petricus said, he threw Silus to the ground.

Ailyn held his hands out in front of him, golden runes appeared in the air then Aram's staff appeared in his hands, he started slamming it into ghouls left and right.

Brawn was being overwhelmed by ghouls pulling them off him and throwing them into the ground, but more kept leaping on him.

Ailyn ran over to him and knocked them away, several more ran at them, Ailyn knocked them back toward the cave entrance with a mighty arcing swing.

Kimba was still drenching the ghouls with the torrent of water, which flooded the cave entrance, the ghouls struggled to get past the pool of rushing water, they began climbing over the walls of the cavern entrance to get to them.

"They just keep coming", Kimba shouted, she stopped the torrent of water then extended both hands toward the cave entrance, she strained as tendrils of life energy began to flow into her, the rock around the cave entrance started to crack, a fissure opened up above it, Kimba threw her hands to the floor and the cave entrance collapsed blocking it off.

Ilutha leaped from boulder to boulder, her curved elven blade in hand, Petricus held the large shield with both hands and slammed it down, Ilutha barely made it underneath as it hit the ground, she leaped between his legs and sliced open a gash into Petricus's other ankle.

She leaped again, making a shallow cut into the back of his tendon, Petricus moved to try to face her, but she was too agile, the damage to his feet was making him slow and unbalanced.

She leaped to avoid being stomped on and again countered with a slash to the tendon, with a loud snap, she severed it and Petricus dropped the shield, he wobbled on his feet.

Brawn picked up a boulder "here catch", he said, throwing it at Petricus, he caught it and the weight made him fall, he crashed down to the floor as Ilutha ran out from under him, he tossed the boulder back at Brawn, it shot out so fast that Brawn hardly had time to react, he

          by Lore Casta Pendragon

tried to move but the boulder glanced him across the shoulder which sent him spinning through the air.

Petricus rolled over onto his stomach as Ilutha tried a frontal assault to his face, he slapped his massive hands together, like he was swatting an insect, he opened his hands and Ilutha collapsed to the floor, he flicked her away like a bug.

Unable to stand Petricus knew he was a sitting duck, Ailyn and Kimba finished off the last of the ghouls, Ailyn smacked them into the flooded water while Kimba froze it over with a layer of ice.

Kimba collapsed to a knee panting, she was exhausted, Ailyn helped her to her feet.

"You did well, get to the ship, let me finish this", Ailyn said, Kimba nodded, the white aura looked like white fire around Ailyn, he walked up to Petricus, Petricus smiled at him, "Ailyn it's me", a familiar voice came from Petricus, "Den?", Ailyn said.

"This monster took my body, now I live within him, he steals people's bodies, memories and abilities", Den's voice came from Petricus's mouth, Ailyn stopped unsure what to do.

Petricus grabbed out at Ailyn, he leaped backward, still unsure what to do, Kimba walked up beside him still panting, "don't worry, I'll do it", Kimba said.

She slammed her fists together and extended one arm, flames flickered from her palm, "Kimba, I'm here too", this time it was Kamdar's voice and Kimba stopped.

"Stop it!", She said lowering her hand, "we're trapped, please save us", Kamdar's voice said, again Petricus reached out, this time for Kimba, Ailyn took two steps and kicked Petricus so hard he flew backward, coming to rest against the corpse of the dragon.

Petricus looked at the beast, then smashed his palm onto it feeling the creature, then smiled, he slammed his hand into the creature's chest wound and tore it open, then wormed himself inside of it.

"What is he doing?", Kimba said trying to hold herself back from vomiting.

Ailyn rushed forward but stopped, Petricus had already disappeared into the dragon's innards, black smokey miasma started rising and curling from the creature, it started to twitch, Ailyn's eyes went wide with horror.

"Get this ship moving", Villias ordered, "we can't fight this thing again, not with everyone laid out like this", Kimba said.

The crew began cutting the lines tying the ship to the sandbags below, "this is bad, get everyone to the ship", Ailyn shouted, he rushed over to Aethor, "father wake up, we gotta go!", Ailyn said gently slapping the side of his face, Aethor opened one eye then grabbed the

		by Lore Casta Pendragon

back of his head, he looked at his hand which was covered in blood, he groaned as Ailyn helped him to his feet.

Kimba moved over to Silus, he was still breathing, horridly injured, she slammed her fists together, water from the cave entrance made its way up to them and surrounded Silus, Kimba spun the water into a vortex and lifted him up to the ship.

"I've got him miss Kindheart", Felix said, Kimba lowered him into Felix's arms drenching him with water, Felix let out a yowl and looked at her disapprovingly then moved to take Silus into the captain's quarters.

"Can you walk?", Ailyn asked, "my head is a blur, but I can manage", Aethor said looking around, "I'll get Ilutha, you grab Wynn", Aethor said moving to her.

Aethor picked her up in his arms and with one mighty leap he landed on the ships deck.

Tendrils of Black miasma in the dragons' wounds coalesced forming new ligaments like black elastic, the blue mane of the beast turned black and the dragon started to roll onto its feet, it's eye's opened and clouded over with black miasma, the pupils were slits of glowing green.

"Such power", Petricus said raising himself on his back legs, his wings extended wide, and fluttered quickly sending a gale of wind around the cavern.

Ailyn helped Wynn to his feet, "thanks lad, I can make it on my own from here", Wynn bellowed.

Brawn walked up to him holding his claymore and put his arm over his shoulder.

"Get to the ship, I'll hold it off", Ailyn said, Wynn and Brawn nodded, Ailyn extended his arms and summoned Aram's staff again, the golden runed appeared in the air, Ailyn grabbed it and the staff became solid in his hands.

Wynn and Brawn made it up the rope ladder and the sky dancer turned to face the dragon, Mech was sitting at the arbalest, bolt loaded and ready, Petricus looked at him and growled.

"Fire!", Mech said and the bolt launched out, Petricus grabbed it in midair then snapped in half, he rushed forward and slashed at the arbalest with his claw, Mech sprawled from the seat, narrowly avoiding being killed as the arbalest shattered and splintered into pieces.

The sky dancer spun like a top, the crew barely held on, Ailyn leaped up from the ground and slammed the staff into Petricus's side, there was an audible crack.

Petricus's dragon eyes went wide and he gasped, falling to the ground, the sky dancer spun toward the cavern cliff, Inaya shot a gust of wind out to stabilize the ship, it slowed its spin and Rayan shot another gust toward the cliff face as the sky dancer pulled away from the wall, "that was too close", Felix said with a sigh.

                                              by Lore Casta Pendragon

Petricus curled up like a snake, his face hidden by his body, Ailyn walked toward him, he held the staff in front of him.

"I'm sorry Den, Kamdar, but I can't let this monster go free, forgive me", Ailyn said, the staff began to glow with the golden runes, Ailyn tucked it under his arm then started to run, he leaped into the air to deliver a decisive blow, when Petricus raised part of his body revealing a mouth full of black fire and smoke, he shot it out at Ailyn, Ailyn's eyes went wide as the flames engulfed him.

"Ailyn!", His friends cried out from the ships deck, Petricus stopped the gout of flames laughing at his own cleverness, Ailyn opened his eyes and stood before him unharmed.

Kimba was on one knee on the deck of the ship both hands extended and panting, a magical ward shattered in front of Ailyn then disappeared, Kimba collapsed unconscious, Felix ran to her, "Kimba, are you alright!", He said, she didn't respond.

Petricus rushed at Ailyn, his mouth open in an attempt to consume him, Ailyn swung the staff and connected with the side of his head, Petricus moved with the blow, mitigating the damage just how Den taught Ailyn to using Aikitai.

Petricus countered by stabbing at Ailyn with his spear-like claws, Ailyn tried to block but could only deflect two as another drove into his side near his hip, he dropped the staff and it disappeared in a flash of light, Petricus looked him in the eye, "interesting skills you have Ailyn, I guess you wouldn't mind me borrowing them", Petricus teased as he opened his jaw, his sharp teeth bore, ready to consume, the heat and rot was intense, Ailyn wanted to scream but gagged instead, blood filled his mouth and his eyes went red.

Ailyn heard a cannon fire and Petricus was hit, he flung his head back in pain, another cannon fired and knocked him back.

He released Ailyn and he dropped to the cavern floor, he landed awkwardly grasping at his wound, he could feel his life force burning away quickly, he didn't have much time left, the staff appeared in his hand again.

"Fire!", Villias shouted and the crew of the sky dancer fired again, Villias had his cannon leg resting on the ships rail, Petricus's thin body whirled around avoiding a cannonball, the other hit his tail making him wince with the pain.

Villias's cannonball smashed Petricus in the chest, cracking the scales and knocking him back, black fire curled in Petricus's mouth.

"Oh, no", Ailyn said, if he aimed that at the ship, it was all over, he'd lose everyone again, he couldn't let that happen.

by Lore Casta Pendragon

Ailyn dug deep, he could feel his life force dwindling like fire flickering on a candle, he held the staff before him, a bright golden light engulfed it, he shot out like a missile and swung the staff as hard as he could, right where the dragon scales were cracked.

A loud crunching sound filled the cavern as Ailyn connected, pieces of dragon scale shattered and the dragon fire spread out over the cavern floor as Petricus flew back splashing through the waterfall, he fell next to the well, his chest was indented and broken.

Petricus's eyes were blurred, he was losing consciousness, he looked into the well, Ailyn landed, then collapsed, he pushed himself up on one knee trying to stand, his eyes were blurring over as well, he knew if he fought on any longer, he'd die.

Aethor leaped down from the ship as Ailyn collapsed, he held Ailyn in his arms.

Petricus heard a voice coming from the well, "Break, The, Seal", Guldamere's dead raspy voice called out, with Petricus's final ounce of strength he reached a clawed talon and dipped it into the well, as soon as it touched the surface an inky blackness spread out from it, covering the well in darkness.

The water rippled violently and rose, taking a humanoid form, Guldamere's black outline rose up from the well, a low cackling evil laugh came from him as his body formed a new.

"You did well son, but we've lost this one, live to fight another day", Aethor said.

He leaped with Ailyn onto the ships deck, "we have to go, now!", Aethor said.

Inaya, Rayan and Villias got into position and the ship started to rise through the hole in the cavern roof.

Guldamere's laugh intensified as a dark shadow began to extend outwards from the cavern, they took off fleeing as fast as the ship could carry them, the darkness followed, it was consuming everything, it caught up to them fast, then past them, they looked out as it covered the land, the sky, everything.

The sun shone with an inky purple light, it was like day turned to night, Guldamere's voice echoed in the minds of everyone in Thalaria that day.

"Endless night, endless insanity, the unfaithful shall fall, none shall sleep, for even in your dreams you cannot escape the god feared", his voice echoed through the land, a chill settled on them, Kimba, Ailyn, Silus and Ilutha all woke up suddenly screaming.

"What's going on?", Felix asked, "We've been cursed", Ilutha said, she was on her back panting heavily, "what do ye mean cursed?", Villias said, "you heard him, he said none shall sleep", Inaya said, "but if we don't sleep won't we die?", Brawn asked, "I think that's the point", Aethor said.

by Lore Casta Pendragon

They all looked to each other, one of the crew stepped up onto the ships rail, fear and resignation covered his face.

"No lad, don't do it", Villias called to him, "it's over, I don't want to suffer", he said as he stepped off the rail and plummeted to the ground below.

by Lore Casta Pendragon

Chapter Twenty-One

Into endless night

Kimba covered her mouth in shock, "this can't be happening", she said in disbelief.

"Guldamere said it's a curse, surely there be a way to break it", Villias asked, "his words, he said endless insanity for the unfaithful, does that mean the church of the god feared would be sparred?", Rayan asked, no one answered, for a while they just stood on the ship not knowing what to do and considering.

Kimba slowly got to her feet, "we can't just lay down and die, if the lich is going to force our hand, then we'll just have to bring the fight to him, the library in Necropyre, if we can get to it, there's a room filled with magic tomes written by Guldamere and Lore Casta Pendragon, perhaps we could find some answers there and break the curse", Kimba suggested.

"If I want to stand a chance at all against him, I'm going to have to collect the final shard from the ronin city to the southwest", Ailyn said, "you're not going anywhere until we've healed our wounded", Ilutha said, Silus groaned as she tended to him.

"He's in bad shape", Ilutha said, Silus coughed, the pain was evident on his face, "you heard his words, none shall sleep, we're out of time, it'll only be a day or two before we lose the ability to fight, if you're going to survive, you have to act now", Silus said, everyone looked his direction, determination covered their faces.

"We have to split up, I'll go to Necropyre to find information on the curse", Kimba said.

"I'll go to the Ronin city and track down the final shard", Ailyn said.

"Take me to Paladin's Reach, I've heard they have an elixir that heals even the direst of wounds", Silus said, Ilutha nodded to him.

"I'll head to the Iron halls and let my king know there's a battle to be fought, we'll organize an offensive", Mech said, "I'll go too, I'll find where our men have gone and rally them for the battle", Brawn said, "I'll go too, the Iron halls are the closest place to the front line, I want to be there when we march on Necropyre and end the lich for good", Wynn bellowed.

"Paladin's Reach be the closest to us, so I'll drop ye to ye destinations and be back to pick ye all up in a day or two, be ready", Villias said as the ship moved to the northwest.

Guldamere stood over the well, it was tainted, covered by an inky blackness, he placed his hands together in prayer, he was transported to the ethereal river of the abyss in a black void, the river ended with a waterfall into a black void, Guldamere snarled at it.

						by Lore Casta Pendragon

"Well played Pendragon, but even you can't stop a god", Guldamere said proudly, Petricus was there in his dragon form his body was limp and he slumped over the falls teetering from the edge, the large form of the abyssal dragon seemed to fight the flow of the river.

Guldamere extended his boney skeletal hand, a black aura surrounded his hand as well as Petricus, the huge body of the dragon lifted, it began floating back toward Guldamere.

"You've done well general, consider this body the reward for your loyalty", he said, voice echoing through the void.

Petricus opened his serpentine eyes, black miasma claws ripped the arbalest bolts from his body, he roared with pain, he slowly clambered to his feet, a black-green miasma surrounded him and he felt invigorated with new life.

Guldamere stayed in the same position opening one eye looking at Petricus, "you are no longer part of the living Petricus", Guldamere said, Petricus could hear Guldamere's voice echoing in his head.

"You are the dracolich, go forth and feast, each life you consume will prolong your own and satiate your hunger", Guldamere said putting his hands together in prayer, bowing his head returning to the living world.

Petricus smirked and bowed before his lord before taking to the sky, the black smokey miasma trailed him like dark contrails.

Guldamere bowed his head once again passing into the abyss.

He waded forward through the ethereal waters until he came to the edge of the falls, he felt the abyss pulling on him, the pull of death was strong for him, but Guldamere was stronger, he extended a skeletal hand over the void below.

Three figures began to rise from the darkness, Violet Valentine, Sin Sonata and Charon rose before him, their souls floated to him in the void, they woke slowly as their ethereal forms took on new life, the inky darkness engulfed them, Guldamere's head rose in the living world as Violet reached a hand out of the well, the sticky blackness clung to her, it felt like it was trying to pull her back under.

A bony skeletal hand surrounded by a black aura reached down and grabbed her hand, Guldamere strained as he pulled against it.

Violet held on with all of her strength as she was pulled free, she sat at the edge of the well, wiping the inky black fluid from her eyes, her dark hair covered her face, she pulled it to the side and looked up at Guldamere, her eyes shone with a glowing purple light, her eyes resembled that of a predator or a cat, her canines had grown out into fangs.

          by Lore Casta Pendragon

Guldamere helped her to her feet, her naked form was only covered by the inky blackness from the well, with a finger gesture Guldamere wrapped her in black miasma which formed into a dress much like the one she used to wear, only this one looked like it was made from the substance that bore her a new, smoke curled from it as she moved.

"Welcome back miss Valentine, undeath suits you", Guldamere said, eyeing her up and down.

Violet's beauty had not tarnished with her lichdom, if anything it heightened it, she felt hunger and lust like she had never felt before, "thank you lord of the dark", Violet said bowing with a smile, showing a great amount of cleavage, her breathy voice had not changed.

"You will need to feed in order to continue your existence here, now go", Guldamere ordered.

Violet pulled the black miasma around her, it dissipated and she disappeared with it.

Charon was the next to immerge, he slithered out of the inky blackness taking the form of a snake, an inky black sack surrounded him, it pulled him back into the well, black miasma surrounded Guldamere's hand forming into a dark taloned claw, it sliced at the inky blackness and Charon slid free.

Curling up he rose before Guldamere, a giant black snake with red stripes and red eyes, he bowed his serpentine head, his tongue wiggled out of his mouth.

"A shame, you no longer possess the ability to speak, you were dead for too long, that is unfortunate, however the more you feed, the stronger you will become, someday you will regain your faculties go forth and consume", Guldamere ordered, with a nod Charon slithered into the shadows.

The next to immerge was Sin, no sooner had his form touched the surface of the well a flash of light ripped open a path and Sin leaped from it, with a flash the ronin katana was back in the saya, he was wearing a white robe and a white kasa, a wide brimmed hat made from straw, "your sword leeches the life of your enemies, find and kill Ailyn Allheart before he reaches the final shard, then bring his corpse to me", Guldamere ordered.

Sin tipped his kasa in acknowledgement, he opened his palm, a small ball of black smoke gathered within it forming into a ball, he grabbed it and threw it at the ground, smoke exploded out from it, it cleared and Sin was gone, Guldamere placed his hands together in prayer once again, he extended a hand into the well, the shadows drew longer and darker.

The inky blackness of the pool began to flow together, it raised itself up forming into the shape of a large man, a foot burst out of it and took a step from the well, it fell away revealing Warden looking rather nonchalant considering he was just brought back from death after so long.

        by Lore Casta Pendragon

"I thought my lord had abandoned me, when I took the plunge into the abyss, I had no delusions of being revived", Warden said.

Guldamere smiled at him, "I spent some time in the lands beyond myself, but I have returned, find your captives and see they pay the price of those who dare try to escape us", Guldamere said.

"Yes, my lord", Warden said with a bow.

"Oh, I hope you don't mind, but I brought a friend back with me this time", he raised an arm which was quickly covered in pure darkness, many eyes opened along it, "we have returned, this time the light won't save them", the creeping dark giggled, Guldamere smiled wickedly as Warden walked off into the shadow on the wall.

Guldamere used much of his power to revive his men and retreated to Necropyre to recover his strength and prepare for his lacrimosa.

The crew of the sky dancer made their way to Paladins Reach, as they arrived the city was covered in scaffolding, they were rebuilding it after the battle that sent the cities entire population scattering to the five corners of Thalaria, thanks to Lore Casta Pendragon's magic.

It seemed a good amount of the citizenry had found their way back to the city, the ship docked close to a balcony at the keep and they were greeted by Paladin's with large crossbows.

"Hold ye fire!", Villias shouted, Link pushed his way through, "Hay!", Kimba yelled from the deck, "lower your weapons", Link ordered.

Locke walked up behind him with an obvious limp, he kept leaning on his sword for support, "finally we might get some answers", Locke said to Link, "lower the rope ladder", Villias ordered.

Ailyn leaped down from the ships deck, Kimba put her fists together and rode down with a vortex of wind, "never mind…", Villias said sarcastically.

"Can someone please explain to me why the day turned dark and why we're having these blasted nightmares, why you have a flying ship and why my kingdom was scattered across the bloody world!", Locke said frustrated.

"There's a lot to unpack there, but I'll try to keep it short, we don't have much time left", Kimba said as she took a deep breath and talked as fast as she could.

"When master Pendragon fought Guldamere he knew he couldn't defeat him by any regular means, he knew that if he perished and left Guldamere here, he would drain every living person of their life force and we'd fail, so he teleported everyone away and dragged Guldamere to the lands beyond with him, he effectively killed him doing so, or so he thought, we were

by Lore Casta Pendragon

teleported to the eastern desert, met up with Silus who changed sides and then met captain Villias, who took us to Oasis, we later found Felix and Mech in the eastern desert, they built this airship from the remains of the flying machine they used in the battle here and Villias's ship, thus the sky dancer had her maiden voyage, we went to the Elven forest and fought a dragon in its lair at an ancient magic well, unfortunately Petricus Postmortus, absorbed the dragon and helped Guldamere revive himself, Guldamere then placed a curse on the land, so if you don't pledge loyalty to the church of the god feared, you'll eventually perish, effectively eliminating all of his enemies at once", Kimba gasped for air.

Link looked at them horrified, "that explains the sky and the night terrors", Link said looking at Locke, "that pretty much explains the lot, I think", Locke said convinced.

A servant brought up a chair as Locke fell backward catching him, his injuries were still raw, "so what brings you here?", Link questioned.

"This is it, we're out of time, unless we stop this curse everyone who has fought against the church of the god feared will die", Ailyn said.

"I see", Locke said looking a little overwhelmed.

"I know you're still recovering from the last battle Lord Lionheart, but we're going to need every bit of help we can to raise an army and finish Guldamere before we're too late", Ailyn pleaded bowing deeply.

"Tell us where to be and you'll have our support", Locke said, Ailyn smiled.

"Thank you, but I have one more favor to ask of you, I need an elixir", Ailyn asked.

"I'm afraid we don't have any left, but if you give me some time, I can get you one", Link said, Ilutha placed Silus on a makeshift stretcher and the crew lowered him down from the ship, Locke scoffed.

"Why should we heal that traitor", Link said scornfully, "my son, as much as I detest this man, if he was willing to die for us, it's the least we can do for him", Locke said.

Locke clicked his fingers and two paladins picked up the stretcher, Ilutha walked over to Link, "lady Ilutha, it's a pleasure to see you again", Link said, "Prince Lionheart, thank you for caring for him", Ilutha said, she turned to Ailyn, "I'll stay with him and make sure he's seen to, you'd best be off, no time to dawdle", Ailyn nodded.

The white aura shown briefly around him, he picked Kimba up unexpectedly and she yelped, Ailyn leaped back up onto the ships deck and placed her down, Kimba felt a little violated but also impressed as she straightened her robe.

"At least warn me if you're going to manhandle me", she said, "next stop, Necropyre", Villias called down as the ship took off.

  by Lore Casta Pendragon

They reached the border of Necropyre a few hours later, "drop us here, Felix and I will make our way into the city on our own, if you come too far into enemy territory, you'll be spotted for sure", Kimba said.

"Be careful Kimba", Ailyn said, she kissed him right in front of Felix who coughed then pulled her away, "well no time to lose, we'll see you again in a day or two", Felix said quickly, they made their way down the rope ladder to the ground below.

Necropyre was just down the mountainside from where they were, the ship took off, and they waved goodbye, Ailyn had a terrible feeling in the pit of his stomach but he knew that time was against them.

He needed to find the last of the shards before the battle began, they flew over the scar toward the living forest, Ailyn could see his old home at riverside village in the distance, Aethor came up beside him a bandage wrapped around his head and placed a hand on his shoulder to comfort him.

"The entrance to the tunnels is north of here, closer to the mountains", Mech shouted, the ship sped off and in no time at all they came to a tunnel with ornate statues of dwarves in armor on the outside.

"This is where we get off", Mech said, Brawn and Wynn jumped off to accompany him, "When we meet again, we'll have an army to back you up, when the time comes", Brawn said.

"Look after yourselves lads", Wynn shouted, Mech flipped a lever on a lamp and it shown with a bright electrical light, "farewell!", He shouted happily, they headed down into the tunnel, the sky dancer took off once more headed south toward the ronin city.

"Captain", Rayan said, "I don't know how much longer we're going to be able to keep the ship flying", the two mages were straining to stand as they crossed the scar toward the ronin city.

"Just a little longer lads, I'll throw in a keg of me best ale if ye can make it there before we crash", Villias said trying to sweeten the deal, Inaya collapsed to the deck sweat covering her brow, Rayan extended another hand to try to pick up the slack, the strain was evident on his face, the ship began to slow and sink, Ailyn grabbed a rag and dabbed it on Inaya's head while Aethor gave her a cup of water.

"Once we pass the gap, we'll go on foot from there", Ailyn said.

A few hours past and Villias took the ship down just outside of a bamboo forest on the southern edge of the scar south of Dawnshire.

"We'll rest here for now, but we'll be off to Paladin's reach to pick up lady Ilutha and Silus, if we don't return in two days, head to the Iron halls", Villias said.

Ailyn and Aethor nodded then leaped down from the ship, they landed on the dusty ground, the ship must have caught the eye of a nightmare creature, as no sooner had they landed a

by Lore Casta Pendragon

large reptilian lizard, sauntered toward them, its long pink tongue flicked out like a whip from its jaw, it's hide was thick and tough.

The white aura around Ailyn began to come into view, the creatures tongue whipped at him with a crack, he leaped up, somersaulting forward and cracked the creature on the nose so hard that there was an audible snapping sound, the creatures jaw snapped shut against the ground, it backstepped back into the bamboo forest and was gone.

The aura faded around Ailyn, Aethor nodded to him and they headed into the dense foliage of the forest, they made their way through the jutting tangle of bamboo until they came to a creek where the bamboo didn't grow as densely.

"So, what did you do before you met mother and moved to Riverside", Ailyn asked, Aethor looked over at him surprised by the question.

"I used to teach soldiers to fight in Dawnshire", Aethor said, "I had a well-respected martial arts school there, but word got out about my affiliation with certain resistance members and I was forced to close the school, I caused some trouble and was run out of town, I headed north, until I came upon Riverside, a girl needed help against some trouble making soldiers and the rest, you can probably guess on your own", Ailyn smiled, Aethor talked to him of their life in Riverside village as they travelled upstream.

After a while they came to a bridge over the river and followed the path, a man wearing rags and a straw hat walked by them to their left, he seemed cautious and agitated.

"Excuse me", Aethor said, his eyes went wide as the man drew his sword, he ducked and the sword sliced the top part of his hair, Aethor spun to his left onto his knee, his back foot spun around and knocked the man legs out, he fell over the rail of the bridge into the water below.

"What was that all about?", Ailyn asked, "the ronin city is under the control of the church of the god feared, we have to be careful", Aethor said, he took the hat the man had dropped and gave it to Ailyn.

"Here, take this", he said, Ailyn looked at him confused, "so your face isn't recognized", Aethor said.

Ailyn took it from him, "you know sometimes I do wonder if that fish did more damage than we thought", Aethor said forcing back a laugh, Ailyn was insulted but couldn't help but smile as he remembered that day by the river with Aidem.

They walked until they passed a small shrine, there was a statue there of a nightmare creature, it's face distorted into an angry snarl, it had four arms and seemed to be doing some kind of dance, a straw hat was tied to a post nearby, Aethor took it and placed it on his head.

Continuing onward, they passed some more people dressed in colorful robes and then some more, the city was in sight now, the buildings were ornate and well-built with wooden structures with sharp edges, they came to the gate as night was falling, there were several

by Lore Casta Pendragon

guards standing on the wall with bows as large as they were, there were several men checking people and carts as they walked toward the city gates, Aethor grabbed Ailyn's shoulder.

"We can't just walk in the front door, we're best to avoid being seen", Aethor said, "how do we get in?", Ailyn asked, Aethor looked around, there was a tree close to the wall hidden by foliage, "we can jump through there", Aethor pointed.

They crouched down and waited for a sentry to pass, Aethor took two steps up the tree, leaped and then another two steps on the wall leaping onto the ledge, Ailyn thought about using his power, but the glowing white aura might give him away.

He followed Aethor's lead, he took two steps up the tree and leaped from it to the wall, he grabbed the ledge by his finger tips and the slanted brick crumbled under his hand, Aethor grabbed his wrist and he hung there, the crumbling brickwork thudded to the ground, the noise attracted the attention of the sentry who started back.

Aethor pulled Ailyn over the ledge, they hung over the other side hanging as the soldier came to check out the noise, he pondered for a moment, but walked away, they sighed in relief.

Dropping down behind a small shop, several pigs grunted and a light flashed on in the shop, they quickly jumped a picket fence and walked out onto the street pulling the kasa hats low over their faces.

The dirt path was lined with ornate lanterns leading up to a curved red bridge, over the bridge they saw an Inn called, 'the luck of the draw'.

"We need to find information on the shard", Ailyn said, "start with the Innkeeper and I'll ask some drunk patrons", Aethor suggested.

They entered the Inn, there were several booths filled with patrons in front with tables closer to the bar at the back, which had some people playing dice games and cards, they went to the bar and were greeted loudly by the barman, "irasshaimase", he bellowed, they kept their heads down and walked to the bar, not used to being welcomed in such a fashion.

"What would you like?", the barman said, Ailyn and Aethor looked at each other then looked at the barman, "whatever you have is fine", Ailyn said.

The barman placed an ornate ceramic wine bottle in front of them then poured an abysmal amount of white liquid from it into tiny little saucers.

Aethor gulped it down then grabbed the bottle taking a large swig, the barman waved his hands trying to stop him, Aethor slammed the bottle down, "wow", he said happily, "strong drink".

Ailyn gulped down his saucer and placed it back on the table, "hmm, not bad", Ailyn said.

by Lore Casta Pendragon

The barman poured him another one, "we're from the north, first time in the city, who run's things around here?", Ailyn asked.

"No one rules in the ronin", the barman said, "without hierarchy how do you decide what needs to be done?", Ailyn asked, Aethor got up and wandered over to a table of people playing dice.

"After the cataclysm our land was mostly destroyed, our leaders were gone, the soldiers that were risen by great lord Guldamere came back to find only a few farmers had survived and the bamboo forest consuming all that was left, with so few of us left we became a collective of lordless ronin, this city was formed by that group and over five hundred years the city has grown into groups of prominent families that contribute to the wellbeing of all, the biggest being the Sonata family", the barman explained.

"Sonata, where have I heard that name before", Ailyn thought to himself.

"Tell me, is one of them named, Sin?", Ailyn asked, the barman hushed him, "don't say his name too loudly, Sin Sonata is one of Guldamere's top officials, he was in charge of the cities defenses, but he went missing some time ago", the barman whispered.

A loud groan came up from the dice table as Aethor won another round, fifteen gold coins were now in front of him.

Ailyn walked up and placed a hand on his shoulder, "aren't we trying to keep a low profile", he whispered.

"Relax, these guys are so desperate to win their money back they'll tell us everything we need to know", Aethor whispered back.

"Did the barman give you any good information?", Aethor asked, "the city is a collective under the rule of Guldamere, the Sonata family holds the majority of the power, Sin's family", Ailyn explained.

"Not much to tell us where to go next", Aethor whispered, he leaned back in his chair winning another round.

"Sorry gentleman, beginners' luck I guess, but I'll tell you what, I'll give some gold pieces to any man who can tell me something interesting about the city, but only if it's more interesting than the last, it's my first time here and I would like to see it all", Aethor said deviously.

The three men at the table looked at each other suspiciously then one man spoke up, "there is a small store run by a poor family who sell's sweet cakes filled with custard for cheap, it's a good place for a snack", the other two men looked at him.

Aethor paused, the information wasn't at all useful but he picked up a gold coin and threw it to him, "Th-thank you", the man stuttered in disbelief, he quickly bowed several times and left in a hurry, the other two men's eyes went wide thinking, Aethor must be drunk.

                              by Lore Casta Pendragon

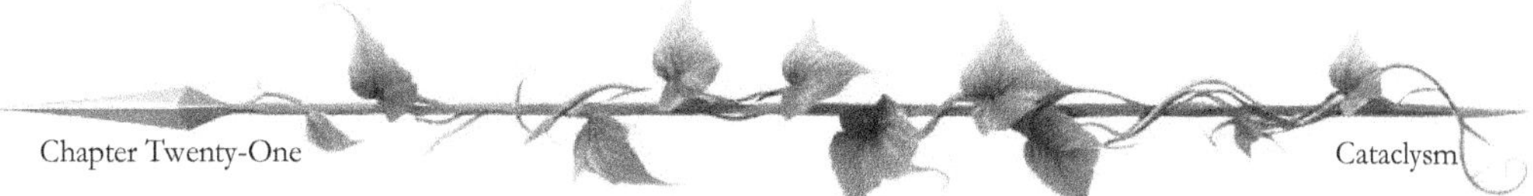

"The temple in the bamboo forest, it's said that it grants people wishes", one man said, Aethor looked at the other man, "where abouts?", "It's along the path to the northwest of town", the third man blurted out, Aethor pocketed some coins then threw them what remained, they quickly snatched them up and left.

Ailyn sat down next to Aethor, "a temple that grants wishes, that certainly sounds like a shard could be there", Ailyn said.

"We should check it out, by the way, how did you manage to win all that coin", he asked, Aethor smiled, "I've got the fastest hands in the world", Aethor said smirking, he picked up a cup of dice and rattled it, he slammed the cup down, but just before it hit the table, Aethor's other hand became a blur of motion, the cup slammed down, Aethor stared Ailyn in the eye and lifted the cup.

Snake eyes plus two, the highest possible roll, "I see, so you cheated them out of their money then gave it back to them for information", Ailyn said, Aethor tapped the side of his nose.

"It's not hard when your opponents are too busy ogling the bar maids and getting drunk", he laughed, Ailyn shook his head, "let's go".

They exited the luck of the draw and headed toward the northwest of town.

One of the men Aethor had cheated watched as they left from around the corner of the Inn, he rushed off to a large building where he was stopped by two guards, they drew katana's and had them at his throat in an instant.

The man dropped to his knees, "I have information, permit me to see my lord", he stammered and the men escorted him inside, he was brought to a room where Sin sat elevated on a platform, sword by his side and wearing a white kasa hat, several beautiful women were pouring tea for him, the man fell to his knees in front of him bowing low.

"My lord your enemy is heading to the temple northwest of town", Sin smiled then waved the man away, one of the guards handed him a bag of coins and grunted nodding toward the door, the man left with the coin.

Sin got up, black smoke curled into a ball in his palm then coalesced and became a solid, he grabbed it and threw it at his feet, the people in the room coughed, it cleared and Sin was gone.

by Lore Casta Pendragon

Chapter Twenty-Two

Sinful Sayonara

Ailyn and Aethor came to the city gate, they climbed onto the roof of a nearby building then used that to leap over the city wall, they quickly ran down a dirt path, the bamboo forest surrounded them, the moon was full and shone with dark purple light, it was dark, but they could see clearly enough.

As they ran, they saw smoke rising overhead and the din of firelight twinkling through the cracks in the bamboo, "don't tell me we're too late", Ailyn said.

They ran faster only to find the temple had been set on fire, "someone must have tipped them off", Ailyn said, Aethor growled in frustration, out of the flaming doorway stepped Sin a torii gate was on fire in front of him, the glowing white shard was in his hand.

"This time we beat you to it", Sin said as he crushed it in his palm, the power flowed into him, a black aura appeared around him.

"Sin!", Ailyn shouted, "good to see you again Ailyn, thanks for finding the shard for me, this time I'll be sure to finish you", Sin said.

He drew his sword in a flash, the torii gate snapped in half as a shockwave cut through it, Ailyn and Aethor leaped above it narrowly avoiding being sliced in half, the soldiers from the city came running from the bamboo forest behind them.

"Damn it all, it's a trap", Aethor said turning to face them, "I'll keep the soldiers busy, you have to get that shard Ailyn, if he gets to Guldamere", Aethor started but Ailyn cut him off, "I know, the only way to get it back now is to finish him", Ailyn said.

Sin leaped down from the burning temple and ran off into the forest, Ailyn pursued him.

Aethor bit into his thumb as the soldiers charged in, his eyes went red as the first of the soldier met him, with a crack Aethor used his dragon kick, side stepping and planting his foot into the man's mid-section.

The man crumbled in half, losing his weapon and shooting back into another soldier, another came in swinging his sword diagonally left and right, Aethor skipped back and back again, he found an opening and back fisted the man to his face, the man's nose broke inward and he fell unconscious as he hit the ground.

The enemy ran around him facing their swords toward him, they surrounded Aethor, slowly and cautiously they walked close, one got too impatient and stabbed at him prematurely, Aethor slapped the sword by the blunt side and moved in fast, he elbowed the man to the mid-section doubling him over.

                    by Lore Casta Pendragon

Aethor grabbed the hilt of the sword and threw the man to the ground, the man to Aethor's left stabbed at him, Aethor avoided it using his keinohenka stepping technique, he moved one eighty degrees around the blade using the sword he stole to slice at the man's heel, it cut through like butter, the man screamed in pain dropping his weapon and grasping at his ankle.

Another soldier came in with a spear stabbing toward Aethor's face, Aethor swung the sword wildly trying to deflect the strikes, they got closer and closer to his face and he almost backed into another soldier who was behind him.

Aethor grabbed the spear shaft twisting around the tip then threw his sword at the other soldier behind, it stuck into his chest.

Aethor pulled the spear wielder forward placing two hands on the spear, in a wave like motion he turned with the weapon, the man lost his grip and Aethor cracked him with the blunt end of it, launching him into the air.

Again, Aethor was surrounded, he heard the twang of a bow string and an arrow pierced him in the back, Aethor cried out in pain.

He spun the spear around and cut the shaft of the arrow off with the blade, another twang sounded out, but this time he was ready, he leaped out to the side and the arrow hit another soldier dropping him.

Aethor followed the sound and threw the spear like a missile, it slammed the archer in the chest splitting his armor and pinning him against a tree, his enemies were shocked at the sheer force of it and stopped attacking, gawking at him.

Furious anger shown on their faces, they began to scream out a war cry in unison, that archer must have been some kind of high-ranking soldier.

Aethor let out a cry of his own and they all came at Aethor at once, he leaped behind the circle of enemies, then jumped forward and bicycle kicked a man in his back, he fell into another man's sword, blood dribbled from his bottom lip.

The other men rushed at him, Aethor countered slashes with punches and kicks dropping men left and right, he no longer cared about the razor-sharp weapons swinging at him, they made cuts into his skin but he kept pressing the attack.

Another arrow slammed into him, he barely felt it, he knocked out a spearman with a kick then threw the spear into the archer, making a shish kebab out of several soldiers.

Aethor pulled the arrow out of his own body and stabbed another man in the eye with it, his bloodlust and rage only increased his strength, he burned with a fury that no man could possibly match, men began to pile up around him, his punches became so forceful that that were leaving indents in steel armor, busting skulls and breaking ribs.

                                    by Lore Casta Pendragon

Aethor walked up to a soldier trying to get to his feet and placed his fingered against the man's steel helmet, he used his short-ranged punch and the helmet caved in with a crunch as the man slammed into the ground, he looked up at the remaining soldiers, his eyes a burning like red fire.

"Demon, he's a demon", a soldier cried, he turned tripping on the bodies of his companions as he retreated, the other soldiers dropped their weapons and ran terrified.

Aethor stood in the fire light, it was only then, being left alone next to the burning temple that he realized how much blood he had lost, it covered the ground, he was covered in gashes, two arrow shafts were sticking out of his back, the red fire in his eyes flickered, then burned out and he fell onto his back.

Ailyn heard the sound of bamboo snapping and dived to the ground, Sin's ranged strike barely missed him and the bamboo trees fell around him, it was dark and he couldn't see much, the white aura began to burn around him illuminating him and the surrounding area.

Ailyn sprinted off to the side, Sin sprinted with him, the moonlight shown rays through the forest, gold runes appeared in the air in front of Ailyn's hands, Aram's staff appeared and his hand clasped around it, Sin sliced through the bamboo and Ailyn came sliding to a stop and swung the back end of the staff around, sparks rang out with the clang of steel.

Ailyn struggled with the weight of the attack but managed to flick the staff pushing the Sin's sword away, Sin instantly withdrew the sword into the saya leaping back.

He landed and followed up with a vertical draw Ailyn moved out to the side but the kasa hat he was wearing came loose, the slash sliced it in half before it hit the ground, Ailyn eyed it warily.

"What's wrong Ailyn, where is all that bravado you had the last time we fought, don't tell me you're afraid", Sin said, he was egging him on, trying to break his concentration, Ailyn knew that one wrong move would end in being severed in two, one wrong move and Guldamere would gain the remaining power and they would lose everything.

Ailyn stood up straight and clasped both hands on the staff, it began to glow with a bright golden light, Sin withdrew his katana and held the tang, ready and waiting.

The white aura burned around Ailyn and black smoke curled around Sin, Ailyn turned bringing the tip of the staff down, he used tenkan, his back foot rotating one hundred eighty degrees around, the staff followed his body movement and he brought it over his head for a vertical strike, a curved golden wave of light extended from the staff toward Sin.

Sin drew his blade horizontally and the two shockwaves met in the middle, they seemed to fold over one another then cancelled each other out.

Ailyn rushed forward, the staff slid forward through his hand stabbing at Sin, Sin raised the tang, blade facing downward and turned his hips away, the staff deflected to the side, Sin

                                    by Lore Casta Pendragon

countered with kotegaeshi, a wrist twist, the sword used the momentum of Ailyn's stab to flick around Sin shoulder for an overhead strike.

Ailyn's eyes went wide, he dropped his hands low and the tip of the staff high, deflecting the sword he also used kotegaeshi, the staff rotating around his left shoulder for an overhead strike, as it came in Sin planted his feet in a horse stance and used kotegaeshi again to the other side, again the overhead strike came back at Ailyn, he saw the challenge and planted his feet as well, he leaned right, deflecting and following up with the overhead slash, again Sin used kotegaeshi.

Ailyn leaned right, they began to pick up speed deflecting and striking, left then right, over and over, sparks flew out like a shower of steel as the two struck at either trying to outpace one another, it was a battle of speed and the victor would be whoever was faster.

The speed and the ring of steel became so fast that Ailyn could no longer even see Sin, all he could focus on was the impact of the sword against his staff and the movement of his body, each hit jarred his wrists, but he wouldn't let up, if he tried to move now it would slow him down too much and he'd be sliced in two, both men started to grunt in pain as their shoulder muscles burned with the effort, Sin slowed for a moment but that was long enough.

Ailyn's staff slammed into Sin's arm with a loud crack, Sin was forced to his knees and his sword flew off and stuck into the ground nearby, Ailyn held the staff above his head ready to finish him, Sin's arms shook, then fell at his sides.

"I trusted you Shin, we were brothers in arms, before I kill you, I need you to tell me why you sided with that monster, why side with Guldamere", Ailyn said, Sin shook his head, "it's Sin, not Shin, don't you see, Guldamere is a force of nature, the force of death itself, the abyss has come to claim the land of Thalaria and the only way forward is to embrace the inevitable, Guldamere will not be stopped, he is immortal, to defy him means to perish forever, but if you accept him, you'll live forever, think about it Ailyn, which side seems more logical to you?", Sin said.

Ailyn's brow furrowed, he understood now, Sin took Ailyn's lack in focus to leap away, he landed on one knee making a symbol with his hands, a tendril of black miasma flicked the sword back to him and he caught it without looking at it.

Sin withdrew the sword in the saya and held a hand palm up, black smoke curled around and formed a large black orb, Sin's fingers clasped around it.

"I can't let you defeat me", Sin said throwing the orb to the ground, it exploded into black smoke which covered the area, everything went pitch black.

Ailyn knew he was in trouble, he remembered the training he did with master Den and closed his eyes listening carefully, Sin came in with a horizontal slash, Ailyn raised the staff and blocked the strike, another to his left and then another to his right, he felt the air around him, he heard the bristling sound of Sin's footsteps in the forest.

 by Lore Casta Pendragon

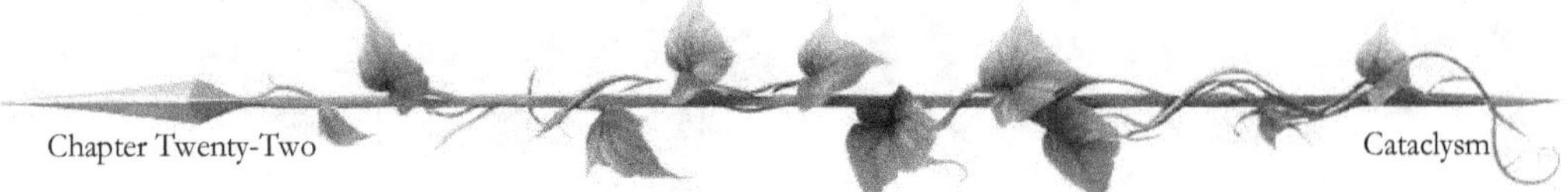

To his right was the snap of a twig, Sin was trying to get behind him, Ailyn turned and swung the staff, he heard the ring of steel followed by a grunt, then a body hitting the ground, Ailyn whirled the staff around him from left to right, the staff glowed with a golden light and the wind picked up around him blowing the smoke away.

Sin leaped in with a jumping overhead strike, the whirling staff knocked it away, Ailyn pressed forward bringing the staff spinning over his head, he tucked the staff under his arm and swung it left, Sin blocked it, but the sheer power of the strike knocked the sword away, Sin almost lost his grip as Ailyn reversed directions.

Again, the staff spun above his head and under his arm as he spun, he struck at Sin to the right, Sin's sword connected but the strength of Ailyn's blow made the sword fly out again, it bounced off the ground.

Sin went to a knee, another overhead spin and Ailyn brought the staff down against Sin's neck, an audible crack reverberated out and Sin slammed to the ground, black miasma kicked up around him then faded in color turning white, it whirled and began to form together, coalescing into a glowing white shard, Ailyn reached out and grabbed it, the light beamed out through his fingers.

"You've done it Ailyn, you've collected all of the shards", Ailyn heard his mother Asta's voice call as the shard spoke to him, "my power is now yours, but be warned, while my power is significant, so was the power of my sisters, you will be outmatched when you confront the lich", the voice said.

"How do I defeat him", Ailyn asked, "death cannot hold him, the only way to defeat him would be to take his power away", the voice faded out.

"How do I take away his power!", Ailyn shouted, but he got no reply, the white around him faded and Ailyn stood there in the dark, he looked down at Sin's body, then looked to the sky, he could still see the smoke from the burning temple.

"Aethor!", Ailyn said rushing back for him, he came into the clearing to see piles of enemy soldiers.

"Father!", Aethor cried out, he heard him cough and leaped over a pile of bodies to find Aethor on the ground in a pool of blood, he was covered in wounds and punctured by arrows.

Ailyn knelt down and lifted Aethor's head, Aethor grabbed his shirt, blood was in his teeth, "did you get the shard?", Aethor asked firmly, "I got it, it's done, what happened here?", Ailyn said, he could see Aethor had lost a lot of blood.

"Sin sent the entire town garrison after us, I couldn't let them interfere, so I fought them off, all of them", Aethor chuckled, cringing in pain.

"You defeated all these men on your own?", Ailyn asked, he looked around at the carnage before him in disbelief, "they could have run, some did, some kept coming", Aethor said, he

by Lore Casta Pendragon

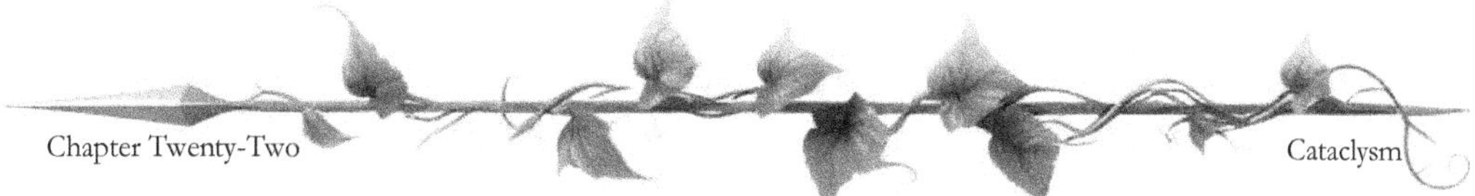

coughed and blood splattered his chest, Ailyn looked around frantically, he didn't know what to do.

"Ailyn", Aethor said, putting his hand on Ailyn's face, "I'm proud of you son, you've grown into a fine man, I know you'll defeat Guldamere, you've come so far, you're the strongest man I've ever known, I love you son", Blood trickled from his wounds and Aethor's strength began to fade.

His hand dropped from Ailyn's face leaving a trail of blood on his cheek, Ailyn held on tighter, tears trickled down Ailyn's face.

"Don't you leave me, not now, father!", Ailyn started to shout as Aethor closed his eyes.

"Aethor!", Ailyn screamed, "wake up!", Ailyn shook him, trying to wake him, but he was gone, Ailyn screamed out a mournful cry, he knelt by his father's body, Aethor's blood soaked his clothes.

Ailyn stayed there for a time, the temple burned near him, he picked up Aethor's lifeless body and walked to the temple placing Aethor inside, he slumped to the ground and watched as the temple burned down with Aethor inside.

He made a cairn from river stones but left no name or marker, he didn't want Guldamere or Petricus to find Aethor's body, so he made sure his father was incinerated.

Ailyn threw out his clenched fist, then slammed it into his chest and held it to his heart, he bowed his head, it was all he could do to express his respect for a man who was so instrumental in showing Ailyn how strong a man could be.

"I'll see you soon father, with mother and brother in the lands beyond", Ailyn said as he walked away.

He headed through the forest until he found where they had left the ship, he eventually made his way out of the bamboo forest and sat on a rocky ledge, he felt a chill grip him, the darkness pushed out from the shadows, Ailyn snarled looking behind him, Guldamere stepped out of the shadows.

"I've been waiting Ailyn, the time is finally upon you to die and grant me the power to ascend to true divinity", Guldamere said calmly.

Ailyn tried to bring forth the power within him, but it wouldn't come, Guldamere walked toward him, a skeletal finger pointed at him, black miasma flowing into it forming into a smokey black spike that continued to grow, Ailyn tried to move but he was frozen with fear,

by Lore Casta Pendragon

he tried to scream but his voice wouldn't come out, the black spike pierced Ailyn's chest and sunk into his heart, he took one last breath and then.

Opened his eyes startled and panting heavily, he was sitting on the rocky ledge, he must have fallen asleep.

Ailyn hugged his knees against the cold of night, sleep brought more terrors, there would be no sleep for him this night, Ailyn crossed his legs, he found calm in his conscious mind and focused into his meditation.

by Lore Casta Pendragon

Chapter Twenty-Three

Paladin's breach

Ilutha waved as the sky dancer flew away, she turned to Link and Locke, "so my prince, we'll need to expedite this elixir or master Silus here won't make it past supper", Ilutha said taking his arm.

Link blushed a little then waved over two paladins who lifted Silus on the stretcher, the paladin's looked at him distastefully, "take him to the infirmary in the keep, keep him alive or you'll be going to the abyss to fetch him", Link ordered firmly, Ilutha smiled up at him, "I like a man who takes charge", she said grabbing at his bicep.

Link's face began to grow red with a smug look of self-satisfaction, "well yes, you know, I like to keep a tight ship around here", Link gloated, Locke shook his head at his son, knowing all too well that Ilutha was just buttering him up because she wanted something, "oh, my boy, you have a lot to learn about women", Locke said following them.

At the keep, Ilutha was tending to Silus's crushed and bruised body as best she good, trying to sooth him with elven lullaby's, Silus went still then screamed out as if in terrible pain, "Cinder don't!", Silus called.

Waking from his nightmare he tried to move which racked his broken body with pain, Ilutha padded a compress on Silus's forehead "hush, your safe, be calm", she said.

Link walked over to them, "how's our patient doing", Link asked, "no good, he's dying, he's burning up and this damned curse won't let him rest, we need to get that elixir to him now, you have to tell me how it's made so we can heal him", Ilutha responded.

Locked walked over, "the secret of the elixir has been guarded by the paladins of the reach for centuries, kept by the paladins alone so the information would never be given to our enemies, we can't let anyone else know of it, what if it fell into enemy hands?", Locke said.

"I know you've had your issues with Silus in the past, but if we're going to restore the world, we are going to need his strength or in a few days we'll be the ones screaming and dying in our beds", Ilutha explained.

"Well put lady Ilutha", Link said, "very well", Locke said slowly eyeing her over his greying brow, "gather the templars and bring them here", Locke ordered to a paladin guarding nearby.

"Yes, my king", he said rushing off.

                                    by Lore Casta Pendragon

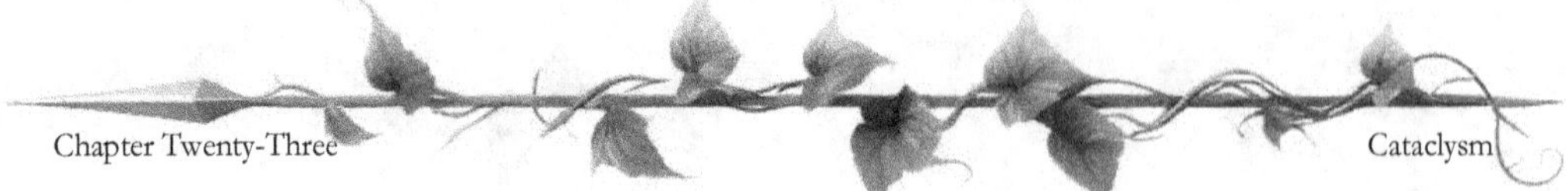

A few minutes later five knights in paladian armor marched in, this armor looked smaller but had a large white robe draped over it with a single red line down the middle.

"Sire?", one of the paladin's said bowing deeply.

"I want you to demonstrate your ability to purify chaos magic for us", Locke said, "certainly sire", the paladins muffled voice said from beneath a crusader type helmet.

A page boy walked in with a pedestal and placed it in the center of the room, it had some sort of laboratory setup on it with a vail underneath it, one of the paladins walked up and placed a gigantic jewel atop it, then returned to his position.

The five men drew longswords from beneath their robes, they held them by the hilt blade down, the swords began to vibrate and ring, a breeze kicked up circling around them, they walked forward spreading out and surrounding the pedestal.

Once there, they raised the swords pointing diagonally forward toward the ceiling, then walked forward and lowered the swords so they overlapped each other to the left around the large gemstone, the ringing of the swords and the wind surrounding them became a torrent the closer they got to each other.

One paladin started to wobble on his feet and another placed his hand on his shoulder, "hang in there, brother", he said.

The paladin straightened with great effort, Ilutha could see that whatever they were doing, it was taking a massive toll on them.

"Are they going to be ok", Ilutha asked Locke, "this ritual can take a man to the brink of death, these men are using their own life energy to purify and liquify chaos magic, the swords resonate with a certain frequency which gathers chaos magic, then the gemstone solidifies it into a physical liquid form, it's an artefact passed down through the line of kings in Paladin's Reach, it's also a fundamental part of our culture, every man turned Paladin had to survive this ritual, that soldier is taking the test for the first time, some have died in the attempt, it is a great shame to bear if one fails the task", Locke explained.

Ilutha looked over them nervously, the gemstone began to glow white, the magic condensed glowing brighter, into the bottom tip of the gemstone and a drop of glowing white liquid fell into the vail, the paladins raised their swords and returned them under their robes, one paladin corked the vail, then walked over and handed it to Locke, Locke brought it up to eye level and examined it, then nodded with a proud look on his face.

"Congratulations paladin, be welcomed by your brothers", Locke said and the templars turned, patted the man on the back and rustled his helmet, they cheered him on happily as they walked off chanting something illegible in the full faced helmets.

Locke walked over to Ilutha and handed her the vial, "all of that for just one drop?", Ilutha said, she looked into the vile to see the small drop of glowing liquid, "that's all we can do, now

                                    by Lore Casta Pendragon

you can see why it takes so long to produce a vial of the stuff, its value is far beyond that of gold", Locke said, "it's not much but it might keep him alive a little longer", Link said.

Ilutha uncorked the vail and poured the drop into Silus's mouth, a bit of color came back into his face, the bruising faded slightly and it seemed to ease a bit of his pain, he did not make a move.

"How often can your templars do this ritual?", Ilutha asked, "no more than once per day and even then it's dangerous", Locke said, "we should be able to pull some of the paladins from their duty for testing", Link said looking at Locke, "send every available paladin to me", Link ordered to a sentinel guard standing nearby who bowed then left swiftly, Link looked at Locke astonished, "are you sure about this, is this man's life worth that of a paladin?", Link questioned, "we'll choose the strongest of them to test first, don't test anyone newly promoted", Locke ordered.

Silus awoke in a hall, he was seated at a round black obsidian table, Guldamere sat at one end and the rest of his inner circle sat around the table, "Silus, how dare you betray us", Warden spat at him abruptly, "traitor", Violet sneered, "silence", Guldamere commanded, his voice echoed off the walls and they fell silent.

"You're dying, Silus", Guldamere said menacingly, "retake your vow to serve and in turn I will give you another chance at life, all you need to do is kill the paladin king and his successor, do this and I'll give you what you've sort all along, your beloved Miss Crowler", Guldamere said, his glowing golden pupils and smokey black eyes penetrating into Silus like a dagger.

He waved a hand a Cinder appeared before them on top of the table, "Silus?", "What's going on?", she said confused.

"Cinder, as much as I want to save you, sacrificing the world to do it, wouldn't leave us with much of a life together, I'll find another way", Silus said, she smiled, light began to emanate from Silus's chest.

Guldamere turned to Petricus who's immense dragon form perched behind him, "they're reviving him, he's at the Reach, go and destroy them!", Guldamere ordered, Petricus spread his four dark wings and flew off.

Guldamere raised a skeletal hand, him and his minions disappeared in a puff of smoke, leaving Silus in an empty black void alone.

Hours later the ritual was repeated several more times by the remaining paladins of the reach, they sat strewn around the hall, drained and tired, those who teetered off to sleep where welcomed with horrid nightmares and brought back to waking.

                                                    by Lore Casta Pendragon

The quiet of the hall erupting into screams of terror, nurses wearing white gowns rushed to comfort them, "it's alright, your fine, it was just a dream, you have to remember not to fall to sleep", one of the nurses said to a paladin.

Link walked through the hall and handed the vial of liquid to Ilutha, "that's the very last of it", Link said, Ilutha walked over to Silus and lifted his head, he woke up confused and trying to speak, Ilutha made sure he drank every drop.

Silus's body made snapping sounds as his bones reset, he opened his eyes in a blur, for a second, he thought he saw Cinders face, "Cinder!", Silus screamed, which then blurred into the face of Ilutha, "I'm still alive?", Silus said sounding disappointed.

"Yes Silus, we still have a job to do", Ilutha said happily.

Silus got up and sat on the side of the bed, "can you walk?", Ilutha asked, "won't know until I try", Silus said attempting to stand, his body was shaking with the effort but he managed to find his feet.

"The elixir will continue to help with the healing process, but you should take it easy for a while", Locke said walking over, "we don't really have the luxury of time on our hands", Silus said.

"Guldamere was haunting my dreams whilst I slept, but I also managed to get information from him, he's revived his inner circle, the dracolich Petricus is heading our way", Ilutha looked around in a panic, "my lords that dragon is more dangerous than you could possibly know, it'll turn the city to ashes", Ilutha explained.

"We can't defeat a dracolich here, we've barely begun to sure up our defenses from the last battle", Locke interjected, they suddenly heard the sound of propellers whirring and ran outside to see the sky dancer coming in to dock at a balcony to the side of the keep, "yar har, matey's!", Villias called.

Ilutha ran out to greet them, "your timing is impeccable Captain", she shouted, waving to them.

Locke, Link and Silus made their way out to the balcony, "I have a plan", Ilutha said to the group, "what if we used the airship to divert the dragon away while you gather your army and head for Necropyre, we'll rendezvous with my forces and the forces of the Iron halls there and hit Guldamere where it hurts", Ilutha suggested.

"With the state the reach is in now, I don't think we could withstand another attack, not without the barrier to protect us and with this curse we won't last long, even behind these walls", Link said to Locke, who nodded his agreement, "considering we only have days left at most, I think a frontal assault would be the best option we have", Locke said.

by Lore Casta Pendragon

"Prepare our forces, we march on Necropyre", the old kings eyes showed a look of determination, he walked off rallying his men who cheered and followed after him.

Petricus was soaring at high speed through the clouds above Thalaria, he let out a loud screeching roar as Paladin's Reach came into view, he swooped down through the clouds at blistering speed toward the city, black fire curled in his mouth as he drew close, flying straight over the massive walls he dowsed the reach in flame, melting stone and setting fire to everything in his path, he turned and hit it again, then once again, but something was wrong.

"Where are the screams?", Petricus thought as he landed on the roof of the keep, he tore it open with large powerful jaws and spear like talons, his long serpentine neck curled in to look around then growled.

"Silus must have warned them", Petricus scoffed in his serpentine voice, "no matter, they can't have gotten far", he said popping his head back out of the hole in the roof, he sniffed the air, hunting for his prey.

The sky dancer flew up from behind the keep, "hold on to your hats", Villias said.

Link, Ilutha, Inaya, Rayan and the crew where all aboard and held on tight to the railings, Inaya and Rayan grunted with the effort as the ship darted off over the dracolich's head, Petricus growled and took off after it and the chase was on.

"Well ye got his attention, now what?", Villias asked, "I hadn't really thought that far yet", Ilutha said, Villias shook his head, "are ye telling me, ye dropped the bait without the hook?", Villias shouted, "head for Oasis", Inaya said, "if we time it right, Amanth may be able to lend us a hand", "ay, that might work, only thing bigger than that dragon be Amanth himself", Villias agreed, "what's an Amanth?", Link asked, "not much of a traveler are ye?", Villias said.

The ship turned and headed to the south east, the dracolich was in pursuit, its wings let off a loud and rapid drumming sound as they beat furiously trying to catch the airship, slowly he was gaining on them.

As Petricus caught up, he saw several cannons that had been moved to the rear of the ship, his head roiled back as black fire filled his jaws, before he could spit, the cannon's fired slamming into his neck, the fire spewed out of the Petricus's mouth in wide arcs as he choked from the impact of the cannonballs, he lost ground snarling hatefully, then continued after them.

"Can't this thing go any faster", Link said, "we're doing everything we can", Inaya said in her long-drawn accent, "if you know how to make a ship fly, be sure to help us out", Rayan added even slower.

by Lore Casta Pendragon

"I don't think we can keep this up much longer, we have to slow him down", Ilutha shouted over the rushing wind.

Petricus caught up to them again, the cannons fired but Petricus twisted his long agile body and avoided the blows, he reached the ship and swung a massive claw at it, Link leaped from the ships deck and slashed at the claw with his sword sinking into the palm, he sprang back and landed back on the ship's rail, he teetered and almost fell.

Petricus snatched the claw back then clawed at the ship with his other claw, Villias put his cannon leg backward on the rail near the ships wheel and fired.

Petricus fell back with a roar, the cannon on Villias's leg smoked from the shot, "ye need to make this thing go faster!", Villias shouted, but the ship was already moving at blistering speed, Inaya and Rayan were struggling to keep the ship going, sweat beaded on their brows.

Petricus came on again spitting fire, "hold on to something", Villias shouted as he moved to avoid the gout of flames that burned toward them, he dodged low and high as Petricus's serpentine form curled after them, Petricus got close and reared up black fire licked his toothy maw, he sent a gout of fire toward the balloon of the ship.

The crew cried out as Villias dumped the controls and the ship darted straight down, they all held on for dear life as the flames narrowly avoided the balloon.

Villias ducked into a large canyon then pulled the ship straight.

Petricus got close, his jaw snapped at the back of the ship splintering away more of the already damaged rear, Villias jolted looking back at rows of huge teeth, he took the ship lower, large rock formations like pillars stuck up from the canyon floor, he dodged left then right each time narrowly avoiding a crash, Petricus was right behind them snapping at them.

Silus watched him closing in, he turned to see a narrow passage leading out, he ran to a nearby cannon, then called for the crew to help him quickly move it from the rear of the ship to the front and loaded it up.

Silus lined up the shot, "on my mark!", he called, "and", he said waiting for ship to line up with his target, "fire!", the cannon exploded and rolled back taking them with it, they rolled to the deck as the cannonball blasted an overhanging rock, a large part of the canyon began to crack and fall as Petricus caught them from behind in his jaw then grabbed onto the rear of the ship with his claws, splintering the deck, he extended both feet to stop them at the narrow passage, he smiled as fire curled from his teeth, "I've got you", Petricus said, the heat of his breath scolding them.

As he hit the canyon wall with his feet the falling rock slammed into him and he dropped spitting fire into the sky, the ship jolted as it ripped from the dracolich's grasp, flying out of the gap leaving him crashing down behind them.

                                        by Lore Casta Pendragon

The canyon opened up to the eastern desert sands, they looked back to see Petricus lifting himself from the sandy canyon floor, he limped slightly for a moment then roared.

"Ye think he'll follow us to Oasis?", Villias said, Silus looked over at him, "he's prideful, he'll follow", he assured them, "that won't delay him long, we gotta go", Villias said as the ship raced over the dunes at full speed.

Ilutha was looking over the rail, the purple hued sun had begun to set, "any sign of him?", She asked, "nothing from this side", Silus replied, Ilutha looked over to see a shadow moving at speed alongside them on the sand, "he's above us!", Ilutha shouted.

Oasis came into view, the large mountainlike beaks of Amanth had begun to close already, "we could be too late", Villias said, the dracolich came down in front of the ship and they slammed straight into him, his spear-like claws grabbed on and sunk into the ship.

"Thought you could escape me", Petricus boomed, his wings started to beat against them slowing the ship, the crew held on against the gale of wind battering them.

Inaya and Rayan blasted the wind back toward him as the ship grew closer to Amanth's mountainous beaks, the ship slowed to a stop just before them.

Inaya and Rayan cried out with the effort of keeping the ship moving, they were almost tapped out.

Petricus held them dead in the air, a smirk formed on his dead face as black fire began to curl from his mouth, the crew all screamed out in terror, all but Silus, he tied a rope to two looped knives at both ends then threw them, he held his hand out like controlling a puppet and the knife soared through a hole in Petricus's face, Silus switched his hands and the knives ducked through another hole on the other side, switching again the knives changed directions going through another hole near the beasts mouth, they sliced a new hole through the flesh, again and again the knives weaved.

Silus closed his hands into fists then pulled them apart and the knives shot out in either direction, the rope pulled tight and Petricus's mouth was sewn shut as he tried to burn them away and incinerate the ship, instead the pressure built in his throat and exploded out the side of his neck.

Petricus roared and his wings stopped beating, Inaya and Rayan gave one final push and the ship lunged forward as Amanth's beaks came together, Link and Ilutha drew swords and dashed toward the claws holding the ship, "hit the brakes!", Link shouted as both him and Ilutha slashed at the clawed fingers severing them one by one.

Inaya and Rayan reversed the wind direction and the ship came to a halt, the dracolich flew back away from the ship but not far enough, the crew turned the cannons toward Petricus and

                                    by Lore Casta Pendragon

Villias raised his cannon leg, "Blow him out of the water", Villias shouted as they fired every cannon in unison.

The cannonballs slammed into Petricus sending him flying between the beaks of Amanth as they closed around him.

He tried to push against them and beat his wings, but it was like trying to push a mountain away, the giant beaks slowly closed around him, black miasma and rotted blood splashed out from between them as Petricus roared a visceral deathly cry and the beaks slammed shut.

The crew cheered and hugged each other triumphantly, "we did it!", Villias cried out.

Inaya and Rayan moved the ship over the peak of Amanth's beaks and brought the ship down near a balcony at the grand Ger in Oasis.

"We cannot go on", Rayan said, "we've done too much", Inaya added, they collapsed to the ships deck.

The crew picked them up and they dropped the gang plank, "let them rest, but don't let them sleep, we'll need them again soon enough", Villias ordered, he began walking down the plank, Emir Azir ran up to them with two large men guarding him, fear and concern on his ragged face.

"My friends, we welcome you here, though we fear what you're coming here might mean, we fear the end is upon us", Azir said taking Villias's hands, "that it might be, Guldamere the god feared placed a curse over all of Thalaria, we'll be gathering our forces at Necropyre for a final assault, though we had to take a detour here due to being chased across the continent by Petricus Postmortus in the form of a dracolich", Villias explained.

"Yes, yes, that does sound terrifying, we have been unable to find any sleep, we are woken by horrid dreams", Azir explained, "that do be part of the curse I'm afraid", Villias said.

Inaya and Rayan appeared leaning over the ship rail barely able to keep themselves standing, they removed their veils and everyone's eyes went wide, it was the first time anyone had actually seen their faces.

"Grand Ezir Amir, we apologize for interrupting, but time is crucial now, we need you to send us all of your available mages", Inaya said sternly, "all of them?", Amir said confused, "how will you be paying for such an endeavor?", Amir laughed in his slow drawling accent.

"We'll repay you with every life in Thalaria", Link said walking down the gang plank, "we do apologize my Ezir, but if we do not reach the Ronin City and then Necropyre within the next day, I fear that Guldamere's curse will consume us all", Rayan said.

Azir looked at the group and looked over the ship, "I shall do this for you, but on one condition", Azir said slowly, "what be ye terms then", Villias said, "do we really have time for this", Link said impatiently, Azir gave him a sideways glance, "when you are done you bring

this ship back to me so my men can copy its composition, it is quite the feat of engineering", Azir said stroking his pointed goatee.

"Deal", Villias said shaking his hand, "excellent, excellent, I will get every available mage to leave immediately", Azir said walking off with his two guards, "get supplies while we are here and tend to the damage to me ship", Villias ordered and the crew got to work, as soon as these mage's are on board we're headed for the Ronin city, its closest to our current location", Villias said, "I just hope the Allhearts found what they were searching for", Ilutha added.

The moon shone with a purple ring in the blackness of night as Azir and his half dozen mages made their way onto the sky dancer, the mages wore the same black robes and Inaya and Rayan and made their way aboard, "this way brothers, sisters, we shall instruct you how to work the ship", Inaya said, having recovered from a few hours rest.

"Ye have me thanks Azir, should we meet again, it'll be in the sun once more", Villias said grabbing Azir's wrist, "take care captain, light speed to you on this endeavor", Azir said, he hopped down from the gang plank, and the ship started to float away.

It wasn't long before the other mages were providing the ship with enough extra power to propel the ship at incredible speed, some sand stalkers raised their heads to look at it from the dunes and the wind whistled as the sky dancer shot by them, they flew over the scar and toward the Ronin City.

Ailyn saw the white balloon of the ship well before it landed from his position near the scar, "if we don't slow down, we'll overshoot it", Link said as it drew close, Ailyn saw that the ship wasn't slowing so he readied himself, as it passed, he leaped up onto the deck catching a rope landing on the railing.

"Ay tis good to have ye back", Villias greeted him, Ailyn's face didn't change, his face was stone determination.

"Where is Aethor?", Ilutha asked, "Aethor, didn't make it", Ailyn said, a tear rolled down his face, "what happened?", Link said.

"We were ambushed by Sin Sonata, the entire city garrison, Aethor stayed behind, he slaughtered the entire guard on his own, but lost his life in the battle", Ailyn explained, Ilutha came up and hugged him to her, "I'm sorry Ailyn, Aethor was an incredible man", Ilutha said, another tear rolled down Ailyn's cheek.

Silus approached him and grabbed his cuff, he didn't say anything but the look on his face was that of condolence, "that be a blow we didn't need at this time, Aethor truly was a force to be reckoned with, I'm sorry for ye loss", Villias said, "did ye get the shard?", Villias asked sternly.

Ailyn looked at him, a piercing stare, the white aura began to burn around him like white fire bigger than it ever had before, "I see", Villias said, the aura faded, "I'm sorry for ye loss boy

by Lore Casta Pendragon

but we can't stand on ceremony, we gotta get this ship moving", Villias shouted and in no time at all the ship was headed for Necropyre.

 by Lore Casta Pendragon

Chapter Twenty-Four

The halls of horror

Mech, Brawn and Wynn made their way down a long tunnel, they came to an ornate iron door carved with dwarven runes, Mech reached up to a large steel knocker and knocked in a sequence, the sound of the metal knocker echoed back through the tunnel.

The door was opened and several dwarven guards welcomed them, "ay, tis good to see you back, Mech, Farin's been waiting for ye", one of the dwarves said, they were escorted deeper, passing a stone bridge over a cavern, down twisting tunnels and across a wide hall with ornate pillars, "the dwarves truly are masters of stonework", Brawn said in awe, "I reckon ye could give em a run for their money", Mech replied.

They entered Farin's chamber where he sat talking with Fyorn and Gear, "by a barghast's beard", Farin exclaimed as they walked in, Farin noticed them first and walked up embracing Mech, both men laughing heartily.

"Where ye been, I thought you'd have perished for sure when ye hadn't returned, can you tell us what's going on out there?", Farin said.

"Ay, I am sorry my king, but there were certain matters that needed my immediate attention, Guldamere has been revived", Mech explained.

"Ay, we figured as much when the sky out there turned dark", Farin said, "as soon as he came back, he placed a curse over the land, none shall sleep unless they bend knee to him, so our time has drawn short", Mech explained.

"That would explain the night terrors we've been having", Farin said, "there isn't much time left for us I'm afraid, we need to raise an army against Guldamere and march on Necropyre immediately, if we don't finish the lich now, every free man left in Thalaria will perish", Mech said.

It took Farin only a minute to decide, "we have no choice then, we'll march every available dwarf on Necropyre as soon as we can get them armored", Farin said.

Brawn walked up to Fyorn and Gear, an intimidating look covered his face, he grinned at them suddenly then grabbed them both in a bear hug which was received with a lot of complaining as Brawn swung them around, he placed them back on the ground laughing with joy.

"It's good to see you alive and well", Brawn said, Wynn walked up and shook hands with them both, "your still kicking old timer", Wynn bellowed to Gear, "oh believe me I didn't think I'd

                              by Lore Casta Pendragon

make it this far either, but the fates have seen me this far, I might as well see the final battle take place", Gear said croakily.

"Did ye find Ailyn?", Fyorn asked, "we did, in the eastern desert, he headed to the ronin city to collect the last shard of power", Mech said.

"I see, I told you he's made of stronger stuff, we've recovered our army here in the Iron halls", Gear said, "finally some good news", Wynn bellowed, "come, you can all take rest while I ready our forces", Farin said ushering them into the feasting hall.

In a few short hours the dwarven and Ailyn's armies were armored, fed and prepared to march, they donned heavy steel armor with an assortment of weapons ranging from battle axes and hammers to crossbows and grenades.

Large wheeled arbalests and cannons where being pulled along by natural gas-powered engines, they lined up in a large central hall at the end of which was a stage, as Farin walked up to address them queen Navi Ironhammer handed him his Iron helm ornate with the crown.

Farin held it under his arm as he took the stage.

"As you are by now aware a great evil has spread throughout our land, an evil which haunts our days as well as our dreams, the Iron halls have stood as solid as the mountains we dwell within and withstood the oppressive rule of the church of the god feared, but that time has now passed, as many of you know too well our time is coming to an end, without rest, we will perish, but while we still have the strength left to fight, we will use that strength to show the lord of the damned that we will not sit idly by and die in our holes, no, we will fight them to the very last, we will defeat the lich of Necropyre and break this curse he has placed on us!", Farin said.

A loud cheer erupted over the hall, "so I ask you now, my people, my kin, will you come with me into the dark, to fight for the light and for our future?", Farin said, which was greeted with an even louder battle cry, "then let us march, for the iron halls and for all the peoples of Thalaria!", Farin shouted and was met with battle cries and cheers of hope as he walked from the stage and through the lines of his men, they peeled in behind him.

Fyorn and Mech walked to either side of him followed by Wynn and Brawn, as he drew close to the end of the hall, he ordered the huge Iron doors to be opened, two dwarves either side swung large hammers knocking out pins holding huge iron chains, they creaked and rumbled as they dropped heavy stone boulders connected to the chains, which in turned large gears and slowly opened the huge doors, the dim light from outside began to shine inwards but then the door stopped as if it was stuck on something.

          by Lore Casta Pendragon

The light in the room got darker as if being pressed in, Farin looked for the men responsible for opening the door, two bodies of dwarves in armor were thrown from the darkness bloodied and lifeless, they landed with a clang and a splat, Farin took a few steps back.

"What is this, are we under attack?", Fyorn said looking around, shadowy clawed hands started reaching around the large Iron doors and the doors began to close again, "it can't be?", Farin said with a horrified expression.

"We destroyed that thing with Lore Cast Pendragon", Mech said, "the creeping dark, it said it would return for us", Farin replied, "grenadiers to the front!", Farin ordered.

A line of dwarves came forward, "pull", Farin said, they pulled the release pins on their flash grenades, "release", Farin ordered.

They threw the grenades into the dark spaces beside the Iron doors, the grenades exploded into flashes of light, a high-pitched screech came from the dark and the clawed hands retreated downwards like black water flowing down, turning smokey and flowing together into a tornado of blackness, it coalesced into the shape of a person, leaving a man standing before them.

"Warden", Fyorn said, Ailyn's men began to murmur, "Guldamere must have brought him back", Brawn said, Warden stood there with his hands clasped behind his back.

"Lord Guldamere has offered sanctuary for the Iron halls, you will be spared if you agree to his terms", Warden's deep booming voice echoed off the walls, "his terms would be nothing less than the enslavement of our people", Farin argued, which was accompanied by the jeers of his men.

"If you disarm and agree to join the church of the god feared, you will be spared and freed from the curse", Warden said, "we'd rather die than be subservient to that monster", Fyorn shouted, "oh and also you'll have to hand over those prisoners to me to be reprocessed", Warden said, more murmurs arose amongst Ailyn's men, "what do you plan on doing to them", Farin said.

"They will be executed of course", Warden said, a hungry glean came to his eye when he said that.

"I've heard enough", Wynn said, "you think you can come in here and start making demands with an entire army in front of you, think again", Wynn's loud voice carried for every man to hear, "if you think your numbers count for something, you're sorely mistaken", Warden said sinking into the darkness on the floor, "the sun's light no longer had the luster it once had, now all the lands of Thalaria are mine to haunt and prey upon", Warden's voice echoed around them, screams of men started to ring out from all around them as men were being grabbed from the darkness by shadowy clawed hands, "everyone get outside!", Farin called, in a mad rush the entire army raced toward the iron doors.

by Lore Casta Pendragon

They crowded around the exit and pushing through, more screams could be heard from behind as more people got picked off, "grenadiers, to the rear, buy us some time", Farin ordered, white flashes of light started pulsating behind them, large shadowy claws wrapped around the door and started to pull it closed, "no!", Fyorn cried out.

He nodded to Brawn who picked him up over the crowd and tossed him toward the door, Fyorn brought the hammers up and slammed them into the door, a powerful clang rang out as the doors burst open, the fingers of the shadow claws tore away into smoke and the army poured out like liquid.

A few stragglers came limping out of the entrance only to be grabbed and dragged back in.

Warden came walking out of the darkness picking at his teeth like he just enjoyed a nice meal, "you rotten bastard", Farin cried out.

"My terms, king of dwarves, pledge your fealty to the church and hand over the fugitives and I'll stop consuming your men", Warden said calmly.

"Seize him!", Farin said, his men marched into a circle around Warden, he smiled as the dwarves closed in.

A pitch-black shadow grew from Warden's feet, the dwarves continued forward as it consumed the ground around them, then large shadow claws began reaching out and grabbing men like black waves in an ocean, the men screamed as they were engulfed by the writhing blackness.

Wynn, Fyorn and Brawn ran forward claymore and hammers swinging, Brawn had a large plank of wood pummeling the shadow claws as they rose, making them burst into plumes of black smoke, Gear moved up with a battalion of grenadiers, "loose", he cried.

The flashes of light made openings in the shadowy mass, Warden let out a painful groan raising his hand to shield his eyes, when he looked back Mech was standing in front of him with his lamp, "Boo", he said opening the latch, a bright light beamed into Warden face.

Warden stumbled backward, a large shadow tentacle whipped out from the floor and collected all four of them, sending them flying, more dwarves took advantage of Warden's lapse in concentration and charged, he recovered before they reached him.

Shadow tentacles whipped out smashing dwarves all around him as they drew close, Brawn tumbled in the dirt and came to rest at the feet of Gear, the old man offered him a hand up, he was covered in bands of flash grenades all tied to a single string which he held on a pin around his thumb, "what are you planning old man?", Brawn said worried.

"don't worry about me, I've seen you throw Fyorn around like he's nothing, surely you can toss a frail old man like me", Gear said with a smile.

									by Lore Casta Pendragon

"Fyorn is a dwarven meatball, you're a cinnamon stick, you'll snap", Brawn said, "quickly Brawn", Gear said eyeing his target, Brawn nodded hesitantly then grabbed Gear by the back of the neck and the back of his pants, he spun him around a few times then threw him over the top of dwarves and shadow tentacles, right toward Warden, Gear's arms flailed, pulling the pins on the flash grenades.

Warden turned to see the old man screaming out as he plummeted down toward him, he raised the shadow tentacles around him like a shield, as Gear fell into him and the grenades detonated in a massive pulsing flash of white light, the shadows eviscerated into black smoke.

The men shielded their eyes and turned away, when they turned back Warden sat there on his knees reaching around obviously blinded by the immense light, Gear was also fumbling around, his clothes had been burned away and his flesh was blistered and burned, blood trickled from painful burn wounds.

He found a pickaxe on the ground and picked it up, he stumbled toward the sound of Wardens growls, then with all the might the old man had left to muster he raised the axe high.

Warden heard him coming and launched a spike made of shadow toward the old man, it penetrated his body and he cried out in pain, fury replaced his pain and he drove the axe straight down into Warden skull, it stuck with a thud of cracking bone and the squish of brain matter, the shadows retreated into the darkness leaving Warden on his knees with an axe imbedded into his skull.

Fyorn ran up and grabbed the wirey old man as he fell, "well played Gear, you clever old bastard", which made gear chuckle a little only to be interrupted by the pain of the gaping hole in this body.

They crowded around him and a dwarven medical team offered their help, Gear just raised a hand to stop them.

"Don't waste the supplies lads, I know where I'm going", Gear said quietly, "do me a favor and tell Ailyn what I did, my lord would be proud of me, today I got to be the hero", Gear smiled.

"Don't ye worry about that old timer, your bravery will be told in the Iron Halls for centuries", Farin assured him, which was accompanied by cheers from his men who removed their helmets, placing them at their chest in a mark of respect.

Gear smiled again as a single tear ran down his face, his head slumped back and he was gone.

Wynn lifted Gear, Farin gave the order and several young dwarves took Gear's body to the Iron Halls and down to the crypts, "what will do with him", Wynn asked.

                                          by Lore Casta Pendragon

"He'll be immortalized in stone as a hero of the Iron Halls", Farin explained, Brawn picked Farin up, several dwarven guardsmen moved to stop him but Brawn bear hugged him, "thank you, Farin", Brawn said sobbing, "ahh ye welcome lad", Farin said kicking Brawn in the crouch to make him let go.

Brawn groaned and dropped him, he landed on his feet and straightened his crowned helm, "we have a lot of ground to cover, let's move out!", Farin commanded and the army lined up in formation, marching toward Necropyre.

                              by Lore Casta Pendragon

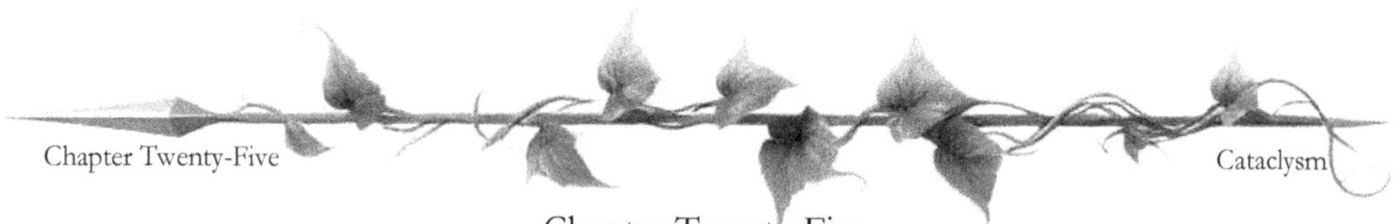

Chapter Twenty-Five

Secrets of Necropyre

Kimba and Felix waved as the sky dancer flew off, Kimba turned to Felix, "it's been a while, ready for another adventure?", Kimba said, "your adventures usually end with me being dragged into something dangerous", Felix jested, "this time will be no different, it's so strange to be back here after all this time", Kimba said sadly.

Felix put his hand on her shoulder, "no time for nostalgia, let's get what we need and get out of here, first things first, how are we going to get into the city?", Felix asked.

"The same way we got out", Kimba said smiling, she put her fist together then placed a hand on Felix, they both started fading from sight like sinking deep into murky water, Felix looked at his hand but it was barely visible, he could only see the air swishing around like ripples in water, "let's go", Kimba said.

They made their way down the path toward the gates of Necropyre, the gates were open, several soldiers and acolytes were guarding the front entrance and checking people as they went through.

Kimba and Felix ducked down and moved slowly behind the guards, one guard noticed the slight warping of the air as they passed, he swayed his hand through the air but touched nothing thinking it was just his imagination, just like that they found themselves back in Necropyre.

The Dutch-style architecture of the buildings mixed with the medieval gothic style of the church gave the city a dreary feel, they ducked into an alleyway beside a shop and Kimba dropped the veil, she panted from the effort of holding it.

"Are you alright miss Kindheart?", Felix asked, "I'm fine Felix, it just takes a lot to hold the veil together, it's like holding your breath for a long time", Kimba explained.

"We need to get to the cathedral of the god feared, the tomes there could help us figure out how to break the curse", she raised the veil again and they headed down the cobbled street avoiding the people and carriages that moved past.

Felix stopped in front of his old house and Kimba almost took her hand away from him, it was still partially burned with a large hole blown into it where the front door had been, it was dilapidated and cordoned off with rope, a sign hung from the rope, it said condemned.

                                                        by Lore Casta Pendragon

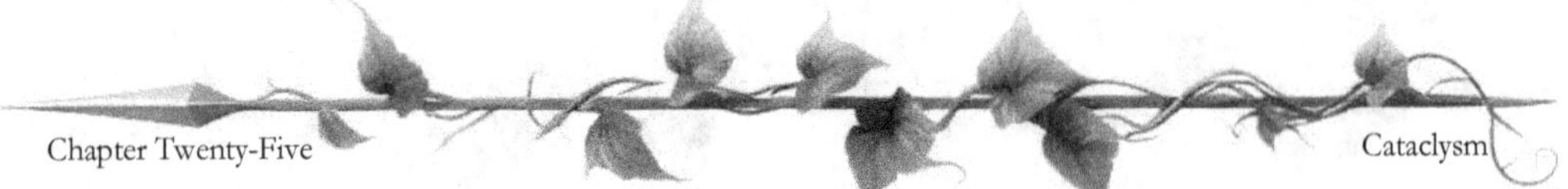

"I built that house with my own hands", Felix said, "It's not like I had a choice though considering no-one else in town would help a Felinine", he said sadly, "shoosh, do you want someone to hear you", Kimba said tugging on him.

With a sigh Felix kept moving down the street, they passed Kamdar's house where Kimba grew up, another family had taken up residence there, "you've got some squatters in your home", Felix said.

"Without Kamdar, it wouldn't be the home I remembered, at least someone is getting some use of it", Kimba said turning away from it, they continued on until they came to the steps of the cathedral, its large triangular pointed spires towered over the city, funnily enough the same acolyte who used to play pranks on Felix with chaos magic still guarded the library entrance.

"I think it time for a little payback", Felix said looking to Kimba, she smiled and nodded her approval, they hunted around the outer garden for a while until they found a bucket and an assortment of garden variety pests, tickle worms, shoe slugs and bullet ants, they placed them carefully into the bucket, Kimba veiled the bucket then they moved behind the acolyte at the door.

Felix carefully tipped the bucket down the back of the acolytes robe, he immediately began both laughing and screaming at the same time, the tickle worms wriggled mercilessly across his skin, making him giggle uncontrollably while the bullet ants poisonous bite stung at him, he tried to slap at them only to feel the shoe slugs burst into large amounts of sticky goo, he tried to wipe it off only to have his hands and fingers stick under the robe which resulted in more stinging from the distressed ants.

Some guards came to see what was going on but upon inspecting the situation thought that the man must have lost his mind and laughed at him as he writhed on the ground laughing and screaming covered in goo, Kimba and Felix tried very hard not to break out in laughter as they ducked into the library.

They made their way behind a bookshelf out of sight and Kimba broke the veil, "oh that felt too good", Felix said, "shh", Kimba tried to say but it was followed a humorous snorting sound, "shoosh, remember where we are", Kimba said still trying not to laugh.

"The library was as she remembered, a large staircase led to an upper floor, and at the back was a barred door where the tomes were kept, although the door looked slightly different, a raven sat perched on the upper railing, watching ever vigilant over the clerks, magic was banned under the law of the church and the tomes were kept under watch at all times.

They snuck behind the book shelf until they came to a gap, the bird looked in the other direction and they dashed to the next row, it looked back almost immediately and they both froze, not knowing if the bird had seen them, no alarm was raised and it continued to look over the library unphased, they let out a collective sigh.

by Lore Casta Pendragon

They snuck around to the barred door avoiding a librarian who was stocking shelves, Kimba looked over at the door, it was charred as it if had been burned, they snuck over to it and Kimba pressed on it, the door frame crumbled as the door swung back, Felix only just managed to stop it from crashing against the wall, the room where the tomes had been was destroyed, burned books laid around the room, Kimba picked one up only to have it fall to ashes in her hand.

Felix took a look around covering his mouth with a handkerchief, he scuffed his foot on a pile of ashes on the floor and noticed a slight breeze pulling at the dust, it was sucked behind a heavy and burned bookshelf.

"Kimba over here", Felix whispered, "what is it?" She said, "give me a hand with this", they pulled on the shelf and it slid out from the wall, behind it was a spiral staircase leading downward.

Kimba put her fists together and summoned a small flame in her hand to light the path, they headed down the dark staircase, it came out into a small room containing more tomes, these ones had escaped the fire.

"Don't open the black ones", Kimba said remembering what happened the last time she was here, Felix nodded, Kimba grabbed one of the blue tomes, "the transference of chaos magic by Lore Casta Pendragon", Kimba said as she read the title.

She stuffed the tome into her sleeve, the book didn't look like it could fit but the magic sleeve in her robe allowed for a lot of storage, Felix looked over an ornate staff with a small crystal attached to the tip, "istaf del alune thundora", Felix read from a plaque beneath it.

Kimba walked up to the end of the room, a large black tome laid on a pedestal, the cover was adorned with black leather in the shape of mournful faces.

"Guldamere's Necronomicon masterworks", Kimba said reading the title, she unlatched the book and it opened by itself, black smokey miasma started flowing out from the pages onto the floor.

"Are you sure you should be touching that?", Felix asked nervously, "this thing is tainted, it smells like rotting corpses, but I need to know how to break Guldamere's curse", Kimba said holding her nose, she began reading the book oblivious to all else, while Felix heard a feint tapping sound coming from the stairs.

He tilted and turned his large ears trying to listen harder as the tapping got closer, he took several slow steps forward then froze in place stunned as the raven from earlier hopped into view down the stairs.

It cawed out loudly and Felix panicked grabbing the staff from the wall, Kimba turned to see what was going on when Felix was about to throw it like a spear to strike the bird, the crystal on the staff glowed then with a great flash of light, a loud explosive crack sounded out.

                                             by Lore Casta Pendragon

A bolt of lightning streaked from the staff and hit the raven which exploded into feathers and black smoke.

"We've been found, we have to get out of here now!", Kimba said tucking the black book into her sleeve, they ran up the spiral stairs and back into the library, it was completely empty now, none of the librarians who were stocking books earlier were there.

They moved out into the center of the room and heard a sound from upstairs behind them, a large serpentine tail whipped out knocking a bookshelf into the door blocking off the exit.

They heard a hissing sound and spun around but couldn't see where it was coming from, the bookshelves began to rock and move around, both Kimba and Felix spotted it at the same time, a gigantically sized black serpent with red stripes, its body moved in a circle around them.

The bookshelves started to slide inward toward them, Felix pulled a mechanical looking tube from his tailcoat, "hold onto me miss Kindheart", Felix said grabbing Kimba around the waist, she held onto him and he hooked it to his belt, he pressed a button on the tube and the mechanism in the tube sprung out.

A grappling hook extended toward the roof, it hooked around a support beam and launched them into the air as the book shelves slammed together being crushed under the force of the serpent constricting them, Kimba and Felix came to a stop half way up.

"Now what?", Kimba asked, "ahh, it was meant to take us, up there", Felix said pointing, Kimba looked down to see the serpent looked up at them it's red piercing eyes glaring at them hungrily, the serpent had a familiar look about it.

"I remember you; you were at the temple of the Aikitai, your Charon, you killed master Den", Kimba said, the snake nodded and seemed to grin, the tube started to give out and they dropped a bit.

Charon's jaw opened below them, black smokey miasma rose out of it, it smelled of death, large fangs extended waiting for them to drop, the tube gave out and they fell, Kimba kicked both legs into Felix and pushed the air between them, they both flew off to either side, the serpents head whipped to face Kimba, she grabbed at her elbow and a fireball flickered into life at her palm.

Charon struck at her before she even hit the ground, she let the fireball go right down his throat, it exploded in the back of his throat and Charon whipped his head back and forth in pain.

Kimba hit the ground running, Felix landed softly on a large pile of books, then got to his feet and brushed himself off.

"Felix, move it!", Kimba called as Charon recovered, his eyes fixed on Felix then he coiled and struck at him, "help me!", Felix screamed as Charon snatched him in his jaw throwing him in the air, "Kimba!", Felix cried out as Charon gulped him down.

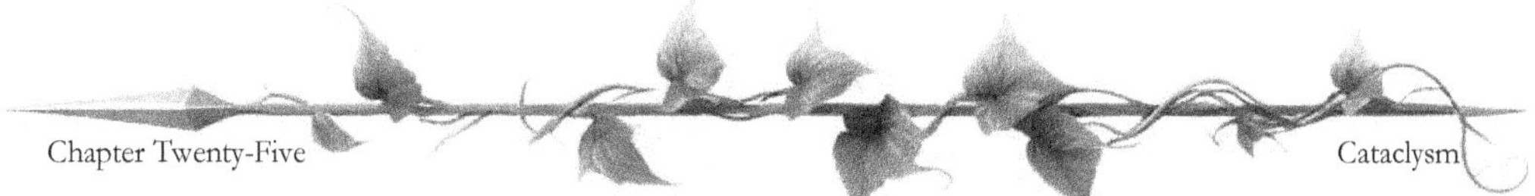

"Oh no", Kimba said softly, her hand covering her mouth, tears began to well up in her eyes, Charon grinned and stared at her, those predatory serpentine eyes seemed to say, "it's your turn", Kimba's face distorted into fury.

Charon struck at her taking a large chunk out of railing but Kimba was quick enough to move out of the way, she extended both hands as she ran and launched fireball after fireball into Charon, the serpent was blasted backward with each hit, Charon avoided one fireball and then another, the large serpents speed was incredible, Charon whipped his tail out and pinned Kimba against the wall.

opening his mouth, the serpent spat a black and green mucus-like liquid at her, Kimba summoned a gust of wind which picked up a table and blocked it, it began to burn through the wood like acid, the rancid smell of it made Kimba gag.

Charon wrapped his tail around her and started to squeeze, Kimba cried out in pain, then summoned a magic ward, which burst out from her like a bubble pushing the snake away, she held both hands extended to either side of her and struggled to keep the ward from breaking as it cracked like glass.

Charon wrapped more of himself around her and the ward started to shatter, Kimba screamed with the effort, but the strength of Charon's muscled serpent body was too much, he grinned as he squeezed, just waiting for the bubble to burst.

Felix was stuck and being held tightly within Charon's body, black green goo, started to burn at him and he cried out in pain, "what a horrible way to go", he thought.

"No, I can't give up, she needs me", Felix said, he had just enough wiggle room to take a mechanical staff from his pocket, he clicked the button and it shot out at either end extending to its full length which opened the space up a little bit, the staff immediately began to hiss from the acid lining touching the ends and Felix knew he didn't have much time, he curled up and crouched by the staff, he pulled out a knife and a roll of tape, he plunged the knife into Charon's stomach lining then taped the knife as best he could to the end of the staff.

He hit the button to retract it and the knife came free, he hit it again and the knife plunged back in, it fizzed and hissed as the black green goo spewed out over it, blood started to gush in as well diluting the acid.

Felix couldn't help but vomit, his fur and skin burned by the fumes and the stomach acids, he kept on hitting the button over and over and the knife hammered in and out cutting through the lining like a carving knife, Kimba's ward shattered and Charon squeezed around her, Kimba was exhausted.

She screamed, then noticed a knife piercing through Charon's body.

Charon's eyes went wide hissing and looking down as Felix cut a small hole through the flesh, he stuck one arm through and then his head and squeezed himself out of the serpent's body.

Charon released Kimba and snapped at Felix, pulling him free but slinging him across the room and straight through a stain glass window on the other side.

"Felix!", Kimba shouted, electricity started crackling around her as she grabbed at her elbow, pointing a finger toward the creature, Charon curled back and struck at her, with a thunderous crack, Kimba shot a lightning bolt which pinned Charon against the far wall, his body thrashed like a worm.

Kimba extended her hands palm up and pieces of splintered wood began to rise and circle around the room, the splintered pieces of wood, stuck into Charon like a pin cushion until he resembled a spikey cactus, he fell to the floor with a crash.

Charon laid still, Kimba limped over to the window, picking up a chair she broke the rest of the glass out then climbed over, Felix was laying against a tree in the grassy garden outside, he wasn't moving.

Kimba rushed over to him, his face was a mess, covered in blood, his skin looked like it had been partially melted, his fur matted, "I'm so sorry Felix", Kimba said sobbing.

"It's alright miss Kindheart, no tears now", Felix said softly, "I have something I need to tell you", he said, Kimba held his hand.

"I have always loved you miss Kindheart, even when we were young, you were my first and only friend", Felix said trying to smile for her, "I know Felix, I love you to", Kimba said sobbing, Felix closed his eyes.

Kimba sobbed into his chest as several soldiers and acolytes surrounded her, a thick black miasma crept in and swirled together coalescing into Guldamere himself, "oh, this is perfect", Guldamere cackled as he put a bony hand on Kimba's shoulder.

                    by Lore Casta Pendragon

Chapter Twenty-Six

The final battle

Ailyn leaned against the rail of the sky dancer; the crew were busy working to repair damages from the battle against Petricus Postmortus in dracolich form.

Silus leaned on the rail beside him, "I know you're hurting, but now isn't the time to be overcome with grief, you've far surpassed all of us in terms of strength, we can see that plain as day, we'll be needing your strength now more than ever", Silus said turning so his back faced the rail.

"I know, if I fail, everything will perish, Guldamere will suck the land dry and enslave us all until there is nothing left but death and darkness", Ailyn said sadly.

"What better motivation do you need", Silus said turning to slap him on the back, Ailyn cringed at the slap but didn't retaliate, he just looked at Silus with an unappreciative smirk.

"Silus, the lich has become too strong, I don't know if I have the strength to defeat him, I'm, I'm afraid of what is going to happen if I lose", Ailyn said, attempting to hold back his grief, he looked at the land flying by below them uncaringly.

"Try not to let the past eat at you, believe me, that's a slippery slope, I've done things that would horrify you and each day I live with what I've done, even so I'd have done it again in a heartbeat if it meant seeing Cinder again and I won't ever stop fighting until I've brought her back and righted that wrong, even if it seems hopeless, I'll never give up and neither should you, you still have someone who cares deeply for you", Silus said, his gruff voice hammering the words home to Ailyn, he nodded to Silus appreciatively.

"There was a time not so long ago, when I was a prisoner in the pit, when I felt like all was lost, when Sin first told me that Aethor was alive, it gave me purpose, I had to find him and it gave me strength, now I've lost him again and that feeling is back", Ailyn said bowing his head.

"Listen to yourself, sobbing like a putz, don't you think for one second that a man like Aethor would ever give in, trust me I know, I tried to break him, had he been in your position, he'd walk straight up to Guldamere and slap him around for a good time, I can tell you that in all my years, there have only been a few who ever bested me and Aethor Allheart was the best of them, no matter what happened the man had a will of steel, a will that could not be broken, you have the same strength of will in you, if he were here now, he wouldn't be sobbing, he'd be preparing for the greatest fight the world has ever seen", Silus said.

Ailyn nodded and stood up straight, "Guldamere will pay for what he's done and if he comes back, I'll kill him again", Ailyn said sternly copying Aethor's words, "we'll all be right there

                                    by Lore Casta Pendragon

with you", Link said, Ailyn turned around to see his friends were behind him listening, he smiled at them.

Villias was still at the flight deck, he peered through an eyeglass, "Necropyre be on the horizon", Villias shouted, "there are armies headed toward the city from the west, the north, the south and another camped in the east", Villias said, "the force to the east is probably ours", Link said, "the elves would be with them too", Ilutha added, "that means the force to the west must be from the Iron halls", Silus said, "I'd imagine my men would also make up a bulk of those forces as well, since we were scattered after the last battle", Ailyn said, Villias's face was scrunched up looking through the eye glass, "then who's is the army from the south?", Ilutha asked.

Ailyn looked over the rail of the ship, "the ronin city and Dawnshire are controlled by the church, chances are they're getting reinforcements from there", Ailyn said, "the force to the north is probably from the northern villages also controlled by the church, Ravenhill was renowned for its mercenaries", Silus added.

"Head west, we'll rendezvous with Farin, it looks like they've fortified the city for battle, it's going to be a four-way fight by the look of things", Ailyn said.

"Heading west!", Villias shouted and the ship turned abruptly, everyone reached to grab something as the ship corrected course, "we really should get seats for this thing", Rayan said.

Farin was leading the march as the dwarven army grew closer to Necropyre, "my king, the sky dancer comes this way", Mech said grinning from ear to ear.

"Would ye look at that, a flying ship, never would I had thought such a thing possible, I bet the elves made it", Farin said, grumbling the last part.

"No actually, it was a boy from Necropyre by the name of Felix Flight, and yours truly of course", Mech said straightening up, "we sure could have used some more of those going into this battle!", Farin said eyeing Mech questioningly, Mech just laughed awkwardly and turned away.

The sky dancer touched down close to Farin's forces and Villias ordered the crew to throw over the rope ladder, Ailyn, Silus and Link all jumped straight over the side, Ailyn landed with a roll, while Silus landed without making a sound, Link landed with a thud and a clang of heavy armor going to one knee.

Brawn, Wynn and Fyorn ran up to greet Ailyn followed by the rest of Ailyn's men, they patted him on the back and where genuinely glad to see him which he was grateful for, though everyone looked a little ragged having trudged so far without rest.

"Ay, Ailyn, did ye get what ye were after", Fyorn asked, Ailyn let the power flow through him and the white aura burned like flame around him, his men all cheered.

 by Lore Casta Pendragon

"Now you have all the shards of power, Guldamere's forces won't stand a chance against you or Aethor, speaking of which where is your old man?", Wynn said his voice boomed over the rabble.

"Aethor didn't make it", Ailyn said his smile turning to a sullen frown as the noise died down, all of Ailyn's men bowed their heads.

"I'm, what?", "How?", Wynn said in disbelief, "he died at the ronin city, he defeated the entire city garrison on his own but passed from his wounds", Ailyn said.

"Did you say he died after fighting an army on his own?", Brawn asked, Ailyn nodded and Brawn blew his breath out flabbergasted, a look of utter amazement on his face.

"A heavy toll, but there will be a heavier toll to pay should we lose this battle", Link said, "Farin, we got a good look at the battlefield, my forces are in the east already engaging the enemy, while the enemy in the north have joined the city, I think our best bet would be to attack the smaller force in the south first then join forces with the Paladins in the west, we'll help them before we assault the city itself as a unified force", Link explained, "that should save us from a flanking maneuver, a decent plan", Farin said.

"By the looks of it, we're going to reach the city before the forces in the south", Silus said, Farin stroked his long beard, "we can draw them to us by using the arbalest to strike at the city walls, they'll think they're flanking us, but we can set up the ambush from higher ground", Farin explained.

"That might just work, or leave us horridly outnumbered if Necropyre pushes the attack from the city walls", Fyorn said concerned, "it's better than a frontal assault", Link replied, "it's worth a try", Wynn said, "alright then, get those arbalests to the front and ready", Farin ordered, his men promptly moved into position.

They set three arbalests facing the walls of Necropyre, toward the northwest and three more facing downhill toward the encroaching ronin army hiding the arbalests in grey hessian sheets so they wouldn't be noticeable.

Ailyn stood with his men, they wore mismatched armors made from modified dwarven armor and whatever they could salvage, most were tied together with cloth or twine, they had an assortment of weapons from hammers to axes to pole arms, one even had pokers from a blacksmith's forge, anything that could be wielded or offer protection.

The dwarves were different, all decked out in fancy steel armor and conical dwarven helms, all wielding axe, hammer and crossbow, standing in spaced lines.

Both armies looked exhausted but also determined, Brawn, Wynn and Link inspected Ailyn's lines while Ilutha, Fyorn and Mech checked the dwarven lines, tugging on armor straps,

by Lore Casta Pendragon

checking to make sure every man and woman were ready for the battle to come, Farin stood in front with Ailyn by his side.

A bell began to toll within the city, the army of Necropyre were prepared and Acolytes were massing along the walls.

Villias was looking through his looking glass on the deck of the sky dancer, he called down to Ailyn, "looks like they've got mages on those walls, be prepared for a rain o' fire", "any sign of Kimba or Felix?", Ailyn asked, Villias shook his head.

Ailyn started to get worried, but Farin put his hand on his shoulder, "don't worry lad, she's got to be one of the strongest mages in Thalaria, I'm sure she found a way out", Farin assured.

Ailyn looked up, Villias was looking to the south, "enemy forces approaching from the southeast", Villias called down, "it's time", Ailyn said.

"Ready the arbalest!", Farin ordered, the dwarves manning the siege weapons aimed them higher by using a crank on the side of the large wooden engines, aiming at the walls of Necropyre.

Farin wielded two dual sided axes adorned with dwarven runes, on his head was a conical helmet with a crown shaped into it, he raised one axe, "on my mark!", Farin cried out, the seconds passed slowly, though they felt like minutes, "fire!", Farin bellowed and the arbalests loosed.

Large wooden spears launched across the field, the acolytes on the wall stood in groups of five spaced out along the wall, they put their hands together in prayer channeling chaos magic into an acolyte at the center of their groups, fireballs exploded into life in their palms.

They released the fireballs but only managed to intercept two of the massive arbalest spears which exploded into splinters before reaching the wall, showering them with burning wooden shrapnel.

Another spear struck true and smashed a huge hole underneath a stone watch tower, the stone began to crumble then slowly leaned and toppled over, the acolytes standing on top fell and met their end on the chattel below.

Farin and Ailyn's men cheered, but the cheers were cut off by a retaliatory shot from the walls, balls of fire rained down toward them, they passed just underneath the sky dancer and down on the lines of men.

"Shields up", Ailyn called, the men raised shields for protection, but as the fireballs hit, the fire swept through them, taking out large groups of men, screams rang out as men burned.

"The southern army has changed directions and are headed this way", Villias called out from the sky dancer, "we should fall back out of range before we lose more men", Link called, Farin nodded.

 by Lore Casta Pendragon

"Fall back and prepare for the assault", Farin called out, the lines remained intact and moved back in unison, turning to face the southeast and the oncoming Ronin forces downhill, as the enemy forces came into sight a mighty war cry sang out.

The Ronin army started sprinting toward them from the bottom of the hill, some on horseback others on foot, the dwarves pulled the hessian sheets from the arbalests facing downhill, "take bow formation", Farin ordered, a line of dwarves pulled out their crossbows and took aim while another two lines stood behind.

"Fire!", Farin called and the arbalests fired, the massive spears took out several ronin soldiers sticking into the ground leaving small craters where they struck, the dwarves loosed a volley of crossbows bolts taking ronin soldiers off their feet.

The dwarves that fired immediately took a knee and began to reload, while the next line of crossbowmen moved forward and took their place, they fired, also taking a knee and began reloading to be replaced by the next line, the result was a constant barrage of crossbow bolts taking out the front lines of cavalry and soldiers.

The ronin army were taking heavy losses as the dwarves advanced, closing the gap with arbalest and crossbow fire, Ailyn waited until they were getting close to the front then raised a hand.

"Charge!", Ailyn called as the white aura began to burn around him, he shot out in front of his men as they called out a mighty battle cry, he looked like a white missile as he encountered the first of the ronin soldiers.

Ailyn punched the first man he encountered so hard that he shattered his body armor and launched him over the head of the men behind him, he moved so fast that his movements were like a blur, men stabbed and struck at him, each attack hit nothing but air and was immediately countered by an intercepting punch or kick, just like Aethor had taught him.

The armies came together and the ring of steel sang out across the battlefield.

Silus was right behind Ailyn, with a flick of his wrists two knives were in his hands, he threw the first knife into the chest of the first man he saw, as the man curled forward Silus performed a barrel roll over him kicking another soldier behind in the chest, he crossed his arms over and into his cloak pulling out three knives on each hand between his fingers, crossing back he threw them all at once, hitting six men, taking them all off their feet.

Brawn and Fyorn smiled at each other and used their signature move, Brawn picked Fyorn up and threw him over the front line, Fyorn flipped forward and brought the hammers down with an earth-shattering crack, the earth beneath him blew outward and men flew out to every side leaving a crater where he landed breaking the enemy line, Wynn took advantage of their

                              by Lore Casta Pendragon

confusion, swinging his large claymore with all of his strength cleaving a pair of soldiers in half.

A soldier rushed at Brawn, he stepped back to avoid the swing of a katana then grabbed the man by the front of his chest plate, he lifted him with one hand and headbutted his face, the man dropped his weapon and went limp, another came in with a spear and Brawn threw the unconscious man at him, both soldiers hit the ground groaning.

Link pulled his golden sword out from his large paladian armor, men slashed and stabbed at him, sparks flew but nothing penetrated, like a charging bull, Link slashed and advanced forward, knocking men off balance and stomping them into the ground, he stuck the golden blade through one man while another came in with an overhead strike of a war hammer, it rang off his helmet which dazed him, but still couldn't penetrate, he retaliated by slashing the man across the face.

Ilutha seemed to dance between the attacking enemies, dual short swords slashing as she moved, cutting high then low, breaking between a narrow gap between two slashing swords while blocking both with either hand and sliding down to her knees, a flick of the wrist and both men dropped screaming, grabbing at their wounds.

She drew a bow from her back and loosed four arrows in quick succession, ridding Wynn, Brawn, Link and Fyorn of a few men rushing their flanks, they nodded to her gratefully then turned back to the fighting as more ronin soldiers came in.

Guldamere sat on his throne, his eyes pools of blackness, his vision cast to dozens of ravens overlooking the city and the battlefield outside.

Violet Valentine stood close by, her dress seemingly made of nothing but skin tight black miasma, the golden pupils of Guldamere's eyes lit up and he took a rasping breath, "the fool brings himself to me willingly", he croaked, voice echoing as if from some far distant place.

The distant rumble of siege fire could be heard not too far away, he reached out a boney hand and summoned Violet closer, he whispered into her ear, she looked at him then let out a hiss, covering her face with her dress she turned away, the black smoke dissipated into the air and she disappeared in a cloud of black smoke.

"Summon the peons, it's time I addressed my adoring followers", Guldamere smirked, "bring the girl to me, after all, it's only fitting that the Allheart boy see her execution".

Soldiers and acolytes of the church of the god feared raced all over the city, pulling every man, woman and child from their houses and ordering them to gather at the courtyard in front of the cathedral of the god feared.

Not a single household was spared until the courtyard was filled with the citizens of Necropyre, Guldamere's men placed themselves at every exit as they waited to hear the

address from Lord Guldamere, several acolytes lined up either side of a podium overlooking the central courtyard.

The darkness grew darker on the podium like the light was too afraid to touch it and out from that darkness stepped Guldamere, the people of Necropyre began to sing praises, grovel and bow before him as he raised his boney hand and silenced them.

Not a single word was spoken, you could hear a pin drop, Guldamere smiled, his voice echoed out enhanced by chaos magic, "my beloved people, today our enemies march upon our great city, they deny our divinity, they try to deny your righteous faith in our church, but do not fear, those who fight in my righteous name, death will not hold you, for I, Lord Guldamere, will bring you back, the old and feeble will again find the strength their youth, the young will find the strength of men, for those who fight in my name shall forever reap the rewards of my divine boon", Guldamere's voice echoed far and wide and his people cried tears of joy, the people began arming themselves, the old and even children, then they were directed toward the city gates.

The people of Necropyre were resolved to die with the promise of Guldamere's boon, Guldamere turned from the podium and walked toward Kimba who was tied and gagged, she was held by two soldiers, several acolytes walked closer to Guldamere as a wave of black miasma passed over them, she was covered in the swirling dark her body felt weightless for a minute then she was no longer on the podium overlooking the battlefield from the walls of Necropyre.

Ailyn stood surrounded by ronin soldiers, they pointed spears and swords at him encircling him, Ailyn held his hands in front of him, golden runes appeared in the air in a line, then faded as Aram's staff became solid in his hands.

The soldiers stabbed in at him, Ailyn raised his back hand grip to his forehead using the tenkan technique, he rotated one hundred eighty degrees and swung the staff knocking spears and swords away then he swung the staff around his head to block the spears from behind.

Once his hands wound up, he was ready and spun back the opposite direction, his feet moving back to where they came, the staff swinging back with his body movement, every soldier who attacked was drawn in and flung back out by the technique.

Ailyn looked like a hurricane in the midst of battle, armored helms shattered and men toppled in a collective groan of pain, crossbow bolts flew past Ailyn taking out a line of ronin soldiers as Farin walked toward him, what was left of the ronin soldiers began to retreat back behind the line of the hills, the sound of clashing steel subsided and was replaced by the moans of the injured and the dying.

                                                                        by Lore Casta Pendragon

Ailyn looked over the battlefield, at his men who had been wounded in the fighting, some were so exhausted they could no longer stand, some who were knocked unconscious woke screaming, there would be no rest for them.

"How long do you think we can keep this up", Ailyn asked Farin, "stick to the plan lad, we either win or we perish", Farin said patting Ailyn on the back, Ailyn felt a little stronger at the reassurance, he could tell by looking at him that Farin was feeling the strain as well, but he refused to show it, he had to be strong for his men, Ailyn nodded at Farin with respect and followed his lead.

"Treat the wounded, all those able to fight, line up!", Ailyn ordered, some ran, some limped, but all those able to fight did so, "we march on the eastern front", Ailyn said, the men followed wearily but determined to see it through.

The gates of Necropyre opened, men, women and children were accompanied by soldiers and the northern mercenaries as they burst out from the gate, the cries of battle rang out.

Villias turned the ship around to face them, then signaled to a crew member to take the wheel, "get them cannons into position", he ordered, "Ailyn, army approaching from the city", Villias called down.

"Get the arbalests into position", Farin ordered, the dwarves wheeled them around to face the city gates.

The crew of the sky dancer had their cannons primed, Mech gave the signal that they were ready, Villias put his leg on the railing, "on my mark", he said.

"Wait!", Ailyn cried out, noticing that some of the people running in the crowd were children, "there are kids in there, hold your fire!", Ailyn panicked.

"Ailyn, if we don't open fire we'll be overrun", Farin said, "I can't do it Farin, we can't, we can't kill children", Ailyn said, Silus put a hand on Ailyn's shoulder walking forward.

"Stand down, I'll take it from here, after all, I'm used to being the one who does what needs to be done", Silus said calmly.

"No, you can't, there are children down there", Ailyn pleaded grabbing Silus by the arm, Silus eyed him sternly, "it's them, or every one of us", Silus said, he shook Ailyn's hand off, then walked to the front, raising one arm.

"On me!", Silus shouted, as his arm came down he said calmly, "fire", arbalest bolts flew past him, the wind bellowing out his cloak as the sound of cannon fire rang out from the sky dancer.

                                            by Lore Casta Pendragon

"Gah!", Villias growled as he reluctantly fired his foot cannon, the artillery smashed into the line of civilians and soldiers alike decimating the front lines, the cries of pain and anguish washed over Ailyn as he fell to his knees.

"What have we done", Ailyn whispered head down, Silus walked back to him, "war is not a game Allheart, you'd best learn to accept sacrifices, before this day ends, you'll be saying goodbye to more than a few kids", Silus said offering a hand.

Ailyn glared up at him, anger burned in his eyes, he reluctantly took his cuff as Silus pulled Ailyn to his feet and they stood for a moment before Ailyn nodded.

"They chose their path, they'd have us all die for that bastard, just like I chose my path when I sided with you", Silus said, Ailyn smiled at him then walked forward.

"Form ranks!", Ailyn shouted, his command echoed out across the battlefield.

Ailyn's companions all lined up behind him as the forces of Necropyre charged in, the power in him burst into white flame.

"Charge!", Ailyn shouted, he burst off like a missile into the enemy ranks slamming a straight line through their defenses, tears stung at his eyes, he hated every moment of this.

Locke Lionheart stood panting side by side with a circle of paladins on the eastern front of the battle, the bodies of sentinel guards and elves laid strewn around them lifeless, werewolves dashed around them looking for any sign of weakness or momentary lapse in concentration.

One paladin got distracted for a moment by a bleeding wound and a werewolf leaped across dragged him away from the circle.

"Eyes up, god damnit!", Locke shouted, the paladin slashed at the beast to try to free himself from its powerful grip, but as it let go, he was jumped on by another three, they tore away pieces of his armor while he screamed, the sharp claws and jaws ripping him apart.

"Close the gap!", Locke commanded and the paladins took a step back to close the circle tighter.

"You fought bravely, Lord Lionheart, but this is the end for you", Violet's voice rang in Locke's ears but he couldn't see her, "show yourself witch!", Locke shouted, with a flash of black smoke she appeared beside two snarling werewolves, she patted them lovingly, her silky dark hair and black smokey dress revealed a lot of breast and leg.

She walked around the outside of the circle, the paladins had swords and shields at the ready, waiting for any who dared to draw close enough.

Violet found a victim and she gave the paladin a sultry look, the paladins eyes locked onto her own, the purple in her eyes glowed while the rest of the world around her went dark, the

by Lore Casta Pendragon

paladin began to lower his sword, the men to either side of him nudged him, but he took no notice.

"What are you doing?", "Raise your arms", the paladins to either side of him said, "what's wrong", asked another, but it was too late.

Violet gestured with a finger for him to come to her and he broke the line, he walked toward her taking off his helm, the werewolves growled violently but violet put her hands out in front of them, "this one is mine", she said as the paladin came close dropping his sword and shield to the ground.

She placed a finger under his chin and she put her face near his, he was enthralled by her.

Violet turned him around and pushed him down onto his knees, making sure the rest of them could watch, "get a hold of yourself soldier!", Locke cried out.

Violet looked at him with a smirk as she placed her fingers over his shoulder, she hissed as long fangs extended from her mouth, she sank them into the man's neck, he acted like it was a pleasurable act as blood burst from the wound soaking his armor, his face became gaunt as his life force was slowly sucked away.

Violet pushed the husk to the ground wiping the blood from her face with her hand, an acolyte offered her a handkerchief to wipe the rest away, "damn you, witch!", Locke said.

"I've certainly had my fill of your men my Lord", she said sarcastically, "I'm afraid it's time for you to die", Violet said.

She patted the werewolves to her sides, "finish them", she said.

The werewolves darted in, Locke stabbed forward his sword splitting the firsts skull in two, the second took out the paladin on his right, one by one the men in the circle were taken out by charging werewolves, Locke watched as the last of the paladins hit the ground fighting for their lives, Locke couldn't pull his sword from the skull of the werewolf so he left it embedded there.

He picked up a tower shield slamming it into the back of a werewolf accosting one of his men.

The beast let out a growl then turned on him, it slammed a muscular grey claw into the shield knocking Locke to the ground, it jumped on him as Locke raised the shield to his face, it was heavy and Locke couldn't budge, it gnawed at him, jaws snapping, then it shuddered and fell to the side whimpering as the paladin he saved severed its spine from behind, he pulled Locke to his feet only to be blasted away by a fireball, Locke hit the ground again losing the tower shield in the explosion.

Looking over to violet she had her hand raised, she blew smoke away from her palm smiling at him.

"Damnit", Locke said, "she's toying with me", Violet gave him a sultry look, Locke looked away then grabbed the dirt with his hands in anger, his eyes went wide then he grabbed the handful of dirt and shoved it into his eyes, he looked back at her, his eyes were scratched and blurred, he saw her eyes glow purple and he knew what she was up to.

Locke got to his feet, his hands falling lifeless to his sides, he stumbled over to her and she smiled placing her hands against his golden chest plate looking up to him, her face drew up to his neck fangs extending viciously "goodbye paladin king", Violent hissed.

Locke pulled a gold dagger from his leg armor and plunged it into her mid-section with a violent thud, Violet's eyes went wide, the fangs retracting and she stepped away shocked and holding the wound.

Locke smiled at her, "fool", her surprise turned to anger as she pulled the dagger out, she placed her hands together in prayer and the wound stitched itself together.

Locke's face turned from devilish satisfaction to horror as she raised a hand to Locke's face and summoned a gout of fire at point blank range.

King Locke Lionheart fell back with the soft clang of steel, "let's get back to Lord Guldamere and tell him the good news", Violet said, with a cloud of black smoke she disappeared from sight.

A child from Necropyre charged at Silus with a what looked to be a kitchen knife, he slapped the blade out of the child's hand then picked him up with one hand by the shirt, the child squirmed, Silus sneered then slammed his fist into the child's stomach, the child lost consciousness immediately then Silus threw him to the ground.

Ailyn and the rest of his companions were finishing off what was left of the army of Necropyre, Ailyn looked up at the walls, the acolytes were still lined up but hadn't made a move, Ailyn eyed them suspiciously, he walked over to Wynn, who finished off a soldier in front of him with one mighty swing of his claymore.

"What do you think they're waiting for?", Ailyn asked, "whatever it is lad, it's not good, and what's worse is that we haven't even seen the lord of darkness himself yet", Wynn bellowed, the strain of fatigue was very apparent on his face, his usually cheery demeanor wasn't there.

Ailyn looked around at his men, at his friends, they all stood stooped and staggered as they walked, the strain of sleeplessness was affecting them all, Ailyn wondered how much longer they could hold.

by Lore Casta Pendragon

Chapter Twenty-Seven

Lacrimosa

Ailyn's eyes felt heavy, they stung with the symptoms of sleep deprivation, his muscles ached from lack of rest.

"Ailyn, rider from the east!", Villias shouted down from the sky dancer, Ailyn saw a cloud of dust rising from a horse, it was being chased by werewolves, the horse slowed as werewolf slashed at it's rear with long claws tearing long wounds into it's flank.

The horse stopped running and limped almost falling under the weight of the rider, another werewolf dashed across taking its throat with large powerful jaws, the rider was thrown to the ground as the horse was taken from under him and devoured by the werewolves, the rider crawled away from them slowly.

Ailyn moved as fast as he could to intercept, followed by Ilutha and Link trailing behind.

As he drew close a werewolf charged at the soldier, teeth bared, claws extended wide, ready to finish his prey, the soldier slowly got to his feet, clearly wounded and limping heavily, he moved determined toward Ailyn, his voice whimpered with every breath, his fear apparent on his face, he reached a hand toward Ailyn like he was reaching for assistance.

Ailyn was fast but so was the man-wolf, it leaped on the soldiers back, sinking its teeth into his shoulder, its great jaws taking most the man torso in its mouth, claws ripped into the paladin's sides.

Ailyn closed the gap and grabbed the beast's arm, he moved around to its rear twisting the muscular arm over his shoulder, he flipped the werewolf over his back and slammed it into the ground like it weighed nothing, it hit the ground with a thud and the sound of breaking ribcage.

The beast let out a growl as it breathed its last breath, Ailyn turned and held the soldier in his arms, the man was struggling to breathe, his wounds were fatal, Ailyn eyed the other beasts warily.

"Lord, Ailyn, the eastern front, was, wiped, out", the soldier said slowly, Ailyn took his hand as the soldier passed, he held out just long enough to see his mission completed.

Werewolves growled at either side of Ailyn, Ilutha leaped in slashing the legs out from under one in one fluent circular motion she finished it with a slash to the throat as it fell.

Link charged in from the other side, slamming his tower shield into the powerful beast, it grabbed around the shield with large talons, and slid backward holding on tight.

                                    by Lore Casta Pendragon

Link pulled back drawing his sword and plunged it into the beast belly, it let go of the shield and slashed at his face, Link just raised the shield smacking the werewolf under the jaw, then with one adept slash he took the beasts head off.

"What did he say?", Ilutha asked, Ailyn placed the soldier on the ground and stood, he turned to face Ilutha, "our eastern forces have been wiped out", Ailyn said, Ilutha's eyes teared up, she covered her mouth with her hand, "I'm sorry Ilutha, we were too late", Ailyn said, "it, can't be", Link said, the blood drained from both their faces, both the armies of Paladin's Reach and the Elven Forest had been Routed.

Ilutha stood there in disbelief while Link walked over to her and held her.

"They will pay for this, I swear it with my last breath, they will pay", Ilutha said, fire in her eyes, Link nodded his agreement, "they think were done, we're just getting started", Link said turning to Ailyn, "let's end this", Ailyn nodded as they began running back to the front line.

"Fall in line", Farin issued the command and the dwarven army formed a line facing the gates of Necropyre, Ailyn's forces fell in behind, Ailyn saw bodies of the young and the old mixed in with the soldiers of Necropyre, it made him sick to the stomach, but he pressed on, the acolytes on the walls had not yet made a move.

"What do you think they're planning?", Farin said, "probably waiting for us to get in range", Ailyn responded, black smoke began to billow over the main gate of Necropyre like a cloud of putrid gas, it faded as Guldamere and Violet stepped out of it and stood atop the gate.

Guldamere held Kimba bound and gagged in his boney hands, his voice echoed out over the battlefield, enhanced by chaos magic.

"You who dare to attack my city, to defy the will of a god, you will suffer deaths uncountable at my hands", Guldamere's words were terrifying, the men became uneasy, knees trembling, like the words carried fear itself, he stroked Kimba's cheek with a boney hand and a tear fell down her face.

"I no longer have to consume the living to survive, but for this one I will make an exception", Guldamere's words hit Ailyn like a ton of bricks, his heart raced and the aura around him burst into life, it glowed like white fire and Ailyn shot toward the gate like a missile, "I have to save her, I have to, if I can save just one thing in this world, please, let it be her", Ailyn said.

On top of the wall, Kimba's face was sorrowful, tied hand and foot, she couldn't do much, Guldamere had her gagged with a rope of black miasma that tasted like rotted flesh, she mumbled something to Guldamere, he waved his bony finger and the gag turned to smoke and disappeared, Kimba coughed a few times then shouted at him.

"I will not be a bargaining chip for you to use", She saw Ailyn rushing in just below the gate, the acolytes on the wall started throwing balls of fire from the top, forcing him to leap back to avoid them, Ailyn summoned Aram's staff.

                                                             by Lore Casta Pendragon

"Please let this work", he said as he aimed up on Kimba, closing one eye.

Ailyn ran forward and threw the staff like a javelin, it soared toward Guldamere at tremendous speed, Guldamere was forced to move back as the light from the staff severed Kimba's bonds, she looked down at Ailyn eyes wide then looked back at Guldamere.

Violet hissed then disappeared into a cloud of black smoke, a black claw rose from the darkness surrounding Guldamere, it reached out to grab Kimba but before it could grasp her, she leaped backward over the wall, Guldamere's shadow claw slammed shut where she was as Kimba plummeted downward.

Ailyn saw her and planted his feet, the ground crumbled beneath him as he shot forward, fireballs from the acolytes above exploding behind him, he ran beside the wall then ran up the side of it, making a beeline for Kimba then kicked off as he got closer, part of the wall collapsed inward under the pressure of his jump and several acolytes on top the wall fell as it cracked and fell away, one of them misfired and a fireball which exploded on the wall behind him, causing even more damage.

Ailyn soared toward Kimba grabbing her out of the air, Kimba screamed as the ground came up to meet them, she slammed her fists together, kicking up a tornado of air to slow their decent, Ailyn landed solidly on the ground knees bent, the earth cratering beneath him.

"Thank you, thank you, I knew you'd save me, I knew it", Kimba said burying her face into his neck, Ailyn's knees were shaking from the impact on the ground and the strain his movements placed on his body.

"Behind you!", Silus shouted charging between Ailyn and a volley of fireballs with a tower shield, the fire exploded around them, Silus let out a groan and winced in pain then dropped the shield, it was red hot, Kimba put her hands up and with a flicker of his dagger Silus severed the black miasma bindings on her feet.

Another volley came at them, Kimba slammed her fists together then extended her hands, white tendrils of chaos magic materialized around her, she whipped her hands forward and the tendrils of magic did the same, they collided with the balls of fire, the ground shook from the ensuing explosions, smoke filled the air, neither side could see the other.

The soldiers and acolytes of Necropyre peered out from over the wall, trying to get a visual, the loud whoop of arbalests being fired was all they heard and seconds later two large ballista bolts smashed into the wall, the wall exploded in a rain of stone, iron and timber.

Men cried out as they fell from the wall, a third bolt sailed over Guldamere's head, his vision followed it as it cleared most of the city and smashed into the front wall of the cathedral of the god feared with a loud rumbling boom and the sound of breaking glass, the front of the building crumbled.

Guldamere snarled and looked back to the wall, he put his hands together and darkness pushed out from him in all directions, his men's knees quivered as a deathly cold embraced them.

"Sire?", An acolyte close to him said, Guldamere gave him a quick sideways glance and fear gripped the man, he turned away shivering in fear too afraid to question further.

Guldamere strained under the effort, a forceful wind blew most of the smoke forward, Ailyn and Silus braced themselves, Ailyn held Kimba behind him and raised his arm over his eyes as the wind billowed past them, they slid backward from the force of it, Ailyn made eye contact with Guldamere, he grinned as black-green miasma began to rise around him.

"This world is full of dead things and I, I am the lord of dead things!", Guldamere shouted, black miasma started rising from the ground around the battlefield, seeping into the dead.

Men, women and children began rising, groaning, broken bones clicking and cracking, flayed skin and bloody wounds not stopping them, ghouls and nightmare creatures rose alongside them, beasts with horrid features, predators of the dark.

"There's so many of them, how many times can he bring them back?", Kimba said, "until there is nothing left of them, and even then, when he brings them back enough times, they come back less than human", Silus replied.

"You fool!", Ailyn shouted at him, "every time you bring something back from the abyss, the more of the abyss comes with it!", Guldamere just smirked, he knew all along the consequences of Necromancy, he didn't care.

"I'll have it all, or no-one will", Guldamere said thrusting his hand forward, the undead and nightmare creatures charged, Link and Ilutha caught up to Ailyn and the five of them stood together as the dead came at them from all sides.

"They're surrounded, we have to help them", Wynn bellowed, Farin raised his axes, "for the future of all, sound the charge!", Farin cried out and a dwarf blew a curled ram's horn, the army charged to meet the undead.

Fyorn grabbed hold of a supply cart and toppled the contents out of it, he nodded to Brawn who took the rear and began running down the hill gaining speed, as they came close to the undead soldier's front line, Brawn pushed as hard as he could and the cart broke through the front line before barreling into a large soldier, splintering into a thousand pieces sending Fyorn flying over the top of them.

He brought the enchanted hammers down and a shockwave of earth blasted outward, ripping undead soldiers apart in a rain of gore, he opened up a hole in the enemy line close to where Ailyn and his companions were.

by Lore Casta Pendragon

"Ye looked like ye could use a hand", Fyorn smiled, he said as he stood from his kneeling position, Ailyn smiled at him shaking his head, then turned to Kimba, "stay behind me, I'll keep them off your back".

Ailyn held out his arms and recalled Aram's staff, two soldiers had found the staff lodged into a stone wall in the city, they were trying to pull it free but they gasped and moved away as gold runes appeared around it and it disappeared, the staff appeared in Ailyn's hands.

"I got your back", Silus added, "we'll take the other sides", Link and Ilutha added, "I'll take out the magic users on the wall", Kimba said focusing, her friends surrounded her in a star formation, the undead came in at them from all sides.

Ailyn was the first to strike, the staff spun above his head then came around like a hurricane collecting three with an audible thud as the staff collided with each of his foes.

Silus was next, he moved so fast between them, they looked like they were standing still, slashing at tendons and severing limbs, when he stopped all his opponents fell.

Ilutha pulled the bow from her back and lined up three arrows to a single shot, all three middled an undead between the eyes.

Link swung his mighty golden sword, each swing connecting with a clang of steel and the crunch of bone, they could strike at him but none could penetrate the thick paladian armor which he wore.

A long line of undead charged forward from their rear, Fyorn let out a mighty war cry as he lifted the enchanted hammers high slamming them into the ground with all his force, a shockwave rippled out in front of him burying the undead under churned earth.

Fyorn was surprised to see a crack began to form in the metalwork of the hammers, "oh, not now, we've still much to do", Fyorn said to the hammers.

In a cloud of acrid black smoke Violet appeared by Guldamere's side, "if it please my lord, I think I'll get revenge on the Kindheart girl", Violet's breathy voice said, "go and have your fun, but be sure to kill the dwarf, those hammers are, a problem", Guldamere croaked.

Violet looked at his rotted face, he seemed so much more otherworldly, so much more distant than he had previously, like the abyss had become a part of him, like he saw the future unfolding before his eyes but didn't care, she knew that he had the power to eliminate them all in a heartbeat, but wondered why he chose to stand there and wait, like he knew that something had to happen before he finished this, she shook the thought from her mind.

"Yes, my, lord", Violet's words came out hesitant as she backed away and turned to the battlefield, she was becoming less trustful of him, "why would he go to all this effort to bring

          by Lore Casta Pendragon

us back if were so beneath him?", She thought, again she tried to shake the thought from her mind.

The acolytes on the wall primed another volley of fire to reign down upon Ailyn's companions.

"Kimba", Silus said looking up as he slashed an undead old hag with his blade, "I can see it, Silan", Kimba said in a familiar tone which earned a raised eyebrow from beneath Silus's wide brimmed hat.

Six thick tendrils of pure white chaos magic rose from Kimba like wings giving her an angelic appearance, the fireballs shot from the walls and the tendrils of chaos magic intercepted them, the fireballs exploded on contact, the tendrils of chaos magic were tattered but unbroken.

Kimba retracted the tendrils then pushed forward pushing the smoke back toward the wall, the acolytes on the wall held on tight, ducking down as a gust of wind washed over them.

Guldamere stood there, never moving an inch, Kimba elongated the tendrils into thin whips and slammed them into the walls sending men falling and stone flying with the impacts, she struck again and again taking out acolytes along the walls.

Guldamere lifted a boney finger and wrapped one tendril heading his way in black miasma, it cancelled out and faded away.

"Now's our chance, storm the city", Farin commanded.

Charging forward, the army followed his lead, slashing at the still rising undead, they pushed past Ailyn and his companions who were still fighting around Kimba.

Wynn sliced undead and nightmare creatures in halves as he rushed forward, his booming war cry could be heard from across the battlefield with every slash from his claymore.

"Full steam ahead, we got a wall to breach", Villias shouted, Mech moved below deck as Rayan and Inaya maneuvered the sky dancer toward the city wall, Kimba's assault faltered and the tendrils of chaos magic dissipated as she dropped to her knee's panting, she wiped sweat from her brow trying to catch her breath.

Ailyn finished off his foes then rushed over to help her, she held out a hand and he helped her to her feet.

"That's it, that's all I could manage", Kimba said exhausted.

"Ye did far more than we could ever have expected lass", Fyorn said turning to her, a cloud of acrid black miasma appeared behind Fyorn, before anyone could act Violet reaved Fyorn's head backwards and plunged a long-jagged dagger down into the front of his throat.

Fyorn let out a garbled cry as blood poured down the front of his chest plate, no one moved from the sudden shock.

                        by Lore Casta Pendragon

Violet threw Fyorn forward pulling the dagger out as a long serpentine tongue licked at the blade.

Link's brow furrowed in anger, he moved forward and slashed at her with his blade, she simply smiled at him and laugh disappearing out of thin air leaving behind an after image of black smoke, Link slashed through it and to either side of him but she was gone.

"No!", Link shouted furiously, "to the depths of the abyss with you, vile witch!", Link screamed in frustration.

"I think that might be exactly what she's doing", Ilutha said intrigued and looking around frantically, gaining another raised eyebrow from Silus.

"She's hopping in and out of it, like creating doorways in and out of one realm and into another, the elves have a sense for these things, she can't stay on the other side for long though, which means, she's going to have to surface soon, like going under water", Ilutha said scanning around them.

"There!", Ilutha pointed close by Ailyn and Kimba, Silus threw a knife as Violet phased back into reality, she raised the dagger to bring it down on Kimba from behind, but Silus's knife struck home and sunk into her chest, the impact knocked her back and she stumbled backward right into Link's golden sword, it stuck her straight through the middle.

Violet's eyes widened as she let out a pained cry, she disappeared into a cloud of smoke and the dagger in her chest dropped to the floor, Link staggered forward as the sword pushed through the smoke.

"Is that it, did we get her?", Kimba asked, "not yet, she's a mage, not to mention she's already dead, there's no telling how fast she could heal from those wounds especially since Guldamere made this field of unending death around us", Link added slashing at an undead soldier who drew too close.

Ilutha's skin went cold, she dive rolled to the side as Violet appeared again in a cloud of black smoke narrowly missing her with the knife before disappearing again.

"Has she already healed from those wounds", Kimba asked, "not completely, I don't think she's entirely human anymore", Ilutha said following the feeling of death as it crept back toward Link, "she's behind you!", Ilutha shouted to Link.

The black smoke appeared behind him, he slashed his sword through it slicing an undead soldier in half, "it's a fake!", Silus shouted, another black puff of smoke behind Ilutha and Violet's dagger sunk between her shoulder blades, Ailyn shot out toward her with a thrust of his staff but hit nothing but smoke.

"You've penetrated me enough, lover boy", Violet laughed mockingly, which gained an angry huff from Kimba, Ilutha fell into Ailyn's arms, "what a wicked trick", Ilutha said as Ailyn took

by Lore Casta Pendragon

the dagger from her back and laid her down, "try not to speak, we'll get help", Ailyn said, but it was already too late, Ilutha's head lulled, the dagger had pierced her heart, Ailyn shook her.

"Ilutha, Ilutha wake up", "Ailyn if you don't get on your feet, you'll have more friends to mourn", Silus warned, the black smoke from Violet's technique left a haze in the air, "little Kimba Kindheart, did Ailyn tell you that I was his first lover", Violet's voice echoed around them.

"I bet that eats you up inside doesn't it", she laughed, Kimba's face went red with anger, "you used him!", Kimba began to shout, but Ailyn cut her off holding out his hand, then whispered under his breathe, "she's coming for you, keep your cool, stay facing forward and get ready", Ailyn said standing in front of her.

Kimba put her fists together under the sleeves of her robe, black smoke appeared behind Kimba as Violet's blade slashed.

Kimba dropped to the ground and Ailyn spun, a quick turn of his hips and Aram's staff knocked the blade from her hand, steel rang as the dagger flew away, Violet's eyes locked onto Ailyn's, the purple glow fixing him onto her, he tried to look away but was enthralled by her.

"She's so beautiful, how could I have struck her, I'm so sorry", he thought lowering the staff, Kimba grabbed her elbow and launched a fireball straight up into Violet's face, Ailyn and Violet flew in opposite directions from the blast.

Silus leaped out grabbing Ailyn under the arms sliding backward, Kimba was coughing from the dust and smoke at the center.

Violet hit the ground beneath a rocky hill clutching her face, she screamed out in anger, "you little bitch, I'm going to keep you alive just so I can keep killing you".

Violet got to her feet, her face burned but healing rapidly, glowing purple eyes locked with Link, he dropped his guard taking a knee.

"Snap out of it Link!", Silus shouted, "that's a good boy, now kill your friends", Violet commanded, Link turned to face Kimba, "Sir Lionheart?", Kimba said, Link didn't respond, he looked at her, hate plastered on his face.

Kimba's heart sank and her shoulders slumped as Link ran at her, Ailyn and Silus jumped in front of him grabbing him by both arms, it was like trying to stop a charging bull and they slid along the ground trying to stop him.

"Get a hold of yourself", Ailyn growled, Violet smiled, "hay boys", she said, they all looked over and were immediately ensnared in her gaze, "oh no, no", Kimba said, "this was too eas…", Violet was saying but was suddenly interrupted by a massive boulder from above, it crushed her into the ground ripping her in half and smearing blood and pieces of Violet over the ground like a wine stain on carpet.

by Lore Casta Pendragon

Brawn stood above her panting with a look of utter brutality on his face, "that was for Fyorn, bitch!", Brawn said.

Ailyn, Silus and Link all snapped out of the trance and were now standing mouths agape at what they were just forced to witness, "we're meant to be the good guys, right?", Ailyn said turning to Link, Silus just stood there pondering that very question, while Link turned and vomited, Brawn jumped down with a splat as he crushed Violet's skull under foot with a grunt.

Ailyn grasped his arm by the cuff, "thanks brawn, you saved us", he said, "long awaited payment for getting us out of the pit alive, I was too late to save our friends, I'm sorry", Brawn said, the grief plastered on his face as he looked at Fyorn.

Kimba ran up and tried to wrap her arms around Brawns big waist, Brawn huffed as she collided with him, "thank you Brawn", she said, he placed his hand on her head with a smile.

They turned to the city, the sky dancer was high above the wall being accosted by fireballs from undead acolytes on the wall, the mages from Oasis were fending off fireballs and arrows with gusts of wind while Villias maneuvered the ship.

"Hurry lads, we can't keep this up for long", Villias shouted, "you sure this will work", Rayan said, "it will, as long as we don't miss", Mech said, both men looked at each other with a worried expression, "that's all the gunpowder left on the ship in this one barrel, we only have one chance, we light the wick then drop it into the gate below", Mech said.

"Not an easy thing to do on a moving ship, with fireballs exploding around us, in high winds", Villias said unassured, a fireball exploded at the side of the ship throwing the ship sideways, several mages fell over the railing as the crew held on for dear life.

"That was a close one, if we get hit, it's a long way down", Villias said, he looked over to see an arrow had stabbed through Mech's chest, "oh no, no, no, no, Mech!", Villias said panicking, Mech slumped to the floor groaning then grabbed Villias by the arm, "give it to me lad, it's, up, to, you, to get us over, to the wall", his voice softened, Villias stood wiping Mech's blood across his lapel, "I'll see it done my friend".

Giving the barrel of powder to Mech, with an oil flint lighter from his coat he shouted, "get us above the wall, we don't have much time", Villias shouted to the crew.

Guldamere watched his army fighting, dying and fighting again, usually he'd admire the death around him with adoration, but he felt nothing, everything within him that once was alive had died, "that final part of the power, when I have it, I'll truly become a god, I'll be able to feel again", he thought to himself looking at his skeletal hand.

"I think it's about time", he said, black miasma pushed Guldamere up from the wall like a rocket launching, propelling himself toward the sky dancer, a black clawed shadow hand reached up onto the deck and he pulled himself over the rail, the crew turned to look and terror crossed their faces as Guldamere slashed two of the crew, they fell into clean slices of

                                    by Lore Casta Pendragon

human meat, the rest of the crew backed off as Guldamere walked casually toward the flight deck, an older sailor with a long grey beard was hiding behind a water barrel and worked up the courage to come at Guldamere with a scimitar, he stabbed it into Guldamere, then looked up into the face of his doom, Guldamere smirked then moved his torn black robe revealing nothing but a skeletal spine at his mid-section, the sword had hit nothing but cloak.

The man lost all bravado as Guldamere grabbed the old sailor by the face, the eerie glow of life force was sucked out of the man, he shriveled into a husk.

"I don't need to devour your souls, but I do find it satisfying when you perish so", Guldamere croaked, he clicked the boney fingers of his free hand and the husk caught fire like kindling, Guldamere threw it onto the deck as it disintegrating into ashes.

The crew began running up to the flight deck, some leaped from the railing to get away, choosing death over oblivion.

Guldamere grabbed the railings with two shadow claws and flung himself onto the flight deck, Villias rushed over drawing a simitar from his belt, he took a swing at Guldamere who caught his wrist lifting him up by the hand until they were face to face, Villias looked into the blackness of Guldamere's eyes, the horror he felt could not be described, it was like looking at the end of his own life.

Stealing his nerves, Villias frowned, "if his lordship wants my soul, then he can take me boot too!", Villias shouted, lifting his cannon leg onto Guldamere's chest, he blasted Guldamere point blank.

Ribcage bones exploded out the back of Guldamere's tattered cloak, which now had a new hole through it, Guldamere growled, throwing Villias to the side, he smashed through the rail and over the side of the ship.

"Captain!", Inaya and Rayan both shouted.

Mech heard the commotion on deck and with a sigh he said, "I'd best get it ready, we won't survive this", his legs wobbled as he got to his feet.

Guldamere turned to Inaya and Rayan, "stay back", Inaya screamed blasting Guldamere with a gust of wind, Rayan added fire creating a massive gout of flame, it engulfed Guldamere burning away part of the ship, the ropes holding the balloon began to burn away and the ship tilted to the side, the gout of fire ceased as Inaya and Rayan fell to the side with the ship only to find Guldamere standing there covered in a shroud of black miasma.

The smoke wisped away revealing Guldamere looking amused, more ropes began to snap and the ship tilted more to one side, Guldamere's shadow claws dug into the timber of the deck to keep him upright, Inaya and Rayan fell toward him and Guldamere grabbed them by the throat, one in each hand, he smirked wickedly and they both screamed while he drained them of life.

        by Lore Casta Pendragon

At the other end of the ship Mech fired a cannon with netting stuffed inside of it, Guldamere deflected the cannonball with a shadow claw but the nets expanded wrapping him up and throwing him to the deck.

Mech rushed over to a rope holding the ship to the balloon and cut it, he raced to the other side and cut another, as each line was cut the ship tilted further, the crew caught on and they sprang into action, he was going to drop Guldamere with the ship.

Some helped cut the lines, others grabbed the netting as Guldamere slashed at it with the shadow claws trying to free himself.

Guldamere growled as the crew threw more netting over him, he put his hands together in prayer, black and green fire burned around him burning away the netting and the crew who held it as he rose to his feet, more of the ship caught fire as shadows extended from Guldamere and under Mech's feet, "one more should do it", Mech said as the ropes began to break and burn away on their own.

Shadow claws rose from the darkness beneath him, Guldamere snatched him up and dragged him forward.

Mech screamed as the shadow claw dug into his ankle.

"Fools, did you think a mere fall could destroy a god", Guldamere cackled, a large spike formed out of black miasma surrounding Guldamere's pointer finger, he pointed it at Mech's eye, the binocular eyeglasses in front of him shattered one after another as it got closer to his eye.

One of the remaining ropes caught fire and broke free, and the ship flipped sideways, Guldamere dropped Mech, stumbling and sinking his claws into the timber deck to stop himself from falling, Mech grabbed onto a rope and swung, but swinging air born he had nowhere left to go but down.

"Now you die", Guldamere said, "Well, this is it lads, been a pleasure sailing the skies with ye", Villias said from the rail above them, Mech and the remaining crew looked over shocked to see the captain still alive with a knife in hand.

Mech nodded to him in resignation, the crew nodded too closing their eyes, Villias looked Guldamere in the eyes as he cut the rope, "you should have known that the captain always goes down with his ship", he cut the rope and the rest snapped away from the balloon, the ship fell from the sky as the balloon caught fire.

Guldamere growled unhooking his claws from the ship, "oh no you don't", Mech said, the crew throwing another fishing net over him and dragged him down with them.

Guldamere desperately clawed at the netting as the sky dancer plummeted down toward Necropyre, it slammed into the wall above the main gate, the gunpowder keg ignited with the burst of fire and the sky dancer, the gate, the crew and the surrounding wall exploded into a

by Lore Casta Pendragon

mass of fire and debris, Guldamere covered himself in black miasma and shot out from the explosion back into the city, smashing through round, stain glass window of the cathedral of the god feared.

Ailyn and Kimba watched as the sky dancer fell, Kimba covered her mouth in disbelief, "Villias!", she cried, but the following explosion was all the finality one needed to see, the sky dancer and her crew were finished, Ailyn's heart sank in his chest, the risen around them fell to the ground once again joining the ranks of the dead.

As the risen surrounding Farin's army collapsed, Wynn had an undead peasant in one hand, it went limp in his big hands, the nightmare creatures were all that was left of Guldamere's forces.

Farin let out a victory cry which was taken up by the rest of the army, "March on the gate, take the city!", Farin commanded as what was left of the combined army charged onward.

"Is it over?", Kimba asked, "as long as Guldamere holds the power, it's never over", Silus said, "we'd better keep up", Ailyn said moving forward, Kimba took him by the arm to stop him.

"Wait!", she said, "I found something in the library, I think you should take a look", Kimba said reaching into her sleeve, she pulled out a two dusty old tomes, Ailyn looked over the cover, "what is it?", "take a look", Kimba said turning the books spines and pointing to the inscriptions, "by Aram Allheart", Ailyn said looking at Kimba surprised, "a tome by Aram?", "Open it", she said.

Ailyn opened the tome to the first few pages, "Aram must have known about Guldamere's plan to use enhanced necromancy, he devised a technique to block its use", she turned a few pages, "this one", she smiled, "is to seal it", Kimba looked at Ailyn with a satisfied grin, "and this one explains how to break the curse".

"We'll take the fight to Guldamere, while you get some study done", Kimba patted Ailyn on the cheek, he was about to protest when Silus came up behind him and gave him a light shove on the back of the shoulder, "don't slack off or there won't be anyone left to save".

Link ruffled his hair passing as well, "study hard", he said mockingly, Brawn shoved his other shoulder giving him a stern nod and a grunt as he past, Ailyn watched as they ran to join Wynn and Farin in front of the gate, with a confused look he watched them go then sat down and opened the tome.

Walking through the now ruined and burning gates of Necropyre, Farin and his men stepped carefully, Farin's eyes darted left and right, the city was covered in an eerie darkness which seemed to push in around his torch light, usually light would taper off over a distance but the light seemed to just stop after a few meters making it hard to see what was ahead.

                    by Lore Casta Pendragon

The city was devoid of life and oddly silent, Farin signaled for his men to part and march either side of the road sensing a trap.

One dwarven soldier heard a door creek, he looked into the open door of a town house, a giant bloodshot eyeball opened up in the darkness, the dwarf screamed as many clawed hands grabbed him, he dropped his weapon and helmet as he was snatched into the darkness of the house.

The soldiers around him fell back, "the creeping dark, it's the creeping dark", they shouted fearfully, "light it up!", Farin said, moving forward with a brigade of grenadiers, they began throwing flashbang grenades through the windows of the house, they heard a visceral shriek and the light of the torches seemed to penetrate a little deeper.

Farin walked inside holding his torch in front, the lower half of his soldier laid in a pool of blood on the floor, Farin backed out slowly, watching the shadows, "it's back from the abyss", Farin said, his face drawing long.

Wynn grabbed Farin by the shoulder pulling him back from the door, looking him in the eye, "what is that thing?".

                              by Lore Casta Pendragon

Chapter Twenty-Eight

Lacrimosa part two

Ailyn's companions ran through the burning gate to join Farin and Wynn inside the city, nightmare creatures were still attacking, but they were vastly outnumbered by the might of the combined forces.

"Why have we stopped", Kimba asked, "the creeping dark, it's been revived, it took some of my men already, I'm not sure if we can fight it here, it's too open and too dark, there's nowhere we could possibly trap it in all this open dark", Farin said.

"Then we'll just have to make it light", Kimba replied slamming her fists together, her fists began to glow with an overwhelmingly bright white light, everyone averted their eyes, Kimba separated her fists and the light coalesced into a large ball which she then threw into the air, it floated up like a balloon the light penetrating much of the darkness in the street, but heavy shadows were still cast from the tall buildings.

Kimba panted as she lowered her hands, sweat beaded on her brow and her eyes drooped, the strain of the battle and the fatigue of the curse was wearing on her heavily.

"That's a decent start lass, at least now we have some safe space to advance", Wynn said, Farin waved his men forward, "stick to the light, lest ye end up in the belly of the creeping dark", Farin shouted, "if it even has a belly", he mumbled walking forward.

Brawn found a large section of broken stone wall which he hefted onto his shoulder, "you know a sword is a much easier weapon to use", Wynn said to him, "you think your puny sword could stop this if I threw it at you?", Brawn replied, Wynn looked at the size of the thing, "probably not", he said concerned, Brawn let out a goofy laugh then continued onward.

The army marched toward the cathedral, their pace slowed the closer they got, not a single man could hold his courage in the face of the confrontation in front of them, their entire lives they were told to revere or fear Guldamere as a god and had witnessed firsthand his terrible power.

Silus pushed past the men to the front line, he showed no fear walking straight past them, the men looked at each other and bolstered their resolve following him, he leaped to the side as a barghast pounced out of the shadows toward him, he sliced it along the side with his knife, the beast tried to stand but the wound made it collapse, a knife struck it in between the eyes and it let out a growl as it died, the men looked at him impressed, "they really are a brainless foe", Silus said confidently.

    by Lore Casta Pendragon

The men's face went from awe to horror in an instant, Silus looked down to see his foot was in the shadow of a nearby building, something wrapped around his ankle and dragged him into the dark, in a flash Silus had a knife in hand and slashed at whatever held him severing it, he got up and sprinted back toward the light of the street but didn't make it, shadow hands grabbed all over him and dragged him back, "damnit, you won't have me", Silus said, he held his hands in front of him like he was controlling a marionette puppet.

The knives in his coat sprung out and moved on their own slashing the claws around him freeing his arms, with a flash two more knives were in hand and he spun slashing so fast he became a blur, eyes began opening in the dark around him, it surrounded him, he held his hands out again and the knives began to circle around him keeping the clawed hands from getting closer.

He reached one hand into his pocket and pulled out two small items, a small grey ball and a shiny black phylactery that looked exactly like him, he threw down the ball and it exploded into a cloud of smoke, the shadow hands reeled back as it burst then reached into the cloud, "I got you", the creeping dark said in a high shrill voice.

It pulled Silus out of the cloud of smoke, a mouth appeared to open from nowhere in the dark lined with teeth that moved in opposite directions like some sort of grinder, it bit down and Silus burst into a cloud of smoke leaving behind a flash grenade, the creeping dark shrieked as the light exploded from the grenade tearing the mouth and eyes to shreds as the light penetrated it, it opened up a path through the darkness and Silus ran from the cloud of smoke and back out onto the light of the street, he put his hands on his knees panting heavily.

"Well, that was a little too close for comfort", he said as the men surrounded him, "did you kill it", one of them stammered, "no, I don't think so, I definitely hurt it though", Silus said straightening his hat.

Guldamere picked himself up from the floor of the cathedral of the god feared, his boney frame clicked as he stood, he caught sight of his reflection in the mirror, his cloak was destroyed, most of it completely torn away, he threw it to the floor in frustration, his skeletal form was mostly broken, half his ribcage was missing.

He put his hands together in prayer, the black miasma that surrounded him folded over him like a smokey black cloak which he wore it like his clothing.

Straightening up he nodded to his reflection then turned to the door, a bloodshot red eye appeared in the dark in front of him, "darkest one, I failed, the man with the big hat, he hurt us", said the shrill high voice of the creeping dark.

"Not to worry, come my pet, lacrimosa is almost at hand", Guldamere said putting his hand on top of the eye.

                                                                    by Lore Casta Pendragon

"I am a god, even if they burn Necropyre to the ground, what does it matter, we have all of eternity to rebuild it, once the power is all mine, existence will bend to my will alone, I think it time that I stopped playing with my food, don't you think?", Guldamere smirked.

"Fetch my Necronomicon, volume seven if you will", the creeping dark closed its eye and seemed to vanish for a minute then came back, a shadow hand carried a book, it looked to be floating in the dimly lit room.

The creeping dark climbed up upon Guldamere's black miasma cloak and sank into it, many small eyes opened on it as the creeping dark seemed to become one with the smokey garment, Guldamere opened the book and placed it down at the Alter, he placing his hands together in prayer.

The front door of the cathedral crashed inward, a piece of heavy stone wall slid to a stop, "what door", brawn said stepping inside, followed by Link, Farin, Wynn, Silus and Kimba, the rest of the combined army waited just beyond the door illuminating it with torchlight.

Guldamere was standing at his alter, head bowed and muttering in prayer.

"It's over lich, your armies are defeated, your walls have been breached, even your church is ruined, lift the curse you've placed on us or else", Link demanded.

Guldamere cackled softly at first, lifting his head his golden eyes stared at Link, it was like looking into death itself, an air of doom set in around them as he cackled loudly, "fools all!", Guldamere shouted at them, "did you think I would let you defile my city unless I wanted you here?", he smirked.

A look of horror engulfed their faces, "it's a trap!", Farin said, outside the combined army saw several pyres of green fire light up along the city walls, the street lamps began to burn with the same fire, it made a pentacle shape throughout the city, "what's going on?", the soldiers said looking around nervously.

"The time has come, lacrimosa begins", Guldamere shouted.

Skulls from around the cathedral started chanting on their own, the companions looked around not knowing what to do, they raised their weapons to fight.

Guldamere cackled as the black miasma around him exploded outward, Link raised his arms to protect himself from whatever was coming, but as soon as the smoke touched him, his body seemed to shrink in his armor, he let out one final death cry as the life was ripped from him, his armor crashing to the floor.

Wynn and Farin turned to run, but were also consumed, it seemed to suck the life straight from their bodies, like they were directly toughing the abyss itself, Silus dashed behind Kimba as she slammed her fists together, a ball of light exploded from her creating a protective shield,

Silus braced her from behind to stop her from falling backward, but the force was too great, they started sliding.

Silus grabbed Kimba by the waist and leaped out of a broken stain glass window which exploded outwards with the pressure.

The combined army saw the black smoke blow out the windows of the cathedral.

As it touched the first few soldiers in the doorway, they immediately died, the men dropped their weapons and ran, they tried ducking down side streets and hiding away but no matter where they ran, the smoke filled the city, everyone in the city, the army of dwarves, Ailyn's men and even a few citizens that were hiding from the war, were all consumed.

Ailyn closed Aram's tome with a sigh, getting to his feet he summoned Aram's staff, the golden runes appeared in the air before him, coalescing into the staff as it appeared.

Ailyn held the staff so it pointed to the sky and closed his eyes, the white flame of the power burned around him and then the staff too began to glow with a pure bright light, it was immense to behold but undamaging to the eye, it was like looking at the sun but it didn't burn.

Ailyn looked over to the city gates, massive pyres of green fire began to appear along the city walls, "oh no", Ailyn said, his heart dropped as he leaped forward, the ground exploded underneath him as he shot toward the city gates.

A wave of black miasma began to pour out of the gates, Ailyn stopped before reaching it, it bellowed around him at great speed, avoiding the light of the staff, Ailyn heard the cries of men ring out in a horrifying chorus as he proceeded into the city, the staff pushed back against the darkness and the billowing miasma.

Silus dug daggers into the stonework of the cathedral wall to make footholds, Kimba held the light shield around them as they climbed out of the cloud of miasma to the steeple at the highest point of the cathedral.

Kimba looked out over the city dropping the light shield, "their all gone", she cried, "I'm afraid that might not be the worst of it", Silus said pointing to the city gates, Kimba looked over to see the miasma hadn't stopped at the city, it was still flowing out like an ocean past the city gates, consuming everything in its path.

"We've failed", Kimba said sobbing as she put her face into Silus's chest, Silus looked down at her, she reminded him of Cinder in so many ways, "I would have like to see her again, just once more", he said holding Kimba close to him.

by Lore Casta Pendragon

Kimba turned her head to see a bright light splitting the blackness at the gate, Silus noticed it too, "Ailyn?", He asked, "who else could it be?", Kimba replied, "then all is not lost, we lost the battle, but we can still make sure Guldamere pays the price for what he's done", Silus said vengefully.

Guldamere reveled in his own maliciousness, the lifeforce of all the living things the black cloud touched flowed into him and fed the incantation more, the creeping dark seemed to sink into his bones and become one with what was left of him.

A bloodshot eye opened upon his palm, he held it up and the sea of black miasma parted from him, he had fed it enough that it would consume everything in Thalaria as it expanded ever outward.

He no longer felt human, he was beyond immortal, he felt as if death could no longer touch him at all, he had become part of the abyss, a nightmare god, the darkness seemed to obey his every command, the darkness lifted Guldamere as the cathedral began to collapsed around him.

Ailyn ran through the streets toward the city center, the hollowed-out husks of men and dwarves laid along the ground, "it may already be too late", Ailyn thought to himself when he heard a cry from above, "Ailyn!", Kimba screamed out as he reached the steps of the crumbling cathedral.

Silus grabbed Kimba and leaped from the steeple as the cathedral came crashing down, Ailyn leaped toward them, grabbing both of them and landing on the far side of the ruin as dust blew around them, "what happened?", Ailyn asked.

"It was a trap, he led us here just so he could start his lacrimosa by feeding on us all", Silus said.

The dust cleared and they turned to see Guldamere, he raised his palm containing the eye of the creeping dark and the bones and husks of the dead began to swirl around him mixing with black miasma, it formed around him into a giant skeletal monstrosity made of the remains of his victims, the behemoth held out one boney hand and shadow claws began forming, grabbing onto one another until they formed the shape of a sword, it solidified seeming to grow solid and sharp.

"This is it, we have no other choice, we have to stop him now", Kimba said slamming her fists together, with a flash Silus had his knives in hand.

"Hay Silus, how many of those do you have left", Ailyn said, "I have enough", Silus said opening his coat, it was lined with knives like chainmail, Ailyn finally understood the purpose of that coat he wore, it was armored and acted like an almost infinite supply of weapons.

                                        by Lore Casta Pendragon

Ailyn reached out with the tip of his staff and tapped the coat with the tip of his staff, the knives began to glow with a soft white light, "that should help", Ailyn said, "neat trick", Silus said with a smirk.

Guldamere saw Ailyn and swung the massive black sword, "you will give me the power now!", The bone behemoth said it's voice reverberating.

Kimba put up a magic ward, the sword hit the barrier and rebounded, but the ward shattered like glass, "you go left, I'll go right, Kimba keep those shields up", Ailyn said as both men dashed off, "easier said than done", Kimba complained, she was exhausted, Ailyn had the power to keep him going, Silus managed to get through on strength of will alone, but Kimba was ready to drop.

Guldamere saw Ailyn as the bigger threat and followed him, swinging the black blade in an arc taking out an entire building in the process, Ailyn tried to leap onto it, but black shadow hands grabbed out at him from the sword, Ailyn grunted slamming the staff down instead and vaulting over it, the hands tried to grab the staff but disintegrated under the intense light, it ate away at the sword which quickly reformed as Guldamere came back for another swing.

Guldamere growled as Silus threw several enchanted daggers into the bone behemoth's back, skull and bone broke away falling to the ground, the enchanted knives nullified the chaos magic holding it together, Silus smiled and winked at Ailyn as Guldamere tried to squash him with a fist, Silus leaped to the side avoiding it easily.

"Traitor!", Guldamere bellowed, swinging the sword at him, Silus backflipped over it, throwing more knives into the boney hand that held the sword, two fingers fell away as Ailyn came in from the other side smashing at the wrist, more bone crumbled and the two raced around avoiding the backswing.

Guldamere slashed across almost collecting the both of them, but Kimba threw up a shield in front of them repelling it, the shield shattered and both Ailyn and Silus stabbed toward the boney wrist holding the sword, with a flash of light the hand was severed, the sword dropped to the ground disintegrating.

Guldamere backed off, Ailyn, Silus and Kimba pressing forward, determination like fire in their eyes.

"Wait!", Guldamere said still backing off, "wait, hear me out", he said, Silus was about to press the attack when a voice cried out, "Silus?", Silus knew that voice, "Silus are you there?", Silus stopped dead in his tracks, "Cinder?", Silus asked, "lord Guldamere said he'll revive me, you just have to switch sides now", Cinder said.

"It's just a trick Silus don't fall for it, we need to finish him", Kimba said, Silus turned to Ailyn, "don't worry I know", Silus said, a smile grew on his scarred face under the brim of his hat.

"Not a chance boney", Silus said, this made Guldamere straighten up.

 by Lore Casta Pendragon

"You already fooled me once with that lie", he said, Guldamere growled, "I am a merciful god, if you give me what I want, I will give you all what you want in return".

Ailyn growled with anger, he shot off like a missile towards the bone behemoth, the tip of the staff glowing a bright white and leaving a trail through the air.

"What I want is a world without you", Ailyn said as he somersaulted up over the staff, the bone behemoth's big boney fist launched at him, but he swung the staff over his head shattering it, then vaulted up over Guldamere's head.

"What I want you've already taken from me!", He screamed bringing the staff down on the bone behemoths skull with a flash of white light, bone shattered in all directions, half the behemoths face broke away as it reeled backward.

Ailyn landed then shot off again leaping at Guldamere bringing the staff across as Guldamere raised what was left of the bone behemoths other arm to defend.

"My brother!", He said slamming the staff into it, shattering the arm into a rain of bone fragments, landing again he swept the staff across in a swallow cut across the bone behemoth's solid base, another explosion of bone fragments shot out.

"My mother!", He shouted as the bone behemoth fell on its back, Ailyn heard Guldamere growl, "and this one is for my father, Aethor!", He screamed leaping above, he could see the cracks forming between the bone constructs ribcage.

'That's got to be where Guldamere is', Ailyn thought, light formed at the tip of the staff into a spear point, "no!", Guldamere cried out, as the spear punched through the bone, it exploded into a densely bright light and bone blew out in every direction.

Kimba saw it coming and put her fists together, Silus leaped behind her as the shield built up in front of her, bone collided with it, they closed their eyes to shield them from the light, it faded and they looked back, the bone behemoth was gone, falling apart.

Ailyn stood over Guldamere on the ground, spear right next to his head, Guldamere held the talon of a large shadow claw stabbed into Ailyn's mid-section, Ailyn grunted and coughed blood.

"You missed", Guldamere said, letting out a ghastly cackling laugh.

He floated up to his feet as Ailyn stumbled back pulling himself free, "damn, you", Ailyn said, coughing up blood as he tried to speak.

"I could have given you anything, but you chose to die instead, you are a fool Allheart, just as your predecessors were", Guldamere said slamming Ailyn with a balled shadow fist, knocking him down hard, Ailyn rolled backward to recover but the pain in his guts was crippling and he fell over some debris, he wobbled as he slowly rose to his feet.

                                        by Lore Casta Pendragon

Guldamere advanced on him, "just like that fool, Aram", the lich croaked.

Ailyn raised his arms to block as his fist hit him again, knocking him back into a broken stone wall, Ailyn slumped against it, "you're going to suffer many deaths at my hands Ailyn", Guldamere smirked, large white tendrils of chaos magic rose up behind him.

Ailyn lifted his head, his eyes flashed red briefly, Guldamere noticed Ailyn looking behind him and turned to see Kimba surrounded by eight white tendrils, two lifted her from the ground while the other six whipped out at Guldamere.

He placed his hands together in prayer, shadow claws grabbed at the first four, but one twisted and smacked Guldamere sideways, the shadow claws disintegrated and the next tendril smacked Guldamere back the other way, the shadows claws burned away under the light then all six tendrils were pummeling him from every angle, Guldamere growled and the air around him went pitch black as a ball of darkness sucked in all of the light, the white tendrils were pulled into it disintegrating.

Guldamere screamed out in hateful rage as a shockwave blew outwards, Kimba slammed her fists together to put up a shield but it immediately shattered and sent her flying backward, she bounced from the ground and smacked her head into a wall, her world went black.

Silus leaped behind some debris and shielded himself with his coat.

"Kimba!", Ailyn Shouted as she hit the wall, the anger exploded within him, his eyes went red, the white aura surrounding him went the color of blood, Guldamere turned to him with a self-satisfied smirk only for it to be quickly replaced with terrible fear as he was struck with a force he'd never experienced in his long life, he was flying through the air, the creeping dark tried to reach out to grab something to slow his decent, but everything it reached for crumbled in its grasp.

Guldamere crashed through the wall of a building and clear out the other side bouncing off the pavement.

"What the hell!", "I didn't even see him move", Guldamere growled.

He got to his feet, Ailyn came round the corner of the building and Guldamere ran the other way down the alley.

Before he reached the end Ailyn stepped around the corner, meeting him face to face, "you're going to pay for that", Ailyn said putting his straightened fingers against Guldamere's boney chest, using Aethor's close range punching technique, Ailyn shattered Guldamere's spine with a loud crack.

The two halves of Guldamere flew to the end of the alleyway, the black miasma around him faded away and the bones crumbled to dust.

        by Lore Casta Pendragon

Ailyn grunted putting his hand on his gut wound, it was bleeding badly, 'I don't have much time left', he thought.

Ailyn went over to where Kimba was, Silus was already there trying to wake her, "where's Guldamere?", Silus asked.

"He's dead, but for how long I don't know", Ailyn said, "is she?", Ailyn said sitting down next to them, "no, but her breathing is faint and she won't wake up", Silus said.

"She's beyond exhausted, she pushed herself to the limits of her power multiple times without a wink of sleep, it's amazing she's breathing at all, I fear the hell she's slipped into, being unable to wake from Guldamere's nightmares", Silus said.

They looked up to see black miasma drifting toward the center of the ruined cathedral, "He's coming", Silus said.

Kimba opened her eyes wide briefly, A look of utter fear gripping her, but closed them again unable to wake completely, Ailyn moved over to her, he put her fists together, his palm glowed with a white light, he placed the tip of his finger against her heart and the color seemed to come back into her face as she opened her eyes, "are you alright?", Ailyn said concerned.

"Thank you, I'll be alright, just give me some time to recover", Kimba said.

"I didn't even have enough left to heal myself, thanks for sharing", she said smiling at him, "what would master Pendragon think of me now", she said disheartened, "I think he'd be proud", Ailyn replied, which made her smile.

Ailyn stood up, Kimba saw the wound and gasped, "how are you still standing?", Kimba said.

"I'm afraid time might be running out, we need to finish this now", Ailyn said taking his hand from the bloody wound.

Silus rested Kimba against a wall then stood up nodded to him and tilted his brimmed hat down, "what's the plan, killing him didn't work", Silus said, "you have to use the staff", Kimba said groggily.

Ailyn and Silus turned to her, "Aram's tome said as much", Ailyn said walking over to where he destroyed the bone behemoth earlier, he pulled Aram's staff from the ground, it still glowed in a soft but brilliant bright white light, the black miasma swirled together at the center of the ruin.

Guldamere's cackling laugh permeated the air as the smoke pulled together in a whirlwind then dissipated revealing Guldamere back in one piece.

"You cannot defeat me Allheart, I am death", Guldamere said holding up a palm, a creepy eye opened upon it and a beam of darkness shot out from it toward Ailyn and Silus, they split in both directions running as it narrowly missed hitting Kimba, she ducked and crawled on her

by Lore Casta Pendragon

hands and knees to hide behind some debris, Guldamere followed Ailyn to the left, everything the death beam touched was dissolving into dust like it was instantly aged thousands of years.

It melted the stone itself into sand, Silus went right and began to arc back in toward Guldamere, the beam sliced back across to cut them off, Ailyn rolled under it and got straight back to his feet, while Silus leaped over it throwing a knife in Guldamere's direction, the creeping dark batted it away with a shadow claw.

"I'm going to revive her Silus, then I'm going to torture her in front of you", Guldamere said, his voice reverberated through the air as he aimed the beam back toward him, Silus ducked behind a wall then took a diagonal path forward leaping over rubble.

"You won't be torturing anyone, anymore", Silus said throwing a knife then somersaulting over a wall, again it was deflected by a shadow hand which disintegrated upon contact.

Guldamere aimed the beam at the thick wall, it wasn't long before it fell away.

Silus ducked down an alleyway then put his back to the wall, panting heavily, he slumped against it checking his bandoliers for more knives, realizing that he was finally out, he took a long-jagged dirk from a holster at his waist, 'last one, not for throwing', he thought to himself.

Ailyn leaped at Guldamere and swung the staff, three shadow hands extended from the creeping dark cloak Guldamere wore, they managed to stop it before it hit, but let out a shriek as the staff burned the dark away, Guldamere stopped his focus on Silus and shot the beam of darkness toward Ailyn at point blank range.

Ailyn couldn't react in time and pulled the staff up to cover his face closing his eyes, he waited for his end, the beam hit the staff with force but the intense light held the beam at bay splitting it around Ailyn and the staff in multiple smaller beams.

Ailyn opened his eyes and held on tight, he thrust the staff back toward the beam and it split around him into multiple streams turning the chattel from the destruction of the city into sand and dust, Kimba ran as the beams shot out over the ruined city almost catching her.

Ailyn strained against the assault taking one step at a time, advancing as the beam chaotically ripped apart things around him.

Silus peeked around the corner to see Ailyn fighting the beam, he leaped up grabbing a drain pipe, then leaped again up onto a balcony, jumping up onto a rail he ran up the wall, then he leaped off and landed on the adjacent roof, then leaped again onto the roof, he took two steps back, took a deep breath in then sprinted and leaped off the ledge.

Silus did a front somersault then took his dirk in both hands, Guldamere was right in his path, a shadow claw reached out to intercept him but Silus slammed the dagger through it and into Guldamere's back barely holding on from the force of the blow.

Ailyn kept pushing forward when the beam suddenly stopped, Guldamere reared up growling, Ailyn took the opportunity and stabbed him with the point of the staff, it burned away at the black miasma that made up the creeping dark cloak, Guldamere lunged forward, gargling out his pain.

Silus took the dagger out and tried to stab again, but a shadow hand grabbed him by the leg, Guldamere reach behind him grabbing Silus and swung him around, Ailyn stepped back to avoid getting struck by his friend.

Guldamere pulled Silus up to eye level with an unimpressed face then ran him through with all five clawed fingers of his shadow hand, "I'll see you again soon traitor", Guldamere said as he slammed Silus into the ground on his back, Silus groaned then was silent.

"You're done, this time you're not coming back!", Ailyn said as he leaped forward, the staff looked like a streak of light slamming it Guldamere, left then right, above, down low then up high, over and over, each time a shadow hand or claw came up to defend it was burned away by the light, with each hit Ailyn became more empowered, hitting even harder but the darkness surrounding Guldamere kept on replenishing him like living armor.

Guldamere had not felt this feeling in a long time, he had not felt anything for a long time, as each subsequent strike impacted, it sounded as if he was trapped inside a large bell and someone kept slamming something into it, each time the bell grew louder, he began to panic and for the first time since he fought Lore Casta Pendragon in Paladins Reach, he felt, fear, he could feel the immense power within being syphoned away, his power, his divinity, he couldn't stand it, then the curse was broken and the sun burst through the darkness.

Ailyn slammed the staff into the side of Guldamere's face, burning away the black miasma shielding him and ripping at his flesh even more, the darkness stitched back together and Guldamere's head turned back to face him, a look of utter disdain and disbelief was plastered upon it.

Ailyn hit him again and again, Guldamere kept turning to him, face regenerating, then as another came in, he stepped in and grabbed Ailyn by the throat with his own boney hand, Ailyn felt the icey hand grasp him, it stung on contact, like frost burn.

Guldamere began draining the life and the source power back from him, Ailyn screamed, then remembered a hand to hand technique that master Den had showed him when he trained at the temple of the Aikitai, he twisted the boney hand at the thumb joint, then swung the staff at Guldamere's arm with one hand, it shattered the bone and Guldamere cried out as he fell

by Lore Casta Pendragon

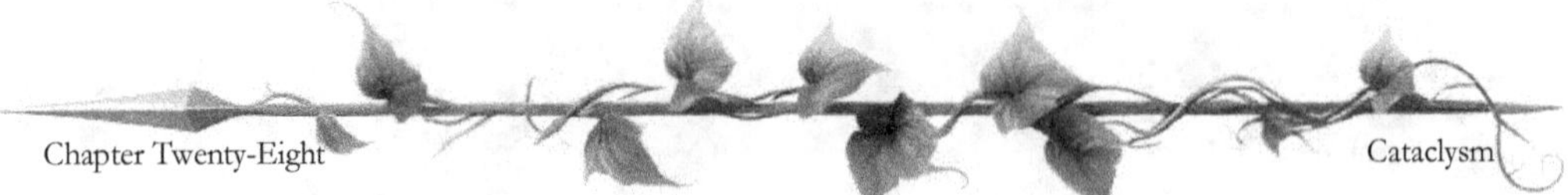

backward, the arm dropping to the ground, Ailyn dropping with it, he tumbled downhill through some rubble and landed right next to Silus, coming to rest lying beside him.

The sun shone straight down into their faces, Ailyn rolled over groaning laying on his back next to Silus.

The wound in his mid-section was bleeding badly and he looked pale, he was exhausted, his vision started to blur and his ears were ringing.

"Get up Ailyn, you've got to finish this", Silus said quietly, his voice echoed in Ailyn's ears, 'Silus, you're still alive?', Ailyn asked, Silus lifted the brim of his hat which covered his face, blood trailed from his mouth but he still smirked at him, the scars on his face seemed even more noticeable in the light.

"Can you stand?", Ailyn asked, "not this time Allheart, this time I won't be coming back", Silus said taking the hat from his head and placing it on top of Ailyn's, then pulled a small vail of white glowing liquid from his pocket.

"Make sure you give the hat to Cinder for me when you're done with it, maybe she'll waste hundreds of years trying to revive me this time, or maybe not", Silus said trying to chuckle which resulted in a groan of pain.

"Also take this, I'm sorry it's a bit gross, it's still got my spit in it after I spat it into the vial, I stashed some of the elixir from paladins reach when they tried to give it to me, after all they said the stuff was worth substantially more than gold", Silus tried to chuckle again.

"An elixir?", Ailyn replied, "you're in worse shape than me you take it".

"You're the only one that can finish him, take the elixir and put an end to Guldamere the god feared", Silus said, "I will, Silus", Ailyn said, it was at that moment looking at Silus that Ailyn finally forgave him completely for what he'd done, he risked everything, his pride, his humanity, his life and hid dignity, all to protect one person.

"You're one hell of a friend Silus, Cinder was lucky to have you, I'll see you in the lands beyond", Ailyn said, Silus smiled, then with his last breath he said, "you can't kill him, but you can't let him live, so drop him into the deepest hole you can find and bury him forever".

with that Silus drew his final breath.

Chapter Twenty-Nine

The final chapter

Ailyn got up raising his head, the warmth of the sun felt good on his face, he took a deep breath, then drank the elixir, it was disgusting but his gut wound healed over leaving a large patch of scar tissue.

Black miasma swirled in behind Ailyn, Guldamere walked out of it, bones from nearby corpses floated over and affixed themselves to him repairing his shattered arm.

"Now what Allheart, got any more friends for me to kill, I've purge Thalaria of all life by now, only you and Pendragons apprentice remain and you cannot kill me, the abyss and I have an accord you see, I granted them access to the world and they granted me safe passage through the void of death, even if we fight until the end of time, I will still reign victorious and only I can bring back the dead, you cannot prevail nor is your fight a righteous one, only I can bring hope to the people of this world, only I can bring life back to the land", Guldamere said looking down at him.

Ailyn sighed heavily then looked up at him, "you're right, I can't beat you, but history has a way of repeating itself", Ailyn said showing him Aram's tome.

"This tome had an interesting note inside of it, a long time ago, three sisters accumulated three sources of immense power, they each used it for the same end, to rid the world of suffering, one of them found the lands beyond, the other found the abyss and the third found a way to prolong life, each thought they were on the correct path, but those paths collided and their world was thrown into a war for power, each one vying for more until there was nothing left, they made an accord and sealed the power away behind a powerful magical seal, one that was never to be broken", Ailyn said.

Guldamere's face grew tight with anger, Kimba walked up behind Ailyn.

"It was you who broke the seal, you who wrought the land, you who brainwashed the people and you who murdered them all!", Kimba shouted, then she turned to Ailyn touching him where the gut wound was, "your wound?", Kimba asked, "a final gift from Silus", Ailyn said not taking his eyes from Guldamere.

"I don't have much left, but I'll help where I can, this will be our last chance, don't you dare fail us", she said giving him a solid pat on the back, Kimba took a few steps back as Ailyn walked forward, runes appeared in the air as Aram's staff appeared.

Ailyn took the fighting pose of the Aikitai, then rushed toward Guldamere who met him by raising two shadow claws, they sliced through the ground before slicing upward toward Ailyn, leaving clawed gashes in the ground.

by Lore Casta Pendragon

Ailyn did a front somersault over the staff, narrowly passing between the claws, then brought the staff streaking down in an arc of white light.

Guldamere raised his arms to defend, the black miasma moved in front of him and solidified, the staff shattered the barrier and drove him onto his knees, the ground beneath him splintered and cracked under the force of the blow.

The creeping dark shrieked and burned in the light, Guldamere growled and darkness pushed out from him, several shadow claws reach out of the darkness and grabbed Ailyn from every side, he held the staff vertically in two hands then closed his eyes focusing.

The light from the staff exploded outwards in a shockwave burning the shadow claws away and repelling the darkness, Guldamere growled in frustration pushing against the light, Ailyn sprung forward the ground splintering underneath him, he thrust the staff forward, the light at the end turning into a spear point.

Ailyn summoned all of his strength and ramming it into Guldamere who cried out with pain as the creeping dark shrieked and burned away in a burst of light, Guldamere flew backward his body shattering against the far wall, black miasma flew out from it as the bones from nearby corpses reformed Guldamere a new.

Guldamere floated in the air, shadow claws formed around his hands, "you're not the only one with a weapon of power", Guldamere shouted putting his hands together, dark purple runes appeared in the air forming into a scythe, Guldamere took hold of it with his shadow claws, then rushed at Ailyn slashing diagonally upward.

Ailyn moved the staff to defend and was surprised when he felt a solid thud as both weapons collided, Ailyn held his ground as Guldamere broke off with a quick backward movement bringing the scythe down on top of him, Ailyn moved the staff to block overhead and was forced to a knee under the strength of the blow.

Guldamere was still far stronger and his arms began to bend as he pressed down, "Ailyn!", Kimba shouted slamming her fists together, "you can do it, you'll find a way, I know you will", she said.

Ailyn looked to the side to see she was crying.

"No, don't!", Ailyn shouted wide eyed, "we'll be together again, in the land beyond", Kimba said, her whole body began to crackle as she got to her feet, her hands opened to the sky as the last of her life energy infused with the spell, Guldamere looked at her with resentment and Ailyn used the distraction to deflect the scythe and roll out to the side, the sky swirled into a mass of grey clouds.

Kimba fell and as she did a lightning bolt of immense power and brightness struck Guldamere causing an explosion of power and light, Ailyn rolled to his feet sliding to a rest, dust kicked up around where Guldamere was hit.

                            by Lore Casta Pendragon

As the dust settled, he could see Guldamere laying prone on the ground, Ailyn ran over and grabbed Kimba in his arms, tears welled up in his eyes and he held her close, her face was gaunt and thin, she gave everything to save him, his eyes caught fire as he placed her gently on the ground turning back to Guldamere who just started pushing himself up from the ground.

Ailyn summoned Aram's staff and walked over as Guldamere looked up at him only to see the staff flying down into his face, Guldamere's head bounced from the ground, Ailyn felt his rage flowing through him, his eyes a blaze of red and body a glow of white fire.

He grunted as he swung the staff over and over slamming it into Guldamere, each hit draining power from Guldamere, each hit growing stronger, Guldamere tried to rise, tried to summon magic, but couldn't, the shadow claws reached out to stop him but Ailyn slammed the staff straight through them, continuing to slam the staff into Guldamere's already decrepit until his body was a battered ruin of rotted flesh and broken bone, tears fell down Ailyn's face.

He stopped the barrage and fell to a sitting position with the staff across his lap as the sky cleared above him, he put his face in his hands and let out a mournful cry, everything he had done only resulted in the death of everything he loved.

He thought back to the pit, where he once tried to end his life, where Shin had told him his father still lived, he should have just ended it there, now he was completely alone, the sole survivor of a holocaust caused by Guldamere the god feared.

He looked to the sky and screamed, "what else could I have done?".

Silence was his answer, a wisp of white light began to rise from Guldamere's body and he heard a familiar voice.

"It's alright Ailyn, all you need do now is take the power", the voice called to him, Ailyn quickly got to his feet and back stepped, "mother?", he said, "I'm not your mother Ailyn", the voice said, "who are you?", Ailyn asked.

"I am Astariel, lady of the lands beyond, I'm the part of the power within you, take the power from Guldamere so that he can never again plague the world, then together we'll seal him and the abyss away like before the cataclysm", Astariel said.

Ailyn watched the wispy line of white light rising from Guldamere's corpse, he reached out and grabbed it, power began to syphon into him, the white aura around him that resembled fire calmed and became a divine glow, the universe seemed to unfold before him, like he could touch every part of it, Ailyn knew he could do anything at all, he could recreate the world a new, he could recreate everything, he could make it better than before, he was a god now, he could do anything, Ailyn grew excited at the possibilities.

But it wouldn't be the same, just an illusion of what was, lacking the souls that inhabited it, those souls now resided in the lands beyond, a place not even he could touch.

by Lore Casta Pendragon

"Seal the Abyss, Ailyn", Astariel's voice called to him in urgency, black miasma rose from Guldamere and he took a rasping breathe, Ailyn held his hand toward Guldamere but hesitated.

"If I sealed the abyss, I'll also seal the dead in the lands beyond", he said.

Ailyn grabbed Guldamere by his boney skull and ripped the skull from his body, "I'll be needing your help for this", he said.

Guldamere's black smokey eyes faded and was replaced by a glowing white light that expanded and washed everything out.

Ailyn was suddenly standing in the ethereal river in an endless black void, Guldamere's skull was in his hand.

Ailyn took a few steps forward, but it felt wrong, like he shouldn't be there, he looked at the skull then looked out over the falls of the abyss.

"You made a deal with this man to being the dead back to life in exchange for entry into Thalaria", Ailyn shouted, "I'm here to offer you a better one".

Silence greeted him, after a long while the river stopped flowing, Ailyn took this as an indication that whatever the abyss was, it was listening, he nodded nervously.

"I offer you one third of the power I hold, for the lives of everyone Guldamere has killed".

A shrill voice began to speak, it was the voice of the creeping dark, "we accept your offer, but we only give you one third in return, give us all of the power and we will have the power to give you all the lives that were ever lost".

Ailyn thought for a moment, "if I gave you this power you could do anything at all, I can't let you do that, my offer stands, I offer one third", Ailyn said.

After a long while the abyss responded, "very well, give me the power", the creeping dark said.

Ailyn held out a hand, a wispy white line of power wormed its way out of it and into the ethereal river.

"That's enough", Ailyn said closing his fist, the river began to run in reverse.

The souls that had been lost in the battle started to flow back up the falls from the abyss, Kimba was the first to the precipice.

Ailyn walked over to her and she stood smiling at him, "I know you could do it she said in an ethereal voice", then her ethereal body faded away.

Ailyn closed his eyes and when he opened them again, he was standing in the ruined cathedral of the god feared.

                                      by Lore Casta Pendragon

Kimba ran over to him and hugged him tightly, tears welled up in Ailyn's eyes, she kissed him and they both laughed, Silus walked up to them, Ailyn looked him in the eye, Silus held out a hand and Ailyn took it, "I take it you won, but how are we here?", Silus asked.

"I made a deal with the abyss in return for the lives lost, we got everyone back, everyone except those lost in the cataclysm", Ailyn said.

Silus's eyes went wide with the realization of what that meant.

"Silus?", Cinder called from behind him, Silus turned slowly with a look of utter disbelief, Cinder stood behind him, not looking a day older then when he lost her, he stood there speechless, she ran to him and leaped on him wrapping her arms around him, tears began to stream from Silus's eyes as he spun with her, he looked at Ailyn, "thank you", was all he managed to say.

"It seems my sacrifice wasn't in vain after all", Lore said walking up behind them, Kimba turned to see Lore walking toward them and embraced him in a welcoming hug, "it seems you've put that power to good use then", Lore said.

"I still have more to do", Ailyn said taking a few steps away.

"To you I offer one third of my power, so you can regain what you have lost", Ailyn said, opening his palm to the ground, a wispy line of energy drew out from it and into the ground at his feet.

"What are you doing", Lore asked, Ailyn didn't respond, the ground started sprouting grass, trees and plants out in front of him, it expanded like a path out of the ruined gates of Necropyre and spread over the blasted land beyond, brilliant green exploded to life, beautiful flowers and even wildlife sprung up from various caves and crevasses dashing off into the distance.

"you did it boy!", Farin said grabbing Ailyn around the waist, he let go and looked at Ailyn with reverence, Ailyn bowed his head and Farin bowed in turn.

Ailyn looked up to see his friends all standing nearby, they started to cheer and applaud, "Wynn, Brawn, Fyorn, Mech, Felix, Gear, Link, Locke, Vince, Villias, Inaya, Rayan, Den, Éoviel, Ilutha", Ailyn said, bowing his head to them all in turn.

Ailyn saw Aethor walking toward him, his mother Asta and his brother Aidem were behind him, Aethor embraced his son, "I'm so damn proud of you", Aethor said, then waved Asta and Aidem over, Asta smiled tearfully and held Ailyn to her chest, "oh, you're so big now", Asta said.

"Mother, I've missed you so much", Ailyn said tearfully, Aidem punched Ailyn in the arm, Ailyn let go of his mother and turned to him, "don't think your better than me just because your bigger than me, I'm still your older brother", Aidem said still looking the same age he did when Ailyn last saw him.

                                              by Lore Casta Pendragon

Ailyn laughed and picked his brother up, "seems you got some catching up to do brother", Ailyn said happily swinging him around, Aidem laughed as Ailyn put him down.

Kamdar walked up to Kimba, she saw him coming and sobbed into his chest, Kamdar held her close, "it's alright, I'm here now", Kamdar said.

They heard the sound of Cinder's scream as their happy reunion was cut short by nightmare creatures surrounding them on all sides, an army of them appeared, Ailyn's companions backed into a circle as the creatures poured in from all sides, the shadows draw long and the creeping dark opened its bloodshot eyes from the darkness.

Ailyn walked forward, "I figured you'd betray me from the start", Ailyn said, the creeping dark just giggled as the nightmare creatures drew closer, snarling, hissing, growling and flexing sharp claws.

Ailyn showed no fear, he simply walked to the corpse of Guldamere, placed the skull back on the corpse which began to move, taking a rasping breathe.

"You!", Guldamere started to croak, but Ailyn held his open palm to him, "one third of the power remains, this I give to you, to reseal the evil you released!", Ailyn shouted.

A wisp of light came from his hand and pushed into Guldamere, Lore started forward to stop him, but Link held him back, "he knows what he's doing, leave him be".

Guldamere rose, cackling to himself, the black miasma exploded out from him knocking everyone but Ailyn to the ground, the last of the power drained from Ailyn and he smiled at Guldamere's as his rotten face turned from elation to horror.

The black miasma started pulling in the darkness from around him, Ailyn's companions backed off and fell to the floor as the creeping dark and all of the nightmare creatures were turned into black smoke and swirled into Guldamere.

"No!", Guldamere and the creeping dark cried out as the spawn of the abyss was sucked into Guldamere in a swirling mass.

Ailyn closed his fist and Guldamere's body turned to stone, sealing the abyss and all of the nightmare creatures within.

Ailyn's companions got up confused but grateful, "you sacrificed all the power in the world to save us, you gave the land life a new, you remade the seal, like the seal of the muses, eons past, you gave everything for us, you truly are a king among men", Lore said reverently.

by Lore Casta Pendragon

He took a knee before Ailyn and bowed.

Silus walked up to him, "you gave Cinder back to me, for that you have my allegiance until my dying day", Silus said joining Lore, Cinder bowing next to him.

Gear walked up to join them, "ever since we met, you've been saving us, you even saved us from death itself, so for that we owe you our lives", Gear said, Ailyn's men bowed reverently behind him.

Farin walked up and bowed before him, "I may be a king in the Irons halls, but it's clear, that you be the king of kings", he said, the dwarves joined him and bowed deeply.

Aethor, Asta and Aidem all smiled at him and bowed their heads.

Locke, Link and Vincent bowed, followed by the rest of the paladins of the reach who lined up behind them, the precession grew as the people of Necropyre lined in behind them to give thanks to their savior.

Aram walked up and bowed to Lore, who wrapped him in a firm embrace, happy tears welled up in Lores eyes, then he turned to Ailyn.

"It's clear we need direction in this new age and there is none better suited in the eyes of all Thalarian's than Ailyn Allheart", Lore shouted, which was met with a hail of cheers and praises for Ailyn Allheart, the new king of Thalaria.

Thus concludes, Cataclysm: The Legends of Thalaria by Lore Casta Pendragon.

Authors note:

I hope you enjoyed this book, after reading over a thousand fantasy novels, I decided to write my own. I wanted to write something to be left behind when I am gone for others to enjoy. Thank you for taking the time to read and enjoy my work, it truly means the world to me, bless you.

To my boys, Theodore and Tenzin, thanks for bringing happiness to my life.

Lore Casta Pendragon is an Australia Author from the Central coast, NSW, Cataclysm is the first novel I wrote and if you would like to see more in the Legends of Thalaria series, show your support by offering a positive review or by reaching out via email.
If you wish to reach out to me you can send an email to: robofthalaria@hotmail.com:

Visit https://Thalaria.com
for Merch and to have a look at the gallery for pictures of your favourite characters.

Copyright 2023, Lore Casta Pendragon.

www.ingramcontent.com/pod-product-compliance
Lightning Source LLC
Chambersburg PA
CBHW082053090726
47909CB00010B/3017